PRAISE FOR LINDA HOWARD

"Already a legend in her own time, Linda Howard
exemplifies the very best of the romance genre.
Her strong characterizations and powerful insight
into the human heart have made her an author
cherished by readers everywhere."

Melinda Helfer,
Romantic Times

"You can't read just one Linda Howard. Once you
indulge in Grant, then you have to have Kell, then
John, and then 'Steve.' We're talking *Midnight
Rainbow*, *Diamond Bay*, *Heartbreaker*, and
White Lies. Enjoy! There are no calories, just
sheer reading pleasure."

Catherine Coulter,
New York Times
bestselling author

"Linda Howard writes with power, stunning
sensuality and a storytelling ability unmatched in
the romance genre. Every book is a treasure for
the reader to savor again and again."

Iris Johansen,
hor of
ancer

HEARTBREAKER

The ranch she'd inherited was nearly bankrupt, and now Michelle was also deeply in debt to John Rafferty, a tough-talking, hard-loving rancher all too ready to bargain. Never would she become his mistress in exchange for canceling the loan. Only by keeping her body out of Rafferty's arms could she prevent him from taking full possession of the heart that was already half his.

WHITE LIES

When the FBI summoned Jay to identify her gravely injured, heavily bandaged ex-husband, she agreed to keep a bedside vigil. Strangely, even unconscious, Steve wasn't at all like the husband she remembered. As he struggled toward awareness, Jay was more drawn to him than ever, and she had a chance to recapture—even embellish—their past. But would the new Steve ever share her cherished memories?

LINDA HOWARD

COLLECTION
VOLUME TWO

HEARTBREAKER

WHITE LIES

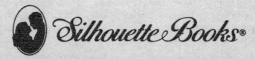

Silhouette Books®

Published by Silhouette Books New York

America's Publisher of Contemporary Romance

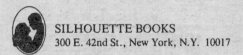

SILHOUETTE BOOKS
300 E. 42nd St., New York, N.Y. 10017

LINDA HOWARD COLLECTION edition published April 1992

HEARTBREAKER © 1987 by Linda Howington
First published as a Silhouette Intimate Moments

WHITE LIES © 1988 by Linda Howington
First published as a Silhouette Special Edition

ISBN: 0-373-48243-4

Printed in the U.S.A.

CONTENTS

Books by Linda Howard

Dear Reader,

Since I still like dangerous men, I noticed John Rafferty immediately when he walked onto the scene in *Diamond Bay,* and he had to have his own book, *Heartbreaker,* which is exactly what he was. Ah, John. He was all fire and sex, a lethal combination of iron will and bone-deep passion. There hadn't been a woman yet who could handle him. Being a woman who has a weakness for dangerous men, how could I resist a challenge like that? I couldn't.

The hero of *White Lies* was a wounded warrior, a dangerous man whose life depended on a woman. He hadn't given me advance warning by walking into another book; he just captured my attention one day and didn't let it go. He was both frighteningly direct and intriguingly layered, with a single-minded determination that never let him swerve from the job at hand. He was like a heat-seeking missile that never gave up, but just kept on pursuing his target. I threw a lot of obstacles in his path, fascinated by his perseverance and his nerve: he tended to go *through* obstacles rather than around them. He was a dangerous man, all right. He sure made my heart beat a little faster.

I hope you enjoy the books. All my best—

Linda Howard

HEARTBREAKER

Chapter 1

She found the paper while she was sorting through the personal things in her father's desk. Michelle Cabot unfolded the single sheet with casual curiosity, just as she had unfolded dozens of others, but she had read only a paragraph when her spine slowly straightened and a tremor began in her fingers. Stunned, she began again, her eyes widening with sick horror at what she read.

Anybody but him. Dear God, anybody but him!

She owed John Rafferty one hundred thousand dollars.

Plus interest, of course. At what percent? She couldn't read any further to find out; instead she dropped the paper onto the littered surface of the desk and sank back in her father's battered old leather chair, her eyes closing against the nausea caused by shock, dread and the particularly sickening feeling of dying hope. She had already been on her knees; this unsuspected debt had smashed her flat.

Why did it have to be John Rafferty? Why not some impersonal bank? The end result would be the same, of course, but the humiliation would be absent. The thought of facing him made her shrivel deep inside, where she protected the tender part of herself. If Rafferty ever even suspected that that tenderness existed, she was lost. A dead duck...or a sitting one, if it made any difference. A gone goose. A cooked goose. Whatever simile she used, it fit.

Her hands were still shaking when she picked up the paper to read it again and work out the details of the financial agreement. John Rafferty had made a personal loan of one hundred thousand dollars to her father, Langley Cabot, at an interest rate two percent lower than the market rate...and the loan had been due four months ago. She felt even sicker. She knew it hadn't been repaid, because she'd gone over every detail of her father's books in an effort to salvage something from the financial disaster he'd been floundering in when he'd died. She had ruthlessly liquidated almost everything to pay the outstanding debts, everything except this ranch, which had been her father's dream and had somehow come to represent a refuge to her. She hadn't liked Florida ten years ago, when her father had sold their home and moved her from their well-ordered, monied existence in Connecticut to the heat and humidity of a cattle ranch in central Florida, but that had been a decade ago, and things changed. People changed, time changed...and time changed people. The ranch didn't represent love or a dream to her; it was, simply, all she had left. Life had seemed so complicated once, but it was remarkable how simple things were when it came down to a matter of survival.

Even now it was hard to just give up and let the inevitable happen. She had known from the beginning that it would be almost impossible for her to keep the ranch and put it back on a paying basis, but she'd been driven to at least *try*. She wouldn't have been able to live with herself if she'd taken the easy way out and let the ranch go.

Now she would have to sell the ranch after all, or at least the cattle; there was no other way she could repay that hundred thousand dollars. The wonder was that Rafferty hadn't already demanded repayment. But if she sold the cattle, what good was the ranch? She'd been depending on the cattle sales to keep her going, and without that income she'd have to sell the ranch anyway.

It was so hard to think of letting the ranch go; she had almost begun to hope that she might be able to hold on to it. She'd been afraid to hope, had tried not to, but still, that little glimmer of optimism had begun growing. Now she'd failed at this, just as she'd failed at everything else in her life: as daughter, wife, and now rancher. Even if Rafferty gave her an extension on the loan, something she didn't expect to happen, she had no real expectation of being able to pay it off when it came due again. The naked truth was that she had no expectations at all; she was merely hanging on.

Well, she wouldn't gain anything by putting it off. She had to talk to Rafferty, so it might as well be now. The clock on the wall said it wasn't quite nine-thirty; Rafferty would still be up. She looked up his number and dialed it, and the usual reaction set in. Even before the first ring sounded, her fingers were locked so tightly around the receiver that her knuckles were white, and her heart had lurched into a fast, heavy pounding that made her feel as if she'd been running. Tension knotted her stomach. Oh, damn! She wouldn't even be able to talk coherently if she didn't get a grip on herself!

The telephone was answered on the sixth ring, and by then Michelle had braced herself for the ordeal of talking to him. When the housekeeper said, "Rafferty residence," Michelle's voice was perfectly cool and even when she asked to speak to Rafferty.

"I'm sorry, he isn't in. May I take a message?"

It was almost like a reprieve, if it hadn't been for the knowledge that now she'd have to do it all over again. "Please have him call Michelle Cabot," she said, and gave the housekeeper her number. Then she asked, "Do you expect him back soon?"

There was only a slight hesitation before the housekeeper said, "No, I think he'll be quite late, but I'll give him your message first thing in the morning."

"Thank you," Michelle murmured and hung up. She should have expected him to be out. Rafferty was famous, or perhaps notorious was a better word, for his sexual appetite and escapades. If he'd quieted down over the years, it was only in his hell-raising. According to the gossip she'd heard from time to time, his libido was alive and well; a look from those hard, dark eyes still made a woman's pulse go wild, and he looked at a lot of women, but Michelle wasn't one of them. Hostility had exploded between them at their first meeting, ten years before, and at best their relationship was an armed standoff. Her father had been a buffer between them, but now he was dead, and she expected the worst. Rafferty didn't do things by half measures.

There was nothing she could do about the loan that night, and she'd lost her taste for sorting through the remainder of her father's papers, so she decided to turn in. She took a quick shower; her sore muscles would have liked a longer one, but she was doing everything she could to keep her electricity bill down, and since she got her water from a well, and the water was pumped by an electric pump, small luxuries had to go to make way for the more important ones, like eating.

But as tired as she was, when she was lying in bed she couldn't go to sleep. The thought of talking to Rafferty filled her mind again, and once more her heartbeat speeded up. She tried to take deep, slow breaths. It had always been like this, and it was even worse when she had to see him face to face. If only he wasn't so big! But he was six feet three inches and about two hundred pounds of muscled masculinity; he was good at dwarfing other people. Whenever he was close, Michelle felt threatened in some basic way, and even thinking of him made her feel suffocated. No other man in the world made her react the way he did; no one else could make her so angry, so wary—or so excited in a strange, primitive way.

It had been that way from the beginning, from the moment she'd met him ten years before. She had been eighteen then, as spoiled as he'd accused her of being, and as haughty as only a teenager standing on her dignity could be. His reputation had preceded him, and Michelle had been determined to show him that *she* couldn't be lumped with all the women who panted after him. As if he would have been interested in a teenager! she thought wryly, twisting on the bed in search of comfort. What a child she'd been! A silly, spoiled, frightened child.

Because John Rafferty *had* frightened her, even though he'd all but ignored her. Or rather, her own reaction had frightened her. He'd been twenty-six, a *man*, as opposed to the boys she was used to, and a man who had already turned a smallish central Florida cattle ranch into a growing, thriving empire by his own force of will and years of back-breaking work. Her first sight of him, towering over her father while the two men talked cattle, had scared her half to death. Even now she could recall her sudden breathlessness, as if she'd been punched in the stomach.

They'd been standing beside Rafferty's horse, and he'd had one arm draped across the saddle while his other hand was propped negligently on his hip. He'd been six feet and three inches of sheer power, all hard muscle and intensity, dominating even the big animal with his will. She'd already heard about him; men laughed and called him a "stud" in admiring tones, and women called him the same thing, but always in excited, half-fearful whispers. A woman might be given the benefit of the doubt after going out with him once, but if she went out with him twice it was accepted that she had been to bed with him. At the time Michelle hadn't even considered that his reputation was probably exaggerated. Now that she was older, she still didn't consider it. There was just something about the way Rafferty looked that made a woman believe all the tales about him.

But even his reputation hadn't prepared her for the real man, for the force and energy that radiated from him. Life burned hotter and brighter in some people, and John Rafferty was one of them. He was a dark fire, dominating his surroundings with his height and powerful build, dominating people with his forceful, even ruthless, personality.

Michelle had sucked in her breath at the sight of him, the sun glinting off his coal-black hair, his dark eyes narrowed under prominent black brows, a neat black mustache shadowing the firm line of his upper lip. He'd been darkly tanned, as he always was from hours of working outside in all seasons; even as she'd watched, a trickle of sweat had run down his temple to curve over his high, bronzed cheekbone before tacking down his cheek to finally drip off his square jaw. Patches of sweat had darkened his blue work shirt under his arms and on his chest and back. But even sweat and dirt couldn't detract from the aura of a powerful, intensely sexual male animal; perhaps they had even added to it. The hand on his hip had drawn her gaze downward to his hips and long legs, and the faded tight jeans had outlined his body so faithfully that her mouth had gone dry. Her heart had stopped beating for a moment, then lurched into a heavy rhythm that made her entire body throb. She'd been eighteen, too young to handle what she felt, too young to handle the man, and her own reaction had frightened her. Because of that, she'd been at her snooty best when she'd walked up to her father to be introduced.

They'd gotten off on the wrong foot and had been there ever since. She was probably the only woman in the world at odds with Rafferty, and she wasn't certain, even now, that she wanted it to be any different. Somehow she felt safer knowing that he disliked her; at least he wouldn't be turning that formidable charm of his on her. In that respect, hostility brought with it a certain amount of protection.

A shiver ran over her body as she lay in bed thinking about both him and what she'd admitted only to herself: she was no more immune to Rafferty than the legion of women who had already succumbed. She was safe only as long as he didn't realize how vulnerable she was to his potent masculinity. He would delight in taking advantage of his power over her, making her pay for all the cutting remarks she'd made to him over the years, and for all the other things he disliked about her. To protect herself, she had to hold him at bay with hostility; it was rather ironic that now she needed his goodwill in order to survive financially.

She had almost forgotten how to laugh except for the social sounds that passed for laughter but held no humor, or how to smile except for the false mask of cheerfulness that kept pity away, but in the darkness and privacy of her bedroom she felt a wry grin curving her mouth. If she had to depend on Rafferty's goodwill for survival, she might as well go out to the pasture, dig a hole and pull the dirt in over herself to save him the time and trouble.

The next morning she loitered around the house waiting for him to call for as long as she could, but she had chores to do, and the cattle wouldn't wait. Finally she gave up and trudged out to the barn, her mind already absorbed with the hundred and one problems the ranch presented every day. She had several fields of hay that needed to be cut and baled, but she'd been forced to sell the tractor and hay baler; the only way she could get the hay cut would be to offer someone part of the hay if they'd do the cutting and baling for her. She backed the pickup truck into the barn and climbed into the hayloft, counting the bales she had left. The supply was dwindling; she'd have to do something soon.

There was no way she could lift the heavy bales, but she'd developed her own system for handling them. She had parked the truck just under the door to the hayloft, so all she had to do was push the bales to the open door and tip them through to land in the truck bed. Pushing the hay wasn't easy; they were supposed to be hundred-pound bales, which meant that she outweighed them by maybe seventeen pounds…if she hadn't lost weight, which she suspected she had, and if the bales weighed only a hundred pounds, which she suspected they didn't. Their weight varied, but some of them were so heavy she could barely move them an inch at a time.

She drove the truck across the pasture to where the cattle grazed; heads lifted, dark brown eyes surveyed the familiar truck, and the entire herd began ambling toward her. Michelle stopped the truck and climbed in back. Tossing the bales out was impossible, so she cut the twine there in the back of the truck and loosened the hay with the pitchfork she had brought along, then pitched the hay out in big clumps. She got back in the truck, drove a piece down the pasture, and stopped to repeat the procedure. She did it until the back of the pickup was empty, and by the time she was finished her shoulders were aching so badly the muscles felt as if they were on fire. If the herd hadn't been badly diminished in numbers from what it had been, she couldn't have handled it. But if the herd were larger, she reminded herself, she'd be able to afford help. When she remembered the number of people who used to work on the ranch, the number needed to keep it going properly, a wave of hopelessness hit her. Logic told her there was no way she could do it all herself.

But what did logic have to do with cold reality? She had to do it herself because she had no one else. Sometimes she thought that was the one thing life seemed determined to teach her: that she could depend only on herself, that there was no one she could trust, no one she could rely on, no one strong enough to stand behind her and hold her up when she needed to rest. There had been times when she'd felt a crushing sense of loneliness, especially since her father had died, but there was also a certain perverse comfort in knowing she could rely on no one but herself. She expected nothing of other people, therefore she wasn't disappointed by any failure on their part to live up to her expectations. She simply accepted facts as they were, without any pretty dressing up, did what she had to do, and went on from there. At least she was free now, and no longer dreaded waking up each day.

She trudged around the ranch doing the chores, putting her mind in neutral gear and simply letting her body go through the motions. It was easier that way; she could pay attention to her aches and bruises when all the chores were finished, but the best way to get them done was to ignore the protests of her muscles and the nicks and bruises she acquired. None of her old friends would ever have believed that Michelle Cabot was capable of turning her dainty hands to rough, physical chores. Sometimes it amused her to imagine what their reactions would be, another mind game that she played with herself to pass the time. Michelle Cabot had always been ready for a party, or shopping, or a trip to St. Moritz, or a cruise on someone's yacht. Michelle Cabot had always been laughing, making wisecracks with the best of them; she'd looked perfectly *right* with a glass of champagne in her hand and diamonds in her ears. The ultimate Golden Girl, that was her.

Well, the ultimate Golden Girl had cattle to feed, hay to cut, fences that needed repair, and that was only the tip of the iceberg. She needed to dip the cattle, but that was something else she hadn't figured out how to manage by herself. There was branding, castrating, breeding…. When she allowed herself to think of everything that needed doing, she was swamped by hopelessness, so she usually didn't dwell on it. She just took each day as it came, slogging along, doing what she could. It was survival, and she'd become good at it.

By ten o'clock that night, when Rafferty hadn't called, Michelle braced herself and called him again. Again the housekeeper answered; Michelle stifled a sigh, wondering if

Rafferty ever spent a night at home. "This is Michelle Cabot. I'd like to speak to Rafferty, please. Is he home?"

"Yes, he's down at the barn. I'll switch your call to him."

So he had a telephone in the barn. For a moment she thought enviously of the operation he had as she listened to the clicks the receiver made in her ear. Thinking about his ranch took her mind off her suddenly galloping pulse and stifled breathing.

"Rafferty." His deep, impatient voice barked the word in her ear, and she jumped, her hand tightening on the receiver as her eyes closed.

"This is Michelle Cabot." She kept her tone as remote as possible as she identified herself. "I'd like to talk to you, if you have the time."

"Right now I'm damned short of time. I've got a mare in foal, so spit it out and make it fast."

"It'll take more time than that. I'd like to make an appointment, then. Would it be convenient for me to come over tomorrow morning?"

He laughed, a short, humorless bark. "This is a working ranch, sugar, not a social event. I don't have time for you tomorrow morning. Time's up."

"Then when?"

He muttered an impatient curse. "Look, I don't have time for you *now*. I'll drop by tomorrow afternoon on my way to town. About six." He hung up before she could agree or disagree, but as she hung up, too, she thought ruefully that he was calling the shots, so it didn't really matter if she liked the time or not. At least she had the telephone call behind her now, and there were almost twenty hours in which to brace herself for actually seeing him. She would stop work tomorrow in time to shower and wash her hair, and she'd do the whole routine with makeup and perfume, wear her white linen trousers and white silk shirt. Looking at her, Rafferty would never suspect that she was anything other than what he'd always thought her to be, pampered and useless.

* * *

It was late in the afternoon, the broiling sun had pushed the temperature to a hundred degrees, and the cattle were skittish. Rafferty was hot, sweaty, dusty and ill-tempered, and so were his men. They'd spent too much time chasing after strays instead of getting the branding and inoculating done, and now the deep, threatening rumble of thunder signaled a summer thunderstorm. The men speeded up their work, wanting to get finished before the storm hit.

Dust rose in the air as the anxious bawling increased in volume and the stench of burning hide intensified. Rafferty worked with the men, not disdaining any of the dirty jobs. It was *his* ranch, his life. Ranching was hard, dirty work, but he'd made it profitable when others had gone under, and he'd done it with his own sweat and steely determination. His mother had left rather than tolerate the life; of course, the ranch had been much smaller back then, not like the empire he'd built. His father, and the ranch, hadn't been able to support her in the style she'd wanted. Rafferty sometimes got a grim satisfaction from the knowledge that now his mother regretted having been so hasty to desert her husband and son so long ago. He didn't hate her; he didn't waste that much effort on her. He just didn't have much use for her, or for any of the rich, spoiled, bored, *useless* people she considered her friends.

Nev Luther straightened from the last calf, wiping his sweaty face on his shirtsleeve, then glancing at the sun and the soaring black cloud bank of the approaching storm. "Well, that's it," he grunted. "We'd better get loaded up before that thing hits." Then he glanced at his boss. "Ain't you supposed to see that Cabot gal today?"

Nev had been in the barn with Rafferty when he'd talked to Michelle, so he'd overheard the conversation. After a quick look at his watch, Rafferty swore aloud. He'd forgotten about her, and he wasn't grateful to Nev for reminding him. There were few people walking the earth who irritated him as much as Michelle Cabot.

"Damn it, I guess I'd better go," he said reluctantly. He knew what she wanted. It had surprised him that she had called at all, rather than continuing to ignore the debt. She was probably going to whine about how little money she had left and tell him that she couldn't *possibly* scrape up that amount. Just thinking about her made him want to grab her and shake her, hard. Or better yet, take a belt to her backside. She was exactly what he disliked most: a spoiled, selfish parasite who'd never done a day's work in her life. Her father had bankrupted himself paying for her pleasure jaunts, but Langley Cabot had always been a bit of a fool where his beloved only child had been concerned. Nothing had been too good for darling little Michelle, nothing at all.

Too bad that darling Michelle was a spoiled brat. Damn, she irritated him! She'd irritated him from the first moment he'd seen her, prissing up to where her father had stood talking to him, with her haughty nose in the air as if she'd smelled something bad. Well, maybe she had. Sweat, the product of physical work, was an alien odor to her. She'd looked at him the way she would have looked at a worm, then dismissed him as unimportant and turned her back to him while she coaxed and wheedled something out of her father with that charming Golden Girl act of hers.

"Say, boss, if you don't want to see that fancy little thing, I'd be happy to fill in for you," Nev offered, grinning.

"It's tempting," Rafferty said sourly, checking his watch again. He could go home and clean up, but it would make him late. He wasn't that far from the Cabot ranch now, and he wasn't in the mood to drive all the way back to his house, shower, and then make the drive again just so he wouldn't offend her dainty nose. She could put up with him as he was, dirt, sweat and all; after all, she was the one begging for favors. The mood he was in, he just might call in that debt, knowing good and well she couldn't pay it. He wondered with sardonic amusement if she would offer to pay it in another way. It would serve her right if he played along; it would make her squirm with distaste to think of letting him have her pampered body. After all, he was rough and dirty and worked for a living.

As he strode over to his truck and slid his long length under the steering wheel, he couldn't keep the image from forming in his mind: the image of Michelle Cabot lying beneath him, her slim body naked, her pale gold hair spread out over his pillow as he moved in and out of her. He felt his loins become heavy and full in response to the provocative image, and he swore under his breath. Damn her, and damn himself. He'd spent years watching her, brooding, wanting her and at the same time wanting to teach her in whatever way it took not to be such a spoiled, selfish snob.

Other people hadn't seen her that way; she could be charming when she chose, and she'd chosen to work that charm on the local people, maybe just to amuse herself with their gullibility. The ranchers and farmers in the area were a friendly group, rewarding themselves for their endless hard work with informal get-togethers, parties and barbecues almost every weekend, and Michelle had had them all eating out of her hand. They didn't see the side of her that she'd revealed to him; she was always laughing, dancing...but never with him. She would dance with every other man there, but never with him. He'd watched her, all right, and because he was a healthy male with a healthy libido he hadn't been able to stop himself from responding physically to her lithe, curved body and sparkling smile, even though it made him angry that he responded to her in any way. He didn't want to want her, but just looking at her made him hungry.

Other men had watched her with hungry eyes, too, including Mike Webster. Rafferty didn't think he'd ever forgive her for what she'd done to Mike, whose marriage had been shaky even before Michelle had burst onto the scene with her flirtatious manner and sparkling laughter. Mike hadn't been any match for her; he'd fallen hard and fast, and the Webster marriage had splintered beyond repair. Then Michelle had flitted on to fresher prey, and Mike had been left with nothing but a ruined life. The young rancher had lost everything he'd worked for, forced to sell his ranch because of the divorce settlement. He was just one more man Michelle had ruined with her selfishness, as she'd ruined her father. Even when Langley was deep in financial trouble he'd kept providing money for Michelle's expensive life-style. Her father had been going under, but he'd still insisted on buying her silks and jewels, and skiing vacations in St. Moritz. It would take a rich man to afford Michelle Cabot, and a strong one.

The thought of being the one who provided her with those things, and the one who had certain rights over her because of it, teased his mind with disturbing persistence. No matter how angry, irritated or disgusted he felt toward her, he couldn't control his physical response to her. There was something about her that made him want to reach out and take her. She looked, sounded and smelled expensive; he wanted to know if she tasted expensive, too, if her skin was as silky as it looked. He wanted to bury his hands in her sunlit hair, taste her wide, soft mouth, and trace his fingertips across the chiseled perfection of her cheekbones, inhale the gut-tightening fragrance of her skin. He'd smelled her the day they'd first met, the perfume in her hair and on her skin, and the sweetness of her flesh beneath it. She was expensive all right, too expensive for Mike Webster, and for the poor sap she'd married and then left, certainly too expensive for her father. Rafferty wanted to lose himself in all that richness. It was a pure, primitive male instinct, the reaction of the male to a ready female. Maybe Michelle was a tease, but she gave out all the right signals to bring the men running, like bees to the sweetest flower.

Right now Michelle was between supporters, but he knew it wouldn't be long before she had another man lined up. Why shouldn't he be that man? He was tired of wanting her and watching her turn her snooty little nose up at him. She wouldn't be able to wrap him around her finger as she was used to doing, but that would be the price she had to pay for her expensive tastes. Rafferty narrowed his eyes against the rain that began to splat against the windshield, thinking about the satisfaction of having Michelle dependent on him for everything she ate and wore. It was a hard, primitive satisfaction. He would use her to satisfy his burning physical hunger for her, but he wouldn't let her get close enough to cloud his mind and judgment.

He'd never paid for a woman before, never been a sugar daddy, but if that was what it took to get Michelle Cabot, he'd do it. He'd never wanted another woman the way he wanted her, so he guessed it evened out.

The threatening storm suddenly broke, sending a sheet of rain sluicing down the windshield to obscure his vision despite the wipers' best efforts. Gusts of wind shoved at the truck, making him fight to hold it steady on the road. Visibility was so bad that he almost missed the turn to the Cabot ranch even though he knew these roads as well as he knew his own face. His features were dark with ill-temper when he drove up to the Cabot house, and his disgust increased as he looked around. Even through the rain, he could tell the place had gone to hell. The yard was full of weeds, the barn and stables had the forlorn look of emptiness and neglect, and the pastures that had once been dotted with prime Brahman cattle were empty now. The little society queen's kingdom had dissolved around her.

Though he'd pulled the truck up close to the house, it was raining so hard that he was drenched to the skin by the time he sprinted to the porch. He slapped his straw hat against his leg to get most of the water off it, but didn't replace it on his head. He raised his hand to knock, but the door opened be-

fore he had a chance. Michelle stood there looking at him
with the familiar disdain in her cool, green eyes. She hesitated for just a moment, as if reluctant to let him drip water
on the carpet; then she pushed the screen door open and
said, "Come in." He imagined it ate at her guts to have to
be nice to him because she owed him a hundred thousand
dollars.

He walked past her, noting the way she moved back so he
wouldn't brush against her. Just wait, he thought savagely.
Soon he'd do more than just *brush* against her, and he'd
make damned certain she liked it. She might turn her nose
up at him now, but things would be different when she was
naked under him, her legs wrapped around his waist while
she writhed in ecstasy. He didn't just want the use of her
body; he wanted her to want him in return, to feel as hungry and obsessed as he did. It would be poetic justice, after
all the men she'd used. He almost wanted her to say something snide, so he'd have a reason to put his hands on her,
even in anger. He wanted to touch her, no matter what the
reason; he wanted to feel her warm and soft in his hands; he
wanted to make her respond to him.

But she didn't cut at him with her tongue as she usually
did. Instead she said, "Let's go into Dad's office," and led
the way down the hall with her perfume drifting behind her
to tease him. She looked untouchable in crisp white slacks
and a white silk shirt that flowed lovingly over her curvy
form, but he itched to touch her anyway. Her sunny pale-
gold hair was pulled back and held at the nape of her neck
with a wide gold clip.

Her fastidious perfection was in direct contrast to his own
rough appearance, and he wondered what she'd do if he
touched her, if he pulled her against him and got her silk
shirt wet and stained. He was dirty and sweaty and smelled
of cattle and horses, and now he was wet into the bargain;
no, there was no way she'd accept his touch.

"Please sit down," she said, waving her hand at one of the leather chairs in the office. "I imagine you know why I called."

His expression became even more sardonic. "I imagine I do."

"I found the loan paper when I was going through Daddy's desk the night before last. I don't want you to think that I'm trying to weasel out of paying it, but I don't have the money right now—"

"Don't waste my time," he advised, interrupting.

She stared up at him. He hadn't taken the chair she'd offered; he was standing too close, towering over her, and the look in his black eyes made her shiver.

"What?"

"This song and dance; don't waste my time doing the whole bit. I know what you're going to offer, and I'm willing. I've been wanting to get in your pants for a long time, honey; just don't make the mistake of thinking a few quickies will make us even, because they won't. I believe in getting my money's worth."

Chapter 2

Shock froze her in place and leeched the color from her upturned face until it was as pale as ivory. She felt disoriented; for a moment his words refused to make sense, rotating in her mind like so many unconnected pieces of a puzzle. He was looming over her, his height and muscularity making her feel as insignificant as always, while the heat and scent of his body overwhelmed her senses, confusing her. He was too close! Then the words realigned themselves, and their meaning slapped her in the face. Panic and fury took the place of shock. Without thinking she drew back from him and snapped, "You must be joking!"

It was the wrong thing to say. She knew it as soon as she'd said it. Now wasn't the time to insult him, not when she needed his cooperation if she wanted to have a prayer of keeping the ranch going, but both pride and habit made her lash back at him. She could feel her stomach tighten even as she lifted her chin to give him a haughty stare, waiting for the reaction that was sure to come after the inadvertent challenge she'd thrown in his teeth. It wasn't safe to challenge Rafferty at all, and now she'd done it in the most elemental way possible.

His face was hard and still, his eyes narrowed and burning as he watched her. Michelle could feel the iron control he exerted to keep himself from moving. "Do I look like I'm joking?" he asked in a soft, dangerous tone. "You've always had some poor sucker supporting you; why shouldn't it be my turn? You can't lead me around by the nose the way you have every other man, but the way I see it, you can't afford to be too choosy right now."

"What would *you* know about being choosy?" She went even whiter, retreating from him a few more steps; she could almost feel his impact on her skin, and he hadn't even moved. He'd had so many women that she didn't even want to think about it, because thinking about it made her hurt deep inside. Had those other women felt this helpless, this overwhelmed by his heat and sexuality? She couldn't control her inborn instincts and responses; she had always sensed her own weakness where he was concerned, and that was what frightened her, what had kept her fighting him all these years. She simply couldn't face being used by him as casually as a stallion would service a mare; it would mean too much to her, and too little to him.

"Don't pull away from me," he said, his voice going even softer, deeper, stroking her senses like dark velvet. It was the voice he would use in the night, she thought dazedly, her mind filled with the image of him covering a woman with his lean, powerful body while he murmured rawly sexual things in her ear. John wouldn't be a subtle lover; he would be strong and elemental, overwhelming a woman's senses. Wildly she blanked the image from her mind, turning her head away so she couldn't see him.

Rage lashed at him when she turned away as if she couldn't bear the sight of him; she couldn't have made it any plainer that she couldn't bear the idea of sleeping with him, either. With three long strides he circled the desk and caught her upper arms in his lean, sinewy hands, pulling her hard against him. Even in his fury he realized that this was the first time he'd touched her, felt her softness and the fragility of her bones. His hands completely encircled her arms, and his fingers wanted to linger, to stroke. Hunger rose again, pushing aside some of the anger. "Don't turn your nose up at me like some Ice Princess," he ordered roughly. "Your little kingdom has gone to hell, honey, in case you haven't noticed. Those fancy playmates of yours don't know you from Adam's housecat now that you can't afford to play. They sure haven't offered to help, have they?"

Michelle pushed against his chest, but it was like trying to move a wall. "I haven't asked them to help!" she cried, goaded. "I haven't asked anyone for help, least of all *you*!"

"Why not me?" He shook her lightly, his eyes narrowed and fierce. "I can afford you, honey."

"I'm not for sale!" She tried to pull back, but the effort was useless; though he wasn't holding her tightly enough to hurt, she was helpless against his steely strength.

"I'm not interested in buying," he murmured as he dipped his head. "Only in renting you for a while." Michelle made an inarticulate sound of protest and tried to turn her head away, but he simply closed his fist in her hair and held her still for his mouth. Just for a moment she saw his black eyes, burning with hunger, then his mouth was on hers, and she quivered in his arms like a frightened animal. Her eyelashes fluttered shut and she sank against him. For years she'd wondered about his mouth, his taste, if his lips would be firm or soft, if his mustache would scratch. Pleasure exploded in her like a fireball, flooding her with heat. Now she knew. Now she knew the warm, heady taste of his mouth, the firm fullness of his lips, the soft prickle of his mustache, the sure way his tongue moved into her mouth as if it were his right to be so intimate. Somehow her arms were around his shoulders, her nails digging through the wet fabric of his shirt to the hard muscle beneath. Somehow she was arched against him, his arms locked tight as he held her and took her mouth so deeply, over and over again. She didn't feel the moisture from his clothing seeping into hers; she felt only his heat and hardness, and dimly she knew that if she didn't stop soon, *he* wouldn't stop at all.

She didn't want to stop. Already she was coming apart inside, because she wanted nothing more than to simply lie against him and feel his hands on her. She'd known it would be like this, and she'd known she couldn't let it happen, couldn't let him get close to her. The feeling was so powerful that it frightened her. *He* frightened her. He would demand too much from her, take so much that there wouldn't be anything left when he moved on. She'd always known instinctively that she couldn't handle him.

It took every bit of inner strength she had to turn her face away from his mouth, to put her hands on his shoulders and push. She knew she wasn't strong enough to move him; when he released her and moved back a scant few inches, she was bitterly aware that it was by his own choice, not hers. He was watching her, waiting for her decision.

Silence filled the room with a thick presence as she struggled to regain her composure under his unwavering gaze. She could feel the situation slipping out of control. For ten years she had carefully cultivated the hostility between them, terrified of letting him discover that just looking at him turned her bones to water. She'd seen too many of his women with stars in their eyes while he gave them his attention, focusing his intense sexual instincts on them, but all too soon he'd moved on to someone else, and the stars had always turned into hunger and pain and emptiness. Now he was looking at her with that penetrating attention, just what she'd always tried to avoid. She hadn't wanted him to notice her as a woman; she hadn't wanted to join the ranks of all those other women he'd used and left. She had enough trouble now, without adding a broken heart, and John Rafferty was a walking heartache. Her back was already to the wall; she couldn't bear anything else, either emotionally or financially.

But his gaze burned her with black fire, sliding slowly over her body as if measuring her breasts for the way they would fit his hands, her hips for the way his would adjust against them, her legs for the way they would wrap around him in the throes of pleasure. He'd never looked at her in that way before, and it shook her down to her marrow. Pure sexual speculation was in his eyes. In his mind he was already inside her, tasting her, feeling her, giving her pleasure. It was a look few women could resist, one of unashamed sexuality, carnal experience and an arrogant confidence that a woman would be ultimately satisfied in his arms. He wanted her; he intended to have her.

And she couldn't let it happen. She'd been wrapped in a silken prison her entire life, stifled first by her father's idealistic adoration, then by Roger Beckman's obsessive jealousy. For the first time in her life she was alone, responsible for herself and finding some sense of worth in the responsibility. Fail or succeed, she needed to do this herself, not run to some man for help. She looked at John with a blank expression; he wanted her, but he didn't like or even respect her, and she wouldn't like or respect herself if she let herself become the parasite he expected her to be.

Slowly, as if her muscles ached, she eased away from him and sat down at the desk, tilting her golden head down so he couldn't see her face. Again, pride and habit came to her aid; her voice was calm and cool when she spoke. "As I said, I don't have the money to repay you right now, and I realize the debt is already delinquent. The solution depends on you—"

"I've already made my offer," he interrupted, his eyes narrowing at her coolness. He hitched one hip up on the desk beside her, his muscled thigh brushing against her arm. Michelle swallowed to alleviate the sudden dryness of her mouth, trying not to look at those powerful, denim-covered muscles. Then he leaned down, propping his bronzed forearm on his thigh, and that was worse, because it brought his torso closer, forcing her to lean back in the chair. "All you have to do is go ahead and accept it, instead of wasting time pretending you didn't like it when I touched you."

Michelle continued doggedly. "If you want repayment immediately, I'll have to sell the cattle to raise the money, and I'd like to avoid that. I'm counting on the sale of the cattle to keep the ranch going. What I have in mind is to sell some of the land to raise the money, but of course that will take longer. I can't even promise to have the money in six months; it just depends on how fast I can find a buyer." She held her breath, waiting for his response. Selling part of the land was the only plan she'd been able to devise, but it all depended on his cooperation.

Slowly he straightened, his dark brows drawing together as he stared down at her. "Whoa, honey, let's backtrack a little. What do you mean, 'keep the ranch going'? The ranch is already dead."

"No, it isn't," she denied, stubbornness creeping into her tone. "I still have some cattle left."

"Where?" His disbelief was evident.

"In the south pasture. The fence on the east side needs repair, and I haven't—" She faltered at the growing anger in his dark face. Why should it matter to him? Their land joined mostly on the north; his cattle weren't in any danger of straying.

"Let's backtrack a little further," he said tightly. "Who's supposed to be working this herd?"

So that was it. He didn't believe her, because he knew there were no cowhands working here any longer. "I'm working the herd," she threw back at him, her face closed and proud. He couldn't have made it any plainer that he didn't consider her either capable or willing when it came to ranch work.

He looked her up and down, his brows lifting as he surveyed her. She knew exactly what he saw, because she'd deliberately created the image. He saw mauve-lacquered toenails, white high-heeled sandals, crisp white linen pants and the white silk shirt, damp now, from contact with his wet clothes. Suddenly Michelle realized that she was damp all along the front, and hectic color rose to burn along her cheekbones, but she lifted her chin just that much higher. Let him look, damn him.

"Nice," he drawled. "Let me see your hands."

Instinctively her hands curled into fists and she glared at him. "Why?"

He moved like a striking rattler, catching her wrist and holding her clenched hand in front of him. She pulled back, twisting in an effort to escape him, but he merely tightened his grip and pried her fingers open, then turned her palm to the light. His face was still and expressionless as he looked down at her hand for a long minute; then he caught her other hand and examined it, too. His grip gentled, and he traced his fingertips over the scratches and half-healed blisters, the forming calluses.

Michelle sat with her lips pressed together in a grim line, her face deliberately blank. She wasn't ashamed of her hands; work inevitably left its mark on human flesh, and she'd found something healing in the hard physical demands the ranch made on her. But no matter how honorable those marks, when John looked at them it was as if he'd stripped her naked and looked at her, as if he'd exposed something private. She didn't want him to know so much about her; she didn't want that intense interest turned on her. She didn't want pity from anyone, but she especially didn't want him to soften toward her.

Then his gaze lifted, those midnight eyes examining every inch of her proud, closed expression, and every instinct in her shrilled an alarm. Too late! Perhaps it had been too late from the moment he'd stepped onto the porch. From the beginning she'd sensed the tension in him, the barely controlled anticipation that she had mistaken for his usual hostility. Rafferty wasn't used to waiting for any woman he wanted, and she'd held him off for ten years. The only time she'd been truly safe from him had been during her brief marriage, when the distance between Philadelphia and central Florida had been more than hundreds of miles; it had been the distance between two totally different life-styles, in both form and substance. But now she was back within reach, and this time she was vulnerable. She was broke, she was alone, and she owed him a hundred thousand dollars. He probably expected it to be easy.

"You didn't have to do it alone," he finally said, his deep voice somehow deeper and quieter. He still held her hands, and his rough thumbs still moved gently, caressingly, over her palms, as he stood and drew her to her feet. She realized that at no time had he hurt her; he'd held her against her will, but he hadn't hurt her. His touch was gentle, but she knew without even trying that she wouldn't be able to pull away from him until he voluntarily let her go.

Her only defense was still the light mockery she'd used against him from the beginning. She gave him a bright, careless smile. "Of course I did. As you so charmingly pointed out, I'm not exactly being trampled by all my friends rushing to my rescue, am I?"

His upper lip curled with contempt for those "friends." He'd never had any patience with the bored and idle rich. "You could've come to me."

Again she gave him that smile, knowing he hated it. "But it would take so *long* to work off a hundred-thousand-dollar debt in that fashion, wouldn't it? You know how I hate being bored. A really good prostitute makes—what?—a hundred dollars a throw? Even if you were up to three times a day, it would still take about a year—"

Swift, dark fury burned in his eyes, and he finally released her hands, but only to move his grip to her shoulders. He held her still while he raked his gaze down her body again. "Three times a day?" he asked with that deceptive softness, looking at her breasts and hips. "Yeah, I'm up to it. But you forgot about interest, honey. I charge a lot of interest."

She quivered in his hands, wanting to close her eyes against that look. She'd taunted him rashly, and he'd turned her words back on her. Yes, he was capable of it. His sexual drive was so fierce that he practically burned with it, attracting women like helpless moths. Desperately she dredged up the control to keep smiling, and managed a little shrug despite his hands on her shoulders. "Thanks anyway, but I prefer shoveling manure."

If he'd lost control of his temper then she would have breathed easier, knowing that she still had the upper hand, by however slim a margin. If she could push him away with insults, she'd be safe. But though his hands tightened a little on her shoulders, he kept a tight rein on his temper.

"Don't push too hard, honey," he advised quietly. "It wouldn't take much for me to show you right now what you really like. You'd be better off telling me just how in hell you think you're going to keep this ranch alive by yourself."

For a moment her eyes were clear and bottomless, filled with a desperation he wasn't quite certain he'd seen. Her skin was tight over her chiseled cheekbones; then the familiar cool mockery and defiance were back, her eyes mossy and opaque, her lips curling a little in the way that made him want to shake her. "The ranch is my problem," she said, dismissing the offer of aid implicit in his words. She knew the price he'd demand for his help. "The only way it concerns you is in how you want the debt repaid."

Finally he released her shoulders and propped himself against the desk again, stretching his long legs and crossing his booted feet at the ankle. "A hundred thousand is a lot of money. It wasn't easy to come up with that much cash."

She didn't need to be told that. John might be a million-aire in assets, but a rancher's money is tied up in land and stock, with the profits constantly being plowed back into the ranch. Cash simply wasn't available for wasting on frivoli-ties. Her jaw tightened. "When do you want your money?" she demanded. "Now or later?"

His dark brows lifted. "Considering the circumstances, you should be trying to sweeten me up instead of snapping at me. Why haven't you just put the ranch and cattle up for sale? You can't run the place anyway, and at least then you'd have money to live on until you find another meal ticket."

"I *can* run it," she flared, turning pale. She had to; it was all she had.

"No way, honey."

"Don't call me honey!" The ragged fury of her own voice startled her. He called every woman "honey." It was a careless endearment that meant nothing, because so many other women had heard it from him. She couldn't stand to think of him lying in the dark with another woman, his voice lazy and dark as they talked and he called her "honey."

He caught her chin in his big, rough hand, turning her face up to his while his thumb rubbed over her lower lip. "I'll call you whatever I want...*honey*, and you'll keep your mouth shut, because you owe me a lot of money that you can't repay. I'm going to think awhile about that debt and what we're going to do about it. Until I decide, why don't you think about this?"

Too late she tried to draw her head back, but he still held her chin, and his warm mouth settled over hers before she could jerk free. Her eyes closed as she tried to ignore the surge of pleasure in her midsection, tried to ignore the way his lips moved over hers and his tongue probed for en-trance. If anything, this was worse than before, because now he was kissing her with a slow assurance that beguiled even as he demanded. She tried to turn her head away, but he forestalled the movement, spreading his legs and pulling her inside the cradle of his iron-muscled thighs. Michelle began shaking. Her hands flattened against his chest, but she could feel his heartbeat pulsing strongly against her palm, feel the accelerated rhythm of it, and she wanted to sink herself into him. Slowly he wedged her head back against his shoulder, his fingers woven into her hair as he held her. There was no way she could turn her head away from him now, and slowly she began to give way to his will. Her mouth opened beneath his, accepting the slow thrust of his tongue as he penetrated her in that small way and filled her with his taste.

He kissed her with shattering absorption, as if he couldn't get enough of her. Even the dim thought that he must have practised his technique with hundreds of women didn't lessen its power. She was utterly wrapped around by him, overwhelmed by his touch and scent and taste, her body tingling and aching with both pleasure and the need to have more of him. She wanted him; she'd always wanted him. He'd been an obsession with her from the moment she had seen him, and she'd spent most of the past ten years running from the power of that obsession, only to wind up practically at his mercy anyway—if he had any mercy.

He lifted his head in slow motion, his dark eyes heavy lidded, his mouth moist from kissing her. Blatant satisfaction was written across his hard face as he surveyed her. She was lying limply against him, her face dazed with pure want, her lips red and swollen. Very gently he put her away from him, holding her with his hands on her waist until she was steady on her feet; then he got to his own feet.

As always when he towered over her, Michelle automatically retreated a step. Frantically she searched for control, for something to say to him to deny the response she'd just given him, but what could she say that he'd believe? She couldn't have been more obvious! But then, neither could he. It was useless to try to regain lost ground, and she wasn't going to waste time trying. All she could do was try to put a halt to things now.

Her face was pale as she faced him, her hands twisted together in a tight knot. "I won't sleep with you to pay that debt, no matter what you decide. Did you come here tonight expecting to whisk me straight up to bed, assuming that I'd choose to turn whore for you?"

He eyed her sharply. "The thought crossed my mind. I was willing."

"Well, I'm not!" Breath rushed swiftly in and out of her lungs as she tried to control the outrage that burned in her at the insult. She had to control it; she couldn't afford to fall apart now.

"I'm glad, because I've changed my mind," he said lazily.

"Gosh, that's big of you!" she snapped.

"You'll go to bed with me, all right, but it won't be because of any money you owe me. When the time comes, you'll spread your legs for me because you want me just the way I want you."

The way he was looking at her made her shiver, and the image his rough words provoked shot through her brain like lightning. He would use her up and toss her away, just as he had all those other women, if she let him get too close to her. "Thanks, but no thanks. I've never gone in for group sex, and that's what it would be like with you!"

She wanted to make him angry, but instead he cupped her knotted-up hands in his palm and lightly rubbed his thumb over her knuckles. "Don't worry, I can guarantee there'll just be the two of us between the sheets. Settle down and get used to the idea. I'll be back out tomorrow to look over the ranch and see what needs to be done—"

"No," she interrupted fiercely, jerking her hands from his grip. "The ranch is mine. I can handle it on my own."

"Honey, you've never even handled a checkbook on your own. Don't worry about it; I'll take care of everything."

His amused dismissal set her teeth on edge, more because of her own fear that he was right than anything else. "I don't want you to take care of everything!"

"You don't know what you want," he replied, leaning down to kiss her briefly on the mouth. "I'll see you tomorrow."

Just like that he turned and walked out of the room, and after a moment Michelle realized he was leaving. She ran after him and reached the front door in time to see him sprinting through the downpour to his truck.

He didn't take her seriously. Well, why should he? Michelle thought bitterly. No one else ever had, either. She leaned on the doorframe and watched him drive away; her shaky legs needed the extra support. Why now? For years she'd kept him at a distance with her carefully manufactured hostility, but all of a sudden her protective barrier had shattered. Like a predator, he'd sensed her vulnerability and moved in for the kill.

Quietly she closed the door, shutting out the sound of rain. The silent house enclosed her, an empty reminder of the shambles of her life.

Her jaw clenched as she ground her teeth together, but she didn't cry. Her eyes remained dry. She couldn't afford to waste her time or strength indulging in useless tears. Somehow she had to hold on to the ranch, repay that debt and hold off John Rafferty....

The last would be the hardest of all, because she'd be fighting against herself. She didn't want to hold him off; she wanted to creep into his iron-muscled arms and feel them close around her. She wanted to feed her hunger for him, touch him as she'd never allowed herself to do, immerse herself in the man. Guilt arose in her throat, almost choking her. She'd married another man wanting John, loving John, *obsessed* with John; somehow Roger, her ex-husband, had sensed it, and his jealousy had turned their marriage into a nightmare.

Her mind burned with the memories, and to distract herself she walked briskly into the kitchen and prepared dinner for one; in this case, a bowl of cornflakes in milk. It was also what she'd had for breakfast, but her nerves were too raw to permit any serious cooking. She was actually able to eat half of the bowlful of cereal before she suddenly dropped the spoon and buried her face in her hands.

All her life she'd been a princess, the darling, pampered apple of her parents' eyes, born to them when they were both nearing forty and had given up hope of ever having children. Her mother had been a gentle, vague person who had passed straight from her father's keeping into that of her husband, and thought that a woman's role in life was to provide a comfortable, loving home for her husband, who supported her. It wasn't an unusual outlook for her generation, and Michelle didn't fault her mother for it. Langley Cabot had protected and spoiled both his wife and his daughter; that was the way life was supposed to be, and it was a source of pride to him that he supported them very well indeed. When her mother died, Michelle had become the recipient of all that protective devotion. Langley had wanted her to have the best of everything; he had wanted her to be happy, and to his way of thinking he had failed as a father and provider if she weren't.

In those days Michelle had been content to let her father shower her with gifts and luxuries. Her life had been humming along just as she had always expected, until the day Langley had turned her world upside down by selling the Connecticut house where she'd grown up, and moved her down to a cattle ranch in central Florida, not far from the Gulf coast. For the first time in her life, Langley had been unmoved by her pleas. The cattle ranch was his dream come true, the answer to some deeply buried need in him that had been hidden under silk shirts, pin-striped suits and business appointments. Because he'd wanted it so badly, he had ignored Michelle's tears and tantrums and jovially assured her that before long she'd have new friends and would love the ranch as much as he did.

In that, he was partially right. She made new friends, gradually became accustomed to the heat, and even enjoyed life on a working cattle ranch. Langley had completely remodeled the old ranch house when he'd bought it, to ensure that his beloved daughter wasn't deprived in any way of the comfort she was accustomed to. So she'd adjusted, and even gone out of her way to assure him of her contentment. He deserved his dream, and she had felt ashamed that she'd tried to talk him out of it. He did so much to make her happy, the least she could do was return as much of the effort as she could.

Then she'd met John Rafferty. She couldn't believe that she'd spent ten years running from him, but it was true. She'd hated him and feared him and loved him all at once, with a teenager's wildly passionate obsession, but she had always seen one thing very clearly: he was more than she could handle. She had never daydreamed of being the one woman who could tame the rake; she was far too vulnerable to him, and he was too strong. He might take her and use her, but she wasn't woman enough to hold him. She was spoiled and pampered; he didn't even like her. In self-defense, she had devoted herself to making him dislike her even more to make certain he never made a move on her.

She had gone to an exclusive women's college back east, and after graduation had spent a couple of weeks with a friend who lived in Philadelphia. During that visit she'd met Roger Beckman, scion of one of the oldest and richest families in town. He was tall and black haired, and he even had a trim mustache. His resemblance to John was slight, except for those points, and Michelle couldn't say that she had consciously married Roger because he reminded her of John, but she was very much afraid that subconsciously she had done exactly that.

Roger was a lot of fun. He had a lazy manner about him, his eyes wrinkled at the edges from smiling so much, and he loved organized crazy games, like scavenger hunts. In his company Michelle could forget about John and simply have fun. She was genuinely fond of Roger, and came to love him as much as she would ever love any man who wasn't John Rafferty. The best thing she could do was forget about John, put him behind her and get on with her life. After all, there had never been anything between them except her own fantasies, and Roger absolutely adored her. So she had married him, to the delight of both her father and his parents.

It was a mistake that had almost cost her her life.

At first everything had been fine. Then Roger had begun to show signs of jealousy whenever Michelle was friendly to another man. Had he sensed that she didn't love him as she should? That he owned only the most superficial part of her heart? Guilt ate at her even now, because Roger's jealousy hadn't been groundless. He hadn't been able to find the true target, so he'd lashed out whenever she smiled at any man, danced with any man.

The scenes had gotten worse, and one night he'd actually slapped her during a screaming fight after a party; she'd made the mistake of speaking to the same man twice while they raided the buffet table. Shocked, her face burning, Michelle had stared at her husband's twisted features and realized that his jealousy had driven him out of control. For the first time, she was afraid of him.

His action had shocked Roger, too, and he'd buried his face in her lap, clinging to her as he wept and begged her forgiveness. He'd sworn never to hurt her again; he'd said he would rather cut off his own hands than hurt her. Shaken to the core, Michelle did what thousands of women did when their husbands turned on them: she forgave him.

But it wasn't the last time. Instead, it got worse.

Michelle had been too ashamed and shocked to tell anyone, but finally she couldn't take any more and pressed charges against him. To her horror, his parents quietly bought off everyone involved, and Michelle was left without a legal leg to stand on, all evidence destroyed. Come hell or high water, the Beckmans would protect their son.

Finally she tried to leave him, but she had gotten no further than Baltimore before he caught up with her, his face livid with rage. It was then that Michelle realized he wasn't quite sane; his jealousy had pushed him over the edge. Holding her arm in a grip that left bruises for two weeks, he made the threat that kept her with him for the next two years: if she left him again, he'd have her father killed.

She hadn't doubted him, nor did she doubt that he'd get away with it; he was too well protected by his family's money and prestige, by a network of old family friends in the law business. So she'd stayed, terrified that he might kill her in one of his rages, but not daring to leave. No matter what, she had to protect her father.

But finally she found a way to escape. Roger had beaten her with a belt one night. But his parents had been in Europe on vacation, and by the time they found out about the incident it was too late to use their influence. Michelle had crept out of the house, gone to a hospital where her bruises and lacerations were treated and recorded, and she'd gotten copies of the records. Those records had bought her a divorce.

The princess would carry the scars to her grave.

Chapter 3

The telephone rang as Michelle was nursing her second cup of coffee, watching the sun come up and preparing herself for another day of chores that seemed to take more and more out of her. Dark circles lay under her heavy-lidded eyes, testimony to hours of twisting restlessly in bed while her mind insisted on replaying every word John had said, every sensation his mouth and hands had evoked. His reputation was well earned, she had thought bitterly in the early hours. Lady-killer. His touch was burningly tender, but he was hell on his women anyway.

She didn't want to answer the phone, but she knew John well enough to know he never gave up once he set his mind on something. He'd be back, and she knew it. If that was him on the telephone, he'd come over if she didn't answer. She didn't feel up to dealing with him in person, so she picked up the receiver and muttered a hello.

"Michelle, darling."

She went white, her fingers tightening on the receiver. Had she conjured him up by thinking about him the night before? She tried *not* to think of him, to keep him locked in the past, but sometimes the nightmare memories surfaced, and she felt again the terror of being so alone and helpless, with no one she could trust to come to her aid, not even her father.

"Roger," she said faintly. There was no doubt. No one but her ex-husband said her name in that caressing tone, as if he adored her.

His voice was low, thick. "I need you, darling. Come back to me, please. I'm begging. I promise I'll never hurt you again. I'll treat you like a princess—"

"No," she gasped, groping for a chair to support her shaking legs. Cold horror made her feel sick. How could he even suggest that she come back?

"Don't say that, please," he groaned. "Michelle, Mother and Dad are dead. I need you now more than ever. I thought you'd come for their funeral last week, but you stayed away, and I can't stand it any longer. If you'll just come back I swear everything will be different—"

"We're divorced," she broke in, her voice thin with strain. Cold sweat trickled down her spine.

"We can be remarried. Please, darling—"

"No!" The thought of being remarried to him filled her with so much revulsion that she couldn't even be polite. Fiercely she struggled for control. "I'm sorry about your parents; I didn't know. What happened?"

"Plane crash." Pain still lingered in his hoarse voice. "They were flying up to the lake and got caught in a storm."

"I'm sorry," she said again, but even if she'd known in time to attend the funeral, she never would have gone. She would never willingly be in Roger's presence again.

He was silent a moment, and she could almost see him rub the back of his neck in the unconscious nervous gesture she'd seen so many times. "Michelle, I still love you. Nothing's any good for me without you. I swear, it won't be the same as it was; I'll never hurt you again. I was just so damned jealous, and I know now I didn't have any reason."

But he did! she thought, squeezing her eyes shut as guilt seeped in to mix with the raw terror evoked by simply hearing his voice. Not physically, but had there been any day during the past ten years when she hadn't thought of John Rafferty? When part of her hadn't been locked away from Roger and every other man because they weren't the heartbreaker who'd stolen her heart?

"Roger, don't," she whispered. "It's over. I'll never come back. All I want to do now is work this ranch and make a living for myself."

He made a disgusted sound. "You shouldn't be working that dinky little ranch! You're used to much better than that. I can give you anything you want."

"No," she said softly. "You can't. I'm going to hang up now. Goodbye, and please don't call me again." Very gently she replaced the receiver, then stood by the phone with her face buried in her hands. She couldn't stop trembling, her mind and body reeling with the ramifications of what he'd told her. His parents were dead, and she had been counting on them to control him. That was the deal she'd made with them; if they would keep Roger away from her, she wouldn't release the photos and medical report to the press, who would have a field day with the scandal. Imagine, a Beckman of Philadelphia nothing but a common wifebeater! That evidence had kept her father safe from Roger's insane threats, too, and now he was forever beyond Roger's reach. She had lived in hell to protect her father, knowing that Roger was capable of doing exactly what he'd threatened, and knowing after the first incident that his parents would make certain Roger was protected, no matter what.

She had honestly liked her in-laws until then, but her affection had died an irrevocable death when they had bought Roger out of trouble the first time he'd really hurt her. She had known their weakness then, and she had forced herself to wait. There was no one to help her; she had only herself. Once she had been desperate enough to mention it to her father, but he'd become so upset that she hadn't pushed it, and in only a moment he'd convinced himself that she'd been exaggerating. Marriage was always an adjustment, and Michelle was spoiled, highly strung. Probably it was just an argument over some minor thing, and the young couple would work things out.

The cold feeling of aloneness had spread through her, but she hadn't stopped loving him. He loved her, she knew he did, but he saw her as more of a doll than a human being. His perfect, loving darling. He couldn't accept such ugliness in her life. She had to be happy, or it would mean he'd failed her in some basic way as a father, protector and provider. For his own sake, he had to believe she was happy. That was his weakness, so she had to be strong for both of them. She had to protect him, and she had to protect herself.

There was no way she would ever go back to Roger. She had dealt with the nightmares and put them behind her; she had picked up the pieces of her life and gone on, not letting the memories turn her into a frightened shell. But the memories, and the fear, were still there, and all it took was hearing Roger's voice to make her break out in a cold sweat. The old feeling of vulnerability and isolation swept over her, making her feel sick.

She jerked around, wrenching herself from the spell, and dashed what was left of her coffee down the drain. The best thing was to be active, to busy herself with whatever came to hand. That was the way she'd handled it when she had finally managed to get away from Roger, globe-trotting for two years because her father had thought that would take her mind off the divorce, and she had let the constant travel distract her. Now she had real work to do, work that left her exhausted and aching but was somehow healing, because it was the first worthwhile work she'd ever done.

It had been eating at him all morning.

He'd been in a bad mood from the moment he'd gotten out of bed, his body aching with frustration, as if he were some randy teenager with raging hormones. He was a long way from being a teenager, but his hormones were giving him hell, and he knew exactly why. He hadn't been able to sleep for remembering the way she'd felt against him, the sweetness of her taste and the silky softness of her body. And she wanted him, too; he was too experienced to be mistaken about something like that. But he'd pushed too hard, driven by ten years of having an itch he couldn't scratch, and she'd balked. He'd put her in the position of paying him with her body, and she hadn't liked that. What woman would? Even the ones who were willing usually wanted a pretty face put on it, and Michelle was haughtier than most.

But she hadn't looked haughty the day before. His frown grew darker. She had tried, but the old snooty coldness was missing. She was dead broke and had nowhere to turn. Perhaps she was scared, wondering what she was going to do without the cushion of money that had always protected her. She was practically helpless, having no job skills or talents other than social graces, which weren't worth a hell of a lot on the market. She was all alone on that ranch, without the people to work it.

He made a rough sound and pulled his horse's head around. "I'll be back later," he told Nev, nudging the horse's flanks with his boot heels.

Nev watched him ride away. "Good riddance," he muttered. Whatever was chewing on the boss had put him in the worst mood Nev had ever seen; it would be a relief to work without him.

John's horse covered the distance with long, easy strides; it was big and strong, seventeen hands high, and inclined to be a bit stubborn, but they had fought that battle a long time ago. Now the animal accepted the mastery of the iron-muscled legs and strong, steady hands of his rider. The big horse liked a good run, and he settled into a fast, smooth rhythm as they cut across pastures, his pounding hooves sending clods of dirt flying.

The more John thought about it, the less he liked it. She'd been trying to work that ranch by herself. It didn't fit in with what he knew of Michelle, but her fragile hands bore the marks. He had nothing but contempt for someone who disdained good honest work and expected someone else to do it for them, but something deep and primitive inside him was infuriated at the idea of Michelle even trying to manage the backbreaking chores around the ranch. Damn it, why hadn't she asked for help? Work was one thing, but no one expected her to turn into a cowhand. She wasn't strong enough; he'd held her in his arms, felt the delicacy of her bones, the greyhound slenderness of her build. She didn't need to be working cattle any more than an expensive thoroughbred should be used to plow a field. She could get hurt, and it might be days before anyone found her. He'd always been disgusted with Langley for spoiling and protecting her, and with Michelle for just sitting back and accepting it as her due, but suddenly he knew just how Langley had felt. He gave a disgusted snort at himself, making the horse flick his ears back curiously at the sound, but the hard fact was that he didn't like the idea of Michelle's trying to work that ranch. It was a man's work, and more than one man, at that.

Well, he'd take care of all that for her, whether she liked it or not. He had the feeling she wouldn't, but she'd come around. She was too used to being taken care of, and, as he'd told her, now it was his turn.

Yesterday had changed everything. He'd felt her response to him, felt the way her mouth had softened and shaped itself to his. She wanted him, too, and the knowledge only increased his determination to have her. She had tried to keep him from seeing it; that acid tongue of hers would have made him lose his temper if he hadn't seen the flicker of uncertainty in her eyes. It was so unusual that he'd almost wanted to bring back the haughtiness that aggravated him so much.... Almost, but not quite. She was vulnerable now, vulnerable to him. She might not like it, but she needed him. It was an advantage he intended to use.

There was no answer at the door when he got to the ranch house, and the old truck was missing from its customary parking place in the barn. John put his fists on his hips and looked around, frowning. She had probably driven into town, though it was hard to think that Michelle Cabot was willing to let herself be seen in that kind of vehicle. It was her only means of transportation, though, so she didn't have much choice.

Maybe it was better that she was gone; he could check around the ranch without her spitting and hissing at him like an enraged cat, and he'd look at those cattle in the south pasture. He wanted to know just how many head she was running, and how they looked. She couldn't possibly handle a big herd by herself, but for her sake he hoped they were in good shape, so she could get a fair price for them. He'd handle it himself, make certain she didn't get rooked. The cattle business wasn't a good one for beginners.

He swung into the saddle again. First he checked the east pasture, where she had said the fence was down. Whole sections of it would have to be replaced, and he made mental notes of how much fencing it would take. The entire ranch was run-down, but fencing was critical; it came first. Lush green grass covered the east pasture; the cattle should be in it right now. The south pasture was probably overgrazed, and the cattle would show it, unless the herd was small enough that the south pasture could provide for its needs.

It was a couple of hours before he made it to the south pasture. He reined in the horse as he topped a small rise that gave him a good view. The frown snapped into place again, and he thumbed his hat onto the back of his head. The cattle he could see scattered over the big pasture didn't constitute a big herd, but made for far more than the small one he'd envisioned. The pasture was badly overgrazed, but scattered clumps of hay testified to Michelle's efforts to feed her herd. Slow-rising anger began to churn in him as he thought of her wrestling with heavy bales of hay; some of them probably weighed more than she did.

Then he saw her, and in a flash the anger rose to boiling point. The old truck was parked in a clump of trees, which was why he hadn't noticed it right off, and she was down there struggling to repair a section of fencing by herself. Putting up fencing was a two-man job; one person couldn't hold the barbed wire securely enough, and there was always the danger of the wire backlashing. The little fool! If the wire got wrapped around her, she wouldn't be able to get out of it without help, and those barbs could really rip a person up. The thought of her lying tangled and bleeding in a coil of barbed wire made him both sick and furious.

He kept the horse at an easy walk down the long slope to where she was working, deliberately giving himself time to get control of his temper. She looked up and saw him, and even from the distance that still separated them he could see her stiffen. Then she turned back to the task of hammering a staple into the fence post, her jerky movements betraying her displeasure at his presence.

He dismounted with a fluid, easy motion, never taking his gaze from her as he tied the reins to a low-hanging tree branch. Without a word he pulled the strand of wire to the next post and held it taut while Michelle, equally silent, pounded in another staple to hold it. Like him, she had on short leather work gloves, but her gloves were an old pair of men's gloves that had been left behind and were far too big for her, making it difficult for her to pick up the staples, so she had pulled off the left glove. She could handle the staples then, but the wire had already nicked her unprotected flesh several times. He saw the angry red scratches; some of which were deep enough for blood to well, and he wanted to shake her until her teeth rattled.

"Don't you have any better sense than to try to put up fencing on your own?" he rasped, pulling another strand tight.

She hammered in the staple, her expression closed. "It has to be done. I'm doing it."

"Not anymore, you aren't."

His flat statement made her straighten, her hand closing tightly around the hammer. "You want the payment right away," she said tonelessly, her eyes sliding to the cattle. She was a little pale, and tension pulled the skin tight across her high cheekbones.

"If that's what I have to do." He pried the hammer from her grip, then bent to pick up the sack of staples. He walked over to the truck, then reached in the open window and dropped them onto the floorboard. Then he lifted the roll of barbed wire onto the truck bed. "That'll hold until I can get my men out here to do it right. Let's go."

It was a good thing he'd taken the hammer away from her. Her hands balled into fists. "I don't want your men out here doing it right! This is still my land, and I'm not willing to pay the price you want for your help."

"I'm not giving you a choice." He took her arm, and no matter how she tried she couldn't jerk free of those long, strong fingers as he dragged her over to the truck, opened the door and lifted her onto the seat. He released her then, slamming the door and stepping back.

"Drive carefully, honey. I'll be right behind you."

She had to drive carefully; the pasture was too rough for breakneck speed, even if the old relic had been capable of it. She knew he was easily able to keep up with her on his horse, though she didn't check the rearview mirror even once. She didn't want to see him, didn't want to think about selling the cattle to pay her debt. That would be the end of the ranch, because she'd been relying on that money to keep the ranch going.

She'd hoped he wouldn't come back today, though it had been a fragile hope at best. After talking to Roger that morning, all she wanted was to be left alone. She needed time by herself to regain her control, to push all the ugly memories away again, but John hadn't given her that time. He wanted her, and like any predator he'd sensed her vulnerability and was going to take advantage of it.

She wanted to just keep driving, to turn the old truck down the driveway, hit the road and keep on going. She didn't want to stop and deal with John, not now. The urge to run was so strong that she almost did it, but a glance at the fuel gauge made her mouth twist wryly. If she ran, she'd have to do it on foot, either that or steal John's horse.

She parked the truck in the barn, and as she slid off the high seat John walked the horse inside, ducking his head a little to miss the top of the doorframe. "I'm going to cool the horse and give him some water," he said briefly. "Go on in the house. I'll be there in a minute."

Was postponing the bad news for a few minutes supposed to make her feel better? Instead of going straight to the house, she walked down to the end of the driveway and collected the mail. Once the mailbox had been stuffed almost every day with magazines, catalogs, newspapers, letters from friends, business papers, but now all that came was junk mail and bills. It was odd how the mail reflected a person's solvency, as if no one in the world wanted to communicate with someone who was broke. Except for past-due bills, of course. Then the communications became serious.

A familiar envelope took her attention, and a feeling of dread welled in her as she trudged up to the house. The electric bill was past due; she'd already had one late notice, and here was another one. She had to come up with the money fast, or the power would be disconnected. Even knowing what it was, she opened the envelope anyway and scanned the notice. She had ten days to bring her account up to date. She checked the date of the notice; it had taken three days to reach her. She had seven days left.

But why worry about the electricity if she wouldn't have a ranch? Tiredness swept over her as she entered the cool, dim house and simply stood for a moment, luxuriating in the relief of being out of the broiling sun. She shoved the bills and junk mail into the same drawer of the entry table where she had put the original bill and the first late notice; she never forgot about them, but at least she could put them out of sight.

She was in the kitchen, having a drink of water, when she heard the screen door slam, then the sharp sound of boot heels on the oak parquet flooring as he came down the hallway. She kept drinking, though she was acutely aware of his progress through the house. He paused to look into the den, then the study. The slow, deliberate sound of those boots as he came closer made her shiver in reaction. She could see him in her mind's eye; he had a walk that any drugstore cowboy would kill for: that loose, long-legged, slim-hipped saunter, tight buttocks moving up and down. It was a walk that came naturally to hell-raisers and heartbreakers, and Rafferty was both.

She knew the exact moment when he entered the kitchen, though her back was to him. Her skin suddenly tingled, as if the air had become charged, and the house no longer seemed so cool.

"Let me see your hand." He was so close behind her that she couldn't turn without pressing against him, so she remained where she was. He took her left hand in his and lifted it.

"They're just scratches," she muttered.

She was right, but admitting it didn't diminish his anger. She shouldn't have any scratches at all; she shouldn't be trying to repair fencing. Her hand lay in his bigger, harder one like a pale, fragile bird, too tired to take flight, and suddenly he knew that the image was exactly right. She was tired.

He reached around her to turn on the water, then thoroughly soaped and rinsed her hand. Michelle hurriedly set the water glass aside, before it slipped from her trembling fingers, then stood motionless, with her head bowed. He was very warm against her back; she felt completely surrounded by him, with his arms around her while he washed her hand with the gentleness a mother would use to wash an infant. That gentleness staggered her senses, and she kept her head bent precisely to prevent herself from letting it drop back against his shoulder to let him support her.

The soap was rinsed off her hand now, but still he held it under the running water, his fingers lightly stroking. She quivered, trying to deny the sensuality of his touch. He was just washing her hand! The water was warm, but his hand was warmer, the rough calluses rasping against her flesh as he stroked her with a lover's touch. His thumb traced circles on her sensitive palm, and Michelle felt her entire body tighten. Her pulse leaped, flooding her with warmth. "Don't," she said thickly, trying unsuccessfully to pull free.

He turned off the water with his right hand, then moved it to her stomach and spread his fingers wide, pressing her back against his body. His hand was wet; she felt the dampness seeping through her shirt in front, and the searing heat of him at her back. The smell of horse and man rose from that seductive heat. Everything about the man was a come-on, luring women to him.

"Turn around and kiss me," he said, his voice low, daring her to do it.

She shook her head and remained silent, her head bent.

He didn't push it, though they both knew that if he had, she wouldn't have been able to resist him. Instead he dried her hand, then led her to the downstairs bathroom and made her sit on the lid of the toilet while he thoroughly cleaned the scratches with antiseptic. Michelle didn't flinch from the stinging; what did a few scratches matter, when she was going to lose the ranch? She had no other home, no other place she wanted to be. After being virtually imprisoned in that plush penthouse in Philadelphia, she needed the feeling of space around her. The thought of living in a city again made her feel stifled and panicky, and she would have to live in some city somewhere to get a job, since she didn't even have a car to commute. The old truck in the barn wouldn't hold up to a long drive on a daily basis.

John watched her face closely; she was distracted about something, or she would never have let him tend her hand the way he had. After all, it was something she could easily have done herself, and he'd done it merely to have an excuse to touch her. He wanted to know what she was thinking, why she insisted on working this ranch when it had to be obvious even to her that it was more than she could handle. It simply wasn't in character for her.

"When do you want the money?" she asked dully.

His mouth tightened as he straightened and pulled her to her feet. "Money isn't what I want," he replied.

Her eyes flashed with green fire as she looked at him. "I'm not turning myself into a whore, even for you! Did you think I'd jump at the chance to sleep with you? Your reputation must be going to your head . . . *stud*."

He knew people called him that, but when Michelle said it, the word dripped with disdain. He'd always hated that particular tone, so icy and superior, and it made him see red now. He bent down until his face was level with hers, their noses almost touching, and his black eyes were so fiery that she could see gold sparks in them. "When we're in bed, honey, you can decide for yourself about my reputation."

"I'm not going to bed with you," she said through clenched teeth, spacing the words out like dropping stones into water.

"The hell you're not. But it won't be for this damned ranch." Straightening to his full height again, he caught her arm. "Let's get that business settled right now, so it'll be out of the way and you can't keep throwing it in my face."

"You're the one who put it on that basis," she shot back as they returned to the kitchen. He dropped several ice cubes in a glass and filled it with water, then draped his big frame on one of the chairs. She watched his muscular throat working as he drained the glass, and a weak, shivery feeling swept over her. Swiftly she looked away, cursing her own powerful physical response to the mere sight of him.

"I made a mistake," he said tersely, putting the glass down with a thump. "Money has nothing to do with it. We've been circling each other from the day we met, sniffing and fighting like cats in heat. It's time we did something about it. As for the debt, I've decided what I want. Deed that land you were going to sell over to me instead, and we'll be even."

It was just like him to divide her attention like that, so she didn't know how to react or what to say. Part of her wanted to scream at him for being so smugly certain she would sleep with him, and part of her was flooded with relief that the debt had been settled so easily. He could have ruined her by insisting on cash, but he hadn't. He wasn't getting a bad deal, by any means; it was good, rich pastureland he was obtaining, and he knew it.

It was a reprieve, one she hadn't expected, and she didn't know how to deal with it, so she simply sat and stared at him. He waited, but when she didn't say anything he leaned back in his chair, his hard face becoming even more determined. "There's a catch," he drawled.

The high feeling of relief plummeted, leaving her sick and empty. "Let me guess," she said bitterly, shoving her chair back and standing. So it had all come down to the same thing after all.

His mouth twisted wryly in self-derision. "You're way off, honey. The catch is that you let me help you. My men will do the hard labor from now on, and if I even hear of you trying to put up fencing again, you'll be sitting on a pillow for a month."

"If your men do my work, I'll still be in debt to you."

"I don't consider it a debt; I call it helping a neighbor."

"I call it a move to keep me obligated!"

"Call it what you like, but that's the deal. You're one woman, not ten men; you're not strong enough to take care of the livestock and keep the ranch up, and you don't have the money to afford help. You're mighty short on options, so stop kicking. It's your fault, anyway. If you hadn't liked to ski so much, you wouldn't be in this position."

She drew back, her green eyes locked on him. Her face was pale. "What do you mean?"

John got to his feet, watching her with the old look that said he didn't much like her. "I mean that part of the reason your daddy borrowed the money from me was so he could afford to send you to St. Moritz with your friends last year. He was trying to hold his head above water, but that didn't matter to you as much as living in style, did it?"

She had been pale before, but now she was deathly white. She stared at him as if he'd slapped her, and too late he saw the shattered look in her eyes. Swiftly he rounded the table, reaching for her, but she shrank away from him, folding in on herself like a wounded animal. How ironic that she should now be struggling to repay a debt made to finance a trip she hadn't wanted! All she'd wanted had been time alone in a quiet place, a chance to lick her wounds and fin-

ish recovering from a brutal marriage, but her father had
thought resuming a life of trips and shopping with her
friends would be better, and she'd gone along with him because it had made him happy.

"I didn't even want to go," she said numbly, and to her
horror tears began welling in her eyes. She didn't want to
cry; she hadn't cried in years, except once when her father
died, and she especially didn't want to cry in front of Rafferty. But she was tired and off balance, disturbed by the
phone call from Roger that morning, and this just seemed
like the last straw. The hot tears slipped silently down her
cheeks.

"God, don't," he muttered, wrapping his arms around
her and holding her to him, her face pressed against his
chest. It was like a knife in him to see those tears on her face,
because in all the time he'd known her, he'd never before
seen her cry. Michelle Cabot had faced life with either a
laugh or a sharp retort, but never with tears. He found he
preferred an acid tongue to this soundless weeping.

For just a moment she leaned against him, letting him
support her with his hard strength. It was too tempting;
when his arms were around her, she wanted to forget everything and shut the world out, as long as he was holding her.
That kind of need frightened her, and she stiffened in his
arms, then pulled free. She swiped her palms over her
cheeks, wiping away the dampness, and stubbornly blinked
back the remaining tears.

His voice was quiet. "I thought you knew."

She threw him an incredulous look before turning away.
What an opinion he had of her! She didn't mind his thinking she was spoiled; her father had spoiled her, but mostly
because he'd enjoyed doing it so much. Evidently John not
only considered her a common whore, but a stupid one to
boot.

"Well, I didn't. And whether I knew or not doesn't
change anything. I still owe you the money."

"We'll see my lawyer tomorrow and have the deed drawn up, and that'll take care of the damned debt. I'll be here at nine sharp, so be ready. A crew of men will be here in the morning to take care of the fencing and get the hay out to the herd."

He wasn't going to give in on that, and he was right; it *was* too much for her, at least right now. She couldn't do it all simply because it was too much for one person to do. After she fattened up the beef cattle and sold them off, she'd have some capital to work with and might be able to hire someone part-time.

"All right. But keep a record of how much I owe you. When I get this place back on its feet, I'll repay every penny." Her chin was high as she turned to face him, her green eyes remote and proud. This didn't solve all her problems, but at least the cattle would be cared for. She still had to get the money to pay the bills, but that problem was hers alone.

"Whatever you say, honey," he drawled, putting his hands on her waist.

She only had time for an indrawn breath before his mouth was on hers, as warm and hard as she remembered, his taste as heady as she remembered. His hands tightened on her waist and drew her to him; then his arms were around her, and the kiss deepened, his tongue sliding into her mouth. Hunger flared, fanned into instant life at his touch. She had always known that once she touched him, she wouldn't be able to get enough of him.

She softened, her body molding itself to him as she instinctively tried to get close enough to him to feed that burning hunger. She was weak where he was concerned, just as all women were. Her arms were clinging around his neck, and in the end it was he who broke the kiss and gently set her away from him.

"I have work to get back to," he growled, but his eyes were hot and held dark promises. "Be ready tomorrow."

"Yes," she whispered.

Chapter 4

Two pickup trucks came up the drive not long after sunrise, loaded with fencing supplies and five of John's men. Michelle offered them all a cup of fresh coffee, which they politely refused, just as they refused her offer to show them around the ranch. John had probably given them orders that she wasn't to do anything, and they were taking it seriously. People didn't disobey Rafferty's orders if they wanted to continue working for him, so she didn't insist, but for the first time in weeks she found herself with nothing to do.

She tried to think what she'd done with herself before, but years of her life were a blank. What *had* she done? How could she fill the hours now, if working on her own ranch was denied her?

John drove up shortly before nine, but she had been ready for more than an hour and stepped out on the porch to meet him. He stopped on the steps, his dark eyes running over her in heated approval. "Nice," he murmured just loud enough for her to hear. She looked the way she should always look, cool and elegant in a pale yellow silk surplice dress, fastened only by two white buttons at the waist. The shoulders were lightly padded, emphasizing the slimness of her body, and a white enamel peacock was pinned to her lapel. Her sunshine hair was sleeked back into a demure twist; oversized sunglasses shielded her eyes. He caught the tantalizing fragrance of some softly bewitching perfume, and his body began to heat. She was aristocratic and expensive from her head to her daintily shod feet; even her underwear would be silk, and he wanted to strip every stitch of it away from her, then stretch her out naked on his bed. Yes, this was exactly the way she should look.

Michelle tucked her white clutch under her arm and walked with him to the car, immensely grateful for the sunglasses covering her eyes. John was a hard-working rancher, but when the occasion demanded he could dress as well as any Philadelphia lawyer. Any clothing looked good on his broad-shouldered, slim-hipped frame, but the severe gray suit he wore seemed to heighten his masculinity instead of restraining it. All hint of waviness had been brushed from his black hair. Instead of his usual pickup truck he was driving a dark gray two-seater Mercedes, a sleek beauty that made her think of the Porsche she had sold to raise money after her father had died.

"You said your men were going to help me," she said expressionlessly as he turned the car onto the highway several minutes later. "You didn't say they were going to take over."

He'd put on sunglasses, too, because the morning sun was glaring, and the dark lenses hid the probing look he directed at her stiff profile. "They're going to do the heavy work."

"After the fencing is repaired and the cattle are moved to the east pasture, I can handle things from there."

"What about dipping, castrating, branding, all the things that should've been done in the spring? You can't handle that. You don't have any horses, any men, and you sure as hell can't rope and throw a young bull from that old truck you've got."

Her slender hands clenched in her lap. Why did he have to be so right? She couldn't do any of those things, but neither could she be content as a useless ornament. "I know I can't do those things by myself, but I can help."

"I'll think about it," he answered noncommittally, but he knew there was no way in hell he'd let her. What could she do? It was hard, dirty, smelly, bloody work. The only thing she was physically strong enough to do was brand calves, and he didn't think she could stomach the smell or the frantic struggles of the terrified little animals.

"It's my ranch," she reminded him, ice in her tone. "Either I help, or the deal's off."

John didn't say anything. There was no point in arguing. He simply wasn't going to let her do it, and that was that. He'd handle her when the time came, but he didn't expect much of a fight. When she saw what was involved, she wouldn't want any part of it. Besides, she couldn't possibly like the hard work she'd been doing; he figured she was just too proud to back down now.

It was a long drive to Tampa, and half an hour passed without a word between them. Finally she said, "You used to make fun of my expensive little cars."

He knew she was referring to the sleek Mercedes, and he grunted. Personally, he preferred his pickup. When it came down to it, he was a cattle rancher and not much else, but he was damned good at what he did, and his tastes weren't expensive. "Funny thing about bankers," he said by way of explanation. "If they think you don't need the money all that badly, they're eager to loan it to you. Image counts. This thing is part of the image."

"And the members of your rotating harem prefer it, too, I bet," she gibed. "Going out on the town lacks something when you do it in a pickup."

"I don't know about that. Ever done it in a pickup?" he asked softly, and even through the dark glasses she could feel the impact of his glance.

"I'm sure *you* have."

"Not since I was fifteen." He chuckled, ignoring the biting coldness of her comment. "But a pickup never was your style, was it?"

"No," she murmured, leaning her head back. Some of her dates had driven fancy sports cars, some had driven souped-up Fords and Chevys, but it hadn't made any difference what they'd driven, because she hadn't made out with any of them. They had been nice boys, most of them, but none of them had been John Rafferty, so it hadn't mattered. He was the only man she'd ever wanted. Perhaps if she'd been older when she'd met him, or if she'd been secure enough in her own sexuality, things might have been different. What would have happened if she hadn't initiated those long years of hostility in an effort to protect herself from an attraction too strong for her to handle? What if she'd tried to get him interested in her, instead of warding him off?

Nothing, she thought tiredly. John wouldn't have wasted his time with a naive eighteen-year-old. Maybe later, when she'd graduated from college, the situation might have changed, but instead of coming home after graduation she had gone to Philadelphia . . . and met Roger.

They were out of the lawyer's office by noon; it hadn't been a long meeting. The land would be surveyed, the deed drawn up, and John's ranch would increase by quite a bit, while hers would shrink, but she was grateful that he'd come up with that solution. At least now she still had a chance.

His hand curled warmly around her elbow as they walked out to the car. "Let's have lunch. I'm too hungry to wait until we get home."

She was hungry, too, and the searing heat made her feel lethargic. She murmured in agreement as she fumbled for her sunglasses, missing the satisfied smile that briefly curled his mouth. John opened the car door and held it as she got in, his eyes lingering on the length of silken leg exposed by the movement. She promptly restored her skirt to its proper position and crossed her legs as she settled in the seat, giving him a questioning glance when he continued to stand in the open door. "Is something wrong?"

"No." He closed the door and walked around the car. Not unless she counted the way looking at her made him so hot that a deep ache settled in his loins. She couldn't move without making him think of making love to her. When she crossed her legs, he thought of uncrossing them. When she pulled her skirt down, he thought of pulling it up. When she leaned back the movement thrust her breasts against her lapels, and he wanted to tear the dress open. Damn, what a dress! It wrapped her modestly, but the silk kissed every soft curve just the way he wanted to do, and all morning long it had been teasing at him that the damned thing was fastened with only those two buttons. Two buttons! He had to have her, he thought savagely. He couldn't wait much longer. He'd already waited ten years, and his patience had ended. It was time.

The restaurant he took her to was a posh favorite of the city's business community, but he didn't worry about needing a reservation. The maître d' knew him, as did most of the people in the room, by sight and reputation if not personally. They were led across the crowded room to a select table by the window.

Michelle had noted the way so many people had watched them. "Well, this is one," she said dryly.

He looked up from the menu. "One what?"

"I've been seen in public with you once. Gossip has it that any woman seen with you twice is automatically assumed to be sleeping with you."

His mustache twitched as he frowned in annoyance. "Gossip has a way of being exaggerated."

"Usually, yes."

"And in this case?"

"You tell me."

He put the menu aside, his eyes never leaving her. "No matter what gossip says, you won't have to worry about being just another member of a harem. While we're together, you'll be the only woman in my bed."

Her hands shook, and Michelle quickly put her menu on the table to hide that betraying quiver. "You're assuming a lot," she said lightly in an effort to counteract the heat she could feel radiating from him.

"I'm not assuming anything. I'm planning on it." His voice was flat, filled with masculine certainty. He had reason to be certain; how many women had ever refused him? He projected a sense of overwhelming virility that was at least as seductive as the most expert technique, and from what she'd heard, he had that, too. Just looking at him made a woman wonder, made her begin dreaming about what it would be like to be in bed with him.

"Michelle, darling!"

Michelle couldn't stop herself from flinching at that particular phrase, even though it was spoken in a lilting female voice rather than a man's deeper tones. Quickly she looked around, grateful for the interruption despite the endearment she hated; when she recognized the speaker, gratefulness turned to mere politeness, but her face was so schooled that the approaching woman didn't catch the faint nuances of expression.

"Hello, Bitsy, how are you?" she asked politely as John got to his feet. "This is John Rafferty, my neighbor. John, this is Bitsy Sumner, from Palm Beach. We went to college together."

Bitsy's eyes gleamed as she looked at John, and she held her hand out to him. "I'm so glad to meet you, Mr. Rafferty."

Michelle knew Bitsy wouldn't pick it up, but she saw the dark amusement in John's eyes as he gently took the woman's faultlessly manicured and bejeweled hand in his. Naturally he'd seen the way Bitsy was looking at *him*. It was a look he'd probably been getting since puberty.

"Mrs. Sumner," he murmured, noting the diamond-studded wedding band on her left hand. "Would you like to join us?"

"Only for a moment," Bitsy sighed, slipping into the chair he held out. "My husband and I are here with some business associates and their wives. He says it's good business to socialize with them occasionally, so we flew in this morning. Michelle, dear, I haven't seen you in so long! What are you doing on this side of the state?"

"I live north of here," Michelle replied.

"You must come visit. Someone mentioned just the other day that it had been forever since we'd seen you! We had the most fantastic party at Howard Cassa's villa last month; you should have come."

"I have too much work to do, but thank you for the invitation." She managed to smile at Bitsy, but she understood that Bitsy hadn't been inviting her to visit them personally; it was just something that people said, and probably her old acquaintances were curious about why she had left their circle.

Bitsy shrugged elegantly. "Oh, work, schmurk. Let someone else take care of it for a month or so. You need to have some fun! Come to town, and bring Mr. Rafferty with you." Bitsy's gaze slid back to John, and that unconsciously hungry look crawled into her eyes again. "You'd enjoy it, Mr. Rafferty, I promise. Everyone needs a break from work occasionally, don't you think?"

His brows lifted. "Occasionally."

"What sort of business are you in?"

"Cattle. My ranch adjoins Michelle's."

"Oh, a *rancher*!"

Michelle could tell by Bitsy's fatuous smile that the other woman was lost in the romantic images of cowboys and horses that so many people associated with ranching, ignoring or simply not imagining the backbreaking hard work that went in to building a successful ranch. Or maybe it was the rancher instead of the ranch that made Bitsy look so enraptured. She was looking at John as if she could eat him alive. Michelle put her hands in her lap to hide them because she had to clench her fists in order to resist slapping Bitsy so hard she'd never even think of looking at John Rafferty again.

Fortunately good manners drove Bitsy back to her own table after a few moments. John watched her sway through the tangle of tables, then looked at Michelle with amusement in his eyes. "Who in hell would call a grown woman *Bitsy*?"

It was hard not to share his amusement. "I think her real name is Elizabeth, so Bitsy is fairly reasonable as a nickname. Of course, she was the ultimate preppy in college, so it fits."

"I thought it might be an indication of her brain power," he said caustically; then the waiter approached to take their orders, and John turned his attention to the menu.

Michelle could only be grateful that Bitsy hadn't been able to remain with them. The woman was one of the worst gossips she'd ever met, and she didn't feel up to hearing the latest dirt on every acquaintance they had in common. Bitsy's particular circle of friends were rootless and a little savage in their pursuit of entertainment, and Michelle had always made an effort to keep her distance from them. It hadn't always been possible, but at least she had never been drawn into the center of the crowd.

After lunch John asked if she would mind waiting while he contacted one of his business associates. She started to protest, then remembered that his men were taking care of the cattle today; she had no reason to hurry back, and, in truth, she could use the day off. The physical strain had been telling on her. Besides, this was the most time she'd ever spent in his company, and she was loathe to see the day end. They weren't arguing, and if she ignored his arrogant certainty that they were going to sleep together, the day had really been rather calm. "I don't have to be back at any certain time," she said, willing to let him decide when they would return.

As it happened, it was after dark before they left Tampa. John's meeting had taken up more time than he'd expected, but Michelle hadn't been bored, because he hadn't left her sitting in the reception area. He'd taken her into the meeting with him, and it had been so interesting that she hadn't been aware of the hours slipping past. It was almost six when they finished, and by then John was hungry again; it was another two hours before they were actually on their way.

Michelle sat beside him, relaxed and a little drowsy. John had stayed with coffee, because he was driving, but she'd had two glasses of wine with her meal, and her bones felt mellow. The car was dark, illuminated only by the dash lights, which gave a satanic cast to his hard-planed face, and the traffic on U.S. 19 was light. She snuggled down into the seat, making a comment only when John said something that required an answer.

Soon they ran into a steady rain, and the rhythmic motion of the windshield wipers added to her drowsiness. The windows began to fog, so John turned the air conditioning higher. Michelle sat up, hugging her arms as the cooler air banished her drowsiness. Her silk dress didn't offer much warmth. He glanced at her, then pulled to the side of the road.

"Why are we stopping?"

"Because you're cold." He shrugged out of his suit jacket and draped it around her, enveloping her in the transferred heat and the smell of his body. "We're almost two hours from home, so why don't you take a nap? That wine's getting to you, isn't it?''

"Mmmm." The sound of agreement was distinctly drowsy. John touched her cheek gently, watching as her eyelids closed, as if her lashes were too heavy for her to hold them open a moment longer. Let her sleep, he thought. She'd be recovered from the wine by the time they got home. His loins tightened. He wanted her awake and responsive when he took her to bed. There was no way he was going to sleep alone tonight. All day long he'd been fighting the need to touch her, to feel her lying against him. For ten years she'd been in his mind, and he wanted her. As difficult and spoiled as she was, he wanted her. Now he understood what made men want to pamper her, probably from the day she'd been placed in her cradle. He'd just taken his place in line, and for his reward he'd have her in his bed, her slim, silky body open for his pleasure. He knew she wanted him; she was resisting him for some reason he couldn't decipher, perhaps only a woman's instinctive hesitance.

Michelle usually didn't sleep well. Her slumber was frequently disturbed by dreams, and she hadn't been able to nap with even her father anywhere nearby. Her subconscious refused to relax if any man was in the vicinity. Roger had once attacked her in the middle of the night, when she'd been soundly asleep, and the trauma of being jerked from a deep, peaceful sleep into a nightmare of violence had in some ways been worse than the pain. Now, just before she slept, she realized with faint surprise that the old uneasiness wasn't there tonight. Perhaps the time had come to heal that particular hurt, too, or perhaps it was that she felt so unutterably safe with John. His coat warmed her; his nearness surrounded her. He had touched her in passion and in anger, but his touch had never brought pain. He tempered his great strength to handle a woman's softness, and she slept, secure in the instinctive knowledge that she was safe.

His deep, dark-velvet voice woke her. "We're home, honey. Put your arms around my neck."

She opened her eyes to see him leaning in the open door of the car, and she gave him a sleepy smile. "I slept all the way, didn't I?"

"Like a baby." He brushed her mouth with his, a brief, warm caress; then his arms slid behind her neck and under her thighs. She gasped as he lifted her, grabbing him around the neck as he'd instructed. It was still raining, but his coat kept most of the dampness from her as he closed the car door and carried her swiftly through the darkness.

"I'm awake now; I could've walked," she protested, her heart beginning a slow, heavy thumping as she responded to his nearness. He carried her so easily, leaping up the steps to the porch as if she weighed no more than a child.

"I know," he murmured, lifting her a little so he could bury his face in the curve of her neck. Gently he nuzzled her jaw, drinking in the sweet, warm fragrance of her skin. "Mmmm, you smell good. Are you clear from the wine yet?"

The caress was so tender that it completely failed to alarm her. Rather, she felt coddled, and the feeling of utter safety persisted. He shifted her in his arms to open the door, then turned sideways to carry her through. Had he thought she was drunk? "I was just sleepy, not tipsy," she clarified.

"Good," he whispered, pushing the door closed and blocking out the sound of the light rain, enveloping them in the dark silence of the house. She couldn't see anything, but he was warm and solid against her, and it didn't matter that she couldn't see. Then his mouth was on hers, greedy and demanding, convincing her lips to open and accept the shape of his, accept the inward thrust of his tongue. He kissed her with burning male hunger, as if he wanted to draw all the sweetness and breath out of her to make it his own, as if the need was riding him so hard that he couldn't get close enough. She couldn't help responding to that need, clinging to him and kissing him back with a sudden wildness, because the very rawness of his male hunger called out to everything in her that was female and ignited her own fires.

He hit the light switch with his elbow, throwing on the foyer light and illuminating the stairs to the right. He lifted his mouth briefly, and she stared up at him in the dim light, her senses jolting at the hard, grim expression on his face, the way his skin had tightened across his cheekbones. "I'm staying here tonight," he muttered harshly, starting up the stairs with her still in his arms. "This has been put off long enough."

He wasn't going to stop; she could see it in his face. She didn't want him to stop. Every pore in her body cried out for him, drowning out the small voice of caution that warned against getting involved with a heartbreaker like John Rafferty. Maybe it had been a useless struggle anyway; it had always been between them, this burning hunger that now flared out of control.

His mouth caught hers again as he carried her up the stairs, his muscle-corded arms holding her weight easily. Michelle yielded to the kiss, sinking against him. Her blood was singing through her veins, heating her, making her breasts harden with the need for his touch. An empty ache made her whimper, because it was an ache that only he could fill.

He'd been in the house a lot over the years, so the location of her room was no mystery to him. He carried her inside and laid her on the bed, following her down to press her into the mattress with his full weight. Michelle almost cried out from the intense pleasure of feeling him cover her with his body. His arm stretched over her head, and he snapped on one of the bedside lamps; he looked at her, and his black eyes filled with masculine satisfaction as he saw the glaze of passion in her slumberous eyes, the trembling of her pouty, kiss-stung lips.

Slowly, deliberately, he levered his knee between hers and spread her legs, then settled his hips into the cradle formed by her thighs. She inhaled sharply as she felt his hardness through the layers of their clothing. Their eyes met, and she knew he'd known before the day even began that he would end it in her bed. He was tired of waiting, and he was going to have her. He'd been patient all day, gentling her by letting her get accustomed to his presence, but now his patience was at an end, and he knew she had no resistance left to offer him. All she had was need.

"You're mine." He stated his possession baldly, his voice rough and low. He raised his weight on one elbow, and with his free hand unbuttoned the two buttons at her waist, spreading the dress open with the deliberate air of a man unwrapping a gift he'd wanted for a long time. The silk caught at her hips, pinned by his own weight. He lifted his hips and pushed the edges of the dress open, baring her legs, then resettled himself against her.

He felt as if his entire body would explode as he looked at her. She had worn neither bra nor slip; the silk dress was lined, hiding from him all day the fact that the only things she had on beneath that wisp of fabric were her panty hose and a minute scrap of lace masquerading as panties. If he'd known that her breasts were bare under her dress, there was no way he could have kept himself from pulling those lapels apart and touching, tasting, nor could he stop himself now. Her breasts were high and round, the skin satiny, her coral-colored nipples small and already tightly beaded. With a rough sound he bent his head and sucked strongly at her, drawing her nipple into his mouth and molding his lips to that creamy, satiny flesh. He cupped her other breast in his hand, gently kneading it and rubbing the nipple with his thumb. A high, gasping cry tore from her throat, and she arched against his mouth, her hands digging into his dark hair to press his head into her. Her breasts were so firm they were almost hard, and the firmness excited him even more.

He had to taste the other one, surround himself with the sweet headiness of her scent and skin.

Slowly Michelle twisted beneath him, plucking now at the back of his shirt in an effort to get rid of the fabric between them. She needed to feel the heat and power of his bare skin under her hands, against her body, but his mouth on her breasts was driving her mad with pleasure, and she couldn't control herself enough to strip the shirt away. Every stroke of his tongue sent wildfire running along her nerves, from her nipples to her loins, and she was helpless to do anything but feel.

Then he left her, rising up on his knees to tear at his shirt and throw it aside. His shoes, socks, pants and underwear followed, flung blindly away from the bed, and he knelt naked between her spread thighs. He stripped her panty hose and panties away, leaving her open and vulnerable to his penetration.

For the first time, she felt fear. It had been so long for her, and sex hadn't been good in her marriage anyway. John leaned over her, spreading her legs further, and she felt the first shock of his naked flesh as he positioned himself for entry. He was so big, his muscled body dominating her smaller, softer one completely. She knew from harsh experience how helpless a woman was against a man's much greater strength; John was stronger than most, bigger than most, and he was intent on the sexual act as males have been from the beginning of time. He was quintessentially male, the sum and substance of masculine aggression and sexuality. Panic welled in her, and her slim, delicate hand pressed against him, her fingers sliding into the curling dark hair that covered his chest. The black edges of fear were coming closer.

Her voice was thready, begging for reassurance. "John? Don't hurt me, please."

He froze, braced over her on the threshold of entry. Her warm, sweet body beckoned him, moistly ready for him, but her eyes were pleading. Did she expect pain? Good God, who could have hurt her? The seeds of fury formed deep in his mind, shunted aside for now by the screaming urges of his body. For now, he had to have her. "No, baby," he said gently, his dark voice so warm with tenderness that the fear in her eyes faded. "I won't hurt you."

He slid one arm under her, leaning on that elbow and raising her so her nipples were buried in the hair on his chest. Again he heard that small intake of breath from her, an unconscious sound of pleasure. Their eyes locked, hers misty and soft, his like black fire, as he tightened his buttocks and very slowly, very carefully, began to enter her.

Michelle shuddered as great ripples of pleasure washed through her, and her legs climbed his to wrap around his hips. A soft, wild cry tore from her throat, and she shoved her hand against her mouth to stifle the sound. Still his black eyes burned down at her. "No," he whispered. "Take your hand away. I want to hear you, baby. Let me hear how good it feels to you."

Still there was that slow, burning push deep into her, her flesh quivering as she tried to accommodate him. Panic seized her again. "Stop! John, please, no more! You're...I can't..."

"Shh, shh," he soothed, kissing her mouth, her eyes, nibbling at the velvety lobes of her ears. "It's okay, baby, don't worry. I won't hurt you." He continued soothing her with kisses and soft murmurs, and though every instinct in him screamed to bury himself in her to the hilt, he clamped down on those urges with iron control. There was no way he was going to hurt her, not with the fear he'd seen in the misty green depths of her eyes. She was so delicate and silky, and so tight around him that he could feel the gentle pulsations of adjustment. His eyes closed as pure pleasure shuddered through him.

She was aroused, but not enough. He set about exciting her with all the sensual skill he possessed, holding her mouth with deep kisses while his hands gently stroked her, and he began moving slowly inside her. So slow, holding himself back, keeping his strokes shallow even though every movement wrung new degrees of ecstasy from him. He wanted her mindless with need.

Michelle felt her control slipping away by degrees, and she didn't care. Control didn't matter, nothing mattered but the heat that was consuming her body and mind, building until all sense of self was gone and she was nothing but a female body, twisting and surging beneath the overpowering male. A powerful tension had her in its grip, tightening, combining with the heat as it swept her inexorably along. She was burning alive, writhing helplessly, wild little pleading sobs welling up and escaping. John took them into his own mouth, then put his hand between their bodies, stroking her. She trembled for a moment on the crest of a great wave; then she was submerged in exploding sensation. He held her safely, her heaving body locked in his arms while he thrust deeply, giving her all the pleasure he could.

When it was over she was limp and sobbing, drenched with both her sweat and his. "I didn't know," she said brokenly, and tears tracked down her face. He murmured to her, holding her tightly for a moment, but he was deep inside her now, and he couldn't hold back any longer. Sliding his hands beneath her hips, he lifted her up to receive his deep, powerful thrusts.

Now it was she who held him, cradling him in her body and with her arms tight around him; he cried out, a deep, hoarse sound, blind and insensible to everything but the great, flooding force of his pleasure.

It was quiet for a long time afterward. John lay on top of her, so sated and relaxed that he couldn't tolerate the idea of moving, of separating his flesh from hers. It wasn't until she stirred, gasping a little for breath, that he raised himself on his elbows and looked down at her.

Intense satisfaction, mingled with both gentleness and a certain male arrogance, was written on his face as he leaned above her. He smoothed her tangled hair back from her face, stroking her cheeks with his fingers. She looked pale and exhausted, but it was the sensuous exhaustion of a woman who has been thoroughly satisfied by her lover. He traced the shape of her elegant cheekbones with his lips, his tongue dipping out to sneak tastes that sent little ripples of arousal through him again.

Then he lifted his head again, curiosity burning in his eyes. "You've never enjoyed it before, have you?"

A quick flush burned her cheeks, and she turned her head on the pillow, staring fixedly at the lamp. "I suppose that does wonders for your ego."

She was withdrawing from him, and that was the last thing he wanted. He decided to drop the subject for the time being, but there were still a lot of questions that he intended to have answered. Right now she was in his arms, warm and weak from his lovemaking, just the way he was going to keep her until she became used to his possession and accepted it as fact.

She was his now.

He'd take care of her, even spoil her. Why not? She was made to be pampered and indulged, at least up to a point. She'd been putting up a good fight to work this ranch, and he liked her guts, but she wasn't cut out for that type of life. Once she realized that she didn't have to fight anymore, that he was going to take care of her, she'd settle down and accept it as the natural order of things.

He didn't have money to waste on fancy trips, or to drape her in jewels, but he could keep her in comfort and security. Not only that, he could guarantee that the sheets on their bed would stay hot. Even now, so soon after having her, he felt the hunger and need returning.

Without a word he began again, drawing her down with him into a dark whirlpool of desire and satisfaction. Michelle's eyes drifted shut, her body arching in his arms. She had known instinctively, years ago, that it would be like this, that even her identity would be swamped with the force of his passion. In his arms she lost herself and became only his woman.

Chapter 5

Michelle woke early, just as the first gray light of dawn was creeping into the room. The little sleep she'd gotten had been deep and dreamless for a change, but she was used to sleeping alone; the unaccustomed presence of a man in her bed had finally nudged her awake. A stricken look edged into her eyes as she looked over at him, sprawled on his stomach with one arm curled under the pillow and the other arm draped across her naked body.

How easy she'd been for him. The knowledge ate at her as she gingerly slipped from the bed, taking care not to wake him. He might sleep for hours yet; he certainly hadn't had much sleep during the night.

Her legs trembled as she stood, the soreness in her thighs and deep in her body providing yet another reminder of the past night, as if she needed any further confirmation of her memory. Four times. He'd taken her four times, and each time it had seemed as if the pleasure intensified. Even now she couldn't believe how her body had responded to him, soaring wildly out of her control. But he'd controlled himself, and her, holding her to the rhythm he set in order to prolong their lovemaking. Now she knew that all the talk about him hadn't been exaggerated; both his virility and his skill had been, if anything, underrated.

Somehow she had to come to terms with the unpleasant fact that she had allowed herself to become the latest of his one-night stands. The hardest fact to face wasn't that she'd been so easily seduced, but her own piercing regret that such ecstasy wouldn't last. Oh, he might come back...but he wouldn't stay. In time he'd become bored with her and turn his predatory gaze on some other woman just as he always had before.

And she'd go on loving him, just as she had before.

Quietly she got clean underwear from the dresser and her bathrobe from the adjoining bath, but she went to the bathroom down the hall to take a shower. She didn't want the sound of running water to awaken him. Right now she needed time to herself, time to gather her composure before she faced him again. She didn't know what to say, how to act.

The stinging hot water eased some of the soreness from her muscles, though a remaining ache reminded her of John's strength with every step she took. After showering she went down to the kitchen and started brewing a fresh pot of coffee. She was leaning against the cabinets, watching the dark brew drip into the pot, when the sound of motors caught her attention. Turning to look out the window, she saw the two pickup trucks from John's ranch pull into the yard. The same men who had been there the day before got out; one noticed John's car parked in front of the house and poked his buddy in the ribs, pointing. Even from that distance Michelle could hear the muffled male laughter, and she didn't need any help imagining their comments. The boss had scored again. It would be all over the county within twenty-four hours. In the manner of men everywhere, they were both proud and slightly envious of their boss's sexual escapades, and they'd tell the tale over and over again.

Numbly she turned back to watch the coffee dripping; when it finished, she filled a big mug, then wrapped her cold fingers around the mug to warm them. It had to be nerves making her hands so cold. Quietly she went upstairs to look into her bedroom, wondering if he would still be sleeping.

He wasn't, though evidently he'd awoken only seconds before. He propped himself up on one elbow and ran his hand through his tousled black hair, narrowing his eyes as he returned her steady gaze. Her heart lurched painfully. He looked like a ruffian, with his hair tousled, his jaw darkened by the overnight growth of beard, his bare torso brown and roped with the steely muscles that were never found on a businessman. She didn't know what she'd hoped to see in his expression: desire, possibly, even affection. But whatever she'd wanted to see wasn't there. Instead his face was as hard as always, measuring her with that narrowed gaze that made her feel like squirming. She could feel him waiting for her to move, to say something.

Her legs were jerky, but she managed not to spill the coffee as she walked into the room. Her voice was only slightly strained. "Congratulations. All the gossip doesn't give you due credit. My, my, you're really something when you decide to score; I didn't even think of saying no. Now you can go home and put another notch in your bedpost."

His eyes narrowed even more. He sat up, ignoring the way the sheet fell below his waist, and held out his hand for the coffee mug. When she gave it to him, he turned it and drank from the place where she'd been sipping, then returned it to her, his eyes never leaving hers.

"Sit down."

She flinched a little at his hard, raspy, early-morning voice. He saw the small movement and reached out to take her wrist, making coffee lap alarmingly close to the rim of the mug. Gently but inexorably he drew her down to sit facing him on the edge of the bed.

He kept his hand on her wrist, his callused thumb rubbing over the fine bones and delicate tracery of veins. "Just for the record, I don't notch bedposts. Is that what's got your back up this morning?"

She gave a small defensive shrug, not meeting his eyes.

She'd withdrawn from him again; his face was grim as he watched her, trying to read her expression. He remembered the fear in her last night, and he wondered who'd put it there. White-hot embers of rage began to flicker to life at the thought of some bastard abusing her in bed, hurting her. Women were vulnerable when they made love, and Michelle especially wouldn't have the strength to protect herself. He had to get her to talk, or she'd close up on him completely. "It had been a long time for you, hadn't it?"

Again she gave that little shrug, as if hiding behind the movement. Again he probed, watching her face. "You didn't enjoy sex before." He made it a statement, not a question.

Finally her eyes darted to his, wary and resentful. "What do you want, a recommendation? You know that was the first time I'd . . . enjoyed it."

"Why didn't you like it before?"

"Maybe I just needed to go to bed with a stud," she said flippantly.

"Hell, don't give me that," he snapped, disgusted. "Who hurt you? Who made you afraid of sex?"

"I'm not afraid," she denied, disturbed by the idea that she might have let Roger warp her to such an extent. "It was just . . . well, it had been so long, and you're a big man. . . ." Her voice trailed off, and abruptly she flushed, her gaze sliding away from him.

He watched her thoughtfully; considering what he'd learned about her last night and this morning, it was nothing short of a miracle that she hadn't knocked his proposal and half his teeth down his throat when he'd suggested she become his mistress as payment of the debt. It also made him wonder if her part in the breakup of Mike Webster's marriage hadn't been blown out of all proportion; after all, a woman who didn't enjoy making love wasn't likely to be fast and easy.

It was pure possessiveness, but he was glad no other man had pleased her the way he had; it gave him a hold on her, a means of keeping her by his side. He would use any weapon he had, because during the night he had realized that there was no way he could let her go. She could be haughty, bad-tempered and stubborn; she could too easily be spoiled and accept it as her due, though he'd be damned if he hadn't almost decided it *was* her due. She was proud and difficult, trying to build a stone wall around herself to keep him at a distance, like a princess holding herself aloof from the peasants, but he couldn't get enough of her. When they were making love, it wasn't the princess and the peasant any longer; they were a man and his woman, writhing and straining together, moaning with ecstasy. He'd never been so hungry for a woman before, so hot that he'd felt nothing and no one could have kept him away from her.

She seemed to think last night had been a casual thing on his part, that sunrise had somehow ended it. She was in for a surprise. Now that she'd given herself to him, he wasn't going to let her go. He'd learned how to fight for and keep what was his, but his single-minded striving over the years to build the ranch into one of the biggest cattle ranches in Florida was nothing compared to the intense possessiveness he felt for Michelle.

Finally he released her wrist, and she stood immediately, moving away from him. She sipped at the coffee she still held, and her eyes went to the window. "Your men got a big kick out of seeing your car still here this morning. I didn't realize they'd be back, since they put up the fencing yesterday."

Indifferent to his nakedness, he threw the sheet back and got out of bed. "They didn't finish. They'll do the rest of the job today, then move the herd to the east pasture tomorrow." He waited, then said evenly, "It bothers you that they know?"

"Being snickered about over a beer bothers me. It polishes up your image a little more, but all I'll be is the most recent in a long line of one-nighters for you."

"Well, everyone will know differently when you move in with me, won't they?" he asked arrogantly, walking into the bathroom. "How long will it take you to pack?"

Stunned, Michelle whirled to stare at him, but he'd already disappeared into the bathroom. The sound of the shower came on. Move in with him? If there was any limit to his gall, she hadn't seen it yet! She sat down on the edge of the bed, watching the bathroom door and waiting for him to emerge as she fought the uneasy feeling of sliding further and further down a precipitous slope. Control of her own life was slipping from her hands, and she didn't know if she could stop it. It wasn't just that John was so domineering, though he was; the problem was that, despite how much she wished it were different, she was weak where he was concerned. She wanted to be able to simply walk into his arms and let them lock around her, to rest against him and let him handle everything. She was so tired, physically and mentally. But if she let him take over completely, what would happen when he became bored with her? She would be right back where she'd started, but with a broken heart added to her problems.

The shower stopped running. An image of him formed in her mind, powerfully muscled, naked, dripping wet. Drying himself with her towels. Filling her bathroom with his male scent and presence. He wouldn't look diminished or foolish in her very feminine rose-and-white bathroom, nor would it bother him that he'd bathed with perfumed soap.

He was so intensely masculine that female surroundings merely accentuated that masculinity.

She began to tremble, thinking of the things he'd done during the night, the way he'd made her feel. She hadn't known her body could take over like that, that she could revel in being possessed, and despite the outdated notion that a man could physically "possess" a woman, that was what had happened. She felt it, instinctively and deeply, the sensation sinking into her bones.

He sauntered from the bathroom wearing only a towel hitched low on his hips, the thick velvety fabric contrasting whitely with the bronzed darkness of his abdomen. His hair and mustache still gleamed wetly; a few drops of moisture glistened on his wide shoulders and in the curls that darkened his broad chest. Her mouth went dry. His body hair followed the tree of life pattern, with the tufts under his arms and curls across his chest, then the narrowing line that ran down his abdomen before spreading again at his groin. He was as superbly built as a triathlete, and she actually ached to touch him, to run her palms all over him.

He gave her a hard, level look. "Stop stalling and get packed."

"I'm not going." She tried to sound strong about it; if her voice lacked the volume she'd wanted, at least it was even.

"You'll be embarrassed if you don't have anything on besides that robe when I carry you into my house," he warned quietly.

"John—" She stopped, then made a frustrated motion with her hand. "I don't want to get involved with you."

"It's a little late to worry about that now," he pointed out.

"I know," she whispered. "Last night shouldn't have happened."

"Damn it to hell, woman, it should've happened a long time ago." Irritated, he dropped the towel to the floor and picked up his briefs. "Moving in with me is the only sensi-

ble thing to do. I normally work twelve hours a day, sometimes more. Sometimes I'm up all night. Then there's the
paperwork to do in the evenings; hell, you know what it
takes to run a ranch. When would I get over to see you?
Once a week? I'll be damned if I'll settle for an occasional
quickie."

"What about *my* ranch? Who'll take care of it while I
make myself convenient to you whenever you get the urge?"

He gave a short bark of laughter. "Baby, if you lay down
every time I got the urge, you'd spend the next year on your
back. I get hard every time I look at you."

Involuntarily her eyes dropped down his body, and a wave
of heat washed over her when she saw the proof of his words
swelling against the white fabric of his underwear. She
jerked her gaze away, swallowing to relieve the dry tight-
ness of her throat. "I have to take care of my ranch," she
repeated stubbornly, as if they were magic words that would
keep him at bay.

He pulled on his pants, impatience deepening the lines
that bracketed his mouth. "I'll take care of both ranches.
Face facts, Michelle. You need help. You can't do it on your
own."

"Maybe not, but I need to try. Don't you understand?"
Desperation edged into her tone. "I've never had a job,
never done anything to support myself, but I'm trying to
learn. You're stepping right into Dad's shoes and taking
over, handling everything yourself, but what happens to me
when you get bored and move on to the next woman? I still
won't know how to support myself!"

John paused in the act of zipping his pants, glaring at her.
Damn it, what did she think he'd do, toss her out the door
with a casual, "It's been fun, but I'm tired of you now?"
He'd make certain she was on her feet, that the ranch was
functioning on a profitable basis, if the day ever came when
he looked at her and *didn't* want her. He couldn't imagine
it. The desire for her consumed him like white-burning fire,

sometimes banked, but never extinguished, heating his body and mind. He'd wanted her when she was eighteen and too young to handle him, and he wanted her now.

He controlled his anger and merely said, "I'll take care of you."

She gave him a tight little smile. "Sure." In her experience, people looked after themselves. Roger's parents had protected him to keep his slipping sanity from casting scandal on *their* family name. Her own father, as loving as he'd been, had ignored her plea for help because he didn't like to think his daughter was unhappy; it was more comfortable for him to decide she'd been exaggerating. The complaint she'd filed had disappeared because some judge had thought it would be advantageous to make friends with the powerful Beckmans. Roger's housekeeper had looked the other way because she liked her cushy well-paid job. Michelle didn't blame them, but she'd learned not to expect help, or to trust her life to others.

John snatched his shirt from the floor, his face dark with fury. "Do you want a written agreement?"

Tiredly she rubbed her forehead. He wasn't used to anyone refusing to obey him whenever he barked out an order. If she said yes, she would be confirming what he'd thought of her in the beginning, that her body could be bought. Maybe he even wanted her to say yes; then she'd be firmly under his control, bought and paid for. But all she said was, "No, that isn't what I want."

"Then what, damn it?"

Just his love. To spend the rest of her life with him. That was all.

She might as well wish for the moon.

"I want to do it on my own."

The harshness faded from his face. "You can't." Knowledge gave the words a finality that lashed at her.

"I can try."

The hell of it was, he had to respect the need to try, even though nature and logic said she wouldn't succeed. She wasn't physically strong enough to do what had to be done, and she didn't have the financial resources; she'd started out in a hole so deep that she'd been doomed to fail from the beginning. She would wear herself to the bone, maybe even get hurt, but in the end it would come full circle and she would need someone to take care of her. All he could do was wait, try to watch out for her, and be there to step in when everything caved in around her. By then she'd be glad to lean on a strong shoulder, to take the place in life she'd been born to occupy.

But he wasn't going to step back and let her pretend nothing had happened between them the night before. She was his now, and she had to understand that before he left. The knowledge had to be burned into her flesh the way it was burned into his, and maybe it would take a lesson in broad daylight for her to believe it. He dropped his shirt and slowly unzipped his pants, watching her. When he left, he'd leave his touch on her body and his taste in her mouth, and she'd feel him, taste him, think of him every time she climbed into this bed without him.

Her green eyes widened, and color bloomed on her cheekbones. Nervously she glanced at the bed, then back at him.

His heart began slamming heavily against his rib cage. He wanted to feel the firmness of her breasts in his hands again, feel her nipples harden in his mouth. She whispered his name as he dropped his pants and came toward her, putting his hands on her waist, which was so slender that he felt he might break her in two if he wasn't careful.

As he bent toward her, Michelle's head fell back as if it were too heavy for her neck to support. He instantly took advantage of her vulnerable throat, his mouth burning a path down its length. She had wanted to deny the force of what had happened, but her body was responding feverishly to him, straining against him in search of the mindless ecstasy he'd given her before. She no longer had the protection of ignorance. He was addictive, and she'd already become hooked. As he took her down to the bed, covering her with his heated nakedness, she didn't even think of denying him, or herself.

Are you on the pill?
No.
Damn. Then, *How long until your next period?*
Soon. Don't worry. The timing isn't right.
Famous last words. You'd better get a prescription.
I can't take the pill. I've tried; it makes me throw up all day long. Just like being pregnant.
Then we'll do something else. Do you want to take care of it, or do you want me to?

The remembered conversation kept replaying in her mind; he couldn't have made it plainer that he considered the relationship to be an ongoing one. He had been so matter-of-fact that it hadn't registered on her until later, but now she realized her acquiescent "I will" had acknowledged and accepted his right to make love to her. It hadn't hit her until he'd kissed her and had driven away that his eyes had been gleaming with satisfaction that had nothing to do with being physically sated.

She had some paperwork to do and forced herself to concentrate on it, but that only brought more problems to mind. The stack of unpaid bills was growing, and she didn't know how much longer she could hold her creditors off. They needed their money, too. She needed to fatten the cattle before selling them, but she didn't have the money for grain. Over and over she tried to estimate how much feed would cost, balanced against how much extra she could expect from the sale of heavier cattle. An experienced rancher would have known, but all she had to go on were the records her father had kept, and she didn't know how accurate they were. Her father had been wildly enthusiastic about his ranch, but he'd relied on his foreman's advice to run it.

She could ask John, but he'd use it as another chance to tell her that she couldn't do it on her own.

The telephone rang, and she answered it absently.

"Michelle, darling."

The hot rush of nausea hit her stomach, and she jabbed the button, disconnecting the call. Her hands were shaking as she replaced the receiver. Why wouldn't he leave her alone? It had been two years! Surely he'd had time to get over his sick obsession; surely his parents had gotten him some sort of treatment!

The telephone rang again, the shrill tone filling her ears over and over. She counted the rings in a kind of frozen agony, wondering when he'd give up, or if her nerves would give out first. What if he just let it keep ringing? She'd have to leave the house or go screaming mad. On the eighteenth ring, she answered.

"Darling, don't hang up on me again, please," Roger whispered. "I love you so much. I have to talk to you or go crazy."

They were the words of a lover, but she was shaking with cold. Roger was already crazy. How many times had he whispered love words to her only moments after a burst of rage, when she was stiff with terror, her body already aching from a blow? But then he'd be sorry that he'd hurt her, and he'd tell her over and over how much he loved her and couldn't live without her.

Her lips were so stiff that she could barely form the words. "Please leave me alone. I don't want to talk to you."

"You don't mean that. You know I love you. No one has ever loved you as much as I do."

"I'm sorry," she managed.

"Why are you sorry?"

"I'm not going to talk to you, Roger. I'm going to hang up."

"Why can't you talk? Is someone there with you?"

Her hand froze, unable to remove the receiver from her ear and drop it onto its cradle. Like a rabbit numbed by a snake's hypnotic stare, she waited without breathing for what she knew was coming.

"Michelle! Is someone there with you?"

"No," she whispered. "I'm alone."

"You're lying! That's why you won't talk to me. Your lover is there with you, listening to every word you're saying."

Helplessly she listened to the rage building in his voice, knowing nothing she said would stop it, but unable to keep herself from trying. "I promise you, I'm alone."

To her surprise he fell silent, though she could hear his quickened breath over the wire as clearly as if he were standing next to her. "All right, I'll believe you. If you'll come back to me, I'll believe you."

"I can't—"

"There's someone else, isn't there? I always knew there was. I couldn't catch you, but I always knew!"

"No. There's no one. I'm here all alone, working in Dad's study." She spoke quickly, closing her eyes at the lie. It was the literal truth, that she was alone, but it was still a lie. There had always been someone else deep in her heart, buried at the back of her mind.

Suddenly his voice was shaking. "I couldn't stand it if you loved someone else, darling. I just couldn't. Swear to me that you're alone."

"I swear it." Desperation cut at her. "I'm completely alone, I swear!"

"I love you," Roger whispered, and hung up.

Wildly she ran for the bathroom, where she retched until she was empty and her stomach muscles ached from heaving. She couldn't take this again; she would have the phone number changed, keep it unlisted. Leaning against the basin, she wiped her face with a wet cloth and stared at her bloodless reflection in the mirror. She didn't have the money to pay for having her number changed and taken off the listing.

A shaky bubble of laughter escaped her trembling lips. The way things were going, the phone service would be disconnected soon because she couldn't pay her bill. That would certainly take care of the problem; Roger couldn't call if she didn't have a telephone. Maybe being broke had some advantages after all.

She didn't know what she'd do if Roger came down here personally to take her back to Philadelphia where she "belonged." If she'd ever "belonged" any one place, it was here, because John was here. Maybe she couldn't go to the symphony, or go skiing in Switzerland, or shopping in Paris. It didn't matter now and hadn't mattered then. All those things were nice, but unimportant. Paying bills was important. Taking care of the cattle was important.

Roger was capable of anything. Part of him was so civilized that it was truly difficult to believe he could be violent. People who'd known him all his life thought he was one of the nicest men walking the face of the earth. And he could be, but there was another part of him that flew into insanely jealous rages.

If he came down here, if she had to see him again...if he touched her in even the smallest way...she knew she couldn't handle it.

The last time had been the worst.

His parents had been in Europe. Roger had accepted an invitation for them to attend a dinner party with a few of his business associates and clients. Michelle had been extremely careful all during the evening not to say or do anything that could be considered flirtatious, but it hadn't been enough. On the way home, Roger had started the familiar catechism: She'd smiled a lot at Mr. So-and-So; had he propositioned her? He had, hadn't he? Why didn't she just admit it? He'd seen the looks passing between them.

By the time they'd arrived home, Michelle had been braced to run, if necessary, but Roger had settled down in the den to brood. She'd gone to bed, so worn out from mingled tension and relief that she'd drifted to sleep almost immediately.

Then, suddenly, the light had gone on and he'd been there, his face twisted with rage as he yelled at her. Terrified, screaming, stunned by being jerked from a sound sleep, she'd fought him when he jerked her half off the bed and began tearing at her nightgown, but she'd been helpless against him. He'd stripped the gown away and begun lashing at her with his belt, the buckle biting into her flesh again and again.

By the time he'd quit, she had been covered with raw welts and a multitude of small, bleeding cuts from the buckle, and she'd screamed so much she could no longer make a sound. Her eyes had been almost swollen shut from crying. She could still remember the silence as he'd stood there by the bed, breathing hard as he looked down at her. Then he'd fallen on his knees, burying his face in her tangled hair. "I love you so much," he'd said.

That night, while he'd slept, she had crept out and taken a cab to a hospital emergency room. Two years had passed, but the small white scars were still visible on her back, buttocks and upper thighs. They would fade with time, becoming impossible to see, but the scar left on her mind by the sheer terror of that night hadn't faded at all. The demons she feared all wore Roger's face.

But now she couldn't run from him; she had no other place to go, no other place where she wanted to be. She was legally free of him now, and there was nothing he could do to make her return. Legally she could stop him from calling her. He was harassing her; she could get a court order prohibiting him from contacting her in any way.

But she wouldn't, unless he forced her to it. She opened her eyes and stared at herself again. Oh, it was classic. A counselor at the hospital had even talked with her about it. She didn't want anyone to know her husband had abused her; it would be humiliating, as if it were somehow her fault. She didn't want people to pity her, she didn't want them to talk about her, and she especially didn't want John to know. It was too ugly, and she felt ashamed.

Suddenly she felt the walls closing in on her, stifling her. She had to get out and *do* something, or she might begin crying, and she didn't want that to happen. If she started crying now, she wouldn't be able to stop.

She got in the old truck and drove around the pastures, looking at the new sections of fence John's men had put up. They had finished and returned to their regular chores. Tomorrow they'd ride over on horseback and move the herd to this pasture with its high, thick growth of grass. The cattle could get their fill without walking so much, and they'd gain weight.

As she neared the house again she noticed how high the grass and weeds had gotten in the yard. It was so bad she might need to move the herd to the yard to graze instead of to the pasture. Yard work had come in a poor second to all the other things that had needed doing, but now, thanks to John, she had both the time and energy to do something about it.

She got out the lawnmower and pushed it up and down the yard, struggling to force it through the high grass. Little green mounds piled up in neat rows behind her. When that was finished, she took a knife from the kitchen and hacked down the weeds that had grown up next to the house. The physical activity acted like a sedative, blunting the edge of fear and finally abolishing it altogether. She didn't have any reason to be afraid; Roger wasn't going to do anything.

Subconsciously she dreaded going to bed that night, wondering if she would spend the night dozing, only to jerk awake every few moments, her heart pounding with fear as she waited for her particular demon to leap screaming out of the darkness and drag her out of bed. She didn't want to let Roger have that kind of power over her, but memories of that night still nagged at the edges of her mind. Someday she would be free of him. She swore it; she promised it to herself.

When she finally went reluctantly up the stairs and paused in the doorway to her delicately feminine room, she was overcome by a wave of memories that made her shake. She hadn't expected this reaction; she'd been thinking of Roger, but it was John who dominated this room. Roger had never set foot in here. John had slept sprawled in that bed. John had showered in that bathroom. The room was filled with his presence.

She had lain beneath him on that bed, twisting and straining with a pleasure so intense that she'd been mindless with it. She remembered the taut, savage look on his face, the gentleness of his hands as he restrained his strength which could too easily bruise a woman's soft skin. Her body tingled as she remembered the way he'd touched her, the places he'd touched her.

Then she realized that John had given her more than pleasure. She hadn't been aware of fearing men, but on some deep level of her mind, she had. In the two years since her divorce she hadn't been out on a date, and she'd managed to disguise the truth from herself by being part of a crowd that included men. Because she'd laughed with them, skied and swam with them—as long as it was a group activity, but never *alone* with a man—she'd been able to tell herself that Roger hadn't warped her so badly after all. She was strong; she could put all that behind her and not blame all men for what one man had done.

She hadn't blamed them, but she'd feared their strength. Though she'd never gone into a panic if a man touched her casually, she hadn't liked it and had always retreated.

Perhaps it would have been that way with John, too, if her long obsession with him hadn't predisposed her to accept his touch. But she'd yearned for him for so long, like a child crying for the moon, that her hunger had overcome her instinctive reluctance.

And he'd been tender, careful, generous in the giving of pleasure. In the future his passion might become rougher, but a bond of physical trust had been forged during the night that would never be broken.

Not once was her sleep disturbed by nightmares of Roger. Even in sleep, she felt John's arms around her.

Chapter 6

She had half expected John to be among the men who rode over the next morning to move the cattle to the east pasture, and a sharp pang of disappointment went through her as she realized he hadn't come. Then enthusiasm overrode her disappointment as she ran out to meet them. She'd never been in on an actual "cattle drive," short as it was, and was as excited as a child, her face glowing when she skidded to a stop in front of the mounted men.

"I want to help," she announced, green eyes sparkling in the early morning sun. The respite from the hard physical work she'd been doing made her feel like doing cartwheels on the lawn. She hadn't realized how tired she'd been until she'd had the opportunity to rest, but now she was bubbling over with energy.

Nev Luther, John's lanky and laconic foreman, looked down at her with consternation written across his weathered face. The boss had been explicit in his instructions that Michelle was not to be allowed to work in any way, which was a damned odd position for him to take. Nev couldn't remember the boss ever wanting anyone *not* to work. But orders were orders, and folks who valued their hides didn't ignore the boss's orders.

Not that he'd expected any trouble doing what he'd been told. Somehow he just hadn't pictured fancy Michelle Cabot doing any ranch work, let alone jumping up and down with joy at the prospect. Now what was he going to do? He cleared his throat, reluctant to do anything that would wipe the glowing smile off her face, but even more reluctant to get in trouble with Rafferty.

Inspiration struck, and he looked around. "You got a horse?" He knew she didn't, so he figured that was a detail she couldn't get around.

Her bright face dimmed, then lit again. "I'll drive the truck," she said, and raced toward the barn. Thunderstruck, Nev watched her go, and the men with him muttered warning comments.

Now what? He couldn't haul her out of the truck and order her to stay here. He didn't think she would take orders too well, and he also had the distinct idea the boss was feeling kinda possessive about her. Nev worked with animals, so he tended to put his thoughts in animal terms. One stallion didn't allow another near his mare, and the possessive mating instinct was still alive and well in humans. Nope, he wasn't going to manhandle that woman and have Rafferty take his head off for touching her. Given the choice, he'd rather have the boss mad about his orders not being followed than in a rage because someone had touched his woman, maybe upset her and made her cry.

The stray thought that she might cry decided him in a hurry. Like most men who didn't have a lot of contact with women, he went into a panic at the thought of tears. Rafferty could just go to hell. As far as Nev was concerned, Michelle could do whatever she wanted.

Having the burden of doing everything lifted off her shoulders made all the difference in the world. Michelle enjoyed the sunshine, the lowing of the cattle as they protested the movement, the tight-knit way the cowboys and their horses worked together. She bumped along the pasture in the old truck, which wasn't much good for rounding up strays but could keep the herd nudging forward. The only problem was, riding—or driving—drag was the dustiest place to be.

It wasn't long before one of the cowboys gallantly offered to drive the truck and give her a break from the dust. She took his horse without a qualm. She loved riding; at first it had been the only thing about ranch life that she'd enjoyed. She quickly found that riding a horse for pleasure was a lot different from riding a trained cutting horse. The horse didn't wait for her to tell it what to do. When a cow broke for freedom, the horse broke with it, and Michelle had to learn to go with the movement. She soon got the hang of it though, and before long she was almost hoping a stray would bolt, just for the joy of riding the quick-moving animal.

Nev swore long and eloquently under his breath when he saw the big gray coming across the pasture. Damn, the fat was in the fire now.

John was eyeing the truck with muted anger as he rode up, but there was no way the broad-shouldered figure in it was Michelle. Disbelieving, his black gaze swept the riders and lighted unerringly on the wand-slim rider with sunny hair tumbling below a hat. He reined in when he reached Nev, his jaw set as he looked at his foreman. "Well?" he asked in a dead-level voice.

Nev scratched his jaw, turning his head to watch Michelle snatch her hat off her head and wave it at a rambunctious calf. "I tried," he mumbled. He glanced back to meet John's narrowed gaze. Damned if eyes as black as hell couldn't look cold. "Hell, boss, it's her truck and her land. What was I supposed to do? Tie her down?"

"She's not in the truck," John pointed out.

"Well, it was so dusty back there that . . . ah, *hell!*"

Nev gave up trying to explain himself in disgust and spurred to head off a stray. John let him go, picking his way over to Michelle. He would take it up with Nev later, though already his anger was fading. She wasn't doing anything dangerous, even if he didn't like seeing her covered with dust.

She smiled at him when he rode up, a smile of such pure pleasure that his brows pulled together in a little frown. It was the first time he'd seen that smile since she'd been back, but until now he hadn't realized it had been missing. She looked happy. Faced with a smile like that, no wonder Nev had caved in and let her do what she wanted.

"Having fun?" he asked wryly.

"Yes, I am." Her look dared him to make something of it.

"I had a call from the lawyer this morning. He'll have everything ready for us to sign the day after tomorrow."

"That's good." Her ranch would shrink by a sizable hunk of acreage, but at least it would be clear of any large debt.

He watched her for a minute, leaning his forearms on the saddle horn. "Want to ride back to the house with me?"

"For a quickie?" she asked tartly, her green eyes beginning to spit fire at him.

His gaze drifted to her breasts. "I was thinking more of a slowie."

"So your men would have even more to gossip about?"

He drew a deep, irritated breath. "I suppose you want me to sneak over in the dead of night. We're not teenagers, damn it."

"No, we're not," she agreed. Then she said abruptly, "I'm not pregnant."

He didn't know if he should feel relieved, or irritated that this news meant it would be several days before she'd let him make love to her again. He wanted to curse, already feeling frustrated. Instead he said, "At least we didn't have to wait a couple of weeks, wondering."

"No, we didn't." She had known that the timing made it unlikely she'd conceive, but she'd still felt a small pang of regret that morning. Common sense aside, there was a deeply primitive part of her that wondered what woman wouldn't want to have his baby. He was so intensely masculine that he made other men pale in comparison, like a blooded stallion matched against scrub stock.

The gray shifted restively beneath him, and John controlled the big animal with his legs. "Actually, I don't have time, even for a quickie. I came to give Nev some instructions, then stop by the house to let you know where I'll be. I have to fly to Miami this afternoon, and I may not be back for a couple of days. If I'm not, drive to Tampa by yourself and sign those papers, and I'll detour on my way back to sign them."

Michelle twisted in the saddle to look at the battered, rusting old truck bouncing along behind the cattle. There was no way she would trust that relic to take her any place she couldn't get back from on foot. "I think I'll wait until you're back."

"Use the Mercedes. Just call the ranch and Nev will have a couple of men bring it over. I wouldn't trust that piece of junk you've been driving to get you to the grocery store and back."

It could have been a gesture between friends, a neighborly loan of a car, even something a lover might do, but Michelle sensed that John intended it to mean more than that. He was maneuvering her into his home as his mistress, and if she accepted the loan of the car, she would be just that much more dependent on him. Yet she was almost cornered into accepting because she had no other way of getting to Tampa, and her own sense of duty insisted that she sign those papers as soon as possible, to clear the debt.

He was waiting for her answer, and finally she couldn't hesitate any longer. "All right." Her surrender was quiet, almost inaudible.

He hadn't realized how tense he'd been until his muscles relaxed. The thought that she might try driving to Tampa in that old wreck had been worrying him since he'd gotten the call from Miami. His mother had gotten herself into financial hot water again, and, distasteful as it was to him, he wouldn't let her starve. No matter what, she was his mother. Loyalty went bone deep with him, a lot deeper than aggravation.

He'd even thought of taking Michelle with him, just to have her near. But Miami was too close to Palm Beach; too many of her old friends were there, bored, and just looking for some lark to spice up their lives. It was possible that some jerk with more money than brains would make an offer she couldn't refuse. He had to credit her with trying to make a go of the place, but she wasn't cut out for the life and must be getting tired of working so hard and getting nowhere. If someone offered to pay her fare, she might turn her back and walk away, back to the jet-set life-style she knew so well. No matter how slim the chance of it happening, any chance at all was too much for him. No way would he risk losing her now.

For the first time in his life he felt insecure about a woman. She wanted him, but was it enough to keep her with him? For the first time in his life, it was important. The hunger he felt for her was so deep that he wouldn't be satisfied until she was living under his roof and sleeping in his bed, where he could take care of her and pamper her as much as he wanted.

Yes, she wanted him. He could please her in bed; he could take care of her. But she didn't want him as much as he wanted her. She kept resisting him, trying to keep a distance between them even now, after they'd shared a night and a bed, and a joining that still shook him with its power.

It seemed as if every time he tried to bring her closer, she backed away a little more.

He reached out and touched her cheek, stroking his fingertips across her skin and feeling the patrician bone structure that gave her face such an angular, haughty look. "Miss me while I'm gone," he said, his tone making it a command.

A small wry smile tugged at the corners of her wide mouth. "Okay."

"Damn it," he said mildly. "You're not going to boost my ego, are you?"

"Does it need it?"

"Where you're concerned, yeah."

"That's a little hard to believe. Is missing someone a two-way street, or will you be too busy in Miami to bother?"

"I'll be busy, but I'll bother anyway."

"Be careful." She couldn't stop the words. They were the caring words that always went before a trip, a magic incantation to keep a loved one safe. The thought of not seeing him made her feel cold and empty. Miss him? He had no idea how much, that the missing was a razor, already slashing at her insides.

He wanted to kiss her, but not with his men watching. Instead he nodded an acknowledgment and turned his horse away to rejoin Nev. The two men rode together for a time, and Michelle could see Nev give an occasional nod as he listened to John's instructions. Then John was gone, kicking the gray into a long ground-eating stride that quickly took horse and rider out of sight.

Despite the small, lost feeling she couldn't shake, Michelle didn't allow herself to brood over the next several days. There was too much going on, and even though John's men had taken over the ranching chores, there were still other chores that, being cowboys, they didn't see. If it didn't concern cattle or horses, then it didn't concern them. Now Michelle found other chores to occupy her time. She painted the porch, put up a new post for the mailbox and spent as much time as she could with the men.

The ranch seemed like a ranch again, with all the activity, dust, smells and curses filling the air. The cattle were dipped, the calves branded, the young bulls clipped. Once Michelle would have wrinkled her nose in distaste, but now she saw the activity as new signs of life, both in the ranch and in herself.

On the second day Nev drove the Mercedes over while one of the other men brought an extra horse for Nev to ride. Michelle couldn't quite look the man in the eye as she took the keys from him, but he didn't seem to see anything unusual about her driving John's car.

After driving the pickup truck for so long, the power and responsiveness of the Mercedes felt odd. She was painfully cautious on the long drive to Tampa. It was hard to imagine that she'd ever been blasé about the expensive, sporty cars she'd driven over the years, but she could remember her carelessness with the white Porsche her father had given her on her eighteenth birthday. The amount of money represented by the small white machine hadn't made any impression on her.

Everything was relative. Then, the money spent for the Porsche hadn't been much. If she had that much now, she would feel rich.

She signed the papers at the lawyer's office, then immediately made the drive back, not wanting to have the Mercedes out longer than necessary.

The rest of the week was calm, though she wished John would call to let her know when he would be back. The two days had stretched into five, and she couldn't stop the tormenting doubts that popped up in unguarded moments. Was he with another woman? Even though he was down there on business, she knew all too well how women flocked to him, and he wouldn't be working twenty-four hours a day. He hadn't made any commitments to her; he was free to take other women out if he wanted. No matter how often she repeated those words to herself, they still hurt.

But if John didn't call, at least Roger didn't, either. For a while she'd been afraid he would begin calling regularly, but the reassuring silence continued. Maybe something or someone else had taken his attention. Maybe his business concerns were taking all his time. Whatever it was, Michelle was profoundly grateful.

The men didn't come over on Friday morning. The cattle were grazing peacefully in the east pasture; all the fencing had been repaired; everything had been taken care of. Michelle put a load of clothing in the washer, then spent the morning cutting the grass again. She was soaked with sweat when she went inside at noon to make a sandwich for lunch.

It was oddly silent in the house, or maybe it was just silent in comparison to the roar of the lawnmower. She needed water. Breathing hard, she turned on the faucet to let the water get cold while she got a glass from the cabinet, but only a trickle of water ran out, then stopped altogether. Frowning, Michelle turned the faucet off, then on again. Nothing happened. She tried the hot water. Nothing.

Groaning, she leaned against the sink. That was just what she needed, for the water pump to break down.

It took only a few seconds for the silence of the house to connect with the lack of water, and she slowly straightened. Reluctantly she reached for the light switch and flicked it on. Nothing.

The electricity had been cut off.

That was why it was so quiet. The refrigerator wasn't humming; the clocks weren't ticking; the ceiling fan was still.

Breathing raggedly, she sank into a chair. She had forgotten the last notice. She had put it in a drawer and forgotten it, distracted by John and the sudden activity around the ranch. Not that any excuse was worth a hill of beans, she reminded herself. Not that she'd had the money to pay the bill even if she had remembered it.

She had to be practical. People had lived for thousands of years without electricity, so she could, too. Cooking was out; the range top, built-in oven and microwave were all electric, but she wasn't the world's best cook anyway, so that wasn't critical. She could eat without cooking. The refrigerator was empty except for milk and some odds and ends. Thinking about the milk reminded her how thirsty she was, so she poured a glass of the cold milk and swiftly returned the carton to the refrigerator.

There was a kerosene lamp and a supply of candles in the pantry, so she would have light. The most critical item was water. She had to have water to drink and bathe. At least the cattle could drink from the shallow creek that snaked across the east pasture, so she wouldn't have to worry about them.

There was an old well about a hundred yards behind the house, but she didn't know if it had gone dry or simply been covered when the other well had been drilled. Even if the well was still good, how would she get the water up? There was a rope in the barn, but she didn't have a bucket.

She did have seventeen dollars, though, the last of her cash. If the well had water in it, she'd coax the old truck down to the hardware store and buy a water bucket.

She got a rope from the barn, a pan from the kitchen and trudged the hundred yards to the old well. It was almost overgrown with weeds and vines that she had to clear away while keeping an uneasy eye out for snakes. Then she tugged the heavy wooden cover to the side and dropped the pan into the well, letting the rope slip lightly through her hands. It wasn't a deep well; in only a second or two there was a distinct splash, and she began hauling the pan back up. When she got it to the top, a half cup of clear water was still in the pan despite the banging it had received, and Michelle sighed with relief. Now all she had to do was get the bucket.

By the time dusk fell, she was convinced that the pioneers had all been as muscular as the Incredible Hulk; every muscle in her body ached. She had drawn a bucket of water and walked the distance back to the house so many times she didn't want to think about it. The electricity had been cut off while the washer had been in the middle of its cycle, so she had to rinse the clothes out by hand and hang them to dry. She had to have water to drink. She had to have water to bathe. She had to have water to flush the toilet. Modern conveniences were damned *in*convenient without electricity.

But at least she was too tired to stay up long and waste the candles. She set a candle in a saucer on the bedside table, with matches alongside in case she woke up during the night. She was asleep almost as soon as she stretched out between the sheets.

The next morning she ate a peanut butter and jelly sandwich for breakfast, then cleaned out the refrigerator, so she wouldn't have to smell spoiled food. The house was oddly oppressive, as if the life had gone out of it, so she spent most of the day outdoors, watching the cattle graze, and thinking.

She would have to sell the beef cattle now, rather than wait to fatten them on grain. She wouldn't get as much for them, but she had to have money *now*. It had been foolish of her to let things go this far. Pride had kept her from asking for John's advice and help in arranging the sale; now she had to ask him. He would know who to contact and how to transport the cattle. The money would keep her going, allow her to care for the remainder of the herd until spring, when she would have more beef ready to sell. Pride was one thing, but she had carried it to the point of stupidity.

Still, if this had happened ten days earlier she wouldn't even have considered asking John's advice. She had been so completely isolated from human trust that any overture would have made her back away, rather than entice her closer. But John hadn't let her back away; he'd come after her, taken care of things over her protests, and very gently, thoroughly seduced her. A seed of trust had been sown that was timidly growing, though it frightened her to think of relying on someone else, even for good advice.

It was sultry that night, the air thick with humidity. The heat added by the candles and kerosene lamp made it unbearable inside, and though she bathed in the cool water she had hauled from the well, she immediately felt sticky again. It was too early and too hot to sleep, so finally she went out on the porch in search of a breeze.

She curled up in a wicker chair padded with overstuffed cushions, sighing in relief as a breath of wind fanned her face. The night sounds of crickets and frogs surrounded her with a hypnotic lullaby, and before long her eyelids were drooping. She never quite dozed, but sank into a peaceful lethargy where time passed unnoticed. It might have been two hours or half an hour later when she was disturbed by the sound of a motor and the crunching of tires on gravel; headlights flashed into her eyes just as she opened them, making her flinch and turn her face from the blinding light. Then the lights were killed and the motor silenced. She sat up straighter, her heart beginning to pound as a tall, broadshouldered man got out of the truck and slammed the door. The starlight wasn't bright, but she didn't need light to identify him when every cell in her body tingled with awareness.

Despite his boots, he didn't make a lot of noise as he came up the steps. "John," she murmured, her voice only a low whisper of sound, but he felt the vibration and turned toward her chair.

She was completely awake now, and becoming indignant. "Why didn't you call? I waited to hear from you—"

"I don't like telephones," he muttered as he walked toward her. That was only part of the reason. Talking to her on the telephone would only have made him want her more, and his nights had been pure hell as it was.

"That isn't much of an excuse."

"It'll do," he drawled. "What are you doing out here? The house is so dark I thought you must have gone to bed early."

Which wouldn't have stopped him from waking her, she thought wryly. "It's too hot to sleep."

He grunted in agreement, bending down to slide his arms under her legs and shoulders. Startled, Michelle grabbed his neck with both arms as he lifted her, then took her place in the chair and settled her on his lap. An almost painful sense of relief filled her as his nearness eased tension she hadn't even been aware of feeling. She was surrounded by his strength and warmth, and the subtle male scent of his skin reaffirmed the sense of homecoming, of rightness. Bonelessly she melted against him, lifting her mouth to his.

The kiss was long and hot, his lips almost bruising hers in his need, but she didn't mind, because her own need was just as urgent. His hands slipped under the light nightgown that was all she wore, finding her soft and naked, and a shudder wracked his body.

He muttered a soft curse. "Sweet hell, woman, you were sitting out here practically naked."

"No one else is around to see." She said the words against his throat, her lips moving over his hard flesh and finding the vibrant hollow where his pulse throbbed.

Heat and desire wrapped around them, sugar-sweet and mindless. From the moment he touched her, she'd wanted only to lie down with him and sink into the textures and sensations of lovemaking. She twisted in his arms, trying to press her breasts fully against him and whimpering a protest as he prevented her from moving.

"This won't work," he said, securing his hold on her and getting to his feet with her still in his arms. "We'd better find a bed, because this chair won't hold up to what I have in mind."

He carried her inside, and as he had done before, he flipped the switch for the light in the entry, so he would be able to see while going up the stairs. He paused when the light didn't come on. "You've got a blown bulb."

Tension invaded her body again. "The power's off."

He gave a low laugh. "Well, hell. Do you have a flashlight? The last thing I want to do right now is trip on the stairs and break our necks."

"There's a kerosene lamp on the table." She wriggled in his arms, and he slowly let her slide to the floor, reluctant to let her go even for a moment. She fumbled for the matches and struck one, the bright glow guiding her hands as she removed the glass chimney and held the flame to the wick. It caught, and the light grew when she put the chimney back in place.

John took the lamp in his left hand, folding her close to his side with his other arm as they started up the stairs. "Have you called the power company to report it?"

She had to laugh. "They know."

"How long will it take them to get it back on?"

Well, he might as well know now. Sighing, she admitted, "The electricity's been cut off. I couldn't pay the bill."

He stopped, his brows drawing together in increasing temper as he turned. "Damn it to hell! How long has it been off?"

"Since yesterday morning."

He exhaled through his clenched teeth, making a hissing sound. "You've been here without water and lights for a day and a half? Of all the damned stubborn stunts... Why in hell didn't you give the bill to me?" He yelled the last few words at her, his eyes snapping black fury in the yellow light from the lamp.

"I don't want you paying my bills!" she snapped, pulling away from him.

"Well, that's just tough!" Swearing under his breath, he caught her hand and pulled her up the stairs, then into her bedroom. He set the lamp on the bedside table and crossed to the closet, opened the doors and began pulling her suitcases from the top shelf.

"What are you doing?" she cried, wrenching the suitcase from him.

He lifted another case down. "Packing your things," he replied shortly. "If you don't want to help, just sit on the bed and stay out of the way."

"Stop it!" She tried to prevent him from taking an armful of clothes from the closet, but he merely sidestepped her and tossed the clothes onto the bed, then returned to the closet for another armful.

"You're going with me," he said, his voice steely. "This is Saturday; it'll be Monday before I can take care of the bill. There's no way in hell I'm going to leave you here. God Almighty, you don't even have water!"

Michelle pushed her hair from her eyes. "I have water. I've been drawing it from the old well."

He began swearing again and turned from the closet to the dresser. Before she could say anything her underwear was added to the growing pile on the bed. "I can't stay with you," she said desperately, knowing events were already far out of her control. "You know how it'll look! I can manage another couple of days—"

"I don't give a damn how it looks!" he snapped. "And just so you understand me, I'm going to give it to you in plain English. You're going with me now, and you won't be coming back. This isn't a two-day visit. I'm tired of worrying about you out here all by yourself; this is the last straw. You're too damned proud to tell me when you need help, so I'm going to take over and handle everything, the way I should have in the beginning."

Michelle shivered, staring at him. It was true that she shrank from the gossip she knew would run through the county like wildfire, but that wasn't the main reason for her reluctance. Living with him would destroy the last fragile buffers she had retained against being overwhelmed by him in every respect. She wouldn't be able to keep any emotional distance as a safety precaution, just as physical distance would be impossible. She would be in his home, in his bed, eating his food, totally dependent on him.

It frightened her so much that she found herself backing away from him, as if by increasing the distance between them she could weaken his force and fury. "I've been getting by without you," she whispered.

"Is this what you call 'getting by'?" he shouted, slinging the contents of another drawer onto the bed. "You were working yourself half to death, and you're damned lucky you weren't hurt trying to do a two-man job! You don't have any money. You don't have a safe car to drive. You probably don't have enough to eat—and now you don't have electricity."

"I know what I don't have!"

"Well, I'll tell you something else you don't have: a choice. You're going. Now get dressed."

She stood against the wall on the other side of the room, very still and straight. When she didn't move his head jerked up, but something about her made his mouth soften. She looked defiant and stubborn, but her eyes were frightened, and she looked so frail it was like a punch in the gut, staggering him.

He crossed the room with quick strides and hauled her into his arms, folding her against him as if he couldn't tolerate another minute of not touching her. He buried his face in her hair, wanting to sweep her up and keep her from ever being frightened again. "I won't let you do it," he muttered in a raspy voice. "You're trying to keep me at a distance, and I'll be damned if I'll let you do it. Does it matter so much if people know about us? Are you ashamed because I'm not a member of your jet set?"

She gave a shaky laugh, her fingers digging into his back. "Of course not. *I'm* not one of the jet set." How could any woman ever be ashamed of him?

His lips brushed her forehead, leaving warmth behind. "Then what is it?"

She bit her lip, her mind whirling with images of the past and fears of the future. "The summer I was nineteen . . . you called me a parasite." She had never forgotten the words or the deep hurt they'd caused, and an echo of it was in her low, drifting voice. "You were right."

"Wrong," he whispered, winding his fingers through the strands of her bright hair. "A parasite doesn't give anything, it only takes. I didn't understand, or maybe I was jealous because I wanted it all. I have it all now, and I won't give it up. I've waited ten years for you, baby; I'm not going to settle for half measures now."

He tilted her head back, and his mouth closed warmly, hungrily, over hers, overwhelming any further protests. With a little sigh Michelle gave in, going up on her tiptoes to press herself against him. Regrets could wait; if this were all she would have of heaven, she was going to grab it with both hands. He would probably decide that she'd given in so she could have an easier life, but maybe that was safer than for him to know she was head over heels in love with him.

She slipped out of his arms and quietly changed into jeans and a silk tunic, then set about restoring order out of the chaos he'd made of her clothes. Traveling had taught her to be a fast, efficient packer. As she finished each case, he carried it out to the truck. Finally only her makeup and toiletries were left.

"We'll come back tomorrow for anything else you want," he promised, holding the lamp for the last trip down the stairs. When she stepped outside he extinguished the lamp and placed it on the table, then followed her and locked the door behind him.

"What will your housekeeper think?" she blurted nervously as she got in the truck. It hurt to be leaving her home. She had hidden herself away here, sinking deep roots into the ranch. She had found peace and healing in the hard work.

"That I should have called to let her know when I'd be home," he said, laughing as relief and anticipation filled him. "I came here straight from the airport. My bag is in back with yours." He couldn't wait to get home, to see Michelle's clothing hanging next to his in the closet, to have her toiletries in his bathroom, to sleep with her every night in his bed. He'd never before wanted to live with a woman, but with Michelle it felt necessary. There was no way he would ever feel content with less than everything she had to give.

Chapter 7

It was midmorning when Michelle woke, and she lay there for a moment alone in the big bed, trying to adjust to the change. She was in John's house, in his bed. He had gotten up hours ago, before dawn, and left her with a kiss on the forehead and an order to catch up on her sleep. She stretched, becoming aware of both her nakedness and the ache in her muscles. She didn't want to move, didn't want to leave the comforting cocoon of sheets and pillows that carried John's scent. The memory of shattering pleasure made her body tingle, and she moved restlessly. He hadn't slept much, hadn't let her sleep until he'd finally left the bed to go about his normal day's work.

If only he had taken her with him. She felt awkward with Edie, the housekeeper. What must she be thinking? They had met only briefly, because John had ushered Michelle upstairs with blatantly indecent haste, but her impression had been of height, dignity and cool control. The housekeeper wouldn't say anything if she disapproved, but then, she wouldn't have to; Michelle would know.

Finally she got out of bed and showered, smiling wryly to herself as she realized she wouldn't have to skimp on hot water. Central air-conditioning kept the house comfortably cool, which was another comfort she had given up in an effort to reduce the bills. No matter what her mental state, she would be physically comfortable here. It struck her as odd that she'd never been to John's house before; she'd had no idea what to expect. Perhaps another old ranch house like hers, though her father had remodeled and modernized it completely on the inside before they had moved in, and it was in fact as luxurious as the home she had been used to. But John's house was Spanish in style, and was only eight years old. The cool adobe-colored brick and high ceilings kept the heat at bay, and a colorful array of houseplants brought freshness to the air. She'd been surprised at the greenery, then decided that the plants were Edie's doing. The U-shaped house wrapped around a pool landscaped to the point that it resembled a jungle lagoon more than a pool, and every room had a view of the pool and patio.

She had been surprised at the luxury. John was a long way from poor, but the house had cost a lot of money that he would normally have plowed back into the ranch. She had expected something more utilitarian, but at the same time it was very much his *home*. His presence permeated it, and everything was arranged for his comfort.

Finally she forced herself to stop hesitating and go downstairs; if Edie intended to be hostile, she might as well know now.

The layout of the house was simple, and she found the kitchen without any problem. All she had to do was follow her nose to the coffee. As she entered, Edie looked around, her face expressionless, and Michelle's heart sank. Then the housekeeper planted her hands on her hips and said calmly, "I told John it was about damned time he got a woman in this house."

Relief flooded through Michelle, because something in her would have shriveled if Edie had looked at her with contempt. She was much more sensitive to what other people thought now than she had been when she was younger and had the natural arrogance of youth. Life had defeated that arrogance and taught her not to expect roses.

Faint color rushed to her cheeks. "John didn't make much of an effort to introduce us last night. I'm Michelle Cabot."

"Edie Ward. Are you ready for breakfast? I'm the cook, too."

"I'll wait until lunch, thank you. Does John come back for lunch?" It embarrassed her to have to ask.

"If he's working close by. How about coffee?"

"I can get it," Michelle said quickly. "Where are the cups?"

Edie opened the cabinet to the left of the sink and got down a cup, handing it to Michelle. "It'll be nice to have company here during the day," she said. "These damn cowhands aren't much for talking."

Whatever Michelle had expected, Edie didn't conform. She had to be fifty; though her hair was still dark, there was something about her that made her look her age. She was tall and broad shouldered, with the erect carriage of a Mother Superior and the same sort of unflappable dignity, but she also had the wise, slightly weary eyes of someone who has been around the block a few times too many. Her quiet acceptance made Michelle relax; Edie didn't pass judgments.

But for all the easing of tension, Edie quietly and firmly discouraged Michelle from helping with any of the household chores. "Rafferty would have both our heads," she said. "Housework is what he pays me to do, and around here we try not to rile him."

So Michelle wandered around the house, poking her head into every room and wondering how long she would be able to stand the boredom and emptiness. Working the ranch by herself had been so hard that she had sometimes wanted nothing more than to collapse where she stood, but there had always been a purpose to the hours. She liked ranching. It wasn't easy, but it suited her far better than the dual roles of ornament and mistress. This lack of purpose made her uneasy. She had hoped living with John would mean doing things with him, sharing the work and the worries with him . . . just as married couples did.

She sucked in her breath at the thought; she was in his— still *his*—bedroom at the time, standing in front of the open closet staring at his clothes, as if the sight of his personal possessions would bring him closer. Slowly she reached out and fingered a shirtsleeve. Her clothes were in the closet beside his, but she didn't belong. This was his house, his bedroom, his closet, and she was merely another possession, to be enjoyed in bed but forgotten at sunrise. Wryly she admitted that if was better than nothing; no matter what the cost to her pride, she would stay here as long as he wanted her, because she was so sick with love for him that she'd take anything she could get. But what she wanted, what she really wanted more than anything in her life, was to have his love as well as his desire. She wanted to marry him, to be his partner, his friend as well as his lover, to belong here as much as he did.

Part of her was startled that she could think of marriage again, even with John. Roger had destroyed her trust, her optimism about life; at least, she'd thought he had. Trust had already bloomed again, a fragile phoenix poking its head up from the ashes. For the first time she recognized her own resilience; she had been altered by the terror and shame of her marriage, but not destroyed. She was healing, and most of it was because of John. She had loved him for so long that her love seemed like the only continuous thread of her life, always there, somehow giving her something to hold on to even when she'd thought it didn't matter.

At last restlessness drove her from the house. She was reluctant to even ask questions, not wanting to interfere with anyone's work, but she decided to walk around and look at everything. There was a world of difference between John's ranch and hers. Here everything was neat and well-maintained, with fresh paint on the barns and fences, the machinery humming. Healthy, spirited horses pranced in the corral or grazed in the pasture. The supply shed was in better shape than her barn. Her ranch had once looked like this, and determination filled her that it would again.

Who was looking after her cattle? She hadn't asked John, not that she'd been given a chance to ask him anything. He'd had her in bed so fast that she hadn't had time to think; then he'd left while she was still dozing.

By the time John came home at dusk, Michelle was so on edge that she could feel her muscles twitching with tension. As soon as he came in from the kitchen his eyes swept the room, and hard satisfaction crossed his face when he saw her. All day long he'd been fighting the urge to come back to the house, picturing her here, under his roof at last. Even when he'd built the house, eight years before, he'd wondered what *she* would think of it, if she'd like it, how she would look in these rooms. It wasn't a grand mansion like those in Palm Beach, but it had been custom built to his specifications for comfort, beauty and a certain level of luxury.

She looked as fresh and perfect as early-morning sunshine, while he was covered with sweat and dust, his jaw dark with a day's growth of beard. If he touched her now, he'd leave dirty prints on her creamy white dress, and he had to touch her soon or go crazy. "Come on up with me," he growled, his boots ringing on the flagstone floor as he went to the stairs.

Michelle followed him at a slower pace, wondering if he already regretted bringing her here. He hadn't kissed her, or even smiled.

He was stripping off his shirt by the time she entered the bedroom, and he carelessly dropped the dirty, sweat-stained garment on the carpet. She shivered in response at the sight of his broad, hair-covered chest and powerful shoulders, her pulse throbbing as she remembered how it felt when he moved over her and slowly let her take his weight, nestling her breasts into that curly hair.

"What've you been doing today?" he asked as he went into the bathroom.

"Nothing," Michelle answered with rueful truthfulness, shaking away the sensual lethargy that had been stealing over her.

Splashing sounds came from the bathroom, and when he reappeared a few minutes later his face was clean of the dust that had covered it before. Damp strands of black hair curled at his temples. He looked at her, and an impatient scowl darkened his face. Bending down, he pried his boots off, then began unbuckling his belt.

Her heart began pounding again. He was going to take her to bed right now, and she wouldn't have a chance to talk to him if she didn't do it before he reached for her. Nervously she picked up his dirty boots to put them in the closet, wondering how to start. "Wait," she blurted. "I need to talk to you."

He didn't see any reason to wait. "So talk," he said, unzipping his jeans and pushing them down his thighs.

She inhaled deeply. "I've been bored with nothing to do all day—"

John straightened, his eyes hardening as she broke off. Hell, he should have expected it. When you acquired something expensive, you had to pay for its upkeep. "All right," he said in an even tone. "I'll give you the keys to the Mercedes, and tomorrow I'll open a checking account for you."

She froze as the meaning of his words seared through her, and all the color washed out of her face. No. There was no way she'd let him turn her into a pet, a chirpy sexual toy, content with a fancy car and charge accounts. Fury rose in her like an inexorable wave, rushing up and bursting out of control. Fiercely she hurled the boots at him; startled, he dodged the first one, but the second one hit him in the chest. "What the hell—"

"No!" she shouted, her eyes like green fire in a face gone curiously pale. She was standing rigidly, her fists clenched at her sides. "I don't want your money or your damned car! I want to take care of my cattle and my ranch, not be left here every day like some fancy...*sex doll*, waiting for you to get home and play with me!"

He kicked his jeans away, leaving him clad only in his briefs. His own temper was rising, but he clamped it under control. That control was evident in his quiet, level voice. "I don't think of you as a sex doll. What brought that on?"

She was white and shaking. "You brought me straight up here and started undressing."

His brows rose. "Because I was dirty from head to foot. I couldn't even kiss you without getting you dirty, and I didn't want to ruin your dress."

Her lips trembled as she looked down at the dress. "It's just a dress," she said, turning away. "It'll wash. And I'd rather be dirty myself than just left here every day with nothing to do."

"We've been over this before, and it's settled." He walked up behind her and put his hands on her shoulders, gently squeezing. "You can't handle the work; you'd only hurt yourself. Some women can do it, but you're not strong enough. Look at your wrist," he said, sliding his hand down her arm and grasping her wrist to lift it. "Your bones are too little."

Somehow she found herself leaning against him, her head resting in the hollow of his shoulder. "Stop trying to make me feel so useless!" she cried desperately. "At least let me go with you. I can chase strays—"

He turned her in his arms, crushing her against him and cutting off her words. "God, baby," he muttered. "I'm trying to protect you, not make you feel useless. It made me sick when I saw you putting up that fence, knowing what could happen if the wire lashed back on you. You could be thrown, or gored—"

"So could you."

"Not as easily. Admit it; strength counts out there. I want you safe."

It was a battle they'd already fought more times than she could remember, and nothing budged him. But she couldn't give up, because she couldn't stand many more days like today had been. "Could you stand it if you had nothing to do? If you had to just stand around and watch everybody else? Edie won't even let me help!"

"She'd damned well better not."

"See what I mean? Am I supposed to just sit all day?"

"All right, you've made your point," he said in a low voice. He'd thought she'd enjoy living a life of leisure again, but instead she'd been wound to the breaking point. He rubbed her back soothingly, and gradually she relaxed against him, her arms sliding up to hook around his neck. He'd have to find something to keep her occupied, but right now he was at a loss. It was hard to think when she was lying against him like warm silk, her firm breasts pushing into him and the sweet scent of woman rising to his nostrils. She hadn't been far from his mind all day, the thought of her pulling at him like a magnet. No matter how often he took her, the need came back even stronger than before.

Reluctantly he moved her a few inches away from him. "Dinner will be ready in about ten minutes, and I need a shower. I smell like a horse."

The hot, earthy scents of sweat, sun, leather and man didn't offend her. She found herself drawn back to him; she pressed her face into his chest, her tongue flicking out to lick daintily at his hot skin. He shuddered, all thoughts of a shower gone from his mind. Sliding his fingers into the shiny, pale gold curtain of her hair, he turned her face up and took the kiss he'd been wanting for hours.

She couldn't limit her response to him; whenever he reached for her, she was instantly his, melting into him, opening her mouth for him, ready to give as little or as much as he wanted to take. Loving him went beyond the boundaries she had known before, taking her into emotional and physical territory that was new to her. It was his control, not hers, that prevented him from tumbling her onto the bed right then. "Shower," he muttered, lifting his head. His voice was strained. "Then dinner. Then I have to do some paperwork, damn it, and it can't wait."

Michelle sensed that he expected her to object and demand his company, but more than anyone she understood about chores that couldn't be postponed. She drew back from his arms, giving him a smile. "I'm starving, so hurry up with your shower." An idea was forming in the back of her mind, one she needed to explore.

She was oddly relaxed during dinner; it somehow seemed natural to be here with him, as if the world had suddenly settled into the natural order of things. The awkwardness of the morning was gone, perhaps because of John's presence. Edie ate with them, an informality that Michelle liked. It also gave her a chance to think, because Edie's comments filled the silence and made it less apparent.

After dinner, John gave Michelle a quick kiss and a pat on the bottom. "I'll finish as fast as I can. Can you entertain yourself for a while?"

Swift irritation made up her mind for her. "I'm coming with you."

He sighed, looking down at her. "Baby, I won't get any work done at all if you're in there with me."

She gave him a withering look. "You're the biggest chauvinist walking, John Rafferty. You're going to work, all right, because you're going to show me what you're doing, and then I'm taking over your bookwork.''

He looked suddenly wary. "I'm not a chauvinist."

He didn't want her touching his books, either. He might as well have said it out loud, because she read his thoughts in his expression. "You can either give me something to do, or I'm going back to my house right now," she said flatly, facing him with her hands on her hips.

"Just what do you know about keeping books?"

"I minored in business administration." Let him chew on that for a while. Since he obviously wasn't going to willingly let her in his office, she stepped around him and walked down the hall without him.

"Michelle, damn it," he muttered irritably, following her.

"Just what's wrong with my doing the books?" she demanded, taking a seat at the big desk.

"I didn't bring you here to work. I want to take care of you."

"Am I going to get hurt in here? Is a pencil too heavy for me to lift?"

He scowled down at her, itching to lift her out of her chair. But her green eyes were glittering at him, and her chin had that stubborn tilt to it, showing she was ready to fight. If he pushed her, she really might go back to that dark, empty house. He could keep her here by force, but he didn't want it that way. He wanted her sweet and willing, not clawing at him like a wildcat. Hell, at least this was safer than riding herd. He'd double-check the books at night.

"All right," he growled.

Her green eyes mocked him. "You're so gracious."

"You're full of sass tonight," he mused, sitting down. "Maybe I should have made love to you before dinner after all, worked some of that out."

"Like I said, the world's biggest chauvinist." She gave him her haughty look, the one that had always made him see red before. She was beginning to enjoy baiting him.

His face darkened but he controlled himself, reaching for the pile of invoices, receipts and notes. "Pay attention, and don't screw this up," he snapped. "Taxes are bad enough without an amateur bookkeeper fouling up the records."

"I've been doing the books since Dad died," she snapped in return.

"From the looks of the place, honey, that's not much of a recommendation."

Her face froze, and she looked away from him, making him swear under his breath. Without another word she jerked the papers from him and began sorting them, then put them in order by dates. He settled back in his big chair, his face brooding as he watched her enter the figures swiftly and neatly in the ledger, then run the columns through the adding machine twice to make certain they were correct.

When she was finished, she pushed the ledger across the desk. "Check it so you'll be satisfied I didn't make any mistakes."

He did, thoroughly. Finally he closed the ledger and said, "All right."

Her eyes narrowed. "Is that all you have to say? No wonder you've never been married, if you think women don't have the brains to add two and two!"

"I've been married," he said sharply.

The information stunned her, because she'd never heard anyone mention his being married, nor was marriage something she readily associated with John Rafferty. Then hot jealousy seared her at the thought of some other woman living with him, sharing his name and his bed, having the right to touch him. "Who . . . when?" she stammered.

"A long time ago. I'd just turned nineteen, and I had more hormones than sense. God only knows why she married me. It only took her four months to decide ranch life wasn't for her, that she wanted money to spend and a husband who didn't work twenty hours a day."

His voice was flat, his eyes filled with contempt. Michelle felt cold. "Why didn't anyone ever mention it?" she whispered. "I've known you for ten years, but I didn't know you'd been married."

He shrugged. "We got divorced seven years before you moved down here, so it wasn't exactly the hottest news in the county. It didn't last long enough for folks to get to know her, anyway. I worked too much to do any socializing. If she married me thinking a rancher's wife would live in the lap of luxury, she changed her mind in a hurry."

"Where is she now?" Michelle fervently hoped the woman didn't still live in the area.

"I don't know, and I don't care. I heard she married some old rich guy as soon as our divorce was final. It didn't matter to me then, and it doesn't matter now."

It was beyond her how any woman could choose another man, no matter how rich, over John. She would live in a hut and eat rattlesnake meat if it meant staying with him. But she was beginning to understand why he was so contemptuous of the jet-setters, the idle rich, why he'd made so many caustic remarks to her in the past about letting others support her instead of working to support herself. Considering that, it was even more confusing that now he didn't want her doing anything at all, as if he wanted to make her totally dependent on him.

He was watching her from beneath hooded lids, wondering what she was thinking. She'd been shocked to learn he'd been married before. It had been so long ago that he never thought about it, and he wouldn't even have mentioned it if her crack about marriage hadn't reminded him. It had happened in another lifetime, to a nineteen-year-old boy busting his guts to make a go of the rundown little ranch he'd inherited. Sometimes he couldn't even remember her name, and it had been years since he'd been able to remember what she looked like. He wouldn't recognize her if they met face to face.

It was odd, because even though he hadn't seen Michelle during the years of her marriage, he'd never forgotten her face, the way she moved, the way sunlight looked in her hair. He knew every line of her striking, but too angular face, all high cheekbones, stubborn chin and wide, soft mouth. She had put her mouth to his chest and tasted his salty, sweaty skin, her tongue licking at him. She looked so cool and untouchable now in that spotless white dress, but when he made love to her she turned into liquid heat. He thought of the way her legs wrapped around his waist, and he began to harden as desire heated his body. He leaned back in his chair, shifting restlessly.

Michelle had turned back to the stack of papers on his desk, not wanting to pry any further. She didn't want to know any more about his ex-wife, and she especially didn't want him to take the opportunity to ask about her failed marriage. It would be safer to get back to business; she needed to talk to him about selling her beef cattle, anyway.

"I need your advice on something. I wanted to fatten the cattle up for sale this year, but I need operating capital, so I think I should sell them now. Who do I contact, and how is transportation arranged?"

Right at that moment he didn't give a damn about any cattle. She had crossed her legs, and her skirt had slid up a little, drawing his eyes. He wanted to slide it up more, crumple it around her waist and completely bare her legs. His jeans were under considerable strain, and he had to force himself to answer. "Let the cattle fatten; you'll get a lot more money for them. I'll keep the ranch going until then."

She turned her head with a quick, impatient movement, sending her hair swirling, but whatever she had been about to say died when their eyes met and she read his expression. "Let's go upstairs," he murmured.

It was almost frightening to have that intense sexuality focused on her, but she was helpless to resist him. She found herself standing, shivering as he put his hand on her back and ushered her upstairs. Walking beside him made her feel vulnerable; sometimes his size overwhelmed her, and this was one of those times. He was so tall and powerful, his shoulders so broad, that when she lay beneath him in bed he blocked out the light. Only his own control and tenderness protected her.

He locked the bedroom door behind them, then stood behind her and slowly began unzipping her dress. He felt her shivering. "Don't be afraid, baby. Or is it excitement?"

"Yes," she whispered as he slid his hands inside the open dress and around to cup her bare breasts, molding his fingers over her. She could feel her nipples throb against his palms, and with a little whimper she leaned back against him, trying to sink herself into his hardness and warmth. It felt so good when he touched her.

"Both?" he murmured. "Why are you afraid?"

Her eyes were closed, her breath coming in shallow gulps as he rubbed her nipples to hard little points of fire. "The way you make me feel," she gasped, her head rolling on his shoulder.

"You make me feel the same." His voice was slow and guttural as the hot pressure built in him. "Hot, like I'll explode if I don't get inside you. Then you're so soft and tight around me that I know I'm going to explode anyway."

The words made love to her, turning her shivers into shudders. Her legs were liquid, unable to support her; if it hadn't been for John's muscular body behind her, she would have fallen. She whispered his name, the single word vibrant with longing.

His warm breath puffed around her ear as he nuzzled the lobe. "You're so sexy, baby. This dress has been driving me crazy. I wanted to pull up your skirt...like this...." His hands had left her breasts and gone down to her hips, and now her skirt rose along her thighs as he gathered the material in his fists. Then it was at her waist, and his hands were beneath it, his fingers spread over her bare stomach. "I thought about sliding my hands under your panties . . . like this. Pulling them down . . . like this."

She moaned as he slipped her panties down her hips and over her buttocks, overcome by a sense of voluptuous helplessness and exposure. Somehow being only partially undressed made her feel even more naked and vulnerable. His long fingers went between her legs, and she quivered like a wild thing as he stroked and probed, slowly building her tension and pleasure to the breaking point.

"You're so sweet and soft," he whispered. "Are you ready for me?"

She tried to answer, but all she could do was gasp. She was on fire, her entire body throbbing, and still he held her against him, his fingers slowly thrusting into her, when he knew she wanted him and was ready for him. He *knew* it. He was too experienced not to know, but he persisted in that sweet torment as he savored the feel of her.

She felt as sexy as he told her she was; her own sensuality was unfolding like a tender flower under his hands and his low, rough voice. Each time he made love to her, she found a little more self-assurance in her own capacity for giving and receiving pleasure. He was strongly, frankly sexual, so experienced that she wanted to slap him every time she thought about it, but she had discovered that she could satisfy him. Sometimes he trembled with hunger when he touched her; this man, whose raw virility gave him sensual power over any woman he wanted, trembled with the need for *her*. She was twenty-eight years old, and only now, in John's hands, was she discovering her power and pleasure as a woman.

Finally she couldn't take any more and whirled away from his hands, her eyes fierce as she stripped off her dress and reached for him, tearing at his clothes. He laughed deeply, but the sound was of excitement rather than humor, and helped her. Naked, already entwined, they fell together to the bed. He took her with a slow, strong thrust, for the first time not having to enter her by careful degrees, and the inferno roared out of control.

Michelle bounced out of bed before he did the next morning, her face glowing. "You don't have to get up," he rumbled in his hoarse, early-morning voice. "Why don't you sleep late?" Actually he liked the thought of her dozing in his bed, rosily naked and exhausted after a night of making love.

She pushed her pale, tousled hair out of her eyes, momentarily riveted by his nudity as he got out of bed. "I'm going with you today," she said, and dashed to beat him to the bathroom.

He joined her in the shower a few minutes later, his black eyes narrowed after her announcement. She waited for him to tell her that she couldn't go, but instead he muttered, "I guess it's okay, if it'll make you happy."

It did. She had decided that John was such an overprotective chauvinist that he would cheerfully keep her wrapped in cotton, so reasoning with him was out of the question. She knew what she could do; she would do it. It was that simple.

Over the next three weeks a deep happiness began forming inside her. She had taken over the paperwork completely, working on it three days out of the week, which gave John more free time at night than he'd ever had before. He gave up checking her work, because he never found an error. On the other days she rode with him, content with his company, and he discovered that he liked having her nearby. There were times when he was so hot, dirty and aggravated that he'd be turning the air blue with savage curses, then he'd look up and catch her smiling at him, and his aggravation would fade away. What did a contrary steer matter when she looked at him that way? She never seemed to mind the dust and heat, or the smells. It wasn't what he'd expected, and sometimes it bothered him. It was as if she were hiding here, burying herself in this self-contained world. The Michelle he'd known before had been a laughing, teasing, social creature, enjoying parties and dancing. This Michelle seldom laughed, though she was so generous with her smiles that it took him a while to notice. One of those smiles made him and all his men a little giddy, but he could remember her sparkling laughter, and he wondered where it had gone.

But it was still so new, having her to himself, that he wasn't anxious to share her with others. They spent the nights tangled together in heated passion, and instead of abating, the hunger only intensified. He spent the days in constant, low-level arousal, and sometimes all he had to do was look at her and he'd be so hard he'd have to find some way of disguising it.

One morning Michelle remained at the house to work in the office; she was alone because Edie had gone grocery shopping. The telephone rang off the hook that morning, interrupting her time and again. She was already irritated with it when it jangled yet again and made her stop what she was doing to answer it. "Rafferty residence."

No one answered, though she could hear slow, deep breathing, as though whoever was on the other end was deliberately controlling his breath. It wasn't a "breather," though; the sound wasn't obscenely exaggerated.

"Hello," she said. "Can you hear me?"

A quiet click sounded in her ear, as if whoever had been calling had put down the receiver with slow, controlled caution, much as he'd been breathing.

He. For some reason she had no doubt it was a man. Common sense said it could be some bored teenager playing a prank, or simply a wrong number, but a sudden chill swept over her.

A sense of menace had filled the silence on the line. For the first time in three weeks she felt isolated and somehow threatened, though there was no tangible reason for it. The chills wouldn't stop running up and down her spine, and suddenly she had to get out of the house, into the hot sunshine. She had to see John, just be able to look at him and hear his deep voice roaring curses, or crooning gently to a horse or a frightened calf. She needed his heat to dispel the coldness of a menace she couldn't define.

Two days later there was another phone call and again, by chance, she answered the phone. "Hello," she said. "Rafferty residence."

Silence.

Her hand began shaking. She strained her ears and heard that quiet, even breathing, then the click as the phone was hung up, and a moment later the dial tone began buzzing in her ear. She felt sick and cold, without knowing why. What was going on? Who was doing this to her?

Chapter 8

Michelle paced the bedroom like a nervous cat, her silky hair swirling around her head as she moved. "I don't feel like going," she blurted. "Why didn't you ask me before you told Addie we'd be there?"

"Because you'd have come up with one excuse after another why you couldn't go, just like you're doing now," he answered calmly. He'd been watching her pace back and forth, her eyes glittering, her usually sinuous movements jerky with agitation. It had been almost a month since he'd moved her to the ranch, and she had yet to stir beyond the boundaries of his property, except to visit her own. He'd given her the keys to the Mercedes and free use of it, but to his knowledge she'd never taken it out. She hadn't been shopping, though he'd made certain she had money. He had received the usual invitations to the neighborhood Saturday night barbecues that had become a county tradition, but she'd always found some excuse not to attend.

He'd wondered fleetingly if she were ashamed of having come down in the world, embarrassed because he didn't

measure up financially or in terms of sophistication with the
men she'd known before, but he'd dismissed the notion almost before it formed. It wasn't that. He'd come to know
her better than that. She came into his arms at night too eagerly, too hungrily, to harbor any feelings that he was so-
cially inferior. A lot of his ideas about her had been wrong.
She didn't look down on work, never had. She had simply
been sheltered from it her entire life. She was willing to
work. Damn it, she insisted on it! He had to watch her to
keep her from trying her hand at bulldogging. He was as bad
as her father had ever been, willing to do just about anything to keep her happy.

Maybe she was embarrassed because they were living together. This was a rural section, where mores and morality
changed slowly. Their arrangement wouldn't so much as
raise an eyebrow in Miami or any other large city, but they
weren't in a large city. John was too self-assured and arrogant to worry about gossip; he thought of Michelle simply
as his woman, with all the fierce possessiveness implied by
the term. She was his. He'd held her beneath him and made
her his, and the bond was reinforced every time he took her.

Whatever her reason for hiding on the ranch, it was time
for it to end. If she were trying to hide their relationship, he
wasn't going to let her get away with it any longer. She had
to become accustomed to being his woman. He sensed that
she was still hiding something of herself from him, carefully preserving a certain distance between them, and it enraged him. It wasn't a physical distance. Sweet Lord, no. She
was liquid fire in his arms. The distance was mental; there
were times when she was silent and withdrawn, the sparkle
gone from her eyes, but whenever he asked her what was
wrong she would stonewall, and no amount of probing
would induce her to tell him what she'd been thinking.

He was determined to destroy whatever it was that pulled
her away from him; he wanted all of her, mind and body. He
wanted to hear her laugh, to make her lose her temper as

he'd used to do, to hear the haughtiness and petulance in her voice. It was all a part of her, the part she wasn't giving him now, and he wanted it. Damn it, was she tiptoeing around him because she thought she *owed* him?

She hadn't stopped pacing. Now she sat down on the bed and stared at him, her lips set. "I don't want to go."

"I thought you liked Addie." He pulled off his boots and stood to shrug out of his shirt.

"I do," Michelle said.

"Then why don't you want to go to her party? Have you even seen her since you've been back?"

"No, but Dad had just died, and I wasn't in the mood to socialize! Then there was so much work to be done...."

"You don't have that excuse now."

She glared at him. "I decided you were a bully when I was eighteen years old, and nothing you've done over the years has changed my opinion!"

He couldn't stop the grin that spread over his face as he stripped off his jeans. She was something when she got on her high horse. Going over to the bed, he sat beside her and rubbed her back. "Just relax," he soothed. "You know everyone who'll be there, and it's as informal as it always was. You used to have fun at these things, didn't you? They haven't changed."

Michelle let him coax her into lying against his shoulder. She would sound crazy if she told him that she didn't feel safe away from the ranch. He'd want to know why, and what could she tell him? That she'd had two phone calls and the other person wouldn't say anything, just quietly hung up? That happened to people all the time when someone had dialed a wrong number. But she couldn't shake the feeling that something menacing was waiting out there for her if she left the sanctuary of the ranch, where John Rafferty ruled supreme. She sighed, turning her face into his throat. She was overreacting to a simple wrong number; she'd felt safe enough all the time she'd been alone at her house. This was just another little emotional legacy from her marriage.

She gave in. "All right, I'll go. What time does it start?"

"In about two hours." He kissed her slowly, feeling the tension drain out of her, but he could still sense a certain distance in her, as if her mind were on something else, and frustration rose in him. He couldn't pinpoint it, but he knew it was there.

Michelle slipped from his arms, shaking her head as she stood. "You gave me just enough time to get ready, didn't you?"

"We could share a shower," he invited, dropping his last garment at his feet. He stretched, his powerful torso rippling with muscle, and Michelle couldn't take her eyes off him. "I don't mind being late if you don't."

She swallowed. "Thanks, but you go ahead." She was nervous about this party. Even aside from the spooky feeling those phone calls had given her, she wasn't certain how she felt about going. She didn't know how much the ranching crowd knew of her circumstances, but she certainly didn't want anyone pitying her, or making knowing remarks about her position in John's house. On the other hand, she didn't remember anyone as being malicious, and she had always liked Addie Layfield and her husband, Steve. This would be a family oriented group, ranging in age from Frank and Yetta Campbell, in their seventies, to the young children of several families. People would sit around and talk, eat barbecue and drink beer, the children and some of the adults would swim, and the thing would break up of its own accord at about ten o'clock.

John was waiting for her when she came out of the bathroom after showering and dressing. She had opted for cool and comfortable, sleeking her wet hair straight back and twisting it into a knot, which she'd pinned at her nape, and she wore a minimum of makeup. She had on an oversize white cotton T-shirt, with the tail tied in a knot on one hip, and loose white cotton drawstring pants. Her sandals consisted of soles and two straps each. On someone else the same ensemble might have looked sloppy, but on Michelle it looked chic. He decided she could wear a feed sack and make it look good.

"Don't forget your swimsuit," he said, remembering that she had always gone swimming at these parties. She'd loved the water.

Michelle looked away, pretending to check her purse for something. "I'm not swimming tonight."

"Why not?"

"I just don't feel like it."

Her voice had that flat, expressionless sound he'd come to hate, the same tone she used whenever he tried to probe into the reason she sometimes became so quiet and distant. He looked at her sharply, and his brows drew together. He couldn't remember Michelle ever "not feeling" like swimming. Her father had put in a pool for her the first year they'd been in Florida, and she had often spent the entire day lolling in the water. After she'd married, the pool had gone unused and had finally been emptied. He didn't think it had ever been filled again, and now it was badly in need of repairs before it would be usable.

But she'd been with him almost a month, and he didn't think she'd been in his pool even once. He glanced out at the balcony; he could just see a corner of the pool, blue and glittering in the late afternoon sun. He didn't have much time for swimming, but he'd insisted, eight years ago, on having the big pool and its luxurious landscaping. For her. Damn it, this whole place was for her: the big house, the comforts, that pool, even the damn Mercedes. He'd built it for her, not admitting it to himself then because he couldn't. Why wasn't she using the pool?

Michelle could feel his sharpened gaze on her as they left the room, but he didn't say anything and, relieved, she realized he was going to let it go. Maybe he just accepted that she didn't feel like swimming. If he only knew how much she wanted to swim, how she'd longed for the feel of cool water on her overheated skin, but she just couldn't bring herself to put on a bathing suit, even in the privacy of his house.

She knew that the little white scars were hardly visible now, but she still shrank from the possibility that someone might notice them. She still felt that they were glaringly obvious, even though the mirror told her differently. It had become such a habit to hide them that she couldn't stop. She didn't dress or undress in front of John if she could help it, and if she couldn't, she always remained facing him, so he wouldn't see her back. It was such a reversal of modesty that he hadn't even noticed her reluctance to be nude in front of him. At night, in bed, it didn't matter. If the lights were on, they were dim, and John had other things on his mind. Still she insisted on wearing a nightgown to bed. It might be off most of the night, but it would be on when she got out of bed in the mornings. Everything in her shrank from having to explain those scars.

The party was just as she had expected, with a lot of food, a lot of talk, a lot of laughter. Addie had once been one of Michelle's best friends, and she was still the warm, talkative person she'd been before. She'd put on a little weight, courtesy of two children, but her pretty face still glowed with good humor. Steve, her husband, sometimes managed to put his own two cents into a conversation by the simple means of putting his hand over her mouth. Addie laughed more than anyone whenever he resorted to that tactic.

"It's an old joke between us," she told Michelle as they put together tacos for the children. "When we were dating, he'd do that so he could kiss me. Holy cow, you look good! Something must be agreeing with you, and I'd say that 'something' is about six-foot-three of pure hunk. God, I used to swoon whenever he spoke to me! Remember? You'd sniff and say he didn't do anything for you. Liar, liar, pants on fire." Addie chanted the childish verse, her eyes sparkling with mirth, and Michelle couldn't help laughing with her.

On the other side of the pool, John's head swiveled at the sound, and he froze, stunned by the way her face lit as she joked with Addie. He felt the hardening in his loins and swore silently to himself, jerking his attention back to the talk of cattle and shifting his position to make his arousal less obvious. Why didn't she laugh like that more often?

Despite Michelle's reservations, she enjoyed the party. She'd missed the relaxed gatherings, so different from the sophisticated dinner parties, yacht parties, divorce parties, fund-raising dinners, et cetera, that had made up the social life John thought she'd enjoyed so much, but had only tolerated. She liked the shrieks of the children as they cannon-balled into the pool, splashing any unwary adult in the vicinity, and she liked it that no one got angry over being wet. Probably it felt good in the sweltering heat, which had abated only a little.

True to most of the parties she'd attended, the men tended to group together and the women did the same, with the men talking cattle and weather, and the women talking about people. But the groups were fluid, flowing together and intermingling, and by the time the children had worn down, all the adults were sitting together. John had touched her arm briefly when he sat down beside her, a small, possessive gesture that made her tingle. She tried not to stare at him like an infatuated idiot, but she felt as if everyone there could tell how warm she was getting. Her cheeks flushed, and she darted a glance at him to find him watching her with blatant need.

"Let's go home," he said in a low voice.

"So soon?" Addie protested, but at that moment they all heard the distant rumble of thunder.

As ranchers, they all searched the night sky for signs of a storm that would break the heat, if only for a little while, and fill the slow-moving rivers and streams. Out to the west, over the Gulf, lightning shimmered in a bank of black clouds.

Frank Campbell said, "We sure could use a good rain. Haven't had one in about a month now."

It had stormed the day John had come over to her ranch for the first time, Michelle remembered, and again the night they'd driven back from Tampa . . . the first time he'd made love to her. His eyes glittered, and she knew he was thinking the same thing.

Wind suddenly kicked up from the west, bringing with it the cool smell of rain and salt, the excitement of a storm. Everyone began gathering up children and food, cleaning up the patio before the rain hit. Soon people were calling out goodbyes and piling into pickup trucks and cars.

"Glad you went?" John asked as he turned onto the highway.

Michelle was watching the lacy patterns the lightning made as it forked across the sky. "Yes, I had fun." She moved closer against him, seeking his warmth.

He held the truck steady against the gusts of wind buffeting it, feeling her breast brush his arm every time he moved. He inhaled sharply at his inevitable response.

"What's wrong?" she asked sleepily.

For answer he took her hand and pressed it to the straining fabric of his jeans. She made a soft sound, and her slender fingers outlined the hard ridge beneath the fabric as her body automatically curled toward him. He felt his jeans open; then her hand slid inside the parted fabric and closed over him, her palm soft and warm. He groaned aloud, his body jerking as he tried to keep his attention on the road. It was the sweetest torture he could imagine, and he ground his teeth as her hand moved further down to gently cup him for a moment before returning to stroke him to the edge of madness.

He wanted her, and he wanted her now. Jerking the steering wheel, he pulled the truck onto the side of the road just as fat raindrops began splattering the windshield. "Why are we stopping?" Michelle murmured.

He killed the lights and reached for her, muttering a graphic explanation.

"John! We're on the highway! Anyone could pass by and see us!"

"It's dark and raining," he said roughly, untying the drawstring at her waist and pulling her pants down. "No one can see in."

She'd been enjoying teasing him, exciting him, exciting herself with the feel of his hardness in her hand, but she'd thought he would wait until they got home. She should have known better. He didn't care if they were in a bedroom or not; his appetites were strong and immediate. She went weak under the onslaught of his mouth and hands, no longer caring about anything else. The rain was a thunderous din, streaming over the windows of the truck as if they were sitting under a waterfall. She could barely hear the rawly sexual things he was saying to her as he slid to the middle of the seat and lifted her over him. She cried out at his penetration, her body arching in his hands, and the world spun away in a whirlwind of sensations.

Later, after the rain had let up, she was limp in his arms as he carried her inside the house. Her hands slid around his neck as he bent to place her gently on the bed, and obeying that light pressure he stretched out on the bed with her. She was exhausted, sated, her body still throbbing with the remnants of pleasure. He kissed her deeply, rubbing his hand over her breasts and stomach. "Do you want me to undress you?" he murmured.

She nuzzled his throat. "No, I'll do it . . . in a minute. I don't feel like moving right now."

His big hand paused on her stomach, then slipped lower. "We didn't use anything."

"It's okay," she assured him softly. The timing was wrong. She had just finished her cycle, which was one reason he'd exploded out of control.

He rubbed his lips over hers in warm, quick kisses. "I'm sorry, baby. I was so damned ready for you, I thought I was going to go off like a teenager."

"It's okay," she said again. She loved him so much she trembled with it. Sometimes it was all she could do to keep from telling him, from crying the words aloud, but she was terrified that if she did he'd start putting distance between them, wary of too many entanglements. It had to end sometime, but she wanted it to last every possible second.

Nothing terrible had happened to her because she'd gone to the party; in fact, the trip home had been wonderful. For days afterward, she shivered with delight whenever she thought about it. There hadn't been any other out of the ordinary phone calls, and gradually she relaxed, convinced that there had been nothing to them. She was still far more content remaining on the ranch than she was either socializing or shopping, but at John's urging she began using the Mercedes to run small errands and occasionally visit her friends on those days when she wasn't riding with him or working on the books. She drove over to her house several times to check on things, but the silence depressed her. John had had the electricity turned back on, though he hadn't mentioned it to her, but she didn't say anything about moving back in. She couldn't leave him, not now; she was so helplessly, hopelessly in love with him that she knew she'd stay with him until he told her to leave.

One Monday afternoon she'd been on an errand for John, and on the return trip she detoured by her house to check things again. She walked through the huge rooms, making certain no pipes had sprung a leak or anything else needed repair. It was odd; she hadn't been away that long, but the house felt less and less like her home. It was hard to remember how it had been before John Rafferty had come storming into her life again; his presence was so intense it blocked out lesser details. Her troubled dreams had almost disappeared, and even when she had one, she would wake to find him beside her in the night, strong and warm. It was becoming easier to trust, to accept that she wasn't alone to face whatever happened.

It was growing late, and the shadows lengthened in the house; she carefully locked the door behind her and walked out to the car. Abruptly she shivered, as if something cold had touched her. She looked around, but everything was normal. Birds sang in the trees; insects hummed. But for a moment she'd felt it again, that sense of menace. It was odd.

Logic told her there was nothing to it, but when she was in the car she locked the doors. She laughed a little at herself. First a couple of phone calls had seemed spooky, and now she was "feeling" things in the air.

Because there was so little traffic on the secondary roads between her ranch and John's, she didn't use the rearview mirrors very much. The car was on her rear bumper before she noticed it, and even then she got only a glimpse before it swung to the left to pass. The road was narrow, and she edged to the right to give the other car more room. It pulled even with her, and she gave it a cursory glance just as it suddenly swerved toward her.

"Watch it!" she yelled, jerking the steering wheel to the right, but there was a loud grinding sound as metal rubbed against metal. The Mercedes, smaller than the other car, was pushed violently to the right. Michelle slammed on the brakes as she felt the two right wheels catch in the sandy soil of the shoulder, pulling the car even harder to that side.

She wrestled with the steering wheel, too scared even to swear at the other driver. The other car shot past, and somehow she managed to jerk the Mercedes back onto the road. Shaking, she braked to a stop and leaned her head on the steering wheel, then sat upright as she heard tires squealing. The other car had gone down the road, but now had made a violent U-turn and was coming back. She only hoped whoever it was had insurance.

The car was a big, blue full-size Chevrolet. She could tell that a man was driving, because the silhouette was so large. It was only a silhouette, because he had something black pulled over his head, like a ski mask.

The coldness was back. She acted instinctively, jamming her foot onto the gas pedal, and the sporty little Mercedes leaped forward. The Chevrolet swerved toward her again, and she swung wildly to the side. She almost missed it...almost. The Chevrolet clipped her rear bumper, and the smaller, lighter car spun in a nauseating circle before sliding off the road, across the wide sandy shoulder, and scraping against an enormous pine before it bogged down in the soft dirt and weeds.

She heard herself screaming, but the hard jolt that stopped the car stopped her screams, too. Dazed, her head lolled against the broken side window for a moment before terror drove the fogginess away. She groped for the handle, but couldn't budge the door. The pine tree blocked it. She tried to scramble across the seat to the other door, and only then realized she was still buckled into her seat. Fumbling, looking around wildly for the Chevrolet, she released the buckle and threw herself to the other side of the car. She pushed the door open and tumbled out in the same motion, her breath wheezing in and out of her lungs.

Numbly she crouched by the fender and tried to listen, but she could hear nothing over her tortuous breathing and the thunder of her heart. Old habits took over, and she used a trick she'd often used before to calm herself after one of Roger's insane rages, taking a deep breath and holding it. The maneuver slowed her heartbeat almost immediately, and the roar faded out of her ears.

She couldn't hear anything. Oh, God, had he stopped? Cautiously she peered over the car, but she couldn't see the blue Chevrolet.

Slowly she realized it had gone. He hadn't stopped. She stumbled to the road and looked in both directions, but the road was empty.

She couldn't believe it had happened. He had deliberately run her off the road, not once, but twice. If the small Mercedes had hit one of the huge pines that thickly lined the road head-on, she could easily have been killed. Whoever the man was, he must have figured the heavier Chevrolet could muscle her off the road without any great risk to himself.

He'd tried to kill her.

It was five minutes before another car came down the road; it was blue, and for a horrible moment she panicked, thinking the Chevrolet was returning, but as it came closer she could tell this car was much older and wasn't even a Chevrolet. She stumbled to the middle of the road, waving her arms to flag it down.

All she could think of was John. She wanted John. She wanted him to hold her close and shut the terror away with his strength and possessiveness. Her voice shook as she leaned in the window and told the young boy, "Please—call John Rafferty. Tell him I've been . . . I've had an accident. Tell him I'm all right."

"Sure, lady," the boy said. "What's your name?"

"Michelle," she said. "My name's Michelle."

The boy looked at the car lodged against the pine. "You need a wrecker, too. Are you sure you're all right?"

"Yes, I'm not hurt. Just hurry, please."

"Sure thing."

Either John called the sheriff's department or the boy had, because John and a county sheriff's car arrived from opposite directions almost simultaneously. It hadn't been much more than ten minutes since the boy had stopped, but in that short length of time it had grown considerably darker. John threw his door open as the truck ground to a stop and was out of the vehicle before it had settled back on its wheels, striding toward her. She couldn't move toward him; she was shaking too violently. Beneath his mustache his lips were a thin, grim line.

He walked all the way around her, checking her from head to foot. Only when he didn't see any blood on her did he haul her against his chest, his arms so tight they almost crushed her. He buried his hand in her hair and bent his head down until his jaw rested on her temple. "Are you really all right?" he muttered hoarsely.

Her arms locked around his waist in a death grip. "I was wearing my seat belt," she whispered. A single tear slid unnoticed down her cheek.

"God, when I got that phone call—" He broke off, because there was no way he could describe the stark terror he'd felt despite the kid's assurance that she was okay. He'd had to see her for himself, hold her, before he could really let himself believe she wasn't harmed. If he'd seen blood on her, he would have gone berserk. Only now was his heartbeat settling down, and he looked over her head at the car.

The deputy approached them, clipboard in hand. "Can you answer a few questions, ma'am?"

John's arms dropped from around her, but he remained right beside her as she answered the usual questions about name, age and driver's license number. When the deputy asked her how it had happened, she began shaking again.

"A...a car ran me off the road," she stammered. "A blue Chevrolet."

The deputy looked up, his eyes abruptly interested as a routine accident investigation became something more. "Ran you off the road? How?"

"He sideswiped me." Fiercely she clenched her fingers together in an effort to still their trembling. "He pushed me off the road."

"He didn't just come too close, and you panicked and ran off the road?" John asked, his brows drawing together.

"No! He pushed me off the road. I slammed on my brakes and he went on past, then turned around and came back."

"He came back? Did you get his name?" The deputy made a notation on his pad. Leaving the scene of an accident was a crime.

"No, he didn't stop. He . . . he tried to ram me. He hit my bumper, and I spun off the road, then into that pine tree."

John jerked his head at the deputy and they walked over to the car, bending down to inspect the damage. They talked together in low voices; Michelle couldn't make out what they were saying, but she didn't move closer. She stood by the road, listening to the peaceful sounds of the deepening Florida twilight. It was all so out of place. How could the crickets be chirping so happily when someone had just tried to commit murder? She felt dazed, as if none of this were real. But the damaged car was real. The blue Chevrolet had been real, as had the man wearing the black ski mask.

The two men walked back toward her. John looked at her sharply; her face was deathly white, even in the growing gloom, and she was shaking. She looked terrified. The Mercedes *was* an expensive car; did she expect him to tear a strip off her hide because she'd wrecked it? She'd never had to worry about things like that before, never had to be accountable for anything. If she'd banged a fender, it hadn't been important; her father had simply had the car repaired, or bought her a new one. Hell, he wasn't happy that she'd wrecked the damn car, but he wasn't a fanatic about cars, no matter how much they cost. It would have been different if she'd ruined a good horse. He was just thankful she wasn't hurt.

"It's all right," he said, trying to soothe her as he took her arm and walked her to the truck. "I have insurance on it. You're okay, and that's what matters. Just calm down. I'll take you home as soon as the deputy's finished with his report and the wrecker gets here.''

Frantically she clutched his arm. "But what about—''

He kissed her and rubbed her shoulder. "I said it's all right, baby. I'm not mad. You don't have to make excuses.''

Frozen, Michelle sat in the truck and watched as he walked back to the deputy. He didn't believe her; neither of them believed her. It was just like before, when no one would believe handsome, charming Roger Beckman was capable of hitting his wife, because it was obvious he adored her. It was just too unbelievable. Even her father had thought she was exaggerating.

She was so cold, even though the temperature was still in the nineties. She had begun to trust, to accept that John stood behind her, as unmoving as a block of granite, his strength available whenever she needed him. For the first time she hadn't felt alone. He'd been there, ready to shoulder her burdens. But suddenly it was just like before, and she was cold and alone again. Her father had given her everything materially, but had been too weak to face an ugly truth. Roger had showered her with gifts, pampering her extravagantly to make up for the bruises and terror. John had given her a place to live, food to eat, mind-shattering physical pleasure…but now he, too, was turning away from a horribly real threat. It was too much effort to believe such a tale. Why would anyone try to kill her?

She didn't know, but someone had. The phone calls…the phone calls were somehow connected. They'd given her the same feeling she'd had just before she got in the car, the same sense of menace. God, had he been watching her at her house? Had he been waiting for her? He could be anywhere. He knew her, but she didn't know him, and she was alone again. She'd always been alone, but she hadn't known it. For a while she'd trusted, hoped, and the contrast with that warm feeling of security made cold reality just that much more piercing.

The wrecker arrived with its yellow lights flashing and backed up to the Mercedes. Michelle watched with detached interest as the car was hauled away from the pine. She didn't even wince at the amount of damage that had been done to the left side. John thought she'd made up a wild tale to keep from having to accept blame for wrecking the car. He didn't believe her. The deputy didn't believe her. There should be blue paint on the car, but evidently the scrapes left by the big pine had obscured it. Maybe dirt covered it. Maybe it was too dark for them to see. For whatever reason, they didn't believe her.

She was utterly silent as John drove home. Edie came to the door, watching anxiously, then hurried forward as Michelle slid out of the truck.

"Are you all right? John left here like a bat out of hell, didn't stop to tell us anything except you'd had an accident."

"I'm fine," Michelle murmured. "I just need a bath. I'm freezing."

Frowning, John touched her arm. It was icy, despite the heat. She wasn't hurt, but she'd had a shock.

"Make some coffee," he instructed Edie as he turned Michelle toward the stairs. "I'll give her a bath."

Slowly Michelle pulled away from him. Her face was calm. "No, I'll do it. I'm all right. Just give me a few minutes by myself."

After a hot but brief shower, she went downstairs and drank coffee, and even managed to eat a few bites of the meal Edie had put back when John tore out of the house.

In bed that night, for the first time she couldn't respond to him. He needed her almost desperately, to reassure himself once again that she was truly all right. He needed to strengthen the bond between them, to draw her even closer with ties as old as time. But though he was gentle and stroked her for a long time, she remained tense under his hands. She was still too quiet, somehow distant from him.

Finally he just held her, stroking her hair until she slept and her soft body relaxed against him. But he lay awake for hours, his body burning, his eyes open. God, how close he'd come to losing her!

Chapter 9

John listened impatiently, his hard, dark face angry, his black eyes narrowed. Finally he said, "It hasn't been three months since I straightened all that out. How the hell did you manage to get everything in a mess this fast?"

Michelle looked up from the figures she was posting in, curious to learn the identity of his caller. He hadn't said much more than hello before he'd begun getting angry. Finally he said, "All right. I'll be down tomorrow. And if you're out partying when I get there, the way you were last time, I'll turn around and come home. I don't have time to cool my heels while you're playing." He hung up the phone and muttered a graphic expletive.

"Who was it?" Michelle asked.

"Mother." A wealth of irritation was in the single word.

She was stunned. "*Your* mother?"

He looked at her for a moment; then his mustache twitched a little as he almost smiled. "You don't have to sound so shocked. I got here by the normal method."

"But you've never mentioned . . . I guess I assumed she was dead, like your father."

"She cut out a long time ago. Ranching wasn't good enough for her; she liked the bright lights of Miami and the money of Palm Beach, so she walked out one fine day and never came back."

"How old were you?"

"Six or seven, something like that. Funny, I don't remember being too upset when she left, or missing her very much. Mostly I remember how she used to complain because the house was small and old, and because there was never much money. I was with Dad every minute I wasn't in school, but I was never close to Mother."

She felt as she had when she'd discovered he had been married. He kept throwing out little tidbits about himself, then dismissing these vital points of his life as if they hadn't affected him much at all. Maybe they hadn't. John was a hard man, made so by a lifetime of backbreaking work and the combination of arrogance and steely determination in his personality. But how could a child not be affected when his mother walked away? How could a young man, little more than a boy, not be affected when his new wife walked out rather than work by his side? To this day John would do anything to help someone who was *trying*, but he wouldn't lift a finger to aid anyone who sat around waiting for help. All his employees were loyal to him down to their last drop of blood. If they hadn't been, they wouldn't still be on his ranch.

"When you went to Miami before, it was to see your mother?"

"Yeah. She makes a mess of her finances at least twice a year and expects me to drop everything, fly down there and straighten it out."

"Which you do."

He shrugged. "We may not be close, but she's still my mother."

"Call me this time," she said distinctly, giving him a hard look that underlined her words.

He grunted, looking irritated, then gave her a wink as he turned to call the airlines. Michelle listened as he booked a flight to Miami for the next morning. Then he glanced at her and said "Wait a minute" into the receiver before putting his hand over the mouthpiece. "Want to come with me?" he asked her.

Panic flared in her eyes before she controlled it and shook her head. "No thanks. I need to catch up on the paperwork."

It was a flimsy excuse, as the accumulated work wouldn't take more than a day, but though John gave her a long, level look, he didn't argue with her. Instead he moved his fingers from the mouthpiece and said, "Just one. That's right. No, not round trip. I don't know what day I'll be coming back. Yeah, thanks."

He scribbled his flight number and time on a notepad as he took the phone from his ear and hung up. Since the accident, Michelle hadn't left the ranch at all, for any reason. He'd picked up the newly repaired Mercedes three days ago, but it hadn't been moved from the garage since. Accidents sometimes made people nervous about driving again, but he sensed that something more was bothering her.

She'd begun totalling the figures she had posted in the ledger. His eyes drifted over her, drinking in her serious, absorbed expression and the way she chewed her bottom lip when she was working. She'd taken over his office so completely that he sometimes had to ask *her* questions about what was going on. He wasn't certain he liked having part of the ranch out of his direct control, but he was damn certain he liked the extra time he had at night.

That thought made him realize he'd be spending the next few nights alone, and he scowled. Once he would have found female companionship in Miami, but now he was distinctly uninterested in any other woman. He wanted

Michelle and no one else. No other woman had ever fit in his arms as well as she did, or given him the pleasure she gave just by being there. He liked to tease her until she lost her temper and lashed back at him, just for the joy of watching her get snooty. An even greater joy was taking her to bed and loving her out of her snooty moods. Thanks to his mother, it was a joy he'd have to do without for a few days. He didn't like it worth a damn.

Suddenly he realized it wasn't just the sex. He didn't want to leave her, because she was upset about something. He wanted to hold her and make everything right for her, but she wouldn't tell him about it. He felt uneasy. She insisted nothing was wrong, but he knew better. He just didn't know what it was. A couple of times he'd caught her staring out the window with an expression that was almost ... terrified. He had to be wrong, because she had no reason to be scared. And of what?

It had all started with the accident. He'd been trying to reassure her that he wasn't angry about the car, but instead she'd drawn away from him as if he'd slapped her, and he couldn't bridge the distance between them. For just an instant she'd looked shocked, even hurt, then she'd withdrawn in some subtle way he couldn't describe, but felt. The withdrawal wasn't physical; except for the night of the accident, she was as sweet and wild in his arms as she'd ever been. But he wanted all of her, mind and body, and the accident had only made his wanting more intense by taunting him with the knowledge of how quickly she could be taken away.

He reached out and touched his fingertips to her cheekbone, needing to touch her even in so small a way. Her eyes cut up to him with a flash of green, their gazes catching, locking. Without a word she closed the ledger and stood. She didn't look back as she walked out of the room with the fluid grace he'd always admired and sometimes hated because he couldn't have the body that produced it. But now he could, and as he followed her from the room he was already unbuttoning his shirt. His booted feet were deliberately placed on the stairs, his attention on the bedroom at the top and the woman inside it.

Sometimes, when the days were hot and slow and the sun was a disc of blinding white, Michelle would feel that it had all been a vivid nightmare and hadn't really happened at all. The phone calls had meant nothing. The danger she'd sensed was merely the product of an overactive imagination. The man in the ski mask hadn't tried to kill her. The accident hadn't been a murder attempt disguised to look like an accident. None of that had happened at all. It was only a dream, while reality was Edie humming as she did housework, the stamping and snorting of the horses, the placid cattle grazing in the pastures, John's daily phone calls from Miami that charted his impatience to be back home.

But it hadn't been a dream. John didn't believe her, but his nearness had nevertheless kept the terror at bay and given her a small pocket of safety. She felt secure here on the ranch, ringed by the wall of his authority, surrounded by his people. Without him beside her in the night, her feeling of safety weakened. She was sleeping badly, and during the days she pushed herself as relentlessly as she had when she'd been working her own ranch alone, trying to exhaust her body so she could sleep.

Nev Luther had received his instructions, as usual, but again he was faced with the dilemma of how to carry them out. If Michelle wanted to do something, how was he supposed to stop her? Call the boss in Miami and tattle? Nev didn't doubt for a minute the boss would spit nails and strip hide if he saw Michelle doing the work she was doing, but she didn't *ask* if she could do it, she simply did it. Not much he could do about that. Besides, she seemed to need the work to occupy her mind. She was quieter than usual, probably missing the boss. The thought made Nev smile. He approved of the current arrangement, and would approve even more if it turned out to be permanent.

After four days of doing as much as she could, Michelle was finally exhausted enough that she thought she could sleep, but she put off going to bed. If she were wrong, she'd spend more hours lying tense and sleepless, or shaking in the aftermath of a dream. She forced herself to stay awake and catch up on the paperwork, the endless stream of orders and invoices that chronicled the prosperity of the ranch. It could have waited, but she wanted everything to be in order when John came home. The thought brought a smile to her strained face; he'd be home tomorrow. His afternoon call had done more to ease her mind than anything. Just one more night to get through without him, then he'd be beside her again in the darkness.

She finished at ten, then climbed the stairs and changed into one of the light cotton shifts she slept in. The night was hot and muggy, too hot for her to tolerate even a sheet over her, but she was tired enough that the heat didn't keep her awake. She turned on her side, almost groaning aloud as her muscles relaxed, and was instantly asleep.

It was almost two in the morning when John silently let himself into the house. He'd planned to take an 8:00 a.m. flight, but after talking to Michelle he'd paced restlessly, impatient with the hours between them. He had to hold her close, feel her slender, too fragile body in his arms before he could be certain she was all right. The worry was even more maddening because he didn't know its cause.

Finally he couldn't stand it. He'd called the airport and gotten a seat on the last flight out that night, then thrown his few clothes into his bag and kissed his mother's forehead. "Take it easy on that damned checkbook," he'd growled, looking down at the elegant, shallow and still pretty woman who had given birth to him.

The black eyes he'd inherited looked back at him, and one corner of her crimson lips lifted in the same one-sided smile that often quirked his mouth. "You haven't told me anything, but I've heard rumors even down here," she'd said smoothly. "Is it true you've got Langley Cabot's daughter living with you? Really, John, he lost everything he owned."

He'd been too intent on getting back to Michelle to feel more than a spark of anger. "Not everything."

"Then it's true? She's living with you?"

"Yes."

She had given him a long, steady look. Since he'd been nineteen he'd had a lot of women, but none of them had lived with him, even briefly, and despite the distance between them, or perhaps because of it, she knew her son well. No one took advantage of him. If Michelle Cabot was in his house, it was because he wanted her there, not due to any seductive maneuvers on her part.

As John climbed the stairs in the dark, silent house, his heart began the slow, heavy rhythm of anticipation. He wouldn't wake her, but he couldn't wait to lie beside her again, just to feel the soft warmth of her body and smell the sweetness of her skin. He was tired; he could use a few hours' sleep. But in the morning... Her skin would be rosy from sleep, and she'd stretch drowsily with that feline grace of hers. He would take her then.

Noiselessly he entered the bedroom, shutting the door behind him. She was small and still in the bed, not stirring at his presence. He set his bag down and went into the bathroom. When he came out a few minutes later he left the bathroom light on so he could see while he undressed.

He looked at the bed again, and every muscle in his body tightened. Sweat beaded on his forehead. He couldn't have torn his eyes away even if a tornado had hit the house at that moment.

She was lying half on her stomach, with all the covers shoved down to the foot of the bed. Her right leg was stretched out straight, her left one drawn up toward the middle of the mattress. She was wearing one of those flimsy cotton shifts she liked, and during the night it had worked its way up to her buttocks. She was exposed to him. His burning gaze slowly, agonizingly moved over the bare curves of her buttocks from beneath the thin cotton garment, to the soft, silky female cleft and folds he loved to touch.

He shuddered convulsively, grinding his teeth to hold back the deep, primal sound rumbling in his chest. He'd gotten so hard, so fast, that his entire body ached and throbbed. She was sound asleep, her breath coming in a deep, slow rhythm. His own breath was billowing in and out of his lungs; sweat was pouring out of him, his muscles shaking like a stallion scenting a mare ready for mounting. Without taking his eyes from her he began unbuttoning his shirt. He had to have her; he couldn't wait. She was moist and vulnerable, warm and female, and . . . his. He was coming apart just looking at her, his control shredded, his loins surging wildly.

He left his clothes on the bedroom floor and bent over her, forcing his hands to gentleness as he turned her onto her back. She made a small sound that wasn't quite a sigh and adjusted her position, but didn't awaken. His need was so urgent that he didn't take the time to wake her; he pulled the shift to her waist, spread her thighs and positioned himself between them. With his last remnant of control he eased into her, a low, rough groan bursting from his throat as her hot, moist flesh tightly sheathed him.

She whimpered a little, her body arching in his hands, and her arms lifted to twine around his neck. "I love you," she moaned, still more asleep than awake. Her words went through him like lightning, his body jerking in response. Oh God, he didn't even know if she said it to him or to some dream, but everything in him shattered. He wanted to hear the words again, and he wanted her awake, her eyes looking into his when she said them, so he'd know who was in her mind. Desperately he sank deeper into her, trying to absorb her body into his so irrevocably that nothing could separate them.

"Michelle," he whispered in taut agony, burying his open mouth against her warm throat.

Michelle lifted, arching toward him again as her mind swam upward out of a sleep so deep it had bordered on unconsciousness. But even asleep she had known his touch, her body reacting immediately to him, opening for him, welcoming him. She didn't question his presence; he was there, and that was all that mattered. A great burst of love so intense that she almost cried out reduced everything else to insignificance. She was on fire, her senses reeling, her flesh shivering under the slamming thrusts of his loins. She felt him deep inside her, touching her, and she screamed into his mouth like a wild creature as sharp ecstasy detonated her nerves. He locked her to him with iron-muscled thighs and arms, holding her as she strained madly beneath him, and the feel of her soft internal shudders milking him sent him blasting into his own hot, sweet insanity.

He couldn't let her go. Even when it was over, he couldn't let her go. He began thrusting again, needing even more of her to satisfy the hunger that went so deep he didn't think it would ever be satisfied.

She was crying a little, her luminous green eyes wet as she clung to him. She said his name in a raw, shaking voice. He hadn't let her slide down to a calm plateau but kept her body tense with desire. He was slow and tender now, gentling her into ecstasy instead of hurling her into it, but the culmination was no less shattering.

It was almost dawn before she curled up in his arms, both of them exhausted. Just before she went to sleep she said in mild surprise, "You came home early."

His arms tightened around her. "I couldn't stand another night away from you." It was the bald, frightening truth. He would have made it back even if he'd had to walk.

No one bothered them the next morning, and they slept until long after the sun began pouring brightly into the room. Nev Luther, seeing John's truck parked in its normal location, came to the house to ask him a question, but Edie dared the foreman to disturb them with such a fierce expression on her face that he decided the question wasn't important after all.

John woke shortly after one, disturbed by the heat of the sunlight streaming directly onto the bed. His temples and mustache were already damp with sweat, and he badly needed a cool shower to drive away the sluggishness of heat and exhaustion. He left the bed quietly, taking care not to wake Michelle, though a purely male smile touched his hard lips as he saw her shift lying in the middle of the floor. He didn't even remember pulling it off her, much less throwing it. Nothing had mattered but loving her.

He stood under the shower, feeling utterly sated but somehow uneasy. He kept remembering the sound of her voice when she said "I love you" and it was driving him crazy. Had she been dreaming, or had she known it was him? She'd never said it before, and she hadn't said it again. The uncertainty knifed at him. It had felt so right, but then, they had always fitted together in bed so perfectly that his memories of other women were destroyed. Out of bed... There was always that small distance he couldn't bridge, that part of herself that she wouldn't let him know. Did she love someone else? Was it one of her old crowd? A tanned, sophisticated jet-setter who was out of her reach now that she didn't have money? The thought tormented him, because he knew it was possible to love someone even when they were far away and years passed between meetings. He knew, because he'd loved Michelle that way.

His face was drawn as he cut the water off with a savage movement. *Love.* God, he'd loved her for years, and lied to himself about it by burying it under hostility, then labeling it as lust, want, need, anything to keep from admitting he was as vulnerable as a naked baby when it came to her. He was hard as nails, a sexual outlaw who casually used and left women, but he'd only prowled from woman to woman so restlessly because none of them had been able to satisfy his hunger. None of them had been the one woman he wanted, the one woman he loved. Now he had her physically, but not mentally, not emotionally, and he was scared spitless. His hands were trembling as he rubbed a towel over his body. Somehow he had to make her love him. He'd use any means necessary to keep her with him, loving her and taking care of her until no one existed in her mind except him, and every part of her became his to cherish.

Would she run if he told her he loved her? If he said the words, would she be uncomfortable around him? He remembered how he'd felt whenever some woman had tried to cling to him, whimpering that she loved him, begging him to stay. He'd felt embarrassment, impatience, pity. Pity! He couldn't take it if Michelle pitied him.

He'd never felt uncertain before. He was arrogant, impatient, determined, and he was used to men jumping when he barked out an order. It was unsettling to discover that he couldn't control either his emotions or Michelle's. He'd read before that love made strong men weak, but he hadn't understood it until now. Weak? Hell, he was terrified!

Naked, he returned to the bedroom and pulled on underwear and jeans. She was a magnet, drawing his eyes to her time and again. Lord, she was something to look at, with that pale gold hair gleaming in the bright sunlight, her bare flesh glowing. She lay on her stomach with her arms under the pillow, giving him a view of her supple back, firmly rounded buttocks and long, sleek legs. He admired her graceful lines and feminine curves, the need growing in him to touch her. Was she going to sleep all day?

He crossed to the bed and sat down on the side, stroking his hand over her bare shoulder. "Wake up, lazybones. It's almost two o'clock."

She yawned, snuggling deeper into the pillow. "So?" Her mouth curved into a smile as she refused to open her eyes.

He chuckled. "So get up. I can't even get dressed when you're lying here like this. My attention keeps wander—" He broke off, frowning at the small white scar marring the satiny shoulder under his fingers. She was lying naked under the bright rays of the afternoon sun, or he might not have noticed. Then he saw another one, and he touched it, too. His gaze moved, finding more of them marring the perfection of her skin. They were all down her back, even on her bottom and the backs of her upper thighs. His fingers touched all of them, moving slowly from scar to scar. She was rigid under his hands, not moving or looking at him, not even breathing.

Stunned, he tried to think of what could have made those small, crescent-shaped marks. Accidental cuts, by broken glass for instance, wouldn't all have been the same size and shape. The cuts hadn't been deep; the scarring was too faint, with no raised ridges. That was why he hadn't felt them, though he'd touched every inch of her body. But if they weren't accidental, that meant they had to be deliberate.

His indrawn breath hissed roughly through his teeth. He swore, his voice so quiet and controlled that the explicitly obscene words shattered the air more effectively than if he'd roared. Then he rolled her over, his hands hard on her shoulders, and said only three words. "Who did it?"

Michelle was white, frozen by the look on his face. He looked deadly, his eyes cold and ferocious. He lifted her by the shoulders until she was almost nose to nose with him, and he repeated his question, the words evenly spaced, almost soundless. "Who did it?"

Her lips trembled as she looked helplessly at him. She couldn't talk about it; she just couldn't. "I don't... It's noth—"

"*Who did it?*" he yelled, his neck corded with rage.

She closed her eyes, burning tears seeping from beneath her lids. Despair and shame ate at her, but she knew he wouldn't let her go until she answered. Her lips were trembling so hard she could barely talk. "John, please!"

"*Who?*"

Crumpling, she gave in, turning her face away. "Roger Beckman. My ex-husband." It was hard to say the words; she thought they would choke her.

John was swearing again, softly, endlessly. Michelle struggled briefly as he swept her up and sat down in a chair, holding her cradled on his lap, but it was a futile effort, so she abandoned it. Just saying Roger's name had made her feel unclean. She wanted to hide, to scrub herself over and over to be rid of the taint, but John wouldn't let her go. He held her naked on his lap, not saying a word after he'd stopped cursing until he noticed her shivering. The sun was hot, but her skin was cold. He stretched until he could reach the corner of the sheet, then jerked until it came free of the bed, and wrapped it around her.

He held her tight and rocked her, his hands stroking up and down her back. She'd been beaten. The knowledge kept ricocheting inside his skull, and he shook with a black rage he'd never known before. If he'd been able to get his hands on that slimy bastard right then, he'd have killed him with his bare hands and enjoyed every minute of it. He thought of Michelle cowering in fear and pain, her delicate body shuddering under the blows, and red mist colored his vision. No wonder she'd asked him not to hurt her the first time he'd made love to her! After her experience with men, it was something of a miracle that she'd responded at all.

He crooned to her, his rough cheek pressed against her sunny hair, his hard arms locked around her. He didn't know what he said, and neither did she, but the sound of his voice was enough. The gentleness came through, washing over her and warming her on the inside just as the heat of his body warmed her cold skin. Even after her shivering stopped he simply held her, waiting, letting her feel his closeness.

Finally she shifted a little, silently asking him to let her go. He did, reluctantly, his eyes never leaving her white face as she walked into the bathroom and shut the door. He started to go into the bathroom after her, alarmed by her silence and lack of color; his hand was on the doorknob when he reined himself under control. She needed to be alone right now. He heard the sound of the shower, and waited with unprecedented patience until she came out. She was still pale, but not as completely colorless as she'd been. The shower had taken the remaining chill from her skin, and she was wrapped in the terry-cloth robe she kept hanging on the back of the bathroom door.

"Are you all right?" he asked quietly.

"Yes." Her voice was muted.

"We have to talk about it."

"Not now." The look she gave him was shattered. "I can't. Not now."

"All right, baby. Later."

Later was that night, lying in his arms again, with the darkness like a shield around them. He'd made love to her, very gently and for a long time, easing her into rapture. In the lengthening silence afterward she felt his determination to know all the answers, and though she dreaded it, in the darkness she felt able to give them to him. When it came down to it, he didn't even have to ask. She simply started talking.

"He was jealous," she whispered. "Insane with it. I couldn't talk to a man at a party, no matter how ugly or happily married; I couldn't smile at a waiter. The smallest things triggered his rages. At first he'd just scream, accusing me of cheating on him, of loving someone else, and he'd ask me over and over who it was until I couldn't stand it anymore. Then he began slapping me. He was always sorry afterward. He'd tell me how much he loved me, swear he'd never do it again. But of course he did.''

John had gone rigid, his muscles shaking with the rage she felt building in him again. In the darkness she stroked his face, giving him what comfort she could and never wondering at the illogic of it.

"I filed charges against him once; his parents bought him out of it and made it plain I wasn't to do such a thing again. Then I tried leaving him, but he found me and carried me back. He . . . he said he'd have Dad killed if I ever tried to leave him again."

"You believed him?" John asked harshly, the first words he'd spoken. She didn't flinch from the harshness, knowing it wasn't for her.

"Oh, yes, I believed him." She managed a sad little laugh. "I still do. His family has enough money that he could have it done and it would never be traced back to him."

"But you left him anyway."

"Not until I found a way to control him."

"How?"

She began trembling a little, and her voice wavered out of control. "The . . . the scars on my back. When he did that, his parents were in Europe; they weren't there to have files destroyed and witnesses bribed until it was too late. I already had a copy of everything, enough to press charges against him. I bought my divorce with it, and I made his parents promise to keep him away from me or I'd use what I had. They were very conscious of their position and family prestige."

"Screw their prestige," he said flatly, trying very hard to keep his rage under control.

"It's academic now; they're dead."

He didn't think it was much of a loss. People who cared more about their family prestige than about a young woman being brutally beaten and terrorized didn't amount to much in his opinion.

Silence stretched, and he realized she wasn't going to add anything else. If he let her, she'd leave it at that highly condensed and edited version, but he needed to know more. It hurt him in ways he'd never thought he could be hurt, but it was vital to him that he know all he could about her, or he would never be able to close the distance between them. He wanted to know where she went in her mind and why she wouldn't let him follow, what she was thinking, what had happened in the two years since her divorce.

He touched her back, caressing her with his fingertips. "Is this why you wouldn't go swimming?"

She stirred against his shoulder, her voice like gossamer wings in the darkness. "Yes. I know the scars aren't bad; they've faded a lot. But in my mind they're still like they were.... I was so scared someone would see them and ask how I got them."

"That's why you always put your nightgown back on after we'd made love."

She was silent, but he felt her nod.

"Why didn't you want *me* to know? I'm not exactly some stranger walking down the street."

No, he was her heart and her heartbreaker, the only man she'd ever loved, and therefore more important to her than anyone else in the world. She hadn't wanted him to know the ugliness that had been in her life.

"I felt dirty," she whispered. "Ashamed."

"Good God!" he exploded, raising up on his elbow to lean over her. "Why? It wasn't your fault. You were the victim, not the villain."

"I know, but sometimes knowledge doesn't help. The feelings were still there."

He kissed her, long and slow and hot, loving her with his tongue and letting her know how much he desired her. He kissed her until she responded, lifting her arms up to his neck and giving him her tongue in return. Then he settled onto the pillow again, cradling her head on his shoulder. She was nude; he had gently but firmly refused to let her put on a gown. That secret wasn't between them any longer, and she was glad. She loved the feel of his warm, hard-muscled body against her bare skin.

He was still brooding, unable to leave it alone. She felt his tension and slowly ran her hand over his chest, feeling the curly hair and small round nipples with their tiny center points. "Relax," she murmured, kissing his shoulder. "It's over."

"You said his parents controlled him, but they're dead. Has he bothered you since?"

She shivered, remembering the phone calls she'd had from Roger. "He called me a couple of times, at the house. I haven't seen him. I hope I never have to see him again." The last sentence was full of desperate sincerity.

"At the house? Your house? How long ago?"

"Before you brought me here."

"I'd like to meet him," John said quietly, menacingly.

"I hope you never do. He's . . . not sane."

They lay together, the warm, humid night wrapped around them, and she began to feel sleepy. Then he touched her again, and she felt the raw anger in him, the savage need to know. "What did he use?"

She flinched away from him. Swearing softly, he caught her close. "Tell me."

"There's no point in it."

"I want to know."

"You already know." Tears stung her eyes. "It isn't original."

"A belt."

Her breath caught in her throat. "He . . . he wrapped the leather end around his hand."

John actually snarled, his big body jerking. He thought of a belt buckle cutting into her soft skin, and it made him sick. It made him murderous. More than ever, he wanted to get his hands on Roger Beckman.

He felt her hands on him, clinging. "Please," she whispered. "Let's go to sleep."

He wanted to know one more thing, something that struck him as odd. "Why didn't you tell your dad? He had a lot of contacts; he could have done something. You didn't have to try to protect him."

Her laugh was soft and faintly bitter, not really a laugh at all. "I did tell him. He didn't believe me. It was easier for him to think I'd made it all up than to admit my life had gone so wrong."

She didn't tell him that she'd never loved Roger, that her life had gone wrong because she'd married one man while loving another.

Chapter 10

"Telephone, Michelle!" Edie called from the kitchen.

Michelle had just come in, and she was on her way upstairs to shower; she detoured into the office to take the call there. Her mind was on her cattle; they were in prime condition, and John had arranged the sale. She would soon be leaving the ranks of the officially broke and entering those of the merely needy. John had scowled when she'd told him that.

"Hello," she said absently.

Silence.

The familiar chill went down her spine. "Hello!" she almost yelled, her fingers turning white from pressure.

"*Michelle.*"

Her name was almost whispered, but she heard it, recognized it. "No," she said, swallowing convulsively. "Don't call me again."

"*How could you do this to me?*"

"Leave me alone!" she screamed, and slammed the phone down. Her legs were shaking, and she leaned on the desk, gulping in air. She was frightened. How had Roger found her here? Dear God, what would John do if he found out Roger was bothering her? He'd be furious.... More than furious. He'd be murderous. But what if Roger called again and John answered? Would Roger ask for her, or would he remain silent?

The initial silence haunted her, reminding her of the other phone calls she had received. She'd had the same horrible feeling from all of them. Then she knew: Roger had made those other phone calls. She couldn't begin to guess why he hadn't spoken, but suddenly she had no doubt about who her caller had been. Why hadn't she realized it before? He had the resources to track her down, and he was sick and obsessive enough to do so. He knew where she was, knew she was intimately involved with another man. She felt nauseated, thinking of his jealous rages. He was entirely capable of coming down here to snatch her away from the man he would consider his rival and take her back "where she belonged."

More than two years, and she still wasn't free of him.

She thought about getting an injunction against him for harassment, but John would have to know, because the telephone was his. She didn't want him to know; his reaction could be too violent, and she didn't want him to get in any trouble.

She wasn't given the option of keeping it from him. He opened the door to the office, a questioning look on his face as he stepped inside; Edie must have told him Michelle had a call, and that was unusual enough to make him curious. Michelle didn't have time to compose her face. He stopped, eyeing her sharply. She knew she looked pale and distraught. She watched as his eyes went slowly, inevitably, to the telephone. He never missed a detail, damn him; it was almost impossible to hide anything from him. She could have done it if she'd had time to deal with the shock, but now all she could do was stand frozen in her tracks. Why couldn't he have remained in the stable five minutes longer? She would have been in the shower; she would have had time to think of something.

"That was him, wasn't it?" he asked flatly.

Her hand crept toward her throat as she stared at him like a rabbit in a snare. John crossed the room with swift strides, catching her shoulders in his big warm hands.

"What did he say? Did he threaten you?"

Numbly she shook her head. "No. He didn't threaten me. It wasn't what he said; it's just that I can't stand hearing—" Her voice broke, and she tried to turn away, afraid to push her self-control any further.

John caught her more firmly to him, tucking her in the crook of one arm as he picked up the receiver. "What's his number?" he snapped.

Frantically Michelle tried to take the phone from him. "No, don't! That won't solve anything!"

His face grim, he evaded her efforts and pinned her arms to her sides. "He's good at terrorizing a woman, but it's time he knows there's someone else he'll have to deal with if he ever calls you again. Do you still remember his number or not? I can get it, but it'll be easier if you give it to me."

"It's unlisted," she said, stalling.

He gave her a long, level look. "I can get it," he repeated.

She didn't doubt that he could. When he decided to do something, he did it, and lesser people had better get out of his way. Defeated, she gave him the number and watched as he punched the buttons.

As close to him as she was, she could hear the ringing on the other end of the line, then a faint voice as someone answered. "Get Roger Beckman on the line," he ordered in the hard voice that no one disobeyed.

His brows snapped together in a scowl as he listened, then he said "Thanks" and hung up. Still frowning, he held her to him for a minute before telling her, "The housekeeper said he's on vacation in the south of France, and she doesn't know when he'll be back."

"But I just talked to him!" she said, startled. "He wasn't in France!"

John let her go and walked around to sit behind the desk, the frown turning abstracted. "Go on and take a shower," he said quietly. "I'll be up in a few minutes."

Michelle drew back, feeling cold all over again. Didn't he believe her? She knew Roger wasn't in the south of France; that call certainly hadn't been an overseas call. The connection had been too good, as clear as a local call. No, of course he didn't believe her, just as he hadn't believed her about the blue Chevrolet. She walked away, her back rigid and her eyes burning. Roger wasn't in France, even if the housekeeper had said he was, but why was he trying to keep his location a secret?

After Michelle left, John sat in the study, pictures running through his mind, and he didn't like any of them. He saw Michelle's face, so white and pinched, her eyes terrified; he saw the small white scars on her back, remembered the sick look she got when she talked about her ex-husband. She'd worn the same look just now. Something wasn't right. He'd see Roger Beckman in hell before he let the man anywhere near Michelle again.

He needed information, and he was willing to use any means available to him to get it. Michelle meant more to him than anything else in the world.

Something had happened the summer before at his neighbor's house over on Diamond Bay, and his neighbor, Rachel Jones, had been shot. John had seen pure hell then, in the black eyes of the man who had held Rachel's wounded body in his arms. The man had looked as if the pain Rachel had been enduring had been ripping his soul out. At the time John hadn't truly understood the depths of the man's agony; at the time he'd still been hiding the truth of his own vulnerability from himself. Rachel had married her black-eyed warrior this past winter. Now John understood the man's anguish, because now he had Michelle, and his own life would be worthless without her.

He'd like to have Rachel's husband, Sabin, with him now, as well as the big blond man who had been helping them. Those two men had something wild about them, the look of predators, but they would understand his need to protect Michelle. They would gladly have helped him hunt Beckman down like the animal he was.

He frowned. They weren't here, but Andy Phelps was, and Phelps had been involved with that mess at Diamond Bay last summer. He looked up a number and punched the buttons, feeling the anger build in him as he thought of Michelle's terrified face. "Andy Phelps, please."

When the sheriff's deputy answered, John said, "Andy, this is Rafferty. Can you do some quiet investigating?"

Andy was a former D.E.A. agent, and, besides that, he had a few contacts it wasn't safe to know too much about. He said quietly, "What's up?"

John outlined the situation, then waited while Andy thought of the possibilities.

"Okay, Michelle says the guy calling her is her ex-husband, but his housekeeper says he's out of the country, right?"

"Yeah."

"Is she sure it's her ex?"

"Yes. And she said he wasn't in France."

"You don't have a lot to go on. You'd have to prove he was the one doing the calling before you could get an injunction, and it sounds as if he's got a good alibi."

"Can you find out if he's really out of the country? I don't think he is, but why would he pretend, unless he's trying to cover his tracks for some reason?"

"You're a suspicious man, Rafferty."

"I have reason to be," John said in a cold, even tone. "I've seen the marks he left on Michelle. I don't want him anywhere near her."

Andy's voice changed as he digested that information, anger and disgust entering his tone. "Like that, huh? Do you think he's in the area?"

"He's certainly not at his home, and we know he isn't in France. He's calling Michelle, scaring her to death. I'd say it's a possibility."

"I'll start checking. There are a few favors I can call in. You might put a tape on your phone, so if he calls back you'll have proof."

"There's something else," John said, rubbing his forehead. "Michelle had an accident a few weeks ago. She said someone ran her off the road, a guy in a blue Chevrolet. I didn't believe her, damn it, and neither did the deputy. No one saw anything, and we didn't find any paint on the car, so I thought someone might have gotten a little close to her and she panicked. But she said he turned around, came back and tried to hit her again."

"That's not your usual someone-ran-me-off-the-road tale," Andy said sharply. "Has she said anything else?"

"No. She hasn't talked about it at all."

"You're thinking it could be her ex-husband."

"I don't know. It might not have anything at all to do with the phone calls, but I don't want to take the chance."

"Okay, I'll check around. Keep an eye on her, and hook a tape recorder up to the phone."

John hung up and sat there for a long time, silently using every curse word he knew. Keeping an eye on her would be easy; she hadn't been off the ranch since the accident, hadn't even gone to check her own house. Now he knew why, and he damned himself and Roger Beckman with equal ferocity. If he'd only paid attention the night of the accident, they might have been able to track down the Chevrolet, but so much time had passed now that he doubted it would ever be found. At least Michelle hadn't connected Beckman with the accident, and John didn't intend to mention the possibility to her. She was scared enough as it was.

It infuriated him that he couldn't do anything except wait for Andy to get back to him. Even then, it might be a dead end. But if Beckman was anywhere in the area, John intended to pay him a visit and make damned certain he never contacted Michelle again.

Michelle bolted upright in bed, her eyes wide and her face chalky. Beside her, John stirred restlessly and reached for her, but didn't awaken. She lay back down, taking comfort in his nearness, but both her mind and her heart were racing.

It was Roger.

Roger had been driving the blue Chevrolet. Roger had tried to kill her. He wasn't in France at all, but here in Florida, biding his time and waiting to catch her out alone. She remembered the feeling she had had before the accident, as if someone were watching her with vile malice, the same feeling the phone calls had given her. She should have tied it all together before.

He'd found out about John. Michelle even knew how he'd found out. Bitsy Sumner, the woman she and John had met in Tampa when they'd gone down to have the deed drawn up, was the worst gossip in Palm Beach. It wouldn't have taken long for the news to work its way up to Philadelphia that Michelle Cabot was very snuggly with an absolute *hunk*, a gorgeous, macho rancher with bedroom eyes that made Bitsy feel so *warm*. Michelle could almost hear Bitsy on the telephone, embroidering her tale and laughing wickedly as she speculated about the sexy rancher.

Roger had probably convinced himself that Michelle would come back to him; she could still hear him whispering how much he loved her, that he'd make it up to her and show her how good it could be between them. He would have gone into a jealous rage when he found out about John. At last he had known who the other man was, confirming the suspicions he'd had all along.

His mind must have snapped completely. She remembered what he'd said the last time he had called: "How could you do this to me?"

She felt trapped, panicked by the thought that he was out there somewhere, patiently waiting to catch her alone. She couldn't go to the police; she had no evidence, only her intuition, and people weren't arrested on intuition. Besides, she didn't put a lot of faith in the police. Roger's parents had bought them off in Philadelphia, and now Roger controlled all those enormous assets. He had unlimited funds at his disposal; who knew what he could buy? He might even have hired someone, in which case she had no idea who to be on guard against.

Finally she managed to go to sleep, but the knowledge that Roger was nearby ate at her during the next few days, disturbing her rest and stealing her appetite away. Despite the people around her, she felt horribly alone.

She wanted to talk to John about it, but bitter experience made her remain silent. How could she talk to him when he didn't believe her about the phone calls or the accident? He had hooked a tape recorder up to the telephone, but he hadn't discussed it with her, and she hadn't asked any questions. She didn't want to know about it if he were only humoring her. Things had become stilted between them since the last time Roger had called, and she felt even less able to approach him than she had before. Only in bed were things the same; she had begun to fear that he was tiring of her, but he didn't seem tired of her in bed. His lovemaking was still as hungry and frequent as before.

Abruptly, on a hot, sunny morning, she couldn't stand it any longer. She had been pushed so far that she had reached her limit. Even a rabbit will turn and fight when it's cornered. She was tired of it all, so tired that she sometimes felt she was dragging herself through water. Damn Roger! What did she have to do to get him out of her life? There had to be something. She couldn't spend the rest of her days peering around every corner, too terrified to even go to a grocery store. It made her angry when she thought how she had let him confine her as surely as if he'd locked her in a prison, and beginning today she was going to do something about it.

She still had the file that had won her a divorce; now that his parents were dead the file didn't mean as much, but it still meant something. It was documented proof that Roger had attacked her once before. If he would only call again, she would have his call on tape, and perhaps she could get him to say something damaging. This was Florida, not Philadelphia; that much money would always be influential, but down here he wouldn't have the network of old family friends to protect him.

But the file was in the safe at her house, and she wanted it in her possession, at John's. She didn't feel secure leaving it in an empty house, even though she kept the door locked. The house could easily be broken into, and the safe was a normal household one; she doubted whether it would prove to be all that secure if anyone truly wanted to open it. If Roger somehow got the file, she'd have no proof at all. Those photographs and records couldn't be replaced.

Making up her mind, she told Edie she was going riding and ran out to the stables. It was a pleasant ride across the pastures to her ranch, but she didn't enjoy it as she normally would have, because of the knot of tension forming in her stomach. Roger had seen her the last time she'd been there, and she couldn't forget the terror she'd felt when she'd seen the blue Chevrolet bearing down on her.

She approached the house from the rear, looking around uneasily as she slid off the horse, but everything was normal. The birds in the trees were singing. Quickly she checked all the doors and windows, but they all seemed tight, with no signs of forced entry. Only then did she enter the house and hurry to the office to open the safe. She removed the manila envelope and checked the contents, breathing a sigh of relief that everything was undisturbed, then slid the envelope inside her shirt and relocked the safe.

The house had been closed up for a long time; the air was hot and stuffy. She felt dizzy as she stood up, and her stomach moved queasily. She hurried outside to the back porch, leaning against the wall and gulping fresh air into her lungs until her head cleared and her stomach settled. Her nerves were shot. She didn't know how much longer she could stand it, but she had to wait. He would call again; she knew it. Until then, there was precious little she could do.

Everything was still calm, quiet. The horse nickered a welcome at her as she mounted and turned toward home.

The stableman came out to meet her as she rode up, relief plain on his face. "Thank God you're back," he said feelingly. "The boss is raising pure hell—excuse me, ma'am. Anyway, he's been tearing the place up looking for you. I'll get word to him that you're back."

"Why is he looking for me?" she asked, bewildered. She had told Edie that she was going riding.

"I don't know, ma'am." He took the horse's reins from her hands as she slid to the ground.

Michelle went into the house and sought out Edie. "What has John in such an uproar?" she asked.

Edie lifted her eyebrows. "I didn't get close enough to ask."

"Didn't you tell him I'd gone riding?"

"Yep. That's when he really blew up."

She thought something might have come up and he couldn't find the paperwork he needed on it, but when she checked the office everything looked just as it had when she'd left that morning. Taking the manila envelope from inside her shirt, she locked it inside John's safe, and only then did she feel better. She *was* safe here, surrounded by John's people.

A few minutes later she heard his truck come up the drive, and judging from its speed, his temper hadn't settled any. More curious than alarmed, she walked out to meet him as the truck skidded to a stop, the tires throwing up a spray of sand and gravel. John thrust the door open and got out, his rifle clutched in his hand. His face was tight, and black fire burned in his eyes as he strode toward her. "Where in hell have you been?" he roared.

Michelle looked at the rifle. "I was out riding."

He didn't stop when he reached her, but caught her arm and hauled her inside the house. "Out riding where, damn it? I've had everyone combing the place for you."

"I went over to the house." She was beginning to get a little angry herself at his manner, though she still didn't know what had set him off. She lifted her nose and gave him a cool look. "I didn't realize I had to ask permission to go to my own house."

"Well, honey bunch, you have to do exactly that," he snapped, replacing the rifle in the gun cabinet. "I don't want you going anywhere without asking me first."

"I don't believe I'm your prisoner," she said icily.

"Prisoner, hell!" He whirled on her, unable to forget the raw panic that had filled him when he hadn't been able to find her. Until he knew what was going on and where Roger Beckman was, he'd like to have her locked up in the bedroom for safekeeping. One look at her outraged face, however, told him that he'd gone about it all wrong, and she was digging her heels in.

"I thought something had happened to you," he said more quietly.

"So you went tearing around the ranch looking for something to shoot?" she asked incredulously.

"No. I went tearing around the ranch looking for you, and I carried the rifle in case you were in any danger."

She balled her hands into fists, wanting to slap him. He wouldn't believe her about a real danger, but he was worried that she might sprain an ankle or take a tumble off a horse. "What danger could I possibly be in?" she snapped. "I'm sure there's not a snake on the ranch that would dare bite anything without your permission!"

His expression became rueful as he stared down at her. He lifted his hand and tucked a loose strand of sun-streaked hair behind her ear, but she still glared at him like some outraged queen. He liked her temper a lot better than the distant manner he'd been getting from her lately. "You're pretty when you're mad," he teased, knowing how that would get her.

For a moment she looked ready to spit. Then suddenly she sputtered, "You jackass," and began laughing.

He chuckled. No one could say "jackass" quite like Michelle, all hoity-toity and precise. He loved it. She could call him a jackass any time she wanted. Before she could stop laughing, he put his arms around her and hauled her against him, covering her mouth with his and slowly sliding his tongue between her lips. Her laughter stopped abruptly, her hands coming up to clutch his bulging biceps, and her tongue met his.

"You worried the hell out of me," he murmured when he lifted his mouth.

"Not all of it, I noticed," she purred, making him grin.

"But I wasn't kidding. I want to know whenever you go somewhere, and I don't want you going over to your place alone. It's been empty for quite a while, and a bum could start hanging around."

"What would a bum be doing this far out?" she asked.

"What would a bum be doing anywhere? Crime isn't restricted to cities. Please. For my peace of mind?"

It was so unusual for John Rafferty to plead for anything that she could only stare at him. It struck her that even though he'd said please, he still expected that she would do exactly as he'd said. In fact, she was only being perverse because he'd been his usual autocratic, arrogant self and made her angry. It suited her perfectly to be cautious, for the time being.

The dizziness and nausea she'd felt at the house must have been the beginning symptoms of some sort of bug, because she felt terrible the next day. She spent most of the day in bed, too tired and sick to worry about anything else. Every time she raised her head, the awful dizziness brought on another attack of nausea. She just wanted to be left alone.

She felt marginally better the next morning, and managed to keep something in her stomach. John held her in his arms, worried about her listlessness. "If you aren't a lot better tomorrow, I'm taking you to a doctor," he said firmly.

"It's just a virus," she sighed. "A doctor can't do anything."

"You could get something to settle your stomach."

"I feel better today. What if you catch it?"

"Then you can wait on me hand and foot until I'm better," he said, chuckling at her expression of horror. He wasn't worried about catching it. He couldn't remember the last time he'd even had a cold.

She was much better the next day, and though she still didn't feel like riding around the ranch, she did spend the morning in the office, feeding information into the computer and catching up on the books. It would be easier if they had a bookkeeping program for the computer; she made a note to ask John about it.

Roger still hadn't called.

She balled her fist. She knew he was somewhere close by! How could she get him to come out of hiding? She could never live a normal life as long as she was afraid to leave the ranch by herself.

But perhaps that was what she would have to do. Obviously Roger had some way of watching the ranch; she simply couldn't believe the blue Chevrolet had been a coincidence, unconnected to Roger. He'd caught her off guard that time, but now she'd be looking for him. She had to draw him out.

When John came to the house for lunch, she had twisted her hair up and put on a bit of makeup, and she knew she looked a lot better. "I thought I'd go to town for a few things," she said casually. "Is there anything you need?"

His head jerked up. She hadn't driven at all since the accident, and now here she was acting as nonchalant about driving as if the accident had never happened at all. Before he had worried that she was so reluctant to go anywhere, but now he wanted her to stay close. "What things?" he asked sharply. "Where exactly are you going?"

Her brows lifted at his tone. "Shampoo, hair conditioner, things like that."

"All right." He made an impatient gesture. "Where are you going? What time will you be back?"

"Really, you missed your calling. You should have been a prison guard."

"Just tell me."

Because she didn't want him to deny her the use of the car, she said in a bored voice, "The drugstore, probably. I'll be back by three."

He looked hard at her, then sighed and thrust his fingers through his thick black hair. "Just be careful."

She got up from the table. "Don't worry. If I wreck the car again, I'll pay for the damages with the money from the cattle sale."

He swore as he watched her stalk away. Damn, what could he do now? Follow her? He slammed into the office and called Andy Phelps to find out if he had any information on Roger Beckman yet. All Andy had come up with was that no one by the name of Roger Beckman had been on a flight to France in the last month, but he might not have gone there directly. It took time to check everything.

"I'll keep trying, buddy. That's all I can do."

"Thanks. Maybe I'm worried over nothing, but maybe I'm not."

"Yeah, I know. Why take chances? I'll call when I get something."

John hung up, torn by the need to do something, anything. Maybe he should tell Michelle of his suspicions, explain why he didn't want her wandering around by herself. But as Andy had pointed out, he really had nothing to go on, and he didn't want to upset her needlessly. She'd had enough worry in her life. If he had his way, nothing would ever worry her again.

Michelle drove to town and made her purchases, steeling herself every time a car drew near. But nothing happened; she didn't see anything suspicious, not even at the spot where the Chevrolet had forced her off the road. Fiercely she told herself that she wasn't paranoid, she hadn't imagined it all. Roger was there, somewhere. She simply had to find him. But she wasn't brave at all, and she was shaking with nerves by the time she got back to the ranch. She barely made it upstairs to the bathroom before her stomach rebelled and she retched miserably.

She tried it again the next day. And the next. Nothing happened, except that John was in the foulest mood she could imagine. He never came right out and forbade her to go anywhere, but he made it plain he didn't like it. If she hadn't been desperate, she would have thrown the car keys in his face and told him what he could do with them.

Roger had been watching her at her house that day. Could it be that he was watching that road instead of the one leading to town? He wouldn't have seen her when she'd gone over to get the file from the safe because she had ridden in from the back rather than using the road. John had told her not to go to her house alone, but she wouldn't have to go to the house. All she had to do was drive by on the road...and if Roger was there, he would follow her.

Chapter 11

She had to be crazy; she knew that. The last thing she wanted was to see Roger, yet here she was trying to find him, even though she suspected he was trying to kill her. No, she wanted to find him *because* of that. She certainly didn't want to die, but she wanted this to be over. Only then could she lead a normal life.

She wanted that life to be with John, but she had never fooled herself that their relationship was permanent, and the mood he was in these days could herald the end of it. Nothing she did seemed to please him, except when they were in bed, but perhaps that was just a reflection of his intense sex drive and any woman would have done.

Her nerves were so raw that she couldn't even think of eating the morning she planned to go to the house, and she paced restlessly, waiting until she saw John get in his pickup and drive across the pastures. She hadn't wanted him to know she was going anywhere; he asked too many questions, and it was hard to hide anything from him. She would only be gone half an hour, anyway, because when it came down to it, she didn't have the courage to leave herself hanging out as bait. All she could manage was one quick drive by; then she would come home.

She listened to the radio in an effort to calm her nerves as she drove slowly down the narrow gravel road. It came as a shock that the third hurricane of the season, Hurricane Carl, had formed in the Atlantic and was meandering toward Cuba. She had completely missed the first two storms. She hadn't even noticed that summer had slid into early autumn, because the weather was still so hot and humid, perfect hurricane weather.

Though she carefully searched both sides of the road for any sign of a car tucked away under the trees, she didn't see anything. The morning was calm and lazy. No one else was on the road. Frustrated, she turned around to drive back to the house.

A sudden wave of nausea hit her, and she had to halt the car. She opened the door and leaned out, her stomach heaving even though it was empty and nothing came out. When the spasm stopped she leaned against the steering wheel, weak and perspiring. This had hung on far too long to be a virus.

She lay there against the steering wheel for a long time, too weak to drive and too sick to care. A faint breeze wafted into the open door, cooling her hot face, and just as lightly the truth eased into her mind.

If this was a virus, it was the nine-month variety.

She let her head fall back against the seat, and a smile played around her pale lips. Pregnant. Of course. She even knew when it had happened: the night John had come home from Miami. He had been making love to her when she woke up, and neither of them had thought of taking precautions. She had been so on edge she hadn't noticed that she was late.

John's baby. It had been growing inside her for almost five weeks. Her hand drifted down to her stomach, a sense of utter contentment filling her despite the miserable way she felt. She knew the problems this would cause, but for the moment those problems were distant, unimportant compared to the blinding joy she felt.

She began to laugh, thinking of how sick she'd been. She remembered reading in some magazine that women who had morning sickness were less likely to miscarry than women who didn't; if that were true, this baby was as secure as Fort Knox. She still felt like death warmed over, but now she was happy to feel that way.

"A baby," she whispered, thinking of a tiny, sweet-smelling bundle with a mop of thick black hair and melting black eyes, though she realized any child of John Rafferty's would likely be a hellion.

But she couldn't continue sitting in the car, which was parked more on the road than off. Shakily, hoping the nausea would hold off until she could get home, she put the car in gear and drove back to the ranch with painstaking caution. Now that she knew what was wrong, she knew what to do to settle her stomach. And she needed to make an appointment with a doctor.

Sure enough, her stomach quieted after she ate a meal of dry toast and weak tea. Then she began to think about the problems.

Telling John was the first problem and, to Michelle, the biggest. She had no idea how he would react, but she had to face the probability that he would not be as thrilled as she was. She feared he was getting tired of her anyway; if so, he'd see the baby as a burden, tying him to a woman he no longer wanted.

She lay on the bed, trying to sort out her tangled thoughts and emotions. John had a right to know about his child, and, like it or not, he had a responsibility to it. On the other hand, she couldn't use the baby to hold him if he wanted to be free. Bleak despair filled her whenever she tried to think of a future without John, but she loved him enough to let him go. Since their first day together she had been subconsciously preparing for the time when he would tell her that he didn't want her any longer. That much was clear in her mind.

But what if he decided that they should marry because of the baby? John took his responsibilities seriously, even to the point of taking a wife he didn't want for the sake of his child. She could be a coward and grab for anything he offered, on the basis that the crumbs of affection that came her way would be better than nothing, or she could somehow find the courage to deny herself the very thing she wanted most. Tears filled her eyes, the tears that came so easily these days. She sniffled and wiped them away.

She couldn't decide anything; her emotions were seesawing wildly between elation and depression. She didn't know how John would react, so any plans she made were a waste of time. This was something they would have to work out together.

She heard someone ride up, followed by raised, excited voices outside, but cowboys were always coming and going at the ranch, and she didn't think anything of it until Edie called upstairs, "Michelle? Someone's hurt. The boys are bringing him in— My God, it's the boss!" She yelled the last few words and Michelle shot off the bed. Afterward she never remembered running down the stairs; all she could remember was Edie catching her at the front door as Nev and another man helped John down from a horse. John was holding a towel to his face, and blood covered his hands and arms, and soaked his shirt.

Michelle's face twisted, and a thin cry burst from her throat. Edie was a big, strong woman, but somehow Michelle tore free of her clutching arms and got to John. He shrugged away from Nev and caught Michelle with his free arm, hugging her to him. "I'm all right," he said gruffly. "It looks worse than it is."

"You'd better get to a doc, boss," Nev warned. "Some of those cuts need stitches."

"I will. Get on back to the men and take care of things." John gave Nev a warning look over Michelle's head, and though one eye was covered with the bloody towel, Nev got the message. He glanced quickly at Michelle, then nodded.

"What happened?" Michelle cried frantically as she helped John into the kitchen. His arm was heavy around her shoulders, which told her more than anything that he was hurt worse than he wanted her to know. He sank onto one of the kitchen chairs.

"I lost control of the truck and ran into a tree," he muttered. "My face hit the steering wheel."

She put her hand on the towel to keep it in place, feeling him wince even under her light touch, and lifted his hand away. She could see thin shards of glass shining in the black depths of his hair.

"Let me see," she coaxed, and eased the towel away from his face.

She had to bite her lip to keep from moaning. His left eye was already swollen shut, and the skin on his cheekbone was broken open in a jagged wound. His cheekbone and brow ridge were already purple and turning darker as they swelled almost visibly, huge knots distorting his face. A long cut slanted across his forehead, and he was bleeding from a dozen other smaller cuts. She took a deep breath and schooled her voice to evenness. "Edie, crush some ice to go on his eye. Maybe we can keep the swelling from getting any worse. I'll get my purse and the car keys."

"Wait a minute," John ordered. "I want to clean up a little; I've got blood and glass all over me."

"That isn't important—"

"I'm not hurt that badly," he interrupted. "Help me out of this shirt."

When he used that tone of voice, he couldn't be budged. Michelle unbuttoned the shirt and helped him out of it, noticing that he moved with extreme caution. When the shirt was off, she saw the big red welt across his ribs and knew why he was moving so carefully. In a few hours he would be too sore to move at all. Easing out of the chair, he went to the sink and washed off the blood that stained his hands and arms, then stood patiently while Michelle took a wet cloth and gently cleaned his chest and throat, even his back. His hair was matted with blood on the left side, but she didn't want to try washing his head until he'd seen a doctor.

She ran upstairs to get a clean shirt for him and helped him put it on. Edie had crushed a good amount of ice and folded it into a clean towel to make a cold pad. John winced as Michelle carefully placed the ice over his eye, but he didn't argue about holding it in place.

Her face was tense as she drove him to the local emergency care clinic. He was hurt. It staggered her, because somehow she had never imagined John as being vulnerable to anything. He was as unyielding as granite, somehow seeming impervious to fatigue, illness or injury. His battered, bloody face was testimony that he was all too human, though, being John, he wasn't giving in to his injuries. He was still in control.

He was whisked into a treatment room at the clinic, where a doctor carefully cleaned the wounds and stitched the cut on his forehead. The other cuts weren't severe enough to need stitches, though they were all cleaned and bandaged. Then the doctor spent a long time examining the swelling around John's left eye. "I'm going to have you admitted to a hospital in Tampa so an eye specialist can take a look at this," he told John.

"I don't have time for a lot of poking," John snapped, sitting up on the table.

"It's your sight," the doctor said evenly. "You took a hell of a blow, hard enough to fracture your cheekbone. Of course, if you're too busy to save your eyesight—"

"He'll go," Michelle interrupted.

John looked at her with one furious black eye, but she glared back at him just as ferociously. There was something oddly magnificent about her, a difference he couldn't describe because it was so subtle. But even as pale and strained as she was, she looked good. She always looked good to him, and he'd be able to see her a lot better with two eyes than just one.

He thought fast, then growled, "All right." Let her think what she wanted about why he was giving in; the hard truth was that he didn't want her anywhere near the ranch right now. If he went to Tampa, he could insist that she stay with him, which would keep her out of harm's way while Andy Phelps tracked down whoever had shot out his windshield. What had been a suspicion was now a certainty as far as John was concerned; Beckman's threat went far beyond harassing telephone calls. Beckman had tried to make it look like an accident when he had run Michelle off the road, but now he had gone beyond that; a bullet wasn't accidental.

Thank God Michelle hadn't been with him as she usually was. At first he'd thought the bullet was intended for him, but now he wasn't so certain. The bullet had been too far to the right. Damn it, if only he hadn't lost control of the truck when the windshield shattered! He'd jerked the wheel instinctively, and the truck had started sliding on the dewy grass, hitting a big oak head-on. The impact had thrown him forward, and his cheekbone had hit the steering wheel with such force that he'd been unconscious for a few minutes. By the time he'd recovered consciousness and his head had cleared, there had been no point in sending any of his men to investigate where the shot had come from. Beckman would have been long gone, and they would only have destroyed any signs he might have left. Andy Phelps could take over now.

"I'll arrange for an ambulance," the doctor said, turning to leave the room.

"No ambulance. Michelle can take me down there."

The doctor sighed. "Mr. Rafferty, you have a concussion; you should be lying down. And in case of damage to your eye, you shouldn't strain, bend over, or be jostled. An ambulance is the safest way to get you to Tampa."

John scowled as much as he could, but the left side of his face was so swollen that he couldn't make the muscles obey. No way was he going to let Michelle drive around by herself in the Mercedes; the car would instantly identify her to Beckman. If he had to go to Tampa, she was going to be beside him every second. "Only if Michelle rides in the ambulance with me."

"I'll be right behind," she said. "No, wait. I need to go back home first, to pick up some clothes for both of us."

"No. Doc, give me an hour. I'll have clothes brought out to us and arrange for the car to be driven back to the house." To Michelle he said, "You either ride with me, or I don't go at all."

Michelle stared at him in frustration, but she sensed he wasn't going to back down on this. He'd given in surprisingly easy about going to the hospital, only to turn oddly stubborn about keeping her beside him. If someone drove the car back to the ranch, they would be stranded in Tampa, so it didn't make sense. This entire episode seemed strange, but she didn't know just why and didn't have time to figure it out. If she had to ride in an ambulance to get John to Tampa, she'd do it. She was still so scared and shocked by his accident that she would do anything to have him well again.

He took her acquiescence for granted, telling her what he wanted and instructing her to have Nev bring the clothes, along with another man to drive the car home. Mentally she threw her hands up and left the room to make the phone call. John waited a few seconds after the door had closed behind her, then said, "Doc, is there another phone I can use?"

"Not in here, and you shouldn't be walking around. You shouldn't even be sitting up. If the call is so urgent it won't wait, let your wife make it for you."

"I don't want her to know about it." He didn't bother to correct the doctor's assumption that Michelle was his wife. The good doctor was a little premature, that was all. "Do me a favor. Call the sheriff's department, tell Andy Phelps where I am and that I need to talk to him. Don't speak to anyone except Phelps."

The doctor's eyes sharpened, and he looked at the big man for a moment. Anyone else would have been flat on his back. Rafferty should have been, but his system must be like iron. He was still steady, and giving orders with a steely authority that made it almost impossible not to do as he said.

"All right, I'll make the call if you'll lie down. You're risking your eyesight, Mr. Rafferty. Think about being blind in that eye for the rest of your life."

John's lips drew back in a feral grin that lifted the corners of his mustache. "Then the damage has probably already been done, doctor." Losing the sight in his left eye didn't matter much when stacked against Michelle's life. Nothing was more important than keeping her safe.

"Not necessarily. You may not even have any damage to your eye, but with a blow that forceful it's better to have it checked. You may have what's called a blowout fracture, where the shock is transmitted to the wall of the orbital bone, the eye socket. The bone is thin, and it gives under the pressure, taking it away from the eyeball itself. A blowout fracture can save your eyesight, but if you have one you'll need surgery to repair it. Or you can have nerve damage, a dislocated lens, or a detached retina. I'm not an eye specialist, so I can't say. All I can tell you is to stay as quiet as possible or you can do even greater damage."

Impatiently John lay down, putting his hands behind his head, which was throbbing. He ignored the pain, just as he ignored the numbness of his face. Whatever damage had been done, was done. So he'd broken his cheekbone and maybe shattered his eye socket; he could live with a battered face or with just one good eye, but he couldn't live without Michelle.

He went over the incident again and again in his mind, trying to pull details out of his subconscious. In that split second before the bullet had shattered the windshield, had he seen a flash that might pinpoint Beckman's location? Had Beckman been walking? Not likely. The ranch was too big for a man to cover on foot. Nor was it likely he would have been on horseback; riding horses were harder to come by than cars, which could easily be rented. Going on the assumption that Beckman had been driving, what route could he have taken that would have kept him out of sight?

Andy Phelps arrived just moments before Nev. For Michelle's benefit, the deputy joked about John messing up his pretty face, then waited while John gave Nev detailed instructions. Nev nodded, asking few questions. Then John glanced at Michelle. "Why don't you check the things Nev brought; if you need anything else, he can bring it to Tampa."

Michelle hesitated for a fraction of a second, feeling both vaguely alarmed and in the way. John wanted her out of the room for some reason. She looked at the tall, quiet deputy, then back at John, before quietly leaving the room with Nev. Something was wrong; she knew it.

Even Nev was acting strangely, not quite looking her in the eye. Something had happened that no one wanted her to know, and it involved John.

He had given in too easily about going to the hospital, though the threat of losing his eyesight was certainly enough to give even John pause; then he had been so illogical about the car. John was never illogical. Nev was uneasy about something, and now John wanted to talk privately to a deputy. She was suddenly certain the deputy wasn't there just because he'd heard a friend was hurt.

Too many things didn't fit. Even the fact that John had had an accident at all didn't fit. He'd been driving across rough pastures since boyhood, long before he'd been old enough to have a driver's license. He was also one of the surest drivers she had ever seen, with quick reflexes and eagle-eyed attention to every other driver on the road. It just didn't make sense that he would lose control of his truck and hit a tree. It was too unlikely, too pat, too identical to her own accident.

Roger.

What a fool she had been! She had considered him as a danger only to herself, not to John. She should have expected his insane jealousy to spill over onto the man he thought had taken her away from him. While she had been trying to draw him out, he had been stalking John. Fiercely her hands knotted into fists. Roger wouldn't stand a chance against John in an open fight, but he would sneak around like the coward he was, never taking the chance of a face-to-face confrontation.

She looked down at the two carryons Edie had packed for them and put her hand to her head. "I feel a little sick, Nev," she whispered. "Excuse me, I have to get to the restroom."

Nev looked around, worry etched on his face. "Do you want me to get a nurse? You do look kinda green."

"No, I'll be all right." She managed a weak smile as she lied, "I never have been able to stand the sight of blood, and it just caught up with me."

She patted his arm and went around the partition to the public restrooms, but didn't enter. Instead she waited a moment, sneaking peeks around the edge of the partition; as soon as Nev turned to sit down while waiting for her, she darted across the open space to the corridor where the examining rooms were. The door to John's room was closed, but not far enough for the latch to catch. When she cautiously nudged it, the door opened a crack. It was on the left side of the room, so John wouldn't be able to see it. Phelps should be on John's right side, facing him; with luck, he wouldn't notice the slight movement of the door, either.

Their voices filtered through the crack.

"—think the bullet came from a little rise just to the left of me," John said. "Nev can show you."

"Is there any chance the bullet could be in the upholstery?"

"Probably not. The trajectory wasn't angled enough."

"Maybe I can find the cartridge. I'm coming up with a big zero from the airlines, but I have another angle I can check. If he flew in, he'd have come in at Tampa, which means he'd have gotten his rental car at the airport. If I can get a match on his description, we'll have his license plate number."

"A blue Chevrolet. That should narrow it down," John said grimly.

"I don't even want to think about how many blue Chevrolets there are in this state. It was a good idea to keep Michelle with you in Tampa; it'll give me a few days to get a lead on this guy. I can get a buddy in Tampa to put surveillance on the hospital, if you think you'll need it."

"He won't be able to find her if the doctor here keeps quiet and if my file is a little hard to find."

"I can arrange that." Andy chuckled.

Michelle didn't wait to hear more. Quietly she walked back down the corridor and rejoined Nev. He was reading a magazine and didn't look up until she sat down beside him. "Feeling better?" he asked sympathetically.

She gave some answer, and it must have made sense, because it satisfied him. She sat rigidly in the chair, more than a little stunned. What she had overheard had verified her suspicion that Roger was behind John's "accident," but it was hard for her to take in the rest of it. John not only believed her about the phone calls, he had tied them in to the blue Chevrolet and had been quietly trying to track Roger down. That explained why he had suddenly become so insistent that she tell him exactly where she was going and how long she would be there, why he didn't want her going anywhere at all. He had been trying to protect her, while she had been trying to bait Roger into the open.

She hadn't told him what she was doing because she hadn't thought he would believe her; she had learned well the bitter lesson that she could depend only on herself, perhaps learned it too well. Right from the beginning John had helped her, sometimes against her will. He had stepped in and taken over the ranch chores that were too much for her; he was literally carrying her ranch until she could rebuild it into a profitable enterprise. He had given her love, comfort, care and concern, and now a child, but still she hadn't trusted him. He hadn't been tiring of her; he'd been under considerable strain to protect her.

Being John, he hadn't told her of his suspicions or what he was doing because he hadn't wanted to "worry" her. It was just like him. That protective, possessive streak of his was bone deep and body wide, defying logical argument. There were few things or people in his life that he cared about, but when he did care, he went full measure. He had claimed her as his, and what was his, he kept.

Deputy Phelps stopped by to chat; Michelle decided to give him an opportunity to talk to Nev, and she walked back to John's room. The ambulance had just arrived, so she knew they would be leaving soon.

When the door opened, he rolled his head until he could see her with his right eye. "Is everything okay?"

She had to grit her teeth against the rage that filled her when she saw his battered, discolored face. It made her want to destroy Roger in any way she could. The primitive, protective anger filled her, pumping into every cell in her body. It took every bit of control she had to calmly walk over to him as if she weren't in a killing rage and take his hand. "If you're all right, then I don't care what Edie packed or didn't pack."

"I'll be all right." His deep voice was confident. He might or might not lose the sight in his eye, but he'd be all right. John Rafferty was made of the purest, hardest steel.

She sat beside him in the ambulance and held his hand all the way to Tampa, her eyes seldom leaving his face. Perhaps he dozed; perhaps it was simply less painful if he kept his right eye closed, too. For whatever reason, little was said during the long ride.

It wasn't until they reached the hospital that he opened his eye and looked at her, frowning when he saw how drawn she looked. She needed the bed rest more than he did; if it hadn't been for his damned eye, and the opportunity to keep Michelle away from the ranch, he would already have been back at work.

He should have gotten her away when he'd first suspected Beckman was behind her accident, but he'd been too reluctant to let her out of his sight. He wasn't certain about her or how much she needed him, so he'd kept her close at hand. But the way she had looked when she saw he was hurt... a woman didn't look like that unless she cared. He didn't know how much she cared, but for now he was content with the fact that she did. He had her now, and he wasn't inclined to let go. As soon as this business with Beckman was settled, he'd marry her so fast she wouldn't know what was happening.

Michelle went through the process of having him admitted to the hospital while he was whisked off, with three—*three!*—nurses right beside him. Even as battered as he was, he exuded a masculinity that drew women like a magnet.

She didn't see him again for three hours. Fretting, she wandered the halls until a bout of nausea drove her to find the cafeteria, where she slowly munched on stale crackers. Her stomach gradually settled. John would probably be here for at least two days, maybe longer; how could she hide her condition from him when she would be with him practically every hour of the day? Nothing escaped his attention for long, whether he had one good eye or two. Breeding wasn't anything new to him; it was his business. Cows calved; mares foaled. On the ranch, everything mated and reproduced. It wouldn't take long for him to discard the virus tale she'd told him and come up with the real reason for her upset stomach.

What would he say if she told him? She closed her eyes, her heart pounding wildly at the thought. He deserved to know. She wanted him to know; she wanted to share every moment of this pregnancy with him. But what if it drove him to do something foolish, knowing that Roger not only threatened her but their child as well?

She forced herself to think clearly. They were safe here in the hospital; this was bought time. He wouldn't leave the hospital when staying here meant that she was also protected. She suspected that was the only reason he'd agreed to come at all. He was giving Deputy Phelps time to find Roger, if he could.

But what if Phelps hadn't found Roger by the time John left the hospital? What evidence did they have against him, anyway? He had had time to have any damage to the Chevrolet repaired, and no one had seen him shoot at John. He hadn't threatened her during any of those phone calls. He hadn't had to; she knew him, and that was enough.

She couldn't run, not any longer. She had run for two years, fleeing emotionally long after she had stopped physically running. John had brought her alive with his fierce, white-hot passion, forcing her out of her protective reserve. She couldn't leave him, especially now that she carried his child. She had to face Roger, face all the old nightmares and conquer them, or she would never be rid of this crippling fear. She could fight him, something she had always been too terrified to do before. She could fight him for John, for their baby, and she could damn well fight him for herself.

Finally she went back to the room that had been assigned to John to wait. It was thirty minutes more before he was wheeled into the room and transferred very carefully to the bed. When the door closed behind the orderlies he said, from between clenched teeth, "If anyone else comes through that door to do anything to me, I'm going to throw them out the window." Gingerly he eased into a more upright position against the pillow, then punched the button that raised the head of the bed.

She ignored his bad temper. "Have you seen the eye specialist yet?"

"Three of them. Come here."

There was no misreading that low demanding voice or the glint in his right eye as he looked at her. He held his hand out to her and said again, "Come here."

"John Patrick Rafferty, you aren't in any shape to begin carrying on like that."

"Aren't I?"

She refused to look at his lap. "You shouldn't be jostled."

"I don't want to be jostled. I just want a kiss." He gave her a slow, wicked grin despite the swelling in his face. "The spirit's willing, but the body's tired as hell."

She bent to kiss him, loving his lips gently with her own. When she tried to lift her head he thrust his fingers into her hair and held her down while his mouth molded to hers, his tongue making teasing little forays to touch hers. He gave a sigh of pleasure and let her up, but shifted his hand to her bottom to hold her beside him. "What've you been doing while I've been lying in cold halls in between bouts of being stuck, prodded, x-rayed and prodded some more?"

"Oh, I've been really entertained. You don't realize what an art mopping is until you've seen a master do it. There's also a four-star cafeteria here, specializing in the best stale crackers I've ever eaten." She grinned, thinking he'd never realize the truth of that last statement.

He returned the grin, thinking that once he would have accused her of being spoiled. He knew better now, because he'd been trying his damnedest to spoil her, and she persisted in being satisfied with far less than he would gladly have given her any day of the week. Her tastes didn't run to caviar or mink, and she'd been content to drive that old truck of hers instead of a Porsche. She liked silk and had beautiful clothes, but she was equally content wearing a cotton shirt and jeans. It wasn't easy to spoil a woman who was happy with whatever she had.

"Arrange to have a bed moved in here for you," he ordered. "Unless you want to sleep up here with me?"

"I don't think the nurses would allow that."

"Is there a lock on the door?"

She laughed. "No. You're out of luck."

His hand moved over her bottom, the slow, intimate touch of a lover. "We need to talk. Will it bother you if I lose this eye?"

Until then she hadn't realized that he might lose the eye as well as his sight. She sucked in a shocked breath, reaching blindly for his hand. He continued to watch her steadily, and slowly she relaxed, knowing what was important.

"It would bother me for your sake, but as for me . . . You can be one-eyed, totally blind, crippled, whatever, and I'll still love you."

There. She'd said it. She hadn't meant to, but the words had come so naturally that even if she could take them back, she wouldn't.

His right eye was blazing black fire at her. She had never seen anyone else with eyes as dark as his, night-black eyes that had haunted her from the first time she'd met him. She looked down at him and managed a tiny smile that was only a little hesitant as she waited for him to speak.

"Say that again."

She didn't pretend not to know what he meant, but she had to take another deep breath. Her heart was pounding. "I love you. I'm not saying that to try to trap you into anything. It's just the way I feel, and I don't expect you to—"

He put his fingers over her mouth. "It's about damn time," he said.

Chapter 12

"You're very lucky, Mr. Rafferty," Dr. Norris said, looking over his glasses. "Your cheekbone seems to have absorbed most of the impact. It's fractured, of course, but the orbital bone is intact. Nor does there seem to be any damage to the eye itself, or any loss of sight. In other words, you have a hell of a shiner."

Michelle drew a deep breath of relief, squeezing John's hand. He winked at her with his right eye, then drawled, "So I've spent four days in a hospital because I have a black eye?"

Dr. Norris grinned. "Call it a vacation."

"Well, vacation's over, and I'm checking out of the resort."

"Just take it easy for the next few days. Remember that you have stitches in your head, your cheekbone is fractured, and you had a mild concussion."

"I'll keep an eye on him," Michelle said with a note of warning in her voice, looking at John very hard. He was probably planning to get on a horse as soon as he got home.

When they were alone again John put his hands behind his head, watching her with a distinct glitter in his eyes. After four days the swelling around his eye had subsided enough that he could open it a tiny slit, enough for him to see with it again. His face was still a mess, discolored in varying shades of black and purple, with a hint of green creeping in, but none of that mattered beside the fact that his eye was all right. "This has been a long four days," he murmured. "When we get home, I'm taking you straight to bed."

Her blood started running wild through her veins again, and she wondered briefly if she would always have this uncontrolled response to him. She'd been completely vulnerable to him from the start, and her reaction now was even stronger. Her body was changing as his baby grew within her, invisible changes as yet, but her skin seemed to be more sensitive, more responsive to his lightest touch. Her breasts throbbed slightly, aching for the feel of his hands and mouth.

She had decided not to tell him about the baby just yet, especially not while his eyesight was still in doubt, and had been at pains during the past four days to keep her uneasy stomach under control. She munched on crackers almost constantly, and had stopped drinking coffee because it made the nausea worse.

She could still see the hard satisfaction that had filled his face when she'd told him she loved him, but he hadn't returned the words. For a horrible moment she'd wondered if he was gloating, but he'd kissed her so hard and hungrily that she had dismissed the notion even though she'd felt a lingering pain. That night, after the lights were out and she was lying on the cot that had been brought in, he had said, "Michelle."

His voice was low, and he hadn't moved. She'd lifted her head to stare through the darkness at him. "Yes?"

"I love you," he had said quietly.

Tremors shook her, and tears leaped to her eyes, but they were happy tears. "I'm glad," she had managed to say.

He'd laughed in the darkness. "You little tease, just wait until I get my hands on you again."

"I can't wait."

Now he was all right, and they were going home. She called Nev to come pick them up, then hung up the phone with hands that had become damp. She wiped them on her slacks and lifted her chin. "Have you heard if Deputy Phelps has found a lead on Roger yet?"

John had been dressing, but at her words his head snapped around and his good eye narrowed on her. Slowly he zipped his jeans and fastened them, then walked around the bed to tower over her threateningly. Michelle's gaze didn't waver, nor did she lower her chin, even though she abruptly felt very small and helpless.

He didn't say anything, but simply waited, his mouth a hard line beneath his mustache. "I eavesdropped," she said calmly. "I had already made the connection between the phone calls and the guy who forced me off the road, but how did you tie everything together?"

"Just an uneasy feeling and a lot of suspicions," he said. "After that last call, I wanted to make certain I knew where he was. There were too many loose ends, and Andy couldn't find him on any airline's overseas passenger list. The harder Beckman was to find, the more suspicious it looked."

"You didn't believe me at first, about the blue Chevrolet."

He sighed. "No, I didn't. Not at first. I'm sorry. It was hard for me to face the fact that anyone would want to hurt you. But something was bothering you. You didn't want to drive, you didn't want to leave the ranch at all, but you wouldn't talk about it. That's when I began to realize you were scared."

Her green eyes went dark. "Terrified is a better word," she whispered, looking out the window. "Have you heard from Phelps?"

"No. He wouldn't call here unless he'd found Beckman."

She shivered, the strained look coming back into her face. "He tried to kill you. I should have known, I should have done something."

"What could you have done?" he asked roughly. "If you'd been with me that day, the bullet would have hit you, instead of just shattering the windshield."

"He's so jealous he's insane." Thinking of Roger made her feel sick, and she pressed her hand to her stomach. "He's truly insane. He probably went wild when I moved in with you. The first couple of phone calls, he didn't say anything at all. Maybe he had just been calling to see if I answered the phone at your house. He couldn't stand for me to even talk to any other man, and when he found out that you and I—" She broke off, a fine sheen of perspiration on her face.

Gently John pulled her to him, pressing her head against his shoulder while he soothingly stroked her hair. "I wonder how he found out."

"Bitsy Sumner," Michelle said shakily.

"The airhead we met in the restaurant?"

"That airhead is the biggest gossip I know."

"If he's that far off his rocker, he probably thinks he's finally found the 'other man' after all these years."

She jumped, then gave a tight little laugh. "He has."

"What?" His voice was startled.

She eased away from him and pushed her hair back from her face with a nervous gesture. "It's always been you," she said in a low voice, looking anywhere except at him. "I couldn't love him the way I should have, and somehow he . . . seemed to know it."

He put his hand on her chin and forced her head around. "You acted like you hated me, damn it."

"I had to have some protection from you." Her green eyes regarded him with a little bitterness. "You had women falling all over you, women with a lot more experience, and who were a lot prettier. I was only eighteen, and you scared me to death. People called you 'Stud!' I knew I couldn't handle a man like you, even if you'd ever looked at me twice."

"I looked," he said harshly. "More than twice. But you turned your nose up at me as if you didn't like my smell, so I left you alone, even though I wanted you so much my guts were tied in knots. I built that house for you, because you were used to a lot better than the old house I was living in. I built the swimming pool because you liked to swim. Then you married some fancy-pants rich guy, damn you, and I felt like tearing the place down stone by stone."

Her lips trembled. "If I couldn't have you, it didn't matter who I married."

"You could have had me."

"As a temporary bed partner? I was so young I thought I had to have it all or nothing. I wanted forever after, for better or worse, and your track record isn't that of a marrying man. Now..." She shrugged, then managed a faint smile. "Now all that doesn't matter."

Hard anger crossed his face, then he said, "That's what you think," and covered her mouth with his. She opened her lips to him, letting him take all he wanted. The time was long past when she could deny him anything, any part of herself. Even their kisses had been restrained for the past four days, and the hunger was so strong in him that it overwhelmed his anger; he kissed her as if he wanted to devour her, his strong hands kneading her flesh with barely controlled ferocity, and she reveled in it. She didn't fear his strength or his roughness, because they sprang from passion and aroused an answering need inside her.

Her nails dug into his bare shoulders as her head fell back, baring her throat for his mouth. His hips moved rhythmically, rubbing the hard ridge of his manhood against her as his self-control slipped. Only the knowledge that a nurse could interrupt them at any moment gave him the strength to finally ease away from her, his breath coming hard and fast. The way he felt now was too private, too intense, for him to allow even the chance of anyone walking in on them.

"Nev had better hurry," he said roughly, unable to resist one more kiss. Her lips were pouty and swollen from his kisses, her eyes half-closed and drugged with desire; that look aroused him even more, because he had put it there.

Michelle slipped out of the bedroom, her clothes in her hand. She didn't want to take a chance on waking John by dressing in the bedroom; he had been sleeping heavily since the accident, but she didn't want to push her luck. She had to find Roger. He had missed killing John once; he might not miss the second time. And she knew John; if he made even a pretense of following the doctor's order to take it easy, she'd be surprised. No, he would be working as normal, out in the open and vulnerable.

He had talked to Deputy Phelps the night before, but all Andy had come up with was that a blue Chevrolet had been rented to a man generally matching Roger's physical description, and calling himself Edward Walsh. The familiar cold chill had gone down Michelle's spine. "Edward is Roger's middle name," she had whispered. "Walsh was his mother's maiden name." John had stared at her for a long moment before relaying the information to Andy.

She wouldn't allow Roger another opportunity to hurt John. Oddly, she wasn't afraid for herself. She had already been through so much at Roger's hands that she simply couldn't be afraid any longer, but she was deathly afraid for John, and for this new life she carried. She couldn't let this go on.

Lying awake in the darkness, she had suddenly known how to find him. She didn't know exactly where he was, but she knew the general vicinity; all she had to do was bait the trap, and he would walk into it. The only problem was that she was the bait, and she would be in the trap with him.

She left a note for John on the kitchen table and ate a cracker to settle her stomach. To be on the safe side, she carried a pack of crackers with her as she slipped silently out the back door. If her hunch was right, she should be fairly safe until someone could get there. Her hand strayed to her stomach. She had to be right.

The Mercedes started with one turn of the ignition key, its engine smooth and quiet. She put it in gear and eased it down the driveway without putting on the lights, hoping she wouldn't wake Edie or any of the men.

Her ranch was quiet, the old house sitting silent and abandoned under the canopy of big oak trees. She unlocked the door and let herself in, her ears straining to hear every noise in the darkness. It would be dawn within half an hour; she didn't have much time to bait the trap and lure Roger in before Edie would find the note on the table and wake John.

Her hand shook as she flipped on the light in the foyer. The interior of the house jumped into focus, light and shadow rearranging themselves into things she knew as well as she knew her own face. Methodically she walked around, turning on the lights in the living room, then moving into her father's office, then the dining room, then the kitchen. She pulled the curtains back from the windows to let the lights shine through like beacons, which she meant them to be.

She turned on the lights in the laundry room, and in the small downstairs apartment used by the housekeeper a long time ago, when there had been a housekeeper. She went upstairs and turned on the lights in her bedroom, where John had taken her for the first time and made it impossible for her to ever be anything but his. Every light went on, both upstairs and downstairs, piercing the predawn darkness. Then she sat down on the bottom step of the stairs and waited. Soon someone would come. It might be John, in which case he would be furious, but she suspected it would be Roger.

The seconds slipped past, becoming minutes. Just as the sky began to take on the first gray tinge of daylight, the door opened and he walked in.

She hadn't heard a car, which meant she had been right in thinking he was close by. Nor had she heard his steps as he crossed the porch. She had no warning until he walked through the door, but, oddly, she wasn't startled. She had known he would be there.

"Hello, Roger," she said calmly. She had to remain calm.

He had put on a little weight in the two years since she had seen him, and his hair was a tad thinner, but other than that he looked the same. Even his eyes still looked the same, too sincere and slightly mad. The sincerity masked the fact that his mind had slipped, not far enough that he couldn't still function in society, but enough that he could conceive of murder and be perfectly logical about it, as if it were the only thing to do.

He carried a pistol in his right hand, but he held it loosely by the side of his leg. "Michelle," he said, a little confused by her manner, as if she were greeting a guest. "You're looking well." It was a comment dictated by a lifetime of having the importance of good manners drilled into him.

She nodded gravely. "Thank you. Would you like a cup of coffee?" She didn't know if there was any coffee in the house, and even if there were, it would be horribly stale, but the longer she could keep him off balance, the better. If Edie wasn't in the kitchen now, she would be in a few minutes, and she would wake John. Michelle hoped John would call Andy, but he might not take the time. She figured he would be here in fifteen minutes. Surely she could handle Roger for fifteen minutes. She thought the brightly lit house would alert John that something was wrong, so he wouldn't come bursting in, startling Roger into shooting. It was a chance, but so far the chances she had taken had paid off.

Roger was staring at her with a feverish glitter in his eyes, as if he couldn't look at her enough. Her question startled him again. "Coffee?"

"Yes. I think I'd like a cup, wouldn't you?" The very thought of coffee made her stomach roll, but making it would take time. And Roger was very civilized; he would see nothing wrong with sharing a cup of coffee with her.

"Why, yes. That would be nice, thank you."

She smiled at him as she got up from the stairs. "Why don't you chat with me while the coffee's brewing? I'm certain we have a lot of gossip to catch up on. I only hope I have coffee; I may have forgotten to buy any. It's been so hot this summer, hasn't it? I've become an iced-tea fanatic."

"Yes, it's been very hot," he agreed, following her into the kitchen. "I thought I might spend some time at the chalet in Colorado. It should be pleasant this time of year."

She found a half-empty pack of coffee in the cabinet; it was probably so stale it would be undrinkable, but she carefully filled the pot with water and poured it into the coffeemaker, then measured out the coffee into the paper filter. Her coffeemaker was slow; it took almost ten minutes to make a pot. The perking, hissing sounds it made were very soothing.

"Please sit down," she invited, indicating the chairs at the kitchen table.

Slowly he took a chair, then placed the pistol on the table. Michelle didn't let herself look at it as she turned to take two mugs from the cabinet. Then she sat down and took another cracker from the pack she had brought with her; she had left it on the table earlier, when she was going around the house turning on all the lights. Her stomach was rolling again, perhaps from tension as much as the effects of pregnancy.

"Would you like a cracker?" she asked politely.

He was watching her again, his eyes both sad and wild. "I love you," he whispered. "How could you leave me when I need you so much? I wanted you to come back to me. Everything would have been all right. I promised you it would be all right. Why did you move in with that brute rancher? *Why did you have to cheat on me like that?*"

Michelle jumped at the sudden lash of fury in his voice. His remarkably pleasant face was twisting in the hideous way she remembered in her nightmares. Her heart began thudding against her ribs so painfully that she thought she might be sick after all, but somehow she managed to say with creditable surprise, "But, Roger, the electricity had been disconnected. You didn't expect me to live here without lights or water, did you?"

Again he looked confused by the unexpected change of subject, but only momentarily. He shook his head. "You can't lie to me anymore, darling. You're still living with him. I just don't understand. I offered you so much more: all the luxury you could want, jewelry, shopping trips in Paris, but instead you ran away from me to live with a sweaty rancher who smells of cows."

She couldn't stop the coldness that spread over her when he called her "darling." She swallowed, trying to force back the panic welling in her. If she panicked, she wouldn't be able to control him. How many minutes did she have left? Seven? Eight?

"I wasn't certain you wanted me back," she managed to say, though her mouth was so dry she could barely form the words.

Slowly he shook his head. "You had to know. You just didn't want to come back. You *like* what that sweaty rancher can give you, when you could have lived like a queen.

Michelle, darling, it's so sick for you to let someone like him touch you, but you enjoy it, don't you? It's *unnatural*!''

She knew all the signs. He was working himself into a frenzy, the rage and jealousy building in him until he lashed out violently. How could even Roger miss seeing why she would prefer John's strong, clean masculinity and earthy passions to his own twisted parody of love? How much longer would it be? Six minutes?

"I called your house," she lied, desperately trying to defuse his temper. "Your housekeeper said you were in France. I wanted you to come get me. I wanted to come back to you."

He looked startled, the rage draining abruptly from his face as if it had never been. He didn't even look like the same man. "You...you wanted..."

She nodded, noting that he seemed to have forgotten about the pistol. "I missed you. We had so much fun together, didn't we?" It was sad, but in the beginning they *had* had fun. Roger had been full of laughter and gentle teasing, and she had hoped he could make her forget about John.

Some of that fun was suddenly echoed in his eyes, in the smile that touched his mouth. "I thought you were the most wonderful thing I'd ever seen," he said softly. "Your hair is so bright and soft, and when you smiled at me, I felt ten feet tall. I would have given you the world. I would have killed for you." Still smiling, his hand moved toward the pistol.

Five minutes?

The ghost of the man he had been faded, and suddenly pity moved her. It wasn't until that moment that she understood Roger was truly ill; something in his mind had gone very wrong, and she didn't think all the psychiatrists or drugs in the world would be able to help him.

"We were so young," she murmured, wishing things could have been different for the laughing young man she had known. Little of him remained now, only moments of remembered fun to lighten his eyes. "Do you remember June Bailey, the little redhead who fell out of Wes Conlan's boat? We were all trying to help her back in, and somehow we all wound up in the water except for Toni. She didn't know a thing about sailing, so there she was on the boat, screaming, and we were swimming like mad, trying to catch up to her."

Four minutes.

He laughed, his mind sliding back to those sunny, goofy days.

"I think the coffee's about finished," she murmured, getting up. Carefully she poured two cups and carried them back to the table. "I hope you can drink it. I'm not much of a coffee-maker." That was better than telling him the coffee was stale because she had been living with John.

He was still smiling, but his eyes were sad. As she watched, a sheen of tears began to brighten his eyes, and he picked up the pistol. "I do love you so much," he said. "You never should have let that man touch you." Slowly the barrel came around toward her.

A lot of things happened simultaneously. The back door exploded inward, propelled by a kick that took it off the hinges. Roger jerked toward the sound and the pistol fired, the shot deafening in the confines of the house. She screamed and ducked as two other men leaped from the inside doorway, the biggest one taking Roger down with a tackle that sent him crashing into the table. Curses and shouts filled the air, along with the sound of wood splintering; then another shot assaulted her ears and strengthened the stench of cordite. She was screaming John's name over and over, knowing he was the one rolling across the floor with Roger as they both struggled for the gun. Then suddenly the pistol skidded across the floor and John was straddling Roger as he drove his fist into the other man's face.

The sickening thudding made her scream again, and she kicked a shattered chair out of her way, scrambling for the two men. Andy Phelps and another deputy reached them at the same time, grabbing John and trying to wrestle him away, but his face was a mask of killing fury at the man who had tried to murder his woman. He slung their hands away with a roar. Sobbing, Michelle threw her arms around his neck from behind, her shaking body against his back. "John, don't, please," she begged, weeping so hard that the words were almost unintelligible. "He's very sick."

He froze, her words reaching him as no one else's could. Slowly he let his fists drop and got to his feet, hauling her against him and holding her so tightly that she could barely breathe. But breathing wasn't important right then; nothing was as important as holding him and having him hold her, his head bent down to hers as he whispered a choked mixture of curses and love words.

The deputies had pulled Roger to his feet and cuffed his hands behind his back, while the pistol was put in a plastic bag and sealed. Roger's nose and mouth were bloody, and he was dazed, looking at them as if he didn't know who they were, or where he was. Perhaps he didn't.

John held Michelle's head pressed to his chest as he watched the deputies take Beckman out. God, how could she have been so cool, sitting across the kitchen table from that maniac and calmly serving him coffee? The man made John's blood run cold.

But she was safe in his arms now, the most precious part of his world. She had said a lot about his tomcatting reputation and the women in his checkered past; she had even called him a heartbreaker. But she was the true heartbreaker, with her sunlight hair and summer-green eyes, a golden woman who he never would have forgotten, even if she'd never come back into his life. Beckman had been obsessed with her, had gone mad when he lost her, and for the first time John thought he might understand. He wouldn't have a life, either, if he lost Michelle.

"I lost twenty years off my life when I found that note," he growled into her hair.

She clung to him, not loosening her grip. "You got here faster than I'd expected," she gasped, still crying a little. "Edie must've gotten up early."

"No, I got up early. You weren't in bed with me, so I started hunting you. As it was, we barely got here in time. Edie would have been too late."

Andy Phelps sighed, looking around the wrecked kitchen. Then he found another cup in the cabinet and poured himself some coffee. He made a face as he sipped it. "This stuff is rank. It tastes just like what we get at work. Anyway, I think I have my pajama bottoms on under my pants. When John called I took the time to dress, but I don't think I took the time to undress first."

They both looked at him. He still looked a little sleepy, and he certainly wasn't in uniform. He had on jeans, a T-shirt, and running shoes with no socks. He could have worn an ape suit for all she cared.

"I need both of you to make statements," he said. "But I don't think this will ever come to trial. From what I saw, he won't be judged mentally competent."

"No," Michelle agreed huskily. "He isn't."

"Do we have to make the statements right now?" John asked. "I want to take Michelle home for a while."

Andy looked at both of them. Michelle was utterly white, and John looked the worse for wear, too. He had to still be feeling the effects of hitting a steering wheel with his face. "No, go on. Come in sometime this afternoon."

John nodded and walked Michelle out of the house. He'd commandeered Nev's truck, and now he led her to it. Someone else could get the car later.

It was a short, silent drive back to the ranch. She climbed numbly out of the truck, unable to believe it was all over.

John swung her up in his arms and carried her into the house, his hard arms tight around her. Without a word to anyone, even Edie, who watched them with lifted brows, he took her straight upstairs to their bedroom and kicked the door shut behind him.

He placed her on the bed as if she might shatter, then suddenly snatched her up against him again. "I could kill you for scaring me like that," he muttered, even though he knew he'd never be able to hurt her. She must have known it, too, because she cuddled closer against him.

"We're getting married right away," he ordered in a voice made harsh with need. "I heard part of what he said, and maybe he's right that I can't give you all the luxuries you deserve, but I swear to God I'll try to make you happy. I love you too much to let you go."

"I've never said anything about going," Michelle protested. Married? He wanted to get married? Abruptly she lifted her head and gave him a glowing smile, one that almost stopped his breathing.

"You never said anything about staying, either."

"How could I? This is your house. It was up to you."

"Good manners be damned," he snapped. "I was going crazy, wondering if you were happy."

"Happy? I've been sick with it. You've given me something that doesn't have a price on it." She lifted her nose at him. "I've heard that mingling red blood with blue makes very healthy babies."

He looked down at her with hungry fire in his eyes. "Well, I hope you like babies, honey, because I plan on about four."

"I like them very much," she said as she touched her stomach. "Even though this is making me feel really ghastly."

For a moment he looked puzzled, then his gaze drifted downward. His expression changed to one of stunned surprise, and he actually paled a little. "You're pregnant?"

"Yes. Since the night you came back from your last trip to Miami."

His right brow lifted as he remembered that night; the left side of his face was still too swollen for him to be able to move it much. Then a slow grin began to widen his mouth, lifting the corners of his mustache. "I was careless one time too many," he said with visible satisfaction.

She laughed. "Yes, you were. Were you trying to be?"

"Who knows?" he asked, shrugging. "Maybe. God knows I like the idea. How about you?"

She reached for him, and he pulled her onto his lap, holding her in his arms and loving the feel of her. She rubbed her face against his chest. "All I've ever wanted is for you to love me. I don't need all that expensive stuff; I like working on the ranch, and I want to build my own ranch up again, even after we're married. Having your baby is . . . just more of heaven."

He laid his cheek on her golden hair, thinking of the terror he'd felt when he'd read her note. But now she was safe, she was his, and he would never let her go. She'd never seen any man as married as he planned to be. He'd spend the rest of his life trying to pamper her, and she'd continue to calmly ignore his orders whenever the mood took her, just as she did now. It would be a long, peaceful life, anchored in hard work and happily shrieking kids.

It would be good.

Their wedding day dawned clear and sunny, though the day before Michelle had resigned herself to having the wedding inside. But Hurricane Carl, after days of meandering around like a lost bee, had finally decided to head west and the clouds had vanished, leaving behind a pure, deep blue sky unmarred by even a wisp of cloud.

Michelle couldn't stop smiling as she dressed. If there were any truth in the superstition that it was bad luck for the groom to see the bride on their wedding day, she and John were in for a miserable life, but somehow she just couldn't believe it. He had not only refused to let her sleep in another room the night before, he'd lost his temper over the subject. She was damn well going to sleep with him where she belonged, and that was that. Tradition could just go to hell as far as he was concerned, if it meant they had to sleep apart. She had noticed that he hadn't willingly let her out of his sight since the morning they had caught Roger, so she understood.

His rather calm acceptance of his impending fatherhood had been a false calm, one shock too many after a nerve-wracking morning. The reality of it had hit him during the night, and Michelle had awakened to find herself clutched tightly to his chest, his face buried in her hair and his muscled body shaking, while he muttered over and over, "A baby. My God, a baby." His hand had been stroking her stomach as if he couldn't quite imagine his child growing inside her slim body. It had become even more real to him the next morning when even crackers couldn't keep her stomach settled, and he had held her while she was sick.

Some mornings weren't bad at all, while some were wretched. This morning John had put a cracker in her mouth before she was awake enough to even open her eyes, so she had lain in his arms with her eyes closed, chewing on her "breakfast." When it became evident that this was going to be a good morning, the bridegroom had made love to the bride, tenderly, thoroughly, and at length.

They were even dressing together for their wedding. She watched as he fastened his cuff links, his hard mouth curved in a very male, very satisfied way. He had found her lace teddy and garter belt extremely erotic, so much so that now they risked being late to their own wedding.

"I need help with my zipper when you've finished with that," she said.

He looked up, and a slow smile touched his lips, then lit his black eyes. "You look good enough to eat."

She couldn't help laughing. "Does this mean we'll have to reschedule the wedding for tomorrow?"

The smile became a grin. "No, we'll make this one." He finished his cuff links. "Turn around."

She turned, and his warm fingers touched her bare back, making her catch her breath and shiver in an echo of delight. He kissed her exposed nape, holding her as the shiver became a sensuous undulation. He wouldn't have traded being with her on this particular morning for all the tradition in the world.

Her dress was a pale, icy yellow, as was the garden hat she had chosen to wear. The color brought out the bright sunniness of her hair and made her glow, though maybe it wasn't responsible for the color in her cheeks or the sparkle in her eyes. That could be due to early pregnancy, or to heated lovemaking. Or maybe it was sheer happiness.

He worked the zipper up without snagging any of the delicate fabric, then bent to straighten and smooth her skirt. He shrugged into his jacket as she applied lipstick and carefully set the hat on her head. The yellow streamers flowed gracefully down her back. "Are we ready?" she asked, and for the first time he heard a hint of nervousness in her voice.

"We're ready," he said firmly, taking her hand. Their friends were all waiting on the patio; even his mother had flown up from Miami, a gesture that had surprised him but, on reflection, was appreciated.

Without the shadow of Roger Beckman hanging over her, Michelle had flowered in just these few days. Until she had made the effort to confront Roger, to do something about him once and for all, she hadn't realized the burden she'd been carrying around with her. Those black memories had stifled her spirit, made her wary and defensive, unwilling to give too much of herself. But she had faced him, and in doing so she had faced the past. She wasn't helpless any longer, a victim of threats and violence.

Poor Roger. She couldn't help feeling pity for him, even though he had made her life hell. At her insistence, John and Andy had arranged for Roger to have medical tests immediately, and it hadn't taken the doctors long to make a diagnosis. Roger had a slow but relentlessly degenerative brain disease. He would never be any better, and would slowly become worse until he finally died an early death, no longer knowing anyone or anything. She couldn't help feeling grief for him, because at one time he'd been a good, kind young man. She wished there were some help for him, but the doctors didn't hold out any hope.

John put his arm around her, seeing the shadows that had come into her eyes. He didn't share her sympathy for Beckman, though perhaps in time he would be able to forget the moment when that pistol had swung toward her. Maybe in a few centuries.

He tilted her head up and kissed her, taking care not to smear her lipstick. "I love you," he murmured.

The sun came back out in her eyes. "I love you, too."

He tucked her hand into the crook of his arm. "Let's go get married."

Together they walked down the stairs and out to the patio, where their friends waited and the sun shone down brightly, as if to apologize for the threat of a storm the day before. Michelle looked at the tall man by her side; she wasn't naive enough to think there wouldn't be storms in their future, because John's arrogance would always make her dig in her heels, but she found herself looking forward to the battles they would have. The worst was behind them, and if the future held rough weather and sudden squalls . . . well, what future didn't? If she could handle John, she could handle anything.

* * * * *

WHITE
LIES

Chapter 1

In ranking the worst days of her life, this one probably wasn't number one, but it was definitely in the top three.

Jay Granger had held her temper all day, rigidly controlling herself until her head was throbbing and her stomach burning. Not even during the jolting ride in a succession of crowded buses had she allowed her control to crack. All day long she had forced herself to stay calm despite the pent-up frustration and rage that filled her, and now she felt as if she couldn't relax her own mental restraints. She just wanted to be alone.

So she silently endured having her toes stepped on, her ribs relocated by careless elbows, and her nostrils assailed by close-packed humanity. It began to rain just before she got off the last bus, a slow, cold rain that had chilled her to the bone by the time she walked the two blocks to her apartment building. Naturally she didn't have an umbrella with her; it was supposed to have been a sunny day. The clouds hadn't cleared all day long.

But at last she reached her apartment, where she was safe from curious eyes, either sympathetic or jeering. She was alone, blessedly alone. A sigh of relief broke from her lips as she started to close the door; then her control cracked and she slammed the door with every ounce of strength in her arm. It crashed against the frame with a resounding thud, but the small act of violence didn't release her tension. Trashing her entire office building might help, or choking Farrell Wordlaw, but both those actions were denied her.

When she thought of the way she had worked for the past five years, the fourteen- and sixteen-hour days, the work she had brought home on the weekends, she wanted to scream. She wanted to throw something. Yes, she definitely wanted to choke Farrell Wordlaw. But that wasn't *appropriate* behavior for a professional woman, a chic and sophisticated executive in a prestigious investment-banking firm. On the other hand, it was entirely appropriate for someone who had just joined the ranks of the unemployed.

Damn them.

For five years she had dedicated herself to her job, ruthlessly stifling those parts of her personality that didn't fit the image. At first it had been mostly because she needed the job and the money, but Jay was too intense to do anything by half measures. Soon she had become caught up in the teeming rat race—the constant striving for success, for new triumphs, bigger and better deals—and that world had been her life for five years. Today she had been kicked out of it.

It wasn't that she hadn't been successful; she had. Maybe too successful. Some people hadn't liked dealing with her because she was a woman. Realizing that, Jay had tried to be as straightforward and aggressive as any man, to reassure her clients that she would take care of them as well as a man could. To that end she had changed her habits of speech, her wardrobe, never let even a hint of a tear sparkle in her eyes, never giggled, and learned how to drink Scotch, though she had never learned to enjoy it. She had paid for such rigid control with headaches and a constant burning in her stomach, but nevertheless she had thrown herself into the role because, for all its stresses, she had enjoyed the challenge. It was an exciting job, with the lure of a fast trip up the corporate ladder, and for the time being, she had been willing to pay the price.

Well, it was over, by decree of Farrell Wordlaw. He was very sorry, but her style just wasn't "compatible" with the image Wordlaw, Wilson & Trusler wanted to project. He deeply appreciated her efforts, et cetera, et cetera, and would certainly give her a glowing reference, as well as two weeks' notice to get her affairs in order. None of that changed the truth, and she knew it as well as he. She was being pushed out to make room for Duncan Wordlaw, Farrell's son, who had joined the firm the year before and whose performance always ranked second, behind Jay's. She was showing up the senior partner's son, so she had to go. Instead of the promotion she'd been expecting, she'd been handed a pink slip.

She was furious, with no way to express it. It would give her the greatest satisfaction to walk out now and leave Wordlaw scrambling to handle her pending work, but the cold, hard fact was that she needed her salary for those two weeks. If she didn't find another well-paying job immediately, she would lose her apartment. She had lived within her means, but as her salary had gone up so had her standard of living, and she had very little in savings. She certainly hadn't expected to lose her job because Duncan Wordlaw was an underachiever!

Whenever Steve had lost a job, he'd just shrugged and laughed, telling her not to sweat it, he'd find another. And he always had, too. Jobs hadn't been that important to Steve; neither had security. Jay gave a tight little laugh as she opened a bottle of antacid tablets and shook two of them into her hand. Steve! She hadn't thought about him in years. One thing was certain, she would never be as uncaring about unemployment as he had been. She liked knowing where her next meal was coming from; Steve liked excitement. He'd needed the hot flow of adrenaline more than he'd needed her, and finally that had ended their marriage.

But at least Steve would never be this strung out on nerves, she thought as she chewed the chalky tablets and waited for them to ease the burning in her stomach. Steve would have snapped his fingers at Farrell Wordlaw and told him what he could do with his two weeks' notice, then walked out whistling. Maybe Steve's attitude was irresponsible, but he would never let a mere job get the best of him.

Well, that was Steve's personality, not hers. He'd been fun, but in the end their differences had been greater than the attraction between them. They had parted on a friendly basis, though she'd been exasperated, as well. Steve would never grow up.

Why was she thinking of him now? Was it because she associated unemployment with his name? She began to laugh, realizing she'd done exactly that. Still chuckling, she ran water into a glass and lifted it in a toast. "To the good times," she said. They'd had a lot of good times, laughing and playing like the two healthy young animals they'd been, but it hadn't lasted.

Then she forgot about him as worry surged into her mind again. She had to find another job immediately, a well-paying job, but she didn't trust Farrell to give her a glowing recommendation. He might praise her to the skies in writing, but then he would spread the word around the New York investment-banking community that she didn't "fit in." Maybe she should try something else. But her experience was in investment banking, and she didn't have the financial reserves to train for another field.

With a sudden feeling of panic, she realized that she was thirty years old and had no idea what she was going to do with her life. She didn't want to spend the rest of it making deals while living on her nerves and an endless supply of antacid tablets, spending all her free time resting in an effort to build up her flagging energy. In reacting against Steve's let-tomorrow-take-care-of-itself-while-I-have-fun-today philosophy, she had gone to the opposite extreme and cut fun out of her life.

She had opened the refrigerator door and was looking at her supply of frozen microwave dinners with an expression of distaste when the doorman buzzed. Deciding to forget about dinner, something she'd done too often lately, she depressed the switch. "Yes, Dennis?"

"Mr. Payne and Mr. McCoy are here to see you, Ms. Granger," Dennis said smoothly. "From the FBI."

"What?" Jay asked, startled, sure she'd misunderstood.

Dennis repeated the message, but the words remained the same.

She was totally dumbfounded. "Send them up," she said, because she didn't know what else to do. FBI? What on earth? Unless slamming your apartment door was somehow against federal law, the worst she could be accused of was tearing the tags off her mattress and pillows. Well, why not? This was a perfectly rotten end to a perfectly rotten day.

The doorbell rang a moment later, and she hurried to open the door, her face still a picture of confusion. The rather nondescript, modestly suited men who stood there both presented badges and identification for her inspection.

"I'm Frank Payne," the older of the two men said. "This is Gilbert McCoy. We'd like to talk to you, if we may."

Jay gestured them into the apartment. "I'm at a total loss," she confessed. "Please sit down. Would you like coffee?"

A look of relief passed over Frank Payne's pleasant face. "Please," he said with heartfelt sincerity. "It's been a long day."

Jay went into the kitchen and hurriedly put on a pot of coffee; then, to be on the safe side, she chewed two more antacid tablets. Finally she took a deep breath and walked out to where the two men were comfortably ensconced on her soft, chic, gray-blue sofa. "What have I done?" she asked, only half-joking.

Both men smiled. "Nothing," McCoy assured her, grinning. "We just want to talk to you about a former acquaintance."

She sank down in the matching gray-blue chair, sighing in relief. The burning in her stomach subsided a little. "Which former acquaintance?" Maybe they were after Farrell Wordlaw; maybe there was justice in the world, after all.

Frank Payne took a small notebook out of his inner coat pocket and opened it, evidently consulting his notes. "Are you Janet Jean Granger, formerly married to Steve Crossfield?"

"Yes." So this had something to do with Steve. She should have known. Still, she was amazed, as if she'd somehow conjured up these two men just by thinking of Steve earlier, something she almost never did. He was so far removed from her life now that she couldn't even form a clear picture in her mind of how he'd looked. But what had he gotten himself into, with his driving need for excitement?

"Does your ex-husband have any relatives? Anyone who might be close to him?"

Slowly Jay shook her head. "Steve is an orphan. He was raised in a series of foster homes, and as far as I know, he didn't stay in touch with any of his foster parents. As for any close friends—" she shrugged "—I haven't seen or heard from him since our divorce five years ago, so I don't have any idea who his friends might be."

Payne frowned, rubbing the deep lines between his brows. "Would you remember the name of a dentist he used while you were married, or perhaps a doctor?"

Jay shook her head, staring at him. "No. Steve was disgustingly healthy."

The two men looked at each other, frowning. McCoy said quietly, "Damn, this isn't going to be easy. We're running into one dead end after another."

Payne's face was deeply lined with fatigue, and something else. He looked back at Jay, his eyes worried. "Do you think that coffee's ready yet, Ms. Granger?"

"It should be. I'll be right back." Without knowing why, Jay felt shaken as she went into the kitchen and began putting cups, cream and sugar on a tray. The coffee had finished brewing, and she transferred the pot to the tray, but then just stood there, staring down at the wafting steam. Steve had to be in serious trouble, really serious, and she regretted it even though there was nothing she could do. It had been inevitable, though. He'd always been chasing after adventure, and unfortunately adventure often went hand in hand with trouble. It had been only a matter of time before the odds caught up with him.

She carried the tray into the living room and placed it on the low table in front of the sofa, her brow furrowed into a worried frown. "What has Steve done?"

"Nothing illegal, that we know of," Payne said hastily. "It's just that he was involved in a . . . sensitive situation."

Steve hadn't done anything illegal, but the FBI was investigating him? Jay's frown deepened as she poured three cups of coffee. "What sort of sensitive situation?"

Payne looked at her with a troubled expression, and suddenly she noticed that he had very nice eyes, clear and strangely sympathetic. Gentle eyes. Not at all the kind of eyes she would have expected an FBI agent to possess. He cleared his throat. "Very sensitive. We don't even know why he was there. But we need, very badly, to find someone who can make a positive identification of him."

Jay went white, the ramifications of that quiet, sinister statement burning in her mind. Steve was dead. Even though the love she'd felt for him had long since faded away, she knew a piercing grief for what had been. He'd been so much fun, always laughing, his brown eyes lit with devilish merriment. It was as if part of her own childhood had died, to know that his laughter had been stilled. "He's dead," she said dully, staring at the cup in her hand as it began to shake, sloshing the coffee back and forth.

Payne quickly reached out and took the cup from her, placing it on the tray. "We don't know," he said, his face even more troubled. "There was an explosion; one man survived. We think it's Crossfield, but we aren't certain, and it's critical that we know. I can't explain more than that."

It had been a long, terrible day, and it wasn't getting any better. She put her shaking hands to her temples and pressed hard, trying to make sense of what he'd told her. "Wasn't there any identification on him?"

"No," Payne said.

"Then why do you think it's Steve?"

"We know he was there. Part of his driver's license was found."

"Why can't you just look at him and tell who he is?" she cried. "Why can't you identify the others and find out who he is by process of elimination?"

McCoy looked away. Payne's gentle eyes darkened. "There wasn't enough left to identify. Nothing."

She didn't want to hear any more, didn't want to know any of the details, though she could guess at the horrible carnage. She was suddenly cold, as if her blood had stopped pumping. "Steve?" she asked faintly.

"The man who survived is in critical condition, but the doctors are what they call 'cautiously optimistic.' He has a chance. Two days ago, they were certain he wouldn't last through the night."

"Why is it so important that you know right now who he is? If he lives, you can ask him. If he dies—" She halted abruptly. She couldn't say the words, but she thought them. If he died, it wouldn't matter. There would be no survivors, and they would close their files.

"I can't tell you anything except that we need to know who this man is. We need to know who died, so certain steps can be taken. Ms. Granger, I *can* tell you that my agency isn't directly involved in the situation. We're merely cooperating with others, because this concerns national security."

Suddenly Jay knew what they wanted from her. They would have been glad if she could have helped them locate any dental or medical records on Steve, but that wasn't their prime objective. They wanted her to go with them, to personally identify the injured man as Steve.

In a dull voice she asked, "Can't they tell if this man matches the general description of any of their own people? Surely they have measurements, fingerprints, that sort of thing?"

She was looking down, so she didn't see the quick wariness in Payne's eyes. He cleared his throat again. "Your husband—ex-husband—and our man are...were...the same general size. Fingerprints aren't possible; his hands are burned. But you know more about him than anyone else we can find. There might be something about him that you recognize, some little birthmark or scar that you remember."

It still confused her; she couldn't understand why they wouldn't be able to recognize their own man, unless he was so horribly mutilated... Shivering, she didn't let herself complete the thought, didn't let the picture form in her mind. What if it *was* Steve? She didn't hate him, had never hated him. He was a rascal, but he'd never been cruel or meanhearted; even after she had stopped loving him, she had still been fond of him, in an exasperated way.

"You want me to go with you," she said, making it a statement instead of a question.

"Please," Payne replied quietly.

She didn't want to, but he had made it seem like her patriotic duty. "All right. I'll get my coat. Where is he?"

Payne cleared his throat again and Jay tensed. She'd already learned that he did that whenever he had to tell her something awkward or unpleasant. "He's at Bethesda Naval Hospital in D.C. You'll need to pack a small suitcase. We have a private jet waiting for us at Kennedy."

Things were moving too fast for her to understand; she felt as if all she could do was follow the path of least resistance. Too much had happened today. First she had been fired, a brutal blow in itself, and now this. The security she had worked so hard to attain for herself had vanished in a few short minutes in Farrell Wordlaw's office, leaving her spinning helplessly, unable to get her feet back on the ground. Her life had been so *quiet* for the past five years; how could all this have happened so quickly?

Numbly she packed two dresses that traveled well, then collected her cosmetics from the bathroom. As she shoved what she needed into a small zippered plastic bag, she was stunned by her own reflection in the mirror. She looked so white and strained, and thin. Unhealthily thin. Her eyes were hollow and her cheekbones too prominent, the result of working long hours and living on antacid tablets. As soon as she returned to the city she would have to begin looking for another job, as well as working out her notice, which would mean more skipped meals.

Then she felt ashamed of herself. Why was she worrying about a job when Steve—or someone—was lying in a hospital bed fighting for his life? Steve had always told her that she worried too much about work, that she couldn't enjoy today because she was always worried about tomorrow. Maybe he was right.

Steve! Sudden tears blurred her eyes as she stuffed the cosmetic bag into her small overnighter. She hoped he would be all right.

At the last moment she remembered to pack fresh underwear. She was rattled, oddly disorganized, but finally she zipped the case and got her purse. "I'm ready," she said as she stepped out of the bedroom.

Gratefully she saw that one of the men had carried the coffee things into the kitchen. McCoy took the case from her hand, and she got her coat from the closet; Payne silently helped her into it. She looked around to make certain all the lights were off; then the three of them stepped into the hallway, and she locked the door behind her, wondering why she felt as if she would never be back.

She slept on the plane. She hadn't meant to, but almost as soon as they were airborne and she relaxed in the comfortable leather seat, her eyelids became too heavy to keep open. She didn't feel Payne spread a light blanket over her.

Payne sat across from her, watching her broodingly. He wasn't quite comfortable with what he was doing, dragging an innocent woman into this mess. Not even McCoy knew how much of a mess it was, how complicated it had become; as far as the other man knew, the situation was exactly the way he'd outlined it to Jay Granger: a simple matter of identification. Only a handful of people knew that it was more; maybe only two others besides himself. Maybe only one other, but that one carried a lot of power. When *he* wanted something done, it was done. Payne had known him for years, but had never managed to be comfortable in his presence.

She looked tired and oddly frail. She was too thin. She was about five-six, but he doubted she weighed much over a hundred pounds, and something about her made him think such thinness wasn't normal for her. He wondered if she was strong enough to be used as a shield.

She was probably very pretty when she was rested, and when she had some meat on her bones. Her hair was nice, a kind of honey brown, as thick and sleek as an otter's coat, and her eyes were dark blue. But now she just looked tired. It hadn't been an easy day for her.

Still, she had asked some questions that had made him uncomfortable. If she hadn't been so tired and upset she might have pinned him down on some things he didn't want to discuss, asked questions in front of McCoy that he didn't want raised. It was essential to the plan that everything be taken at face value. There could be no doubt at all.

The flight from New York to Bethesda was a short one, but the nap refreshed her, gave her back a sense of balance. The only thing was, the more alert she felt, the more unreal this entire situation seemed. She checked her watch as Payne and McCoy escorted her off the private jet when they landed at Washington National and into a government car waiting on the tarmac for them, and was startled to see that it was only nine o'clock. Only a few hours had passed, yet her life had been turned upside down.

"Why Bethesda?" she murmured to Payne as the car purred down the street, a few flakes of snow drifting down like flower petals on a light breeze. She stared at the snowflakes, wondering absently if an early-winter snowstorm would keep her from getting home. "Why not a civilian hospital?"

"Security." Payne's quiet voice barely reached her ears. "Don't worry. The best trauma experts were called in to work on him, civilian and military. We're doing the best we can for your husband."

"Ex-husband," Jay said faintly.

"Yes. Sorry."

As they turned onto Wisconsin Avenue, which would eventually take them to the Naval Medical Center, the snow became a little heavier. Payne was glad she hadn't asked any more questions about why the man was in a military hospital instead of, say, Georgetown University Hospital. Of course, he'd told her the truth, as far as it went. Security *was* the reason he was at Bethesda. It just wasn't the only reason. He watched the snow swirling down and wondered if all the loose threads could possibly be woven into a believable whole.

When they reached the medical center, only Payne got out of the car with her; McCoy nodded briefly in farewell and drove away. Snowflakes quickly silvered their hair as Payne took her elbow and hurried her inside, where the welcome warmth just as quickly melted the lacy flakes. No one paid them any attention as they took an elevator upward.

When the elevator doors opened, they stepped out into a quiet corridor. "This is the ICU floor," Payne said. "His room is this way."

They turned to the left, where double doors were guarded by two stern young men in uniform, both of whom wore pistols. Payne must have been known on sight, for one of the guards quickly opened a door for them. "Thank you," Payne said courteously as they passed.

The unit was deserted, except for the nurses who monitored all the life-support systems and continually checked on the patients, but still Jay sensed a quiet hum that pervaded every corner of the unit—the sound of the machines that kept the patients alive or aided in their recovery. For the first time it struck her that Steve must be hooked up to one or more of those machines, unable to move, and her steps faltered. It was just so hard to take in.

Payne's hand remained under her elbow, unobtrusively providing her with support. He stopped before a door and turned to her, his clear gray eyes full of concern. "I want to prepare you a little. He's badly injured. His skull was fractured, and the bones in his face were crushed. He's breathing through a trach tube. Don't expect him to look like the man you remember." He waited a moment, watching her, but she didn't say anything, and finally he opened the door.

Jay stepped into the room, and for a split second both her heart and lungs seemed to stop functioning. Then her heart lurched into rhythm again, and she drew a deep, painful breath. Tears sprang to her eyes as she stared at the inert form on the white hospital bed, and his name trembled soundlessly on her lips. It didn't seem possible that this . . . *this* could be Steve.

The man on the bed was almost literally a mummy. Both legs were broken and encased in pristine plaster casts, supported by a network of pulleys and slings. His hands were wrapped in bandages that extended almost to his elbows. His head and face were swathed in gauze, with extra-thick pads over his eyes; only his lips, chin and jaw were visible, and they were swollen and discolored. His breath whistled faintly but regularly from the tube in his throat, and various other tubes ran into his body. Monitors overhead recorded every detail of his bodily functions. And he was still. He was so still.

Her throat was so dry that speaking was painful. "How can I possibly identify him?" she asked rawly. "You *knew* I couldn't. You knew how he looks!"

Payne was watching her with sympathy. "I'm sorry, I know it's a shock. But we need for you to try. You were married to Steve Crossfield. You know him better than any other person on earth. Maybe there's some little detail you remember, a scar or a mole, a birthmark. Anything. Take your time and look at him. I'll be just outside."

He went out and closed the door behind him, leaving her alone in the room with that motionless figure and the quiet beeping of the monitors, the weak whistle of his breathing. Her hands knotted into fists, and tears blurred her eyes again. Whether this man was Steve or not, a pity so acute it was painful filled her.

Somehow her feet carried her closer to the bed. She carefully avoided the tubes and wires while never looking away from his face—or as much of his face as she could see. Steve? Was this really Steve?

She knew what Payne wanted. He hadn't actually spelled it out, but he hadn't needed to. He wanted her to lift the sheet away and study this man while he lay there unconscious and helpless, naked except for the bandages over his wounds. He thought she would have a wife's intimate knowledge of her husband's body, but five years is a long time. She could remember Steve's grin, and the devilish sparkle in his chocolaty brown eyes, but other details had long since faded from her mind.

It wouldn't matter to this man if she stripped back the sheet and looked at him. He was unconscious; he might well die, even now, with all these miracle machines hooked up to his body. He would never know. And as Payne would say, she would be doing her country a service if she could somehow identify this man as Steve Crossfield, or as definitely not.

She couldn't stop looking at him. He was so badly hurt. How could anyone be injured this critically and still live? If he were granted a lucid moment, right now, would he even want to live? Would he be able to walk again? Use his hands? See? Think? Or would he take stock of his injuries and tell the doctors, "Thanks, guys, but I think I'll take my chances at the Pearly Gates."

But perhaps he had a tremendous will to live. Perhaps that was what had kept him alive this long, an unconscious, deep-seated will to *be*. Fierce determination could move mountains.

Hesitantly she stretched out her hand and touched his right arm, just above the bandages that covered his burns. His skin was hot to the touch, and she jerked her fingers back in surprise. Somehow she had thought he would be cold. This intense heat was another sign of how brightly life still burned inside him, despite his stillness. Slowly her hand returned to his arm, lightly resting on the smooth skin just below the inside of his elbow, taking care not to disturb the IV needle that dripped a clear liquid into a vein.

He was warm. He was alive.

Her heart was pounding in her chest, some intense emotion welling up in her until she thought she would burst from the effort of trying to control it. It staggered her to think of what he had been through, yet he was still fighting, defying the odds, his spirit too fierce and proud to just let go. If she could have, she would have suffered the pain in his place.

And his body had been invaded enough. Needles pierced his veins; wire and electrodes picked up and broadcast his every heartbeat. As if he didn't have enough wounds already, the doctors had made more to insert drainage tubes in his chest and side, and there were other tubes, as well. Every day a host of strangers looked at him and treated him as if he were nothing but a slab of meat, all to save his life.

But she wouldn't invade his privacy, not in this manner. Modesty might not mean anything to him, but it was still his choice to make.

All her attention was focused on him; nothing else in the world existed in this moment except the man lying so still in the hospital bed. Was this Steve? Would she feel some sense of familiarity, despite the disfiguring swelling and the bandages that swathed him? She tried to remember.

Had Steve been this muscular? Had his arms been this thick, his chest this deep? He could have changed, gained weight, done a lot of physical work that would have developed his shoulders and arms more, so she couldn't go by that. Men got heavier in the chest as they matured.

His chest had been shaved. She looked at the dark stubble of body hair. Steve had had chest hair, though not a lot of it.

His beard? She looked at his jaw, what she could see of it, but his face was so swollen that she couldn't find anything familiar. Even his lips were swollen.

Something wet trickled down her cheek, and in surprise she dashed her hand across her face. She hadn't even realized she was crying.

Payne reentered the room and silently offered her his handkerchief. When she had wiped her face he led her away from the bedside, his arm warm and comforting around her waist, letting her lean on him. "I'm sorry," he finally offered. "I know it isn't easy."

She shook her head, feeling like a fool for breaking down like that, especially in light of what she had to tell him. "I don't know. I'm sorry, but I can't tell if he's Steve, or not. I just . . . can't."

"Do you think he could be?" Payne asked insistently.

Jay rubbed her temples. "I suppose so. I can't *tell*. There are so many bandages—"

"I understand. I know how difficult it is. But I need something to tell my superiors. Was your husband that tall? Was there anything at all familiar about him?"

If he understood, why did he keep pushing? Her headache was getting worse by the second. "I just don't know!" she cried. "I guess Steve is that tall, but it's hard to tell when he's lying down. Steve has dark hair and brown eyes, but I can't even tell that much about this man!"

Payne looked down at her. "It's on his medical sheet," he said quietly. "Brown hair and brown eyes."

For a moment the import of that didn't register; then her eyes widened. She hadn't felt any sense of recognition for the man at all, but she was still dazed by the storm of emotion he *had* caused in her: pity, yes, but also awe, that he was still alive and fighting, and an almost staggering respect for the determination and sheer guts he must have.

Very faintly, her face white, she said, "Then he must be Steve, mustn't he?"

A flash of relief crossed Payne's face, then was gone before she could be certain it was there. He nodded. "I'll notify our people that you've verified his identity. He's Steve Crossfield."

Chapter 2

When Jay awoke the next morning she lay very still in the bed, staring around the unfamiliar hotel room and trying to orient herself. The events of the previous day were mostly a blur, except for the crystal-clear memory she had of the injured man in the hospital. Steve. That man was Steve.

She should have recognized him. Even though it had been five years, she had once loved him. *Something* about him should have been familiar, despite the disfiguring bruises and swelling. An odd feeling of guilt assailed her, though she knew it was ridiculous, but it was as if she had let him down somehow, reduced him to the level of being too unimportant in her life for her to remember how he looked.

Grimacing, Jay got out of bed. There she went again, letting things matter too much to her. Steve had constantly told her to lighten up, and his tone had sometimes been full of impatience. That was another area where they had been incompatible. She was too intense, too involved with everyday life and the world around her, while Steve had skated blithely on the surface.

She was free to return to New York that morning, but she was reluctant to do so. It was only Saturday; there was no hurry as long as she returned in time to go to work Monday morning. She didn't want to sit in her apartment all weekend long and brood about being unemployed, and she wanted to see Steve again. That seemed to be what Payne wanted, too. He hadn't mentioned making arrangements for her return to New York.

She had been so exhausted that for once she had slept deeply, and as a result the shadows beneath her eyes weren't as dark as they usually were. She stared into the bathroom mirror, wondering if being fired might have been a blessing in disguise. The way she had been pushing herself had been hard on her health, burning away weight she couldn't afford to lose, drawing the skin tightly over her facial bones so that she looked both haggard and emaciated, especially without makeup. She made a face at herself in the mirror. She'd never been a beauty and never would be, but she had once been pretty. Her dark blue eyes and swath of sleek, heavy, golden-honey-brown hair were her best features, though the rest of her face could be described as ordinary.

What would Steve say if he could see her now? Would he be disappointed, and bluntly say so?

Why couldn't she get him out of her mind? It was natural to be concerned about him, to feel sharp sympathy because of his terrible injuries, but she couldn't stop herself from wondering what he would think, what he would say, about her. Not the Steve he had been before, that charming but unreliable will-o'-the-wisp, but the man he was now: harder, stronger, with the fierce will to survive that had kept him alive in the face of overwhelming odds. What would that man think of her? Would he still want her?

The thought made her face flame, and she jerked away from the mirror to turn on the shower. She must be going mad! He was an invalid. Even now, it wasn't by any means certain that he would survive, despite his fighting nature. And even if he did, he might not function as well as he had before. The surgery to save his sight might not have worked; they wouldn't know until the bandages came off. He might have brain damage. He might not be able to walk, talk or feed himself.

Helplessly she felt hot tears begin to slide down her cheeks again. Why should she cry for him now? Why couldn't she stop crying for him? Every time she thought of him she started crying, which was ridiculous, when she hadn't even been able to recognize him.

Payne was calling for her at ten, so she forced herself to stop crying and get ready. She managed that with plenty of time to spare, then found, surprisingly, that she was hungry. She usually didn't eat breakfast, sustaining herself with an endless supply of coffee until lunch, when her stomach would be burning and she wouldn't be able to eat much. But already the strain of her job was fading away, and she wanted food.

She ordered breakfast from room service and received it in a startlingly short length of time. Falling on the tray like a famine victim, she devoured the omelet and toast in record time; when Payne knocked on her door, she had been finished for almost half an hour.

Without seeming to, Payne studied her face with sharp eyes that noted and analyzed every detail. She'd been crying. This was really getting to her, and though that was exactly what they wanted, he still regretted that she had to be hurt. She also looked immeasurably better this morning, with a bit of color in her face. Her marvelous eyes were bigger and brighter than he had remembered, but part of that was the result of her tears. He only hoped she wouldn't have to shed too many more.

"I've already called to check on his condition," he reported, taking her arm. "Good news. His vital signs are improving. He's still unconscious, but his brain waves are increasing in activity and the doctors are more optimistic than they've been. He's really done better than anyone expected.''

She didn't point out that they had expected him to die, so anything was better than that. She didn't want to think about how close he had come to dying. In some way she didn't understand, Steve had become too important to her during those minutes when she had stood beside his bed and touched his arm.

The big white naval hospital was much busier that morning than it had been the night before, and two different guards stood at the doors to the ICU wing where Steve's room was located. Again they seemed to know Payne on sight. Jay wondered how many times he had been here to see Steve, and why he would have felt it necessary to be there at all. As he had that morning, he could have checked on Steve's condition by phone. Whatever Steve had gotten himself into must be extremely important, and Payne wanted to be on hand the instant he recovered consciousness, if ever.

Payne left her to enter the room on her own, saying he wanted to talk to someone. Jay nodded absently, her attention already focused on Steve. She pushed open the door and walked in, leaving Payne standing in the hall practically in midsentence. A wry, faintly regretful smile touched his mouth as he looked at the closed door; then he turned and walked briskly down the hall.

Jay stared at the man in the bed. Steve. Now that she was seeing him again, it was a little hard to accept that he *was* Steve. She had known Steve as vibrant, burning with energy; he was so still now that it threw her off balance.

He was still in the same position he'd been in the night before; the machines were still quietly humming and beeping, and fluids were still being fed into his veins through needles. The strong scent of hospital antiseptic burned her nose, and suddenly she wondered if, in some corner of his mind, he was aware of the smell. Could he hear people talking, though he was unable to respond?

She walked to the bed and touched his arm as she had the night before. The heat of his skin tingled against her fingertips despite the coolness of the controlled temperature. The mummylike expanse of bandages robbed him of individuality, and his lips were so swollen they looked more like caricatures than the lips of the man she had once kissed, loved, married, fought with and finally divorced. Only the hot bare skin of his arm made him real to her.

Did he feel anything? Was he aware of her touch?

"Steve?" she whispered, her voice trembling. It felt so funny to talk to a motionless mummy, knowing that he was probably so deep in his coma that he was unaware of everything, and that even if by some miracle he could hear her, he wouldn't be able to respond. But even knowing all that, something inside compelled her to try. "I...it's Jay." Sometimes he'd called her Jaybird, and when he'd really wanted to aggravate her he'd called her Janet Jean. Her nickname had evolved when she'd been a very young child. Her parents had called her Janet Jean, but her elder brother, Wilson, had shortened it to J.J., which had naturally become Jay. By the time she'd started school, her name was, irrevocably, Jay.

"You've been hurt," she told Steve, still stroking his arm. "But you're going to be all right. Your legs have been broken, and they're both in casts. That's why you can't move them. They have a tube in your throat, helping you to breathe, and that's why you can't talk. You can't see because you have bandages over your eyes. Don't worry about anything. They're taking good care of you here."

Was it a lie that he was going to be all right? Yet she didn't know what else to tell him. If he could hear her, she had to reassure him, not give him something else to worry about.

Clearing her throat, she began telling him about the past five years, what she'd been doing since the divorce. She even told him about being fired, and how badly she'd wanted to punch Farrell Wordlaw right in the nose. How badly she still wanted to punch him in the nose.

The voice was calm and infinitely tender. He didn't understand the words, because unconsciousness still wrapped his mind in layers of blackness, but he heard the voice, felt it, like something warm touching his skin. It made him feel less alone, that tiny, dim contact. Something hard and vital in him focused on the contact, yearning toward it, forcing him upward out of the blackness, even though he sensed the fanged monsters that waited for him, waiting to tear at his flesh with hot knives and brutal teeth. He would have to endure that before he could reach the voice, and he was very weak. He might not make it. Yet the voice reached out to him, pulling at him like a magnet, lifting him out of the deep senselessness that had held him.

"I remember the doll I got for Christmas when I was four years old," Jay said, talking automatically now. Her voice was low and dreamy. "She was soft and floppy, like a real baby, and she had curly brown hair and big brown eyes, with inch-long lashes that closed when I laid her down. I named her Chrissy, for my very best friend in the world. I lugged that doll around until she was so ragged she looked like a miniature bag lady. I slept with her, I put her on the chair beside me when I ate, and I rode miles around and around the house on my tricycle with her on the seat in front of me. Then I began to grow up, and I lost interest in Chrissy. I put her on the shelf with my other dolls and forgot about her. But the first time I saw you, Steve, I thought, 'He's got Chrissy eyes.' That's what I used to call brown eyes when I was little and didn't know my colors. You have Chrissy eyes."

His breathing seemed to be slower, deeper. She couldn't be certain, but she thought there was a different rhythm to the rise and fall of his chest. The sound of his breathing whistled in and out through the tube in his throat. Her fingers gently rubbed his arm, maintaining the small contact even though something inside her actually hurt from touching his skin.

"I almost told you a couple of times that you have Chrissy eyes, but I didn't think you'd like it." She laughed, the sound warm in the room filled with impersonal, humming machines. "You were always so protective of your macho image. A devil-may-care adventurer shouldn't have Chrissy eyes, should he?"

Suddenly his arm twitched, and the movement so startled her that she jerked her hand away, her face pale. Except for breathing, it was the first time he'd moved, even though she knew it was probably an involuntary muscle spasm. Her eyes flew to his face but there was nothing to see there. Bandages covered the upper two-thirds of his head, and his bruised lips were immobile. Slowly she reached out and touched his arm again, but he lay still under her touch, and after a moment she resumed talking to him, rambling on as she dragged up childhood memories.

Frank Payne silently opened the door and stopped in his tracks, listening to her low murmurings. She still stood by the bed; hell, she probably hadn't moved an inch from the man's side, and she had been in here—he checked his watch—almost three hours. If she had been the guy's wife, he could have understood it, but she was his *ex*-wife, and she was the one who had ended the marriage. Yet there she stood, her attention locked on him as if she were *willing* him to get better.

"How about some coffee?" he asked softly, not wanting to startle her, but her head jerked around anyway, her eyes wide.

Then she smiled. "That sounds good." She walked away from the bed, then stopped and looked back, a frown knitting her brows together. "I hate to leave him alone. If he understands anything at all, it must be awful to just lie there, trapped and hurting and not knowing why, thinking he's all alone."

"He doesn't know anything," Payne assured her, wishing it was different. "He's in a coma, and right now it's better that he stays in it."

"Yes," Jay agreed, knowing he was right. If Steve were conscious now, he would be in terrible pain.

That first faint glimmer of awareness had faded; the warm voice had gone away and left him without direction. Without that to guide him, he sank back into the blackness, into nothingness.

Frank lingered over the bad cafeteria food and the surprisingly good coffee. It wasn't great coffee; it truly wasn't even good coffee, but it was better than he'd expected. The next batch might not be as good, so he wanted to enjoy this one as long as he could. Not only that, he didn't know exactly how to bring up the subject he'd been skating around all during lunch, but he had to do it. The Man had made it plain: Jay Granger had to stay. He didn't want her to identify the patient and leave; he wanted her to become emotionally involved, at least enough to stay. And what the Man wanted, he got.

Frank had sighed. "What if she falls in love with him? Hell, you know what he's like. He has women crawling all over him. They can't resist him."

"She may be hurt," the Man had conceded, though the steel never left his voice. "But his life is on the line, and our options are limited. For whatever reason, Steve Crossfield was there when it went down. We know it, and they know it. We don't have a list of possibilities to choose from. Crossfield is the *only* choice."

He hadn't needed to say more. Since Crossfield was the only choice, his ex-wife was also the only choice by reason of being the only person who could identify him.

"Did McCoy buy it?" the Man had asked abruptly.

"The whole nine yards." Then Frank's voice had sharpened. "You don't think Gilbert McCoy is—"

The Man interrupted. "No. I know he isn't. But McCoy's a damned sharp agent. If he bought it, that means we're doing a good job of making things look the way we want."

"What happens if she's with him when he wakes up?"

"It doesn't matter. The doctors say he'll be too confused and disoriented to make sense. They're monitoring him, and they'll let us know when they start bringing him out of it. We can't keep her out of his room without it looking suspicious, but watch it. If he starts making sense, get her out of the room fast, until we can talk to him. But there's not too much danger of that happening."

"You're stirring that coffee to death." Jay's voice broke in on his thoughts, and he looked up at her, then down at the coffee. He'd been stirring it so long that it had cooled. He grimaced at the waste of not-bad coffee.

"I've been trying to think of how to ask something of you," he admitted.

Jay gave him a puzzled look. "There's only one way. Just ask."

"All right." He took a deep breath. "Don't go back to New York tomorrow. Will you stay here with Steve? He needs you. He's going to need you even more."

The words hit her hard. Steve had never needed her. She had been too intense, wanting more from him, from their relationship, than he had in him to give. He'd always wanted a slight distance between them, mentally and emotionally, claiming that she "smothered" him. She remembered the time he'd shouted those words at her; then she thought of the man lying so still in the hospital bed, and again she felt that unnerving sense of unreality.

Slowly she shook her head. "Steve is a loner. You should know that from the information you have on him. He doesn't need me now, won't need me when he wakes up, and probably won't like the idea of anyone taking care of him, least of all his ex-wife."

"He'll be very confused when he wakes up. You'll be a lifeline to him, the only face he knows, someone he can trust, someone who'll reassure him. He's in a drug-induced coma...the doctors can tell you more about it than I can. But they've said he'll be very confused and agitated, maybe even delirious. It'll help if someone he knows is there."

Practicality made her shake her head again. "I'm sorry, Mr. Payne. I don't think he'd want me there, but I wouldn't stay anyway, if I could. I was fired from my job yesterday. I have two weeks' notice to work out. I can't afford not to work those two weeks, and I have to find another job."

He whistled through his teeth. "You had a bitch of a day, didn't you?"

She had to laugh, in spite of the seriousness of the situation. "That's a good description of it, yes." The longer she knew Frank Payne, the more she liked him. There was nothing outstanding about him: he was of medium height, medium weight, with graying brown hair and clear gray eyes. His face was pleasant, but not memorable. Yet there was a steadiness in him that she sensed and trusted.

He looked thoughtful. "It's possible we can do something about your situation. Let me check into it before you book a flight back. Would you like a chance to tell your boss to go take a flying leap?"

Jay gave him a very sweet smile, and this time he was the one who laughed.

It wasn't until later that she realized the request meant they were certain Steve would live. She was back in Steve's room, standing by his bed, and she gently squeezed his arm as relief filled her. "You're going to make it," she whispered. It was almost sundown, and she had spent most of the day standing beside his bed. Several times a nurse or an orderly had requested that she step outside, but except for that and the time she had spent with Frank at lunch, she had been with Steve. She had talked until her throat was dry, talked until she couldn't think of anything else to say and silence had fallen again, but even then she had kept her hand on his arm. Maybe he knew she was there.

A nurse came in and gave Jay a curious look but didn't ask her to leave the room. Instead she checked the monitors and made notes on a pad. "It's odd," she murmured. "But maybe not. Somehow I think our boy knows when you're here. His heartbeat is stronger and his respiration rate settles down if you're here with him. When you left for lunch his vital signs deteriorated, then picked back up when you returned. I've noticed the same thing happen every time we've asked you to leave the room. Major Lunning is going to be interested in these charts."

Jay stared at the nurse, then at Steve. "He *knows* I'm here?"

"Not consciously," the nurse said hastily. "He isn't going to wake up and talk to you, not with the barbiturate dose he's getting. But who knows what he senses? You've been talking to him all day, haven't you? Part of it must be getting through, on some level. You must be really important to him, for him to respond to you like this."

The nurse left the room. Stunned, Jay looked back at Steve. Even if he somehow sensed her presence, why would it affect him like that? Yet she couldn't ignore the nurse's theory, because she had noticed herself that the rhythm of his breathing had changed. It was almost impossible for her to believe, because Steve had never needed her in any way. He had enjoyed her for a time, but something in him had kept her at a small but significant distance. Because he couldn't return love of any depth, he hadn't allowed himself to accept a deep love. All Steve had ever wanted was a superficial sort of relationship, a light, playful love that could end with no regrets. Theirs had ended in just that way, and she had seldom thought of him after they had parted. Why should she be important to him now?

Then she gave a low laugh as understanding came to her. Steve wasn't responding to *her*; he was responding to a touch and a voice meant for him personally, rather than the impartial, automatic touches and words of the healers surrounding him. Anyone else would have done just as well. Frank Payne could have stood there and talked to him with the same result.

She said as much an hour later, when Major Lunning studied the charts and stroked his jaw, occasionally glancing at her with a thoughtful expression. Frank stood to one side, careful to keep his face blank, but his sharp gaze didn't miss anything.

Major Lunning was one of the top military doctors, a man devoted to both healing and the military. He wasn't stationed at Bethesda, but he hadn't questioned the orders that had gotten him up in the middle of the night and brought him there. He and several other doctors had been given the task of saving this man's life. At the time they hadn't even known his name. Now there was a name on his chart, but they still had no inkling why he was so important to the powers that be. It didn't make any difference; Major Lunning would use whatever weapon or procedure he could find to help his patient. Right now, one of those weapons was this too-thin young woman with dark blue eyes and a full, passionate-looking mouth.

"I don't think we can ignore the pattern, Ms. Granger," the Major said frankly. "It's your voice he responds to, not mine, not Mr. Payne's, not any of the nurses'. Mr. Crossfield isn't in a deep coma. He's breathing on his own and still has reflexes. It isn't unreasonable to think that he can hear you. He may not understand and he certainly can't respond, but it's entirely possible that he hears."

"But I understood that his coma is drug-induced," Jay protested. "When people are drugged, aren't they totally unconscious?"

"There are different levels of consciousness. Let me explain his injuries more completely. He has simple fractures of both legs, nothing that will prevent him from walking normally. He has second-degree burns on his hands and arms, but the worst of the burns are on his palms and fingers, as if he grabbed a hot pipe, or perhaps put his hands up to shield his face. His spleen was ruptured, and we removed it. One lung was punctured and collapsed. But the worst of his injuries were to his head and face. His skull was fractured, and his facial bones were simply shattered.

"We performed surgery immediately to repair the damage, but to control the swelling of the brain and prevent further damage, we have to administer large doses of barbiturates. That keeps him in a coma. Now, the deeper the coma, the less the brain functions. In a deep coma the patient may not even be able to breathe for himself. The level of the coma depends in part on the patient's tolerance for the drugs, which varies from person to person. Mr. Crossfield's tolerance seems to be a bit higher than usual, so his coma isn't as deep as it could be. We haven't increased the dosage, because it hasn't been necessary. In time we'll gradually decrease the dosage and bring him out of the coma. He's going to make it on his own, but I'll tell you frankly, he definitely does better when you're with him. There's still a lot we don't know about the mind and how it affects the body, but we know it does."

"Are you saying he'll get well faster if I'm here?"

The Major grinned. "That's it in a nutshell."

Jay felt tired and confused, as if she'd spent hours in a house of mirrors trying to find her way out but instead finding only one deceitful reflection after another. It wasn't just these people, all insisting that she stay; part of it was inside. Something happened when she touched Steve, something she didn't understand. She certainly hadn't felt it before, even when they'd been married. It was as if he were more than he had been, somehow different in ways she sensed but couldn't define.

She wished they hadn't put this responsibility on her. She didn't want to stay. This strange feeling she had for Steve made her feel threatened. If she left now, it wouldn't have a chance to develop. But if she stayed... She hadn't been devastated by their divorce, five years earlier, because their love had never grown, never gone any deeper. In the end it had simply faded away. But Steve was different now; he'd changed in those five years, into a man whose power she could feel even when he was unconscious. If she fell in love with him again, she might never get over it.

But if she left, she would feel guilty because she hadn't helped him.

She needed to find another job. She had to get back to New York and begin doing something to keep her life from disintegrating. But she was tired of the frantic pushing and maneuvering, the constant dealing. She didn't want to go, but she was afraid to stay.

Frank saw the tension in her face, felt it vibrating through her. "Let's walk down to the lounge," he said, stepping forward to take her arm. "You need a break. See you later, Major."

Major Lunning nodded. "Try to talk her into staying. This guy really needs her."

Out in the hall, Jay murmured, "I hate it when people talk around me, as if I'm not there. I'm tired of being maneuvered." She was thinking of her job when she said that, but Frank gave her a sharp look.

"I don't mean to put you in a difficult position," he said diplomatically. "It's just that we badly need to talk to your husband...sorry, ex-husband. I keep forgetting. At any rate, we're willing to do whatever is possible to aid in his recovery."

Jay put her hands in her pockets, slowing her steps as she considered something. "Is Steve going to be arrested because of what he was doing, whatever it was?"

Frank didn't have any hesitation on that score. "No," he said with absolute certainty. The man was going to get nothing but the best medicine and best protection his country could provide him; Frank only wished he could tell Jay why, but that wasn't possible. "We think he was simply in the wrong place at the wrong time, an innocent bystander, if you will. But given his background, we think it likely he would have picked up on the situation. It's even possible he was trying to help when everything blew up in his face."

"Literally."

"Yes, unfortunately. Anything he can remember will help us."

They reached the lounge and he opened the door so she could precede him. They were alone, thank heavens. He went over to the coffee machine and fed coins into it. "Coffee?"

"No, thank you," Jay replied tiredly as she sat down. Her stomach was blessedly calm, and she didn't want to upset it now with the noxious brew that usually came from those machines. She hadn't noticed before how tired she was, but now fatigue was washing over her in great waves that made her feel giddy.

Frank sat down opposite her, cradling the plastic cup in his hands. "I talked to my superior, explained your situation," he began. "Would you stay if you didn't have to worry about finding another job?"

She let her eyelids droop as she rubbed her forehead in an effort to force herself to concentrate on what he'd said. She couldn't remember ever having been as tired as she was now, as if all energy had drained from her. Even her mind felt numb. All day long she had focused so fiercely on Steve that everything else had blurred, and now that she had let herself relax, exhaustion had crashed in on her, a deep lassitude that was mental as well as physical.

"I don't understand," she murmured. "I have to work at a job to make money. And even if you've somehow lined one up for me, I can't work and stay here, too."

"Staying here would be your job," Frank explained, wishing he didn't have to push her. She looked as if it were all she could do to sit erect. But maybe she would be more easily convinced now, with fatigue dulling her mind. "We'll take care of your apartment and living expenses. It's that important to us."

Her eyelids lifted and she stared at him incredulously. "You'd *pay* me to stay here?"

"Yes."

"But I don't want money to stay with him! I *want* to help him, don't you understand that?"

"But you can't, because of your financial position," Frank said, nodding. "What we're offering to do is take care of that for you. If you were independently wealthy, would you hesitate to stay?"

"Of course not! I'll do whatever I can to help him, but the idea of taking money for it is ugly."

"We aren't paying you to stay with him, we're paying you so you *can* stay with him. Do you see the difference?"

She had to be going mad, because she did see the difference between the two halves of the hair he had just split. And his eyes were so kind that she instinctively trusted him, even though she sensed a lot going on that she didn't understand.

"We'll get an apartment for you close by, so you can spend more time with him," Frank continued, his voice soothing and reasonable. "We'll also keep your New York apartment for you, so you'll have that to go back to. If you give me the word now, we can have a place here ready for you to move into on Monday."

There had to be arguments she could use, but she couldn't think of any. Frank was sweeping all obstacles out of the way; it would make her feel mean and petty if she refused to do what he wanted, when he had gone to so much trouble and they—whoever *they* were—so badly wanted her to remain.

"I'll have to go home," she said helplessly. "To New York, that is. I need more clothes, and I'll have to quit my job." Suddenly she laughed. "If it's possible to quit a job you've already been fired from."

"I'll make the travel arrangements for you."

"How long do you think I'll be here?" She was estimating a two- or three-week stay, but she wanted to be certain. She would have to do something about her mail and utilities.

Frank's gaze was level. "A couple of months, at least. Maybe longer."

"Months!"

"He'll have to have therapy."

"But he'll be conscious then. I thought you only wanted me to stay until the worst was over!"

He cleared his throat. "We'd like you to stay until he's dismissed from the hospital, at least." He had been trying to break the idea to her gradually, first by just getting her here, then convincing her that Steve needed her, then talking her into staying for the duration. He only hoped it would work.

"But why?"

"He'll need you. He'll be in pain. I haven't told you before, but he needs more surgery on his eyes. It will probably be six to eight weeks before he'll get the bandages off his eyes for good. He's going to be confused, in pain, and they'll put him through more pain in therapy. To top it all off, he won't be able to see. Jay, you're going to be his lifeline."

She sat there numbly, staring at him. It looked as if, after all this time and now that it was too late, Steve was going to need her more than either of them had ever thought.

Chapter 3

It felt strange to be back in New York. Jay had flown back on Sunday afternoon and had spent the hours packing her clothes and other personal possessions, but even her apartment had felt strange, as if she no longer belonged there. She packed automatically, her mind on the hospital room in Bethesda. How was he doing? She had spent the morning with him, constantly talking and stroking his arm, yet she felt frantic at spending such a long time away from him.

On Monday morning she dressed for work for the last time, and was conscious of a deep sense of relief. Until it had been lifted, she hadn't been aware what a burden that job had been, how desperately she had been driving herself to compete. Competition was a fine thing, but not at the expense of her health, though part of it could be blamed on her own intensity. She had channeled all her temper, interests and energy into that job, leaving nothing as an escape valve. She was lucky she hadn't developed an ulcer, rather than the less severe stress symptoms of a nervous stomach, constant headaches and disturbed sleep.

When she reached her office in the high-rise office building that housed many such firms, she scrounged around until she located a cardboard box, then swiftly cleaned out her desk, depositing all her personal items in the carton. There weren't many: a tube of lipstick, an extra pair of panty hose, a small pack of tissues, an expensive gold ballpoint pen, two small prints from the wall. She had just finished and was reaching for the phone to call Farrell Wordlaw to request a meeting when the intercom buzzed.

"Mr. Clements with EchoSystems on line three, Ms. Granger."

Jay depressed the button. "Please transfer all my calls to Duncan Wordlaw."

"Yes, Ms. Granger."

Taking a deep breath, Jay dialed Farrell on the inter-office line. Two minutes later she walked purposefully into his office.

He smiled benignly at her, as if he hadn't cut her off at the knees three days before. "You're looking well, Jay," he said smoothly. "Is something on your mind?"

"Not much," she replied. "I just wanted to let you know that I won't be able to work out the two weeks' notice you gave me. I came in this morning to clean out my desk, and I left instructions for all my calls to be transferred to Duncan."

It gave her a measure of satisfaction to see him blanch. "That's very unprofessional!" he snapped, surging to his feet. "We were counting on you to tie up the loose ends—"

"And train Duncan how to do my job," she interrupted, her voice ironic.

His tone was threatening. "Under these circumstances, I don't see how I can give you the positive recommendation I had planned. You won't work again in investment banking, not without a favorable reference."

Her dark blue eyes were steady and cold as she stared at him. "I don't plan to work in investment banking, thank you."

From that he decided she must already have another job, which took away the leverage he had been planning to use on her. Jay watched him, practically seeing the wheels turning as he considered his options. She was really leaving them in the lurch, and it was his fault, because he had fired her. "Well, perhaps I was too hasty," he said, forcing his voice to show warm paternalism. "It will certainly leave a black eye on this firm, and on you, if the matters on your desk aren't handled properly. Perhaps if I add two weeks' salary as severance pay, you'll reconsider leaving us so precipitately?"

She was supposed to fall back in line when he waved the magic carrot of money in front of her nose. "Thank you, but no," she declined. "It isn't possible. I won't be in town."

Panic began to edge into his face. If the deals she had been handling fell through, it would cost the firm millions of dollars in fees. "But you can't do that! Where will you be?"

Already Jay could imagine panicky phone calls from Duncan. She gave Farrell a cool smile. "Bethesda Naval Hospital, but I won't be accepting any calls."

He looked absolutely stunned. "The . . . the naval hospital?" he croaked.

"It's a family emergency," she explained as she walked out the door.

When she was outside again with the small cardboard box tucked under her arm, she laughed out loud from the sheer joy of being unemployed, of being able to put that look of panic in Farrell Wordlaw's eyes. It was almost as good as if she had been able to strangle him. And now she was free to return to Steve, drawn by the powerful compulsion to be with him that she could neither understand nor resist.

She had come up on a commuter flight, but because of the amount of luggage and personal furnishings she was taking back to D.C., Frank had arranged for her to take a charter flight back, and she was pleasantly surprised when he met her at the airport. "I didn't know you were going to be here!" she exclaimed.

He couldn't help smiling at her. Her eyes were sparkling like the ocean, and the lines of tension were gone from her face. She looked as if she had thoroughly enjoyed walking out of her job, and he said as much.

"It was...satisfying," she admitted, smiling at him. "How is Steve today?"

Frank shrugged. "Not as well as he was before you left." It was damned strange, but it was true. His pulse was weaker and faster, his breathing shallow and ragged. Even though he was unconscious, the man needed Jay.

Her eyes darkened with worry and she bit her lip. The urge to get back to Steve grew more intense, like invisible chains pulling at her.

But first she had to get settled in the apartment Frank had gotten for her, something that took up too much time and ate at her patience. The apartment was about half the size of her place in New York, really only two rooms—the living room and bedroom. The kitchen was a cubbyhole in a corner, and there was a crowded little alcove for dining. But the apartment was comfortable, especially since she planned to spend most of her time at the hospital, anyway. This was simply a place to sleep and have a few meals.

"I've arranged for you to have a car," Frank said as he carried in the last case. He grinned at her surprised look. "This isn't New York. You'll need a way to get around." He produced the keys from his pocket and dropped them on the table. "You can come and go at the hospital as you like. You have clearance to see Steve at any hour. I won't be around all the time, the way I have been, but whenever I'm gone another agent will be on hand."

"Are you going to the hospital with me now?"

"Now?" he asked, looking surprised in turn. "Aren't you going to unpack?"

"I can unpack later tonight. I'd rather see Steve now."

"All right." Privately he thought the plan was working a little too well, but that couldn't be helped. "Why don't you follow me in your car, so you can get used to the streets and learn the way to the hospital? Uh . . . you do drive, don't you?"

Smiling, she nodded. "I've only lived in New York for the past five years. Everywhere else I've lived, I needed a car. But I warn you, I haven't driven very much in that time, so give me a chance to get used to it again."

Actually, driving a car was a lot like riding a bicycle: once you had learned, the skill wasn't forgotten. After taking a moment to familiarize herself with the instrumentation, Jay followed Frank's car without difficulty. She had always been a steady, deliberate driver; Steve had been the daredevil, driving too fast, taking chances.

It wasn't until she stepped into his hospital room and approached the bed that she felt a knot of tension deep inside begin to loosen. She stared down at his bandaged head, with only his bruised, swollen lips and jaw visible, and her heart slammed painfully against her ribs. With infinite care she laid her fingers on his arm and began talking.

"I'm here. I had to go back to New York yesterday to pack my things and quit my job. Remind me to tell you about that someday. Anyway, I'm going to be staying here with you until you're better."

The voice was back. Slowly it penetrated the black layers that shrouded his mind, forming a tiny link with his consciousness. He still didn't understand the words, but he wasn't aware that he didn't understand. The voice simply was, like light where before there had been nothing. Sometimes the voice was calm and sometimes it rippled with amusement. He wasn't aware of the amusement, only of the change in tone.

He wanted more. He needed to get closer to the sound, and he began trying to fight his way out of the dark fog in his mind. But every time he tried, a vicious, burning pain that permeated his entire body began gnawing at him, and he would withdraw, back into the protecting blackness. Then the voice would lure him out again, until the beast attacked once more and he had to retreat.

His arm twitched the way it had once before, and again the movement startled Jay into jerking her hand away. She stopped talking and stared at him. Then, with only a slight pause, she replaced her hand on his arm and resumed what she had been saying. Her heart was pounding. It had to be an involuntary twitching of muscles forced into one position for too long. He couldn't be trying to respond, because the barbiturates they were feeding him literally shut down most of his brain functions. Most, but not all, Major Lunning had said. If Steve was aware of her, could he be trying to communicate?

"Are you awake?" she asked softly. "Can you twitch your arm again?"

His arm was motionless under her fingers, and with a sigh she again took up her rambling discourse. For a moment the feeling had been so strong that she had been convinced he was awake, despite everything they had told her.

She was back at the hospital the next morning before the sun was little more than a graying of the eastern sky. She hadn't slept well, partly because of the unfamiliar surroundings, but she couldn't place all the blame on being in a strange apartment. She had lain awake in the darkness, her mind churning as she tried to analyze and diminish her absurd conviction that, for a moment, Steve had actually been trying to reach out to her in the only way he could. But, for all her analyzing, logic meant nothing whenever she remembered the feeling that had burned through her.

Stop it! she scoffed at herself as she rode the elevator up to the ICU. Her imagination was running away with her, fueled by her own characteristic tendency to totally immerse herself in her interests. She had never been one of those cool, aloof people who could dole out their emotions in careful measure, though she had nearly wrecked her health by trying to be that way. Because she so badly wanted Steve to recover, she was imagining responses where there were none.

His room was bright with lights, despite the hour, since light or darkness hardly mattered to him in his condition. She supposed the nurses left the lights on for convenience. She closed the door, enclosing them in a private cocoon, then walked to his bed. She touched his arm. "I'm here," she said softly.

He drew a deep breath, his chest shuddering slightly.

It hit her hard, jerking at her like a rope that had suddenly been pulled taut. That deep sense of mutual awareness stretching between them, a communication that went beyond logic, beyond speech, was there again, stronger this time. He knew she was there. Somehow he recognized her. And he was fighting to reach her.

"Can you hear me?" she whispered shakily, her eyes locked on him. "Or do you somehow sense my touch? Is that what it is? Can you feel it when I touch your arm? You must be scared and confused, because you don't know what happened and you're trying to reach out, but you can't seem to make anything work. You're going to be all right, I promise you, but it's going to take time."

The voice. Something in it drew him, despite the pain that waited to claw him whenever he left the darkness. He feared the pain, but he wanted the warmth of the voice more. He wanted to be closer to it... to her. At some point too dim for him to remember or even comprehend, he had realized it was a woman's voice. It held tenderness and the only hint of security in the black swirling emptiness of his mind and world. He knew very little, but he knew that voice; some primal instinct in him recognized it and yearned for it, giving him the strength to fight the pain and the darkness. He wanted her to know he was there.

His arm twitched, the movement somehow too slow to be an involuntary spasm of cramped muscles. This time Jay didn't jerk her hand away. Instead she rubbed her fingertips over his skin, while her eyes fastened on his face.

"Steve? Did you mean to jerk your arm? Can you do it again?"

Odd. Some of the words made sense. Others made no sense at all. But she was there, closer, the voice clearer. He could see only darkness, as if the world had never been, but she was much nearer now. Pain racked his body, great waves of it that made sweat bead on his skin, but he didn't want to let go after getting this far, didn't want to fall back down into the black void.

His arm? Yes. She wanted him to move his arm. He didn't know if he could. It hurt so damned bad he didn't know if he could hold on, if he could try anymore. Would she go away if he didn't move his arm? He couldn't bear being left alone again, where everything was so cold and dark and empty, not after getting this close to her warmth.

He tried to scream, and couldn't. The pain was incredible, tearing him apart like a wild animal with fangs and claws, ripping at him.

He moved his arm.

The movement was barely there, a twitch so light she would have missed it if her hand hadn't been on his arm. He had broken out in a sweat, his chest and shoulders glistening under the bright fluorescent lights. Her heart was pounding as she leaned closer to him, her gaze riveted on his lips.

"Steve, can you hear me? It's Jay. You can't talk because you have a tube in your throat. But I'm right here. I won't leave you."

Slowly his bruised lips parted, as if he were trying to form words that refused to take shape. Jay hung over him, breathing suspended, her chest aching, as he struggled to force his lips and tongue through the motions of speech. She felt the force of both his desperation and dogged determination as, against all logic, he fought pain and drugs to be able to say one word. It was as if he *couldn't* give up, no matter what it cost him. Something in him wouldn't let him give up.

Again he tried, his swollen, discolored lips moving in agonized deliberation. His tongue moved, doing its part to shape the word that would remain soundless:

"Hurt."

The pain in her chest became acute, and abruptly she gulped in deep breaths of air. She didn't feel the tears sliding down her cheeks. Gently she patted his arm. "I'll be right back. They'll give you something so you won't hurt any longer. I'm only leaving you for a minute, and I promise I'll be back."

She flew to the door and jerked it open, stumbling into the hall. She must have been there a lot longer than it seemed, because the third shift had gone home and the first shift was back on duty. Frank and Major Lunning were standing at the nurses' station, talking in low, urgent voices that didn't carry; both men looked up as she ran toward them, and a sort of disbelieving horror filled Frank's eyes.

"He's awake!" she choked. "He said that he hurts. Please, you have to give him something—"

They bolted past her, practically shoving her to the side. Frank said, "This wasn't supposed to happen," in a voice so hard she wasn't certain it was his.

But it had to be, even though the words didn't make any sense. What wasn't supposed to happen? Steve wasn't supposed to wake up? Had they lied to her? Had they expected him to die after all? No, that couldn't be it, or Frank wouldn't have gone to so much trouble to get her to stay.

Nurses were scurrying into Steve's room, but when Jay tried to enter she was firmly escorted back into the hallway. She stood outside, listening to the muted furor of voices inside, chewing on her bottom lip and wiping the slow-welling tears from her cheeks. She should be in there. Steve needed her.

Inside the room, Frank watched as Major Lunning swiftly checked Steve's vital signs and brain-wave activity. "No doubt about it," the major confirmed absently as he worked. "He's coming out of it."

"He's on barbiturates, for God's sake!" Frank protested. "How can he come out of it until you lessen the dosage?"

"He's fighting it off. He's got one hell of a constitution, and that woman out there in the hall has a strong effect on him. Adrenaline is a powerful stimulant. Enough of it, and people perform superhuman feats of strength and endurance. His blood pressure is up and his cardiac output has increased, all signs of adrenaline stimulation."

"Are you going to increase the dosage?"

"No. The coma was to keep his brain from swelling and causing more damage. I was almost ready to begin bringing him out of it anyway. He's just moved up the timetable a little. We'll have to keep him on drugs for the pain, but he won't be in a coma. He'll be able to wake up."

"Jay thought he said that he hurt. Can he feel pain, as drugged as he is?"

"If he was conscious enough to communicate, he was conscious enough to feel pain."

"Can he understand what we're saying?"

"It's possible. I'd say he definitely hears us. Understanding is something else entirely."

"How long will it be before we can question him?"

Major Lunning gave him a severe look. "Not until the swelling in his face and throat subside enough for me to remove the trach tube. I'd say another week. And don't expect him to be a fount of information. He may never remember what happened to him, and even if he eventually does, it could be months in the future."

"Is there any danger that he might reveal some classified information to Jay?" Frank didn't want to say too much. Major Lunning knew that Steve was a very important patient, but he didn't know any of the details.

"It isn't likely. He'll be too dazed and confused, maybe even delirious, and at any rate, he still isn't able to talk. I promise you, you'll be the first to see him when we take the trach tube out."

Frank stared at the still form on the bed; he had been unconscious for so long, it was hard to accept that he could hear or feel, that he had even made an attempt to communicate. But knowing what he knew about the man, Frank realized he should have been prepared for something like this. The man never gave up, never stopped fighting, even when the odds were so strong against him that anyone else would have walked away, and because of that he had survived in many instances when others wouldn't, just as he had this time. Most people never saw past the easy grin to that enormous, fearsome determination.

"What's the likelihood of permanent brain damage?" he asked quietly, remembering that Steve could hear, and there was no way of telling how much he could understand.

Major Lunning sighed. "I don't know. He received excellent, immediate care, and that counts for a lot. It may be so minimal that you won't be able to tell the difference, but I wouldn't put my money on anything right now. I simply can't tell. The fact that he woke up and responded to Ms. Granger is totally out of the expected range. He leap-frogged over several stages of recovery. I've never seen anything like it before. Normally the stages are stupor, where it would take vigorous stimulation to rouse him at all, then delirium and extreme agitation, as if the electrical processes of his brain had gone wild. Then he would become quieter, but he'd be very confused. In the next stage he would be like an automaton. He'd be able to answer questions, but unable to perform any but the simplest physical tasks. The higher brain functions return gradually."

"And the stage he's at now?"

"He was able to communicate, as if he were in the automaton stage, but I think he's lapsed back now. It must have taken a tremendous effort for him to do that much."

"As you cut down on the barbiturates, he'll be able to communicate more?"

"Perhaps. This one incident may not be repeated. He may revert to the more classical stages of recovery."

Exasperated, Frank said, "Is there *anything* you're certain of?"

Major Lunning gave him a long, level look. "Yes. I'm certain that his recovery depends on Ms. Granger. Keep her around. He'll need her."

"Is it safe for her to be with him while you bring him off the drugs?"

"I insist on it. She may keep him calm. I sure as hell don't want him thrashing around with that tube in his chest. Will she be able to take it?"

Frank lifted his brows. "She's stronger than she looks." And Jay was oddly devoted to Steve in a way that he hadn't expected and could not quite understand. It was as if something pulled her to him, but there wasn't any basis for that kind of attraction. Maybe later, when he was awake—his effect on women had always had his superiors shaking their heads in disbelief. But he was little more than a mummy now, unable to use the charm for which he was famous, so it had to be something else.

He had to let the Man know what had happened.

Suddenly the door was shoved open and Jay entered, giving them a hard, bright look that dared them to throw her out again. "I'm staying," she said flatly, moving to Steve's side and putting her hand on his arm. Her chin lifted stubbornly. "He needs me, and I'm going to be here."

Major Lunning looked from her to Steve, then at Frank. "She's staying," he said mildly, then consulted the file in his hand. "Okay, I'm going to begin decreasing the barbiturates now, to completely bring him out of the coma. It will take from twenty-four to thirty-six hours, and I don't know how he's going to react, so I want him under full-time observation." He glanced up at Jay. "Ms. Granger—may I call you Jay?"

"Please," she murmured.

"A nurse will be in here with him most of the time until he's completely off the drugs. His reaction may be unpredictable. If anything happens, it's important that you move away from the bed and not hinder anything we have to do. Do you understand?"

"Yes."

"Can I trust you not to faint and get in the way?"

"Yes."

"All right. I'll hold you to that." His stern military gaze measured her, and he must have been reassured by what he saw, because he gave an abrupt nod of approval. "It won't be easy, but I think you'll hold up."

Jay turned her attention back to Steve, dismissing everyone else in the room as if they no longer existed. She couldn't help it. He crowded everyone else out of her consciousness, flattening them into one-dimensional cartoon characters. Nothing mattered except him, and since his agonized attempt to talk to her, the feeling was even stronger than before. It shattered her and terrified her, because it was so far outside her previous experience, but she couldn't fight it. It was so strange; Steve was exerting far more power over her now than he ever had before, when he'd had full use of his senses and body, and his full range of charm. He was motionless and, for the most part, insensate, but something deep and primal pulled her to him. Just being in the same room with him made her heart settle into a stronger rhythm, heating her flesh as her blood raced through her veins, energizing her.

"I'm back," she murmured, touching his arm. "You can go to sleep now. Don't worry, don't fight the pain...just let it go. I'm here with you, and I won't leave. I'll watch over you, and I'll be here when you wake up again."

Slowly his breathing settled into an easier rhythm and his pulse rate dropped. His blood pressure lowered. Air hissed from the tube in his throat in what would have been a faint sigh had the tube not been in place. Jay stood by his bed, her fingers lightly stroking his arm as he slept.

Where are you? He came awake, screaming silently as he clawed his way through the shrouding darkness and pain into an even greater horror. The pain was like being eaten alive, but he could bear that because despite its force, it was secondary to the horrible emptiness. God, was he buried alive? He couldn't move, couldn't see, couldn't make a sound, as if his body had died but his mind had remained alive. Terrified, he tried again to scream and couldn't.

Where was he? What had happened?

He didn't know. God help him, he didn't know!

"I'm here," the voice crooned soothingly. "I know you're frightened and don't understand, but I'm here. I'll stay with you."

The voice. It was familiar. It had been in his dreams. No, not dreams. Something deeper than that. It was in his guts, his bones, his cells, his genes, his chromosomes. It was part of him, and he focused on it with an intense, almost painful recognition. Yet it was oddly alien, connected to nothing his conscious mind could produce.

"The doctors say you're probably very confused," the voice continued. It was a calm, tender voice, with a slightly husky catch in it, as if she had been crying. She. Yes. It was definitely a woman. He had a vague memory of that voice calling to him, pulling him out of a strange, suffocating darkness.

She began reciting a litany of injuries, and he listened to her voice with fierce concentration, only gradually realizing that she was talking about him. He was injured. Not dead, not buried alive.

The tidal wave of relief exhausted him.

She was still there the next time he surfaced, and this time the initial terror was of shorter duration. Fractionally more alert, he decided she was hoarse rather than teary.

She was always there. He had no concept of time, only of pain and darkness, but gradually he became aware that there were two darknesses. One was in his mind, paralyzing his thoughts, but he could fight it. Slowly that darkness was becoming less. Then there was the other darkness, the absence of light, the inability to see. Again he would have panicked if she hadn't been there. Over and over she explained, as if she knew he would only gradually comprehend her words. He wasn't blind; there were bandages over his eyes, but he wasn't blind. His legs were broken, but he would walk again. His hands were burned, but he would use them again. There was a tube in his throat to help him breathe; soon the tube would be removed and he would talk again.

He believed her. He didn't know her, but he trusted her.

He tried to think, but words boomeranged around in his head until he couldn't make sense of them. He didn't know... There was so much he didn't know. He didn't know anything. But he couldn't catch the words and arrange them in proper order so he'd know what it was he didn't know. It just didn't make sense, and he was too tired to fight.

Finally he woke to find that his thoughts were clearer, the confusion different, because the words made sense even though nothing else did. She was there. He could feel her hand on his arm, could hear her slightly hoarse voice. Did she stay with him all the time? How long had it been? It seemed forever, and it nagged at him, because he felt as if he should know exactly.

There was so much he wanted to know, and he couldn't ask. Frustration ate at him, and his arm flexed beneath her fingers. God, what would happen to him if she left? She was the one link he had to the world outside the prison of his own body, his link to sanity, the only window in his world of darkness. And suddenly the need to know coalesced inside him into a single thought, a single word: *Who?*

His lips formed the word and gave birth to it in silence. Yes, that was the word he'd wanted. Everything he wanted to know was summed up in that one small word.

Jay gently laid her fingers over his swollen lips. "Don't try to talk," she whispered. "Let's use a spelling system. I'll recite the alphabet, and whenever I get to the letter you want, twitch your arm. I'll do the alphabet over and over until we've spelled out whatever you want to say. Can you do that? One twitch for yes, two twitches for no."

She was exhausted; it had been two days since the first time he had woken up, and she had been with him for most of that time. She had talked until her voice was almost gone, her words giving him a bridge out of his coma into reality. She knew when he was awake, sensed that he was terrified, felt his struggle to understand what had happened. But this was the first time his lips had moved, and she was so tired she hadn't been able to grasp what he'd been trying to say. The alphabet game was the only way she could think of for them to communicate, but she didn't know if he'd be able to concentrate enough for it to work.

His arm twitched. Just once.

She drew a deep breath, forcing her exhaustion away. "All right. Here we go. A...B...C...D..."

She began to give up hope as she slowly ran through the alphabet and his arm lay motionless under her hand. It had been a long shot, anyway. Major Lunning had said it could be days before Steve's mind would be clear enough for him to really understand what was going on around him. Then she said "W," and his arm twitched.

She stopped. "W?"

His arm twitched. Once, for "Yes."

Joy shot through her. "Okay, W is the first letter. Let's go for the second one. A...B..."

His arm twitched on the H.

And again on the O.

He stopped there.

Jay was astounded. "*Who?* Is that it? You want to know who I am?"

His arm twitched. *Yes.*

He didn't know; he really didn't know. She couldn't remember if she had mentioned who she was, except when she had first begun talking to him. Had she thought he would remember her voice after not seeing him for five years?

"I'm Jay," she said gently. "Your ex-wife."

Chapter 4

He was very still. Jay had the impression that she could feel him withdrawing, though he didn't move a muscle. A surprisingly sharp pain bloomed inside, and she chided herself for it. What had she expected? He couldn't get up and hug her, he couldn't speak, and he was probably exhausted. She knew all that, yet she still had the feeling that he was pulling back from her. Did he resent being so dependent on her? Steve had always been aloof in a curious sort of way, holding people away from him. Or maybe he resented the fact that she was here with him now, rather than some impersonal nurse. After all, a certain degree of independence remained when the service was detached, done because it was a job. Personal service carried a price that couldn't be paid in dollars, and Steve wouldn't like that.

She schooled her voice to a calmness she didn't feel. "Do you have any more questions?"

Two twitches. *No.*

She had been pushed away so many times that she recognized it now, even as subtle and unspoken as the message was. It hurt. She closed her eyes, fighting for the control that would let her speak again. It was a moment before she managed it. "Do you want me to stay in here with you?"

He was still for a long moment. Then his arm twitched. And twitched again. *No.*

"All right. I won't bother you again." Her control was shot, her voice thin and taut. She didn't wait to see if he made any response, but turned and walked out. She felt almost sick. Even now, it was an effort to walk out and leave him alone. She wanted to stay with him, protect him, fight for him. God, she would even take his pain on herself if she could. But he didn't want her. He didn't need her. She had been right all along in thinking that he wouldn't appreciate her efforts on his behalf, but the pull she thought she had felt between them had been so strong that she had ignored her own good sense and let Frank talk her into staying.

Well, at least she should let Frank know that her sojourn here was over, and that she would be leaving. Her problems hadn't changed; she still had to find a new job. Digging a coin out of her purse, she found a pay phone and called the number Frank had given her. He hadn't spent as much time at the hospital these past two days as he had before; in fact, he hadn't been there at all that day.

He answered promptly, and hearing his calm voice helped. "This is Jay. I wanted you to know that my job is over. Steve doesn't want me to stay with him anymore."

"What?" He sounded startled. "How do you know?"

"He told me."

"How in blue blazes did he do that? He can't talk, and he can't write. Major Lunning said he should still be pretty confused, anyway."

"He's a lot better this morning. We worked out a system," she explained tiredly. "I recite the alphabet, and he signals with his arm when I get to the letter he wants. He can spell out words and answer questions. One twitch means 'Yes' and two twitches means 'No.'"

"Have you told Major Lunning?" Frank asked sharply.

"No, I haven't seen him. I just wanted to let you know that Steve doesn't want me with him."

"Have Lunning paged. I want to talk to him. Now."

For such a pleasant man, Frank could be commanding when he chose, Jay thought as she went to the nurses' station and requested that Major Lunning be paged. It was five minutes before he appeared, looking tired and rumpled, and dressed in surgicals. He listened to Jay, then, without a word, walked to the pay phone and talked quietly to Frank. She couldn't make out what he was saying, but when he hung up he called a nurse and went directly into Steve's room.

Jay waited in the hallway, struggling to handle her feelings. Though she knew Steve and had expected this, it still hurt. It hurt more now than it had when they had divorced. She felt oddly...betrayed, and bereft, as if she had lost part of herself, and she hadn't felt that way before. She hadn't felt so strongly connected to him before. Well, this was just another classic example of her own intensity leading her to read things into a situation that simply weren't there. Would she ever learn?

Major Lunning was in Steve's room a long time, and a phalanx of nurses came and went. Within half an hour Frank arrived, his face taut and set. He squeezed Jay's arm comfortingly as he went past, but he didn't stop to talk. He, too, disappeared into Steve's room, as if something dreadfully important were going on in there.

Jay moved to the visitors' lounge, sitting quietly with her hands folded in her lap while she tried to plan what she should do next. Return to New York, obviously, and get a job. But the idea of hurling herself back into the business world left her cold. She didn't want to go back. She didn't want to leave Steve. Even now, she didn't want to leave him.

Almost an hour later Frank found her in the lounge. He looked at her sharply before going to the coffee machine and

buying two cups. Jay looked up and managed a smile fo
him as he approached. "Do I really look as if I need that?
she asked wryly, nodding toward the coffee.

He extended a cup toward her. "I know. It tastes wors
than it looks. Drink it anyway. If you don't need it now, yo
will in a minute."

She took the cup and sipped the hot liquid, grimacing a
the taste. It was a mystery how anyone could take simpl
water and coffee and make them taste so horrible. "Wh
will I need it in a minute? It's over, isn't it? Steve told me t
go away. It's obvious that he doesn't want me here, so m
presence will only upset him and slow his recovery."

"It isn't over," Frank said, looking down at his own cof
fee, and his flat tone made Jay look at him sharply. H
looked haggard, with worry etching new lines into his face

A cold chill ran down her spine and she sat up straight
"What's wrong?" she asked. "Has he relapsed?"

"No."

"Then what's wrong?"

"He doesn't remember," Frank said simply. "Anything
He has amnesia."

Frank had been right; she did need the coffee. She dran
that cup, then got another one. Her head was reeling, an
she felt as if she'd been punched in the stomach. "What els
can go wrong?" she asked, talking mostly to herself, bu
Frank knew what she meant.

He sighed. They hadn't counted on this. They had needed
him awake, able to talk, able to understand what needed to
be done. This latest development had thrown a monkey
wrench into the whole plan. He didn't even know who he
was! How could he protect himself if he didn't know who he
had to be on guard against? He couldn't recognize friends
or enemies.

"He's been asking for you," Frank said, taking her hand.
She started, already rising to her feet, but he tugged on her

hand and she sank back into her chair. "We've been asking him a lot of questions," he continued. "We used your system, though it takes a while. When you told him you were his ex-wife, it confused him, scared him. He couldn't remember you, and he didn't know what to do. Remember, he's still easily confused. It's hard for him to concentrate, though he's getting better fast."

"Are you certain he's asking for me?" Jay asked, her heart pounding. Out of everything he had said, her emotions had centered on his first sentence.

"Yes. He spelled out your name over and over."

The instinct to go to him was so strong it was almost painful. She forced herself to sit still, to understand more. "He has total amnesia? He doesn't remember anything?"

"He doesn't even know his own name." Frank sighed again, a heavy sound. "He doesn't remember anything about the explosion or why he was there. Nothing. A total blank. Damn it!" The last expressed his helpless frustration.

"What does Major Lunning think?"

"He said total amnesia is extremely rare. More often it's a sort of spot amnesia that blocks out the accident itself and anything that happened a short while before it. With the head trauma Steve suffered, amnesia wasn't that unexpected, but this..." He made a helpless gesture.

She tried to think of what she had read about amnesia, but all that came to mind was the dramatic use often made of it on soap operas. Invariably the amnesiac recovered his full memory during a highly dramatic moment, just in time to prevent a murder or keep from being murdered himself. It was good melodrama, but that was all it was.

"Will he regain his memory?"

"Probably. Part of it, at least. There's no way to be certain. It might start coming back almost immediately, or it could take months before he begins remembering anything.

Major Lunning said that his memory will come back in bits and pieces, usually the oldest memories first.''

Might. Probably. Could. Usually. What it all added up to was that they simply didn't know. In the meantime Steve lay in his bed, unable to talk, unable to see, unable to move. All he could do was hear and think. What would it be like to be so cut adrift from everything familiar, even himself? He had no point of reference for anything. The thought of the inner terror he must be feeling squeezed her heart.

"Are you still willing to stay?" Frank asked, his clear eyes filled with concern. "Knowing that it might take months or even years?"

"Years?" she echoed faintly. "But you only wanted me to stay until the surgery on his eyes was completed."

"We didn't know then that he wouldn't remember anything. Major Lunning said that being around familiar things and people would help stimulate his memory, give him a feeling of stability."

"You want me to stay until he regains his memory," Jay stated, putting it into words. The idea frightened her. The longer she stayed with Steve, the more strongly she reacted to him. What would happen to her if she fell in love with him far more deeply than she had the first time, only to lose him again when he returned to his footloose life? She was afraid that she already cared too much to simply walk away. How could she walk away when he needed her?

"He needs you," Frank said, echoing her thoughts. "He's asking for you. He responds to you so strongly that he keeps confounding Major Lunning's predictions. And we need you, Jay. We need you to help him in any way you can, because we need to know what he knows."

"If sentiment won't get me, try patriotism?" she asked tiredly, leaning her head back against the padded orange vinyl chair. "It wasn't necessary. I won't leave him. I don't know what's going to happen, or how we'll handle it if he doesn't get his memory back soon, but I won't leave him."

She got up and walked out, and Frank sat there for a moment staring at the cup still in his hands. From what she'd just said, he knew that Jay sensed she was being manipulated, but she was willing to let them do it because Steve was so important to her. He had to talk to the Man about this latest development, and he wondered what would happen. They had counted on Steve's willing participation, on his talents and skills. Now they had to let him walk out on the streets as helpless as a baby because he couldn't recognize the dangers, or take the risk of telling him things that could set back his recovery. Major Lunning had been adamant that upsetting him would be the worst thing they could do. He needed quiet and tranquillity, a stable emotional base; his memory would return faster under those conditions. No matter what decision the Man reached, Steve was at risk. And if Steve was at risk, so was Jay.

It was hard for Jay to enter Steve's room after the emotional battering she had taken. She needed time to get herself under control, but she felt the pull between them again; it was growing so strong she no longer had to be in the room with him, touching him. He needed her right now, far more than she needed time. She opened the door and felt his attention center on her, though not even his head moved. It was as if he were holding his breath.

"I'm back," she said quietly, walking to his bed and putting her hand on his arm. "It seems I can't stay away."

His arm twitched urgently, several times, and she got the message. "All right," she said, and began reciting the alphabet.

Sorry.

What could she say? Deny that she'd been upset? He would know better. He felt the pull just as she did, because he was on the other end of that invisible rope. He turned his face slightly toward her, his bruised lips parted as he waited for her answer.

"It's all right," she said. "I didn't realize what a shock I had just given you."

Yes.

It was odd how much expression he could put in a single motion, but she felt his wryness and sensed that he was still shocked. Shocked, but in control. His control was astounding.

She began spelling again.

Afraid.

The admission hit her hard; it was something the old Steve never would have admitted, but the man he had become was so much stronger that he could admit it and lose nothing of his strength. "I know, but I'll stay with you as long as you want me," she promised.

What happened? He made it a question by a slight upward movement of his arm.

Keeping her voice calm, Jay told him about the explosion but didn't give him any of the details. Let him think that he'd simply been in an accident.

Eyes?

So he hadn't understood everything she'd told him before and needed reassuring. "You'll have more surgery on your eyes, but the prognosis is good. You'll see again, I promise."

Paralyzed?

"No! You've broken both legs and they're in casts. That's why you can't move them."

Toes.

"Your toes?" she asked in bewilderment. "They're still there."

His lips moved in a very slight, painful smile. *Touch them.*

She bit her lip. "Okay." He wanted her to touch his toes so he'd know he still had feeling in them, as a reassurance that he wasn't paralyzed. She walked to the foot of the bed and firmly folded her hands over his bare toes, letting his cool flesh absorb the heat from her palms. Then she returned to his side and touched his arm. "Did you feel that?"

Yes. Again he gave that painful fraction of a smile.

"Anything else?"

Hands.

"They're burned, and in bandages, but they're not third-degree burns. Your hands will be fine."

Chest. Hurts.

"You have a collapsed lung, and a tube in your chest. Don't do any tossing around."

Funny.

She laughed. "I didn't know anyone could be silent and sarcastic at the same time."

Throat.

"You have a trach tube because you weren't breathing well."

Face broken?

She sighed. He wanted to know, not be protected. "Yes, some bones in your face were broken. You aren't disfigured, but the swelling made it hard for you to breathe. As soon as the swelling goes down, they'll take the trach tube out."

Lift the sheet and check my—

"I will not!" she said indignantly, halting her spelling when she realized where his words were heading. Then she had to laugh because he actually managed to look impatient. "Everything is still there, believe me."

Functional?

"You'll have to find that out on your own!"

Prissy.

"I'm not prissy, and you behave or I'll have a nurse change your tube. Then you'll find out the hard way what you want to know." As soon as she said the words she felt herself blushing, and it didn't help that he was smiling again. She hadn't meant to sound the way she had.

The effort of concentrating for so long had tired him, and after a minute he spelled *Sleep*.

"I didn't mean to tire you out," she murmured. "Go to sleep."

Stay?

"Yes, I'm staying. I won't go back to my apartment without telling you." Her throat felt thick at his need for reassurance, and she stood by the bed with her hand on his arm until his breathing changed into the deep, steady rhythm of sleep.

Even then she was reluctant to take her hand away, and she stood beside him for a long time. A smile kept curving her lips. His personality was so strong that it came through despite his limited means of communication. He wanted the truth about his condition, not vague promises or medical double-talk. He might not know his name, but that hadn't changed the man he was. He was strong, much stronger than he had been before. Whatever had happened to him in the past five years had tempered him, like steel subjected to the hottest fires. He was harder, stronger, tougher, his will-power so fierce it was like an energy field emanating from him. Oh, he had been a charming rascal before, devilishly reckless and daring, with a glint in his eye that had turned many feminine heads. But now he was... dangerous.

The word startled her, but when she examined it, she re-alized that it described exactly the man he had become. He was a dangerous man. She didn't feel threatened by him, but danger didn't necessarily constitute a threat. He was dangerous because of his steely, implacable will; when this man decided to do something, it wasn't safe to get in his way. At some time in the past five years, something had drastically changed him and she wasn't sure she wanted to know what it was. It must have been something cataclysmic, something awful, to have so focused his character and determination. It was as if he had been stripped down to the bare essentials of human existence, forced to discard all his personality traits that weren't necessary to survival and adopt new ones that were. What was left was hard and pure, unbreakable and curiously resilient. This was a man who wouldn't admit defeat; he didn't know what it was.

Her heart was beating heavily as she stood looking down at him, her attention so focused on him that they might have been the only two people in the world. He awed her, and he attracted her so strongly that she jerked her hand away from his arm as soon as the thought formed. Dear God! She would be a fool to let herself get caught in that trap again. Even more now than before, Steve was essentially alone, his personality so honed that he was complete unto himself. She had walked away relatively unscathed before, but what would happen to her this time if she let herself care too much? She felt scared, not only because she was teetering on the edge of heartbreak, but because she was even daring to think of getting too close to him. It was like watching a panther in a cage, standing outside the bars and knowing you were safe, but feeling the danger that was barely restrained.

Making love with him before had been ... fun, passionate in a playful way. What would it be like now? Was the playfulness gone? She thought it must be. His lovemaking would be intense and elemental now, as he was, like getting caught up in a storm.

She became aware that she could barely breathe, and she forced herself to walk away from his bed. She didn't want him to mean that much to her. And she was very much afraid that he already did.

"What do we do?" Frank asked quietly, his clear eyes meeting shuttered black ones.

"We play out the hand," the Man answered just as quietly. "We have to. If we do anything out of the ordinary now, it could tip someone off, and he isn't able to recognize his enemies."

"Any luck in tracing Piggot?"

"We lost him in Beirut, but we know he hooked up with his old pals. He'll surface again, and we'll be waiting."

"We just have to keep our guy alive until we can neutralize Piggot," Frank said, his tone turning glum.

"We'll do it. One way or the other, we have to keep Piggot's cutthroats from getting their hands on him."

"When he gets his memory back, he isn't going to like what we've done."

A brief smile touched the Man's hard mouth. "He'll raise mortal hell, won't he? But I'm not taking any chance with the protected-witness program until he's able to look out for himself, and maybe not even then. It's been penetrated before, and could be again. Everything hinges on getting Piggot."

"You ever wish you were back in the field, so you could hunt him yourself?"

The Man leaned back, hooking his hands behind his head. "No. I've gotten domesticated. I like going home at night to Rachel and the kids. I like not having to watch my back."

Frank nodded, thinking of the time when the Man's back had been a target for every hit man and terrorist in the business. He was safe now, out of the mainstream . . . as far as was generally known. A very small group of people knew otherwise. The Man officially didn't exist; even the people who followed his orders didn't know the orders came from him. He was buried so deeply in the bowels of bureaucracy, protected by so many twists and turns, that there was no way to connect him to the job he actually did. The President knew about him, but Frank doubted the vice president did, or any department secretary, the Chiefs of Staff or the head of the agency that employed him. Whoever was President next might not know about him. The Man decided for himself whom he could trust; Frank was one of those people. And so was the man in Bethesda Naval Hospital.

* * *

Two days later, they took the tube out of Steve's chest because his collapsed lung had healed and reinflated. When they let Jay into his room again she hung over the side of his bed, stroking his arm and shoulder until his breathing settled down and the fine mist of perspiration on his body began to dry.

"It's over, it's over," she murmured.

He moved his arm, a signal that he wanted to spell, and she began reciting the alphabet.

Not fun.

"No," she agreed.

More tubes?

"There's one in your stomach, for feeding you." She felt his muscles tense as if in anticipation of the pain he knew would come, and he spelled out a terse expletive. Her hand moved over his chest in sympathy, feeling the coarseness of his hair as it grew out, and avoiding the wound where the tube had entered his body.

He took a deep breath and forced himself to slowly relax. *Raise head.*

It took her a few seconds to figure that one out. He must be incredibly sore from lying flat for so long, unable to shift his legs or lift his arms. The only time his arms were moved was when the bandages were changed. She pressed the control that raised the head of the bed, lifting him only an inch or so at a time, keeping her hand on his arm so he could signal her when he wanted her to stop. He took several more deep breaths as his weight shifted to his hips and lower back, then moved his arm to halt her. His lips moved in silent curse, his muscles tightening against the pain, but after a moment he adjusted and began to relax again.

Jay watched him, her deep blue eyes mirroring the pain he felt, but he was improving daily, and seeing the improvements filled her with heady joy. The swelling in his face was subsiding; his lips were almost normal again, though dark bruises still stained his jaw and throat.

She could almost feel his impatience. He wanted to talk, he wanted to see, he wanted to walk, to be able to shift his own weight in the bed. He was imprisoned in his body and he didn't like it. She thought it must be close to hell to be cut off from his own identity as he was, as well as being so completely constrained by his injuries. But he wasn't giving in; he asked more questions every day, trying to fill the void of memories by making new ones, maybe hoping that some magic word would take him back to himself. Jay talked to him even when he didn't ask questions, idle conversation that, she hoped, gave him basic information and perspective. Even if it just filled the silence, that was something. If he didn't want her to talk he would tell her.

A movement of his arm alerted her, and she began the alphabet.

When married?

She caught her breath. It was the first personal question he'd asked her, the first time he'd wanted to know about their past relationship. "We were married for three years," she managed to say calmly. "We divorced five years ago."

Why?

"It wasn't a hostile divorce," she mused. "Or a hostile marriage. I guess we simply wanted different things out of life. We grew apart, and finally the divorce seemed more like a formality than any wrenching change in our lives."

What did you want?

Now that was a twenty-thousand-dollar question. What did she want? She had been certain of her life up until the Friday when she had been fired and Frank Payne had brought Steve back into her life. Now she wasn't certain at all; too many changes had happened all at once, jolting her life onto a different track entirely. She looked at Steve and felt him waiting patiently for her answer.

"Stability, I guess. I wanted to settle down more than you did. We had fun together, but we weren't really suited to each other."

Children?

The thought startled her. Oddly, when they had been married, she hadn't been in any hurry to start a family. "No, no children." She hadn't been able to visualize having Steve's children. Now...oh God, now the idea shook her to the bones.

Remarried?

"No, I've never remarried. I don't think you have, either. When Frank notified me of your accident, he asked if you had any other relatives or close friends, so you must have stayed single."

He'd been listening closely, but his interest suddenly sharpened. She could feel it, like a touch against her skin.

No family?

"No. Your parents are dead, and if you had any relatives, I never knew about them." She skated around telling him that he'd been orphaned at an early age and raised in foster homes. Not having a family seemed to disturb him, though he'd never given any indication that it bothered him while they had been married.

He lay very still and the line of his mouth was grim. She sensed there was a lot he wanted to ask her, but the very complexity of his questions stymied him. To get his mind off the questions he couldn't ask and the answers he wouldn't like, she began to tell him about how they had met, and slowly his mouth relaxed.

"...and since it was our first date, I was a little stiff. More than a little stiff, if you want the truth. First dates are torment, aren't they? It had been raining off and on all day, and water was standing in the streets. We walked out to your car, and a passing truck hit this huge puddle just as we reached the curb. We were both drenched, from the head down. And we stood there laughing at each other like complete fools. I don't even want to think what I looked like, but you had muddy water dripping off your nose."

His lips were twitching, as if it hurt him to smile but he couldn't stop the movement. *What did we do?*

She chuckled. "There wasn't a lot we could do, looking the way we did. We went back to my apartment, and while our clothes were washing we watched television and talked. We never did make it to the party we'd been going to. One date led to another, and five months later we were married."

He asked one question after another, like a child listening to fairy tales and wanting more. Knowing that he was reaching for the part of himself that was lost due to the blankness of his memory, she tirelessly recounted places they had gone and the things they'd done, people they had known, hoping that some little detail would provide the spark needed to bring it all back. Her voice began to grow hoarse, and finally he managed a small shake of his head.

Sorry.

She pressed his arms, understanding. "Don't worry," she said softly. "It will all come back. It will just take time."

But the days passed and still his memory didn't return—not even a glimmer of a link to the past. She could feel his intense concentration on every word she uttered, as if he were willing himself to remember. Even now, his control was phenomenal; he never allowed himself to become frustrated or lose his temper. He just kept trying, keeping his feelings under control as if he sensed that any emotional upheaval could set his recovery back. Total recovery was his aim, and he worked toward it with a single-minded concentration that never wavered.

Frank was there the day they took the trach tube from Steve's throat, and he waited in the hall with Jay, holding her hand. She looked at him questioningly, but he merely shook his head. Several minutes later a hoarse cry of pain from Steve's room made her jerk, and Frank's hand tight-

ened on hers. "You can't go in there," he said softly.
"They're removing his stomach tube, too."

The cry had been Steve's; the first sound he'd made had
been one of pain. She began to tremble, every instinct she
had screaming at her to go to him, but Frank held her still.
There were no other sounds from the room, and finally the
door opened and the doctors and nurses exited. Major
Lunning was last, and he paused to talk to Jay.

"He's all right," he said, smiling a little at her tense face.
"He's breathing just fine, and talking. I won't tell you what
his first words were. But I want to warn you that his speaking voice won't be the way you remember it; his larynx was
damaged, and his voice will always sound hoarse. It will
improve some, but he'll never sound the way he did before."

"I'd like to talk to him now," Frank said, looking down
at Jay, and she understood that there were things he wanted
to tell Steve, even though Steve didn't remember what had
happened.

"Good luck," Major Lunning said, smiling wryly at
Frank. "He doesn't want you, he wants Jay, and he was
pretty autocratic about it."

Knowing just how autocratic he could be, Frank wasn't
surprised. But he still needed to ask Steve some questions,
and if this was his lucky day, the questions just might trigger some return of memory. Patting Jay's hand again, he
went into Steve's room and firmly closed the door behind
him.

Less than a minute later, he opened the door and looked
at Jay, his expression both frustrated and amused. "He
wants you, and he isn't cooperating until he gets you."

"Did you think I would?" a raspy voice demanded behind him. "Jay, come here."

She began trembling again at the sound of that rough,
deep voice, so much rougher and deeper than she remembered. It was almost gravelly, and it was wonderful. Her

knees felt rubbery as she crossed the room to him, but she wasn't aware of actually walking. She was just there, somehow, clinging to the railing of his bed in an effort to hold herself upright. "I'm here," she whispered.

He was silent a moment; then he said, "I want a drink of water."

She almost laughed aloud, because it was such a mundane request that could have been made of anyone, but then she saw the tension in his jaw and lips and realized that, again, he was checking out his condition, and he wanted her with him. She turned to the small plastic pitcher that was kept full of crushed ice, which she used to keep his lips moist. The ice had melted enough that she was able to pour the glass half full of water. She stuck a straw into it and held it to his lips.

Gingerly he sucked the liquid into his mouth and held it for a moment, as if letting it soak into his membranes. Then, slowly, he swallowed, and after a minute he relaxed. "Thank God," he muttered hoarsely. "My throat still feels swollen. I wasn't sure I could swallow, and I sure as hell didn't want that damned tube back."

Behind Jay, Frank turned a smothered laugh into a cough.

"Anything else?" she asked.

"Yes. Kiss me."

Chapter 5

When she opened the door to Steve's room the next morning, he turned his head on the pillow and said, "Jay." His voice was harsh, almost guttural, and she wondered if he'd just awakened.

She paused, her attention caught as she stared at his bandaged eyes. "How did you know?" The nurses were in and out, so how could he have guessed her identity?

"I don't know," he said slowly. "Maybe your smell, or just the feel of you in the room. Maybe I recognize the rhythm of your walk."

"My smell?" she asked blankly. "I'm not using perfume, so if you smell me from that distance something's wrong!"

His lips curved in a smile. "It's a fresh, faintly sweet smell. I like it. Do I get a good-morning kiss?"

Her heart gave a giant leap, just as it had the day before when he'd demanded that she kiss him. She had given him a light, tender kiss, barely brushing her lips against his, while Frank, in the background, had pretended to be invisible; but it had taken her pulse a good ten minutes to settle down afterward. Now, even while her mind shouted at her to be cautious, she crossed the room to him and bent down to give him another light kiss, letting her lips linger for only a second. But when she started to draw away, he increased the pressure, his mouth molding itself to hers, and her heart slammed wildly against her rib cage as excitement shot through her.

"You taste like coffee," she managed to say when she finally forced herself to stand upright again, breaking the contact.

His lips had been slightly parted, with a disturbing sensuality, but at her words they took on a smug line. "They wanted me to drink tea or apple juice—" he made it sound like hemlock "—but I talked them into letting me have coffee."

"Oh?" she asked dryly. "How? By refusing to drink anything until you had your coffee?"

"It worked," he said, not sounding at all repentant. She could imagine how helpless the nurses were against his relentless will.

Despite the fact that she no longer needed to communicate with him in their old way, her hand went to his arm in habit, and she was so used to the contact that she didn't notice it. "How are you feeling?" she asked, then winced at the triteness of the question, but she was still rattled from the effects of his kiss.

"Like hell."

"Oh."

"How long have I been here?"

To her surprise, she had to stop and count the days. She had become so involved with him that time had ceased to mean anything, and it was difficult to recall. "Three weeks."

"Then I have three more weeks in these casts?"

"I think so, yes."

"All right." He said it as if giving his permission, and she felt that he would give them three weeks and not one day longer, or he would take the casts off himself. He lifted his left arm. "I'm minus a couple of needles today. They took the IVs out about an hour ago."

"I hadn't even noticed!" she exclaimed, smiling a little at the note of pride in his ruined voice. She wondered if she would ever get used to its harshness, but at the same time tiny shivers went down her spine every time she heard it.

"And I refused the pain medication. I want my head clear. There were a lot of questions I wanted to ask before, but it took so much time and effort, and my brain was so foggy from the drugs, that it was just too much trouble. Now I want to know what's going on. Where am I? I've heard you call the doctor Major, so I know I'm in a military hospital. The question is, why?"

"You're in Bethesda," she said.

"A naval hospital?" Astonishment roughened his voice even more.

"Frank said you were brought here for security reasons. There are guards posted at every entrance to this wing. And this was a central location for all the surgeons they pulled in for you."

"Major Lunning isn't navy," he said sharply.

"No." It was astonishing that he could lose the most basic of memories, those of himself, yet retain the knowledge that Bethesda was a naval hospital and that major wasn't a navy rank. She watched the stillness of his mouth as he studied the implications of what she had just told him.

"Then someone with a lot of influence wanted me here. Langley, probably."

"Who?"

"Company headquarters, baby. CIA." She felt a chill of dread as he continued, "Maybe the White House, but Langley is the most likely bet. What about Frank Payne?"

"He's FBI. I trust him," she said steadily.

"Damn, this is getting deep," he muttered. "All these different departments and military branches coordinating just isn't normal. What's going on? Tell me about the explosion."

"Didn't Frank tell you?"

"I didn't ask for or volunteer any information. I didn't know him."

Yes, that was like Steve. He had always held back, watching cautiously, though she had already married him before she began noticing that particular trait. He used his charm like a shield, so that most people would have described him as outgoing and spontaneous, when in fact he was just the opposite. He had held people away, not trusting them and not allowing anyone close to him, but they never noticed, because he was such an actor. Now she sensed that the shield was gone. People could take him as he was or leave him; he didn't care. It was a hard attitude, but she found that she liked it better. It was real, without pretense or subterfuge. And for the first time, he was letting her get close to him. He needed her, trusted her. Perhaps it was only because of the extenuating circumstances, but it was happening, and it stunned her.

"Jay?" he prompted.

"I don't know exactly what happened," she explained. "I don't know why you were there. They don't know either."

"Who is 'they'?"

"Frank. The FBI."

"And whoever else he's working for," he added dryly. "Go on."

"Frank told me that you weren't doing anything illegal that they know of. Perhaps you were only an innocent bystander, but you have a reputation for sniffing out trouble, and they think you might know something about what happened to their operation. They had set up a sting, or whatever you want to call it, but someone had planted a bomb at the meeting site. You were the only survivor."

"What kind of sting?"

"I don't know. All Frank has said is that it involved national security."

"And they're afraid their guy's cover was blown, but they don't know, because the players on the other side were disintegrated, too," he said, as if to himself. "It could have been a double double-cross, and the bomb was meant for the others. Damn! No wonder they want me to get my memory back! But all that doesn't explain one thing. Why are you involved?"

"They brought me here to identify you," she said, absently stroking his arm as she had for so many hours.

"Identify me? Didn't they know?"

"Not for certain. Part of your driver's license was found, but they still weren't certain if you were...you, or their agent. Apparently you and the agent were about the same height and weight, and your hands were burned, so they weren't able to get your fingerprints for identification." She paused as something nagged at her memory, but she couldn't bring the elusive detail into focus. For a moment it was close; then Steve's next question splintered her concentration.

"Why did they ask you? Wasn't there anyone else who could identify me? Or did we stay close after our divorce?"

"No, we didn't. It was the first time I'd seen you in five years. You've always been pretty much a loner. You weren't the type for bosom buddies. And you don't have any family, so that left me."

He moved restlessly, his mouth drawing into a hard line as he uttered a brief, explicit curse. "I'm trying to get a handle on this," he said tersely. "And I keep running into this damned blank wall. Some of what you tell me seems so familiar, and I think, yeah, that's me. Then part of it is as if you're telling me about some stranger, and I wonder if I really know. Hell, how *can* I know?" he finished with raw frustration.

Her fingers glided over his arm, giving him what comfort she could. She didn't waste her breath mouthing platitudes because she sensed they would only make him furious. As it was, he had already used up his small store of energy with the questions he had asked her, and he lay there in silence for several minutes, his chest rising and falling too quickly. Finally the rhythm of his breathing slowed, and he muttered, "I'm tired."

"You've pushed yourself too far. It's only been three weeks, you know."

"Jay."

"What?"

"Stay with me."

"I will. You know I will."

"It's…strange. I can't even picture your face in my mind, but part of me knows you. Maybe biblical knowledge goes deeper than mere memory."

His harsh voice gave rough edges to the words, but Jay felt as if an electrical charge had hit her body, making her skin tingle. Her mind filled with images, but not those of memory; her imagination manufactured new ones—of this man with his harder soul and ruined voice, bending over her, taking her in his arms, moving between her legs in a more complete possession than she had ever known before. Her own breath shortened as her breasts grew tight and achy, and her insides turned liquid. Another tingle jolted her, making her feel as if she were on the verge of physical ecstasy, and merely from his words, his voice. The violence of her response shocked her, scared her, and she jerked away from his bed before she could control the motion.

"Jay?" He was concerned, even a little alarmed, as he felt her move away from him.

"Go to sleep," she managed to say, her voice almost under control. "You need the rest. I'll be here when you wake up."

He lifted his bandaged hand. "How about holding my hand?"

"I can't do that. It would hurt you."

"It would blend in with all the other pain," he said groggily. He was losing strength rapidly. "Just touch me until I go to sleep, all right?"

Jay felt his request go straight through her heart. That he should ask anything of her still staggered her, but his need to be touched was almost more than she could bear. She stepped back to the bed, folding her hand over his arm. At the first touch she felt him begin to relax, and within two minutes he was asleep.

She stepped outside, feeling the need to escape, though she wasn't certain exactly what she was escaping from. It was Steve, and yet it was something else, something inside her that was growing more and more powerful. It scared her; she didn't want it, yet she was helpless to stop it. She had never responded to him like that before, not even in the first wild, heady days of their marriage. It's just the situation, she told herself, trying to find comfort in the thought. It was just her tendency to throw herself wholly into something, concentrating on it too intensely, that made her feel like this. But comfort eluded her and despair welled in her heart, because analyzing her emotions didn't change them. God help her, she was falling in love with him again, with even less reason than she'd had the first time. For most of the past three weeks he'd been little more than a mummy, incapable of movement or speech, yet she had felt drawn to him, tied to him; and loving him now was much more dangerous than it had been before. He was a different, stronger, harder man. Even when he'd been unconscious, she had felt his fierce inner power, and her need to know what had happened to him to cause that change was so strong it almost hurt.

A nurse, the one who had first noticed Steve's unconscious reaction to Jay's presence, stopped beside her. "How is he? He refused his pain medication this morning."

"He's asleep now. He tires very easily."

The nurse nodded, her bright blue eyes meeting Jay's darker ones. "He has the most incredible constitution I've ever seen. He's still in a great deal of pain, but he just seems to ignore it. Normally it would be at least another week before we began tapering off the pain medication." Admiration filled her voice. "Did the coffee upset his stomach?"

Jay had to laugh. "No. He was rather smug about it."

"He was certainly determined to get that coffee. Maybe we can start him on a soft diet tomorrow, so he can begin regaining his strength."

"Do you know when he'll be transferred out of intensive care?"

"I really don't know. Major Lunning will have to make that decision." The nurse smiled as she took her leave, returning to the central station.

Jay walked to the visitors' lounge to buy a soft drink, and she took advantage of the room's emptiness to give herself some much-needed privacy. She was filled with a vague uneasiness, and she couldn't pinpoint the reason. Or reasons, she thought. Part of it was Steve, of course, and her own unruly emotional response to him. She didn't want to love him again, but she didn't know how to fight it, only that she had to. She *could not* love him again. It was too risky. She knew that, fiercely told herself over and over that she wouldn't allow it to happen, even as she acknowledged that it might already be too late.

The other part of her uneasiness was also tied to Steve, but she wasn't certain why. That aggravating sense of having missed something kept nagging at her, something that she should have seen but hadn't. Perhaps Steve sensed it too, judging by all the questions he'd asked; he didn't quite trust Frank, though she supposed that was to be expected, given

Steve's situation. But Jay knew that she would trust Frank with her life, and with Steve's. So why did she keep feeling that she should know more than she did? Was Steve in danger because of what he had witnessed? Had Steve actually been involved in the deal? She would have had to be naive not to realize that the vast majority of the facts had been kept from her, but she didn't expect Frank to spout out everything he knew. No, it wasn't that. It was something that she should have seen, something that was obvious, and she'd missed it entirely. It was some little detail that didn't fit, and until she could pinpoint what it was, she wouldn't be able to get rid of that nagging uneasiness.

Steve was taken out of intensive care two days later and moved to a private room, and the navy guards shifted location. The new room had a television, something the ICU room had lacked, and Steve insisted on listening to every news program he could, as if he were searching for clues that would tie all the missing pieces together for him again. The problem was that he seemed to be interested in all the world situations and could discuss the politics of others nations as easily as domestic issues. That disturbed Jay; Steve had never been particularly political, and the depth of his current knowledge revealed that he had become deeply involved. Given that, it became more likely that he had also been more involved in the situation that had nearly killed him than perhaps even Frank knew. Or perhaps Frank did know, after all. He had had several long, private conversations with Steve, but Steve remained guarded. Only with Jay did he lose his wariness.

His various injuries kept him bed-bound much longer than he should have been, but he wasn't able to negotiate with crutches due to his burned hands. His physical inactivity ate at him, eroding his patience and good humor. He quickly decided which television shows he liked, discarding all game shows and soap operas, but even the ones he liked lacked something, since so much of the action was visual. Merely being able to listen frustrated him, and soon he wanted the set on only for the news. Jay did everything she could think of to entertain him; he liked it when she read the newspaper to him, but for the most part he just wanted to talk.

"Tell me what you look like," he said one morning.

The demand flustered her. It was oddly embarrassing to be asked to describe oneself. "Well, I have brown hair," she began hesitantly.

"What shade of brown? Reddish? Gold?"

"Gold, I guess, but on the dark side. Honey-colored."

"Is it long?"

"No. It's almost to my shoulders, and very straight."

"What color are your eyes?"

"Blue."

"Come on," he chided after a minute when she didn't add anything. "How tall are you?"

"Medium. Five-six."

"How tall am I? Did we fit together well?"

The thought made her throat tighten. "You're six feet, and yes, we did dance well together."

He turned his bandaged eyes toward her. "I wasn't talking about dancing, but so what? When I get out of these casts, let's go dancing again. Maybe I haven't forgotten how."

She didn't know if she could stand being in his arms again, not with her responses running wild every time she heard his harsh, cracked voice. But he was waiting for her to answer, so she said lightly, "It's a date."

He lifted his hands. "The bandages come off tomorrow. Next week I have the final surgery on my eyes. The casts come off in two weeks. Give me a month to build up my strength. By then the bandages should be off my eyes, and we'll do the town."

"You're only giving yourself a month to get your strength back? Isn't that a little ambitious?"

"I've done it before," he said, then went very still. Jay held her breath as she watched him, but after a minute he swore softly. "Damn it, I *know* things, but I can't remember them. I know what foods I like, I know the name of every head of state of every nation mentioned in the news, I can even recall what they look like, but I don't know my own face. I know who won the last World Series, but not where I was when it was played. I know the smell of the canals in Venice, but I can't remember ever being there." He paused a minute, then said very quietly, "Sometimes I want to take this place apart with my bare hands."

"Major Lunning told you what to expect," Jay said, still shaken by what he'd said. How deeply had he involved himself in the gray world Frank had hinted at? She was very much afraid that Steve was no longer an adventurer, but a player. "Stop feeling sorry for yourself. He said your memory would probably come back in dribbles."

A slow grin touched his lips, deepening the lines that bracketed his mouth and drawing her helpless, fascinated gaze. His lips seemed firmer, fuller, as if they were still slightly swollen, or perhaps it was because his face was thinner and older. "Sorry," he said. "I'll have to watch that."

His wry humor, especially when he had good reason to occasionally feel sorry for himself, only reminded her again of his hard inner strength and was one more blow against the shaky guard she had set up around her heart. She had to laugh at him, just as she had years before, but there was a difference now. Before, Steve had used humor as a wall to hide behind; now the wall was gone, and she could see the real man.

She was with him the next morning when the bandages came off his burned hands for good. She had been in there before when the bandages were changed, so she had seen the raw blisters on his palms and fingers when they had looked much worse than they did now. Patches of reddened skin were still visible all the way to his elbows, but his hands had caught the worst of it. Now that the danger of infection was past, the new, tender skin would heal faster without the bandages, but his hands would be too painful for him to use them much for a while.

When she compared how he looked now to the way he had looked the first time she had seen him, hooked to all those machines and monitors, with so many tubes running into his body, it seemed nothing short of a miracle. It had been only four weeks, but he had been little more than a vegetable then, and now he exerted the force of his personality over everyone who entered his room, even the doctors. His face had been swollen and bruised before; now the hard line of his jaw and the precise cut of his lips fascinated her. She knew that plastic surgeons had rebuilt his shattered face, and she wondered about the changes she would see when the bandages were completely gone and she was able to truly see him for the first time. His jaw was a little different, a little squarer, leaner, but that was to be expected, since he had lost so much weight after he'd been injured. His beard seemed darker, because he was so pale. She was very well acquainted with his jaw and beard, since she had to shave him every morning. The nurses had done it until he became conscious and made it known he wanted Jay to shave him, and no one else.

He no longer had a thick swath of gauze wrapped around his skull. There was a big, jagged white scar that ran diagonally from the top of his head, at a point directly above his right ear, to the back and left of his skull, but his hair was already longer than that of the average military recruit in boot camp, and it was beginning to cover the scar. The new hair was dark and glossy, having never been exposed to the sun. His eyes were still covered with bandages, but though the gauze pads and wrapping were much smaller now than they had been before, the upper bridge of his nose and the curve of his cheekbones were still covered. The bandages tantalized her; she wanted to see his new face, to judge for herself how well the plastic surgeon had done his job. She wanted to be able to apply his identity to his face, to look into his dark eyes and see all the things she'd looked for in their marriage and hadn't been able to find.

"Your hands are tender," the doctor who'd been caring for Steve's burns said as he cut away the last of the bandages and signaled for a nurse to clean them. "Be careful with them until all this new skin has toughened. They're stiff right now, but use them, exercise them. You don't have any tendon or ligament damage, so in time you'll have full use of them again."

Slowly, painfully, Steve flexed his fingers, wincing as he did so. He waited until the doctor and nurses had left the room, then said, "Jay?"

"I'm here."

"How do they look?"

"Red," she answered honestly.

He flexed them again, then cautiously rubbed the fingers of his right hand over his left one, then reversed the procedure. "It feels strange," he said, smiling a little. "They're damned tender, like he said, but the skin feels as smooth as a baby's butt. I don't have any calluses now." The smile faded abruptly, replaced with a frown. "I had callused hands." Again he explored his hands, as if trying to find something familiar in the touch, slowly rubbing his fingertips together.

She laughed softly. "One summer, you played so much sandlot baseball that your hands were as tough as leather. You had calluses on your calluses."

He still looked thoughtful; then his mood changed and he said, "Come sit by me, on the bed."

Curious, she did as he said, sitting facing him. The head of his bed had been raised to an upright position, so he was sitting erect and they were on the same level. Abruptly she noticed how much she had to look up at him. His bare shoulders and chest, despite the weight he had lost, still dwarfed her, and again she wondered what sort of work he had done that had developed his torso to that degree.

Tentatively he reached out, and his hand touched her hair. Realizing why he had wanted her to sit there, she remained still while his fingers sifted through the strands. He didn't say anything. He lifted his other hand, and his palms cupped her face, his fingers gliding lightly over her forehead and brow, down the bridge of her nose, over her lips and jaw and chin before sliding down the length of her throat.

Her breath had stopped, but she hadn't noticed. Slowly he laced his fingers around her neck as if measuring it, then traced the hollows of her collarbones out to her shoulders. "You're too thin," he murmured, cupping the balls of her shoulders in his palms. "Don't you eat enough?"

"Actually, I've gained a little weight," she whispered, beginning to shake at his warm touch.

Calmly, deliberately, he moved his hands down to her breasts and molded his fingers over them. Jay inhaled sharply, and he said, "Easy, easy," as he stroked the soft mounds.

"Steve, no." But her eyes were closing as warm pleasure built in her, her blood beating slowly and powerfully through her veins. His thumbs rubbed over her nipples and she quivered, her breasts beginning to tighten.

"You're so soft." His voice roughened even more. "God, how I've wanted to touch you. Come here, sweetheart."

He ignored the pain in his hands as he pulled her against him, and he wrapped his arms around her as he had dreamed of doing so many times since her voice had charmed him out of the darkness. He felt her slenderness, her softness, her warmth, and the gut-wrenching pleasure of her breasts flattening against the hard planes of his chest. He smelled the sweetness of her skin, felt the thick silk of her hair, and with a harsh, muffled sound of want, of need, he sought her mouth.

He already knew her mouth. He would beg, cajole, insist until she would give him a kiss in the morning and again at night before she left. He knew it was wide and full and soft, and that her lips trembled each time she kissed him. Now he slanted his mouth to cover hers, pressing hard until her lips parted and gave him the entrance he sought. He could feel her shaking in his arms as he moved his tongue into her mouth and tasted her sweetness. Damn, how had he been fool enough to let her get away from him five years before? Not being able to remember making love to her made him furious because he wanted to know what she liked, how it felt to be inside her, if they had been as good together as every instinct he possessed told them they would be. She belonged to him; he knew it, felt it, as if they were tied together. He deepened the kiss, forcing her to respond to him the way he knew she could, the way he knew she wanted to. Finally she shivered convulsively, and her tongue met his as her arms crept up around his neck.

He shouldn't be this strong, Jay thought dimly, not after all he's been through. But his arms were hard, and so tight around her that her ribs were being squeezed. Steve had never been this aggressive before; he certainly hadn't been a passive man, but now he was kissing her with naked demand, forcing their relationship into an intimacy that frightened her. He wanted her more than he ever had during their marriage, but now his attention was intensely focused on her because of the circumstances.

"We shouldn't do this," she managed to say, turning her head aside to free her mouth from the hungry pressure of his. She brought her hands down and pushed lightly at his shoulders.

"Why not?" he murmured, taking advantage of the vulnerability of her throat with slow kisses. His tongue touched the sensitive hollow below her ear, and her hands tightened on his shoulders as wonderful little ripples of pleasure radiated over her skin. His lack of sight didn't hinder him; he knew his way around a woman's body. Instinct went deeper than memory.

Both conscience and her sense of self-protection made Jay push at his shoulders again, and this time he slowly released her. "We can't let ourselves get involved again," she said in a low voice.

"We're both free," he pointed out.

"As far as we know. Steve, you could have met someone in the past five years who you really care about. Someone could be waiting for you to come home. Until you get your memory back, you can't be certain that you're free. And...and I think we should be cautious about jumping back into a relationship without knowing more than we do."

"No one's waiting for me," he said with harsh certainty.

Her movements were jerky with agitation as she slid off the bed and walked to the window. The morning sky was a leaden color, and snow flurries were drifting aimlessly on the light wind. "You can't know that," she insisted, and turned back to look at him.

His face was turned toward her even though he couldn't see her, and the hard line of his mouth told her he was angry. The sheet was around his waist, baring his broad shoulders and chest, as he had disdained both pajamas and a hospital gown, though he had finally consented to wear the pajama bottoms with the legs cut off and the seams slit so they would fit over the casts on his legs. He was thin, pale and weak from what he'd been through, but somehow the impression he gave was one of power. Nor was he all that weak, not if the strength she had just felt in him was any measure. He must have been incredibly strong before the accident. Those five years when she hadn't seen him were becoming even more of a mystery.

"So you've stayed here with me all this time just because you have a Florence Nightingale complex?" he asked sharply. It was the first time she had refused him anything, and he didn't like it at all. If he could have walked, he would have come after her, sightless or not, weak or not, even though he was still in pain most of the time. None of that would have stopped him, and for the first time she was grateful for his broken legs.

"I never hated you," she tried to explain, knowing that she owed him at least the effort. "I don't think we were all that deeply in love, certainly not enough to make our marriage work. Frank asked me to stay because he thought you would need me, given your condition. Even Major Lunning said it would help if you were around someone familiar, someone you knew before the accident. So...I stayed."

"Don't give me that crap." Her attempt to explain had made him even more furious, and it was a type of anger she hadn't seen before. He was very still and controlled, his guttural voice little more than a whisper. Chills ran up her spine because she could feel his temper like both ice and fire, lashing out at her even though he hadn't moved. "Do you think that because I can't see, I couldn't tell you were turned on just now? Try again, sweetheart."

Jay began to get angry at the harsh demand in his voice. "All right, if you want the truth, here it is. I don't trust you. You were always too restless to settle down and try to build a life together. You were always leaving on another of your 'adventures,' looking for something I couldn't give you. Well, I don't want to go through that again. I don't want to get involved with you again. You want me now, and you may need me a little, but what happens when you're well? Another pat on the head and a kiss on the cheek while I get to watch you ride off into the sunset? Thanks, but no thanks. I have more sense now than I did before."

"Is that why you start shaking every time I touch you? You want to get involved again, all right, but you're afraid."

''I said I don't trust you. I didn't say I was afraid of you. Why should I trust you? You were still looking for trouble when that explosion almost killed you!''

Abruptly she realized that she was all but yelling at him, while his voice hadn't risen at all. She turned and walked out, then leaned against the wall outside his door until both the temper and the shaking subsided. She felt sick, not because of their argument, but because he was right. She *was* afraid. She was terrified. And it was too late to do anything about it, because she was in love with him again, despite all her warnings and lectures to herself against it. She didn't know him anymore. He had changed; he was harder, rougher, far more dangerous. He was still a leaver, probably far more involved in the situation than Frank had wanted her to know.

But it didn't make any difference. She had loved him before when it had gone against her better judgement, and she loved him now when it made even less sense. God help her, she had left herself wide open for a lot of pain, and there was nothing she could do.

Chapter 6

Steve lay quietly, forcing the lingering cloudiness of anesthesia from his mind. He was instinctively still, like an animal in the jungle, until he was aware enough to know what was going on. A man could lose his life by moving before he knew where his enemies were. If they thought he was dead, he gained the advantage of surprise by lying still and not letting them know he was still alive until he could recover enough to make his move. He tried to open his eyes, but something covered them. They had him blindfolded. But that didn't make sense; why blindfold someone they thought was dead?

He listened, trying to locate his captors. The usual jungle sounds were absent, and gradually he realized that he was too cold to be in a jungle. The smell was all wrong, too; it was a sharp, medicinal odor, like disinfectant. This place smelled like a hospital.

The realization was like a curtain going up, and abruptly he knew where he was and what had happened, and at the same time the hazy recollection of the steamy jungle swiftly faded. The final surgery on his eyes was over, and he was in Recovery. "Jay!" It took an incredible amount of effort to call for her, and his voice sounded strange, even worse than usual, so deep and hoarse it was almost like an animal's cry. "Jay!"

"Everything's all right, Mr. Crossfield," a calm voice said soothingly. "You've had your surgery, and everything is just fine. Lie still, and we'll have you back in your room in a few minutes."

It wasn't Jay's voice. It was a nice voice, but it wasn't what he wanted. His throat was dry; he swallowed, and winced a little because his throat was so raw and sore. That's right; they'd had a tube down it. "Where's Jay?" he croaked, like a frog.

"Is Jay your wife, Mr. Crossfield?"

"Yes." Ex-wife, if they wanted to get technical. He didn't care about the labels. Jay was his.

"She's probably waiting for you in your room."

"Take me there."

"Let's wait a few more minutes—"

"Now." The single word was guttural, the steely command naked. He didn't try to dress it up in polite phrases, because it was all he could do to say a few words at a time. He was still groggy, but he fixed his thoughts on Jay with single-minded determination. He began groping for the rail on the side of the bed.

"Mr. Crossfield, wait! You're going to pull the IV out of your arm!"

"Good," he muttered.

"Calm down, we're going to take you to your room. Just lie still while I get an orderly."

A minute later he felt the bed begin to move. It was a curiously relaxing movement, and he began to go to sleep again but forced himself to stay alert. He couldn't afford to relax until Jay was with him; there was damned little he knew about who he was or what was going on, but Jay was the one constant in his life, the one person he trusted. She had been there from the beginning, as far back as his memory reached, and further.

"Here we are," the nurse said cheerfully. "He couldn't wait to get back to his room, Mrs. Crossfield. He was asking for you and kicking up a fuss."

"I'm here, Steve," Jay said, and he thought she sounded anxious. He noticed that she didn't correct the nurse about her name, and fierce satisfaction filled him. The name didn't mean much to him, but it was a name he'd once shared with Jay, one of the links that bound her to him.

He was lifted onto his bed, and he could feel them fussing around him for a few more minutes. It was getting harder to stay awake. "Jay!"

"I'm here."

He reached out with his left hand toward her voice, and her slim, cool fingers touched him. Her hand felt so small and fragile in his.

"The doctor said everything went perfectly," she said, her voice somewhere above him in the darkness. "You'll get the bandages off for good in about two weeks."

"Then I'm outta here," he murmured. His hand tightened around hers, and he gave in to the lingering effects of the anesthesia.

When he woke again, it was without the initial confusion, but he was still groggy. Impatiently he forced his mind out of lethargy, and it was so habitual now to ignore the pain in his mending body that he truthfully didn't even notice it. At some unknown point in his life he had learned that the human body could be forced to superhuman feats if the brain knew how to ignore pain. Evidently he had learned that lesson so well that it was second nature to him now.

Now that he was more awake, he didn't have to call for Jay to know she was in the room. He could hear her breathing, hear the pages of a magazine turning as she sat by the bed. He could smell the faint, sweet scent of her skin, a scent that identified her immediately to him whenever she entered the room. Then there was that other awareness, the physical awareness that was like an electrical charge, making his skin tingle with pleasure and excitement at her closeness, or even at the mere thought of her.

He hadn't kissed her since their argument the week before, but he was only biding his time. She had been upset, and he didn't want that, didn't want to push her. Maybe he hadn't been much of a prize before, but she still felt something for him, or she wouldn't be here now, and when the time came he would capitalize on those feelings. She was his; he knew it with a bone-deep sense of possession that overrode everything else.

He wanted her. The strength of his sexual need for her surprised him, given his current physical condition, but the stirring in his loins every time she touched him was proof that certain instincts were stronger than pain. Every day the pain was a little less, and every day he wanted her a little more. It was basic. Whenever two people were attracted to each other, the urge to mate became overwhelming; it was nature's way of propagating the species. Intense physical desire and hot, frequent lovemaking reinforced the bond between two people. They became a couple, because back in the human species' first primitive days, it took two people to provide care for their helpless young. In current times one parent could raise a child quite well, and modern medicine had made it possible for a woman not to become pregnant if she didn't want to, but the old instincts were still there. The sexual drive was still there, a man's need to make love to his woman and make certain she knew she was his. He understood the basis of the biological need programmed into his genes, but understanding didn't lessen its power.

Amnesia was a curious thing. When he examined it unemotionally, he was interested in its oddities. He had lost all conscious knowledge of whatever had happened to him before he'd come out of the coma, but a lot of unconscious knowledge evidently hadn't been affected. He could remember different World Series and Super Bowls, and how Niagara Falls looked. That wasn't important. Interesting, but not important.

Equally interesting, and far more important, were the things he knew about both obscure Third World nations and major powers without remembering how he came by the knowledge. He couldn't bring his own face to mind, but somehow that didn't negate what he knew was fact. He knew the desert, the hot, dry heat and blood-sizzling sun. He also knew the jungle, the stifling heat and humidity, the insects and reptiles, the leeches, the shrieking birds, the stench of rotting vegetation.

Taking those bits and pieces of himself that he could recognize, he was able to piece together part of the puzzle. The jungle part was easy. Jay had told him that he was thirty-seven; he was just the right age to have been in Vietnam during the height of the war in the late sixties. The rest of it, all added together, could have only one logical explanation: he was far more involved in the situation than Jay had been told.

He had wondered if scopolamine or Pentothal would be successful on an amnesia victim, or if the amnesia effectively sealed off his memories even from the powerful drugs available today. If what he might know was important enough for him to warrant this kind of red-carpet treatment, then it would have been worth Frank Payne's effort to at least have tried the drugs. They hadn't tried, and that told him something else: Payne knew Steve had been indoctrinated to resist any chemical prying into his brain. Therefore he must be a trained field operative.

Jay didn't know. She really thought he had simply been in the wrong place at the wrong time. She had said that when they had been married, he had constantly been taking off on one "adventure" after another, so he must have kept her in the dark and just let her think that he was footloose, rather than worrying her with the knowledge of just how dangerous his work was, and that the odds were even he wouldn't return from any given trip.

He had fitted that many pieces of the puzzle together, but there were still a lot of little things that didn't make sense to him. He had noticed, as soon as the bandages were taken off his hands, that his fingertips were oddly smooth. It wasn't the smoothness of scar tissue; his hands were so sensitive, with their new, healing skin, that he could tell the difference between the burned areas and his fingertips. He was positive his fingertips hadn't been burned; rather, his fingerprints had been altered or removed altogether, probably the latter. Recently, too, most likely here in this hospital. The question was: Why? Who were they hiding his identity from? They knew who he was, and he was evidently on good terms with them, or they wouldn't have gone to such extraordinary lengths to save his life. Jay knew who he was. Was someone out there hunting for him? And, if so, was Jay in danger simply because she was with him?

Too many questions, and he didn't know the answers to any of them. He could ask Payne, but he wasn't certain he'd get a straight answer from the man. Payne was hiding something. Steve didn't know what it was, but he could hear a faint note of guilt in the man's voice, especially when he spoke to Jay. What had they gotten Jay involved in?

He heard the door to his room open and he lay motionless, wanting to know the identity of his visitor without them knowing he was awake. He had noticed that cautiousness in himself before; it fit in with what he had deduced.

''Is he awake yet?''

It was Frank Payne's quiet voice, and that special note was there again, the guilt and the . . . affection. Yeah, that's what it was. Payne liked Jay and worried about her, but he was still using her. It made Steve feel even less inclined to cooperate. It made him mad, to think they could be putting Jay in any danger.

"He went to sleep as soon as they got him in bed, and he hasn't stirred since. Have you talked to the doctor?"

"No, not yet. How did it go?"

"Wonderfully. The doctor doesn't think there's any permanent damage. He has to lie as quietly as possible for a few days, and his eyes may be sensitive to bright light after the bandages come off, but he probably won't even need glasses."

"That's good. He should be leaving here in another couple of weeks, if everything goes all right."

"It's hard to think of not coming here every day," Jay mused. "It won't seem normal. What happens when he's released?"

"I need to talk to him about that," Payne answered. "It can wait a few days, until he's more active."

Steve could hear the worry in Jay's voice and wondered at it. Did she know something, after all? Why else would she worry about what happened to him when he left the hospital? He had news for her, though; wherever she went, that was where he intended to go, and Frank Payne could take those ideas of his and become real friendly with them.

Two more weeks of biding his time. He didn't know if he could do it. It was hard to force himself to exercise the patience he needed to allow his body to heal, and there were still weeks of rehabilitation ahead before he regained his full strength. He'd have to push himself harder than the therapists would, but he could sense his own limits, and he knew they were more elastic than the therapists could guess. It was just one more piece of the puzzle.

He decided to let himself "wake up" and began shifting restlessly. The IV needle tugged at his hand. "Jay?" he called in a groggy tone, then cleared his throat and tried again. "Jay?" He never quite got used to hearing his own voice the way it was now, so harsh and strained, gravelly in texture. Another little oddity. He couldn't remember his own voice, but he knew this one wasn't right.

"I'm here." Her cool fingers touched his arm.

How many times had he heard those two words, and how many times had they provided him with a link to consciousness? They seemed embedded in his mind, as if they were his one memory. Hell, they probably were. He reached for her with his free hand. "Thirsty."

He heard the sound of water pouring; then a straw touched his lips and he gratefully sucked the cold liquid into his dry mouth and down his raw throat. She took the straw away after only a couple of swallows. "Not too much at first," she said in that calm way of hers. "The anesthesia may make you sick."

He moved his hand and felt the needle tugging at it again. Swift irritation filled him. "Get a nurse to take this damned needle out."

"You need glucose after surgery to keep from going into shock," she argued. "And it probably has an antibiotic in it—"

"Then they can give me pills," he rasped. "I don't like being restricted like this." It was bad enough that his legs were still in casts; he'd had enough of having to lie still to last him a lifetime.

She was silent for a moment, and he could sense her understanding. Sometimes it was as if they didn't need words, as if there were a link between them that transcended the verbal. She knew exactly how frustrated it made him to have to lie in bed day after day; it was not only boring, it went against every survival instinct he possessed. "All right," she finally said, her cool fingers drifting against his arm. "I'll get a nurse."

He listened as she left the room, then lay quietly, waiting to see if Frank Payne would identify himself. It was a subtle game; he didn't even know why he was playing it. But Payne was hiding something, and Steve didn't trust him.

He'd do anything he could to gain an edge, even if it was something so trivial as pretending to sleep while he eavesdropped. He hadn't even learned anything, other than that Payne had "plans" for him.

"Are you in any pain?" Frank asked.

Steve cautiously turned his head. "Frank?" Another part of the game, pretending he didn't recognize the other man's voice.

"Yes."

"No, not much pain. Groggy." That much was true; the anesthesia made him feel limp and sleepy. But he could force himself to mental alertness, and that was the important part. He would rather be in pain than be so doped up he didn't know what was going on around him. The barbiturate coma had been a nightmare of darkness, of *nothingness*, which he didn't want to experience again, even in a mild form. Even amnesia was better than that total lack of self.

"That's the last of it. No more surgery, no more tubes, no more needles. When the casts come off your legs, you can start getting back to your old shape." Frank had a quiet voice, and there was often a note of familiarity in it, as if they had known each other well.

His words touched a chord of recognition in Steve; his old shape hadn't been bulky muscles, but rather speed and stamina, a steely core of strength that kept him going when other men would have collapsed.

"Is Jay in any danger?" he asked, cutting through the cautious maneuvering to what was most important to him.

"Because of what you may have seen?"

"Yes."

"We don't anticipate any danger," Frank replied, his voice cautious. "You are important to us only because we need to know exactly what happened, and you might provide us with some answers."

Steve smiled wryly. "Yeah, I know. Important enough to cut through red tape and coordinate two, maybe three, separate agencies, as well as pulling in people from different branches of the service and from the private sector. I'm just an innocent bystander, aren't I? Jay may buy that, but I don't. So cut the crap and give me a yes or no answer. Is Jay in any danger?''

"No," Frank said firmly, and after a second Steve gave a fractional nod, all he could manage. Regardless of what Frank was hiding, he was still fond of Jay and protective of her. Jay was safe enough. Steve could deal with the rest later; Jay was what mattered now.

His legs were thin and weak after having been encased in plaster for six weeks; he ran his hands down them, getting himself accustomed to their peculiar lightness. He could move them, but his movements were jerky and uncontrolled. For the past couple of days he had been sitting in a wheelchair or in the bedside chair, letting his body adjust to movement and different postures. His hands had healed enough that he had been able to stand, using a walker for support, for a few minutes each day. His store of knowledge was increasing all the time. He now knew that even when he was bent forward to hold the walker, he was several inches taller than Jay. He wanted to take her in his arms and hold her against him, to feel her soft body adjust to his size as he bent his head to kiss her. He'd been holding off, taking it slow, but now that was at an end.

Jay watched him massage his thighs and calves, his long fingers kneading the muscles with sure strokes. He was scheduled for a session in physical therapy that afternoon, but he wasn't waiting for someone else to do the work for him. He had been like a coiled spring since the surgery on his eyes: tense, waiting, but under iron control. It had been a month and a half since the explosion, and perhaps lesser people would still have been lying in bed and taking pills for the pain, but Steve had been pushing himself from the moment he'd regained consciousness. His hands had to be tender, but he used them and never winced. His ribs and legs had to hurt, but he didn't let that stop him. He never complained of a headache, though Major Lunning had told Jay he would probably have headaches for several months.

She glanced at her watch. He'd been massaging his legs for half an hour. "I think that's enough," she said firmly. "Don't you want to go back to bed?"

He straightened up in the wheelchair and his teeth flashed in a grin. "Baby, I'm so tired of that bed, the only way you could get me back in it would be if you crawled in there with me."

He looked so wickedly masculine that she felt herself weakening even as she tried to warn herself against his charm. He wasn't above using his appeal as a wounded warrior to get to her, blast his hide. She couldn't even look at him without getting wobbly kneed, and sometimes the way she felt about him welled up in her like a flood tide, pleasure and pain so sharply mingled that she would almost moan aloud. Every day he was stronger; every day he conquered new territory, exerted his will over another aspect of his life. It was both amazing and frightening to watch him and to realize the extent of his willpower as he dealt with his situation. He was so fiercely controlled and determined that it was almost inhuman, but at the same time he let her see how very human he was; he depended on her now more than she had ever imagined possible, and the vulnerability he revealed to her was all the more shattering because she knew how rare it was.

"Get the walker for me," he ordered now, turning his bandaged eyes toward her expectantly, as if waiting for her to protest.

Jay pursed her lips, looking at him, then shrugged and placed the walker in front of him. If he suffered a setback, it would be his own fault for refusing to accept his limitations. "All right," she said calmly. "Go ahead and fall. Break your legs again, crack your head open again and spend a few more months in here. I'm sure that will thrill the nurses."

He chuckled at her acerbity, a reaction that was becoming more frequent as he healed. He regarded it as a measure of his recovery; while he had been ill and helpless, she hadn't refused him anything. He liked finding this bite to her personality. A passive woman wouldn't suit him at all, but Jay suited him in every way, at all times.

"I won't fall," he assured her, levering himself into an upright position. He had to support most of his weight on his arms, but his feet moved when he told them to. Jerkily, true, but on command.

"And heee's offf aaand *stumbling*!" Jay cried in dry imitation of a racetrack announcer, her irritation plain.

He gave a shout of laughter and did stumble, but caught himself with the walker. "You're supposed to guide me, not make fun of me."

"I refuse to help you push yourself too hard. If you fall, it will be your own fault."

A crooked smile twisted his lips and her heart speeded up at the roguish charm it gave his face. "Ah, baby," he cajoled. "I'm not pushing too hard, I promise. I know how much I can do. Come on, guide me down the hall."

"No," she said firmly.

Two minutes later she was walking slowly by his side as he maneuvered the walker, and his reluctant legs, down the hall. At the end of the corridor, the Navy guard watched alertly, examining everyone and everything. It was like that every time Steve left his room, though he didn't realize he was guarded so closely. Jay felt a chill as her eyes met those of the guard and he nodded politely; no matter how calm everything seemed, the guards' presence reminded her that Steve had been involved in something highly dangerous. Wouldn't his amnesia put him in even more danger? He didn't even know he was being threatened or by whom. No wonder those guards were necessary! But realizing just how necessary they were terrified her. This was all part of the large gray area Frank hadn't explained, but she knew it was there.

"This is far enough," Steve said, and cautiously turned around. He turned exactly 180 degrees and took two steps before stopping, his head turning back to her. "Jay?"

"Sorry." Hastily she moved to his side. How had he known how far to turn? Why wasn't he more uncertain of his movements? He walked slowly, still supporting most of his weight on his arms and hands, but he seemed deliberate and sure. He was slowed by his injuries but not thwarted. He wouldn't let himself give in; he didn't look on his injuries as something to be recovered from, but rather as something to be conquered. He would handle this on his own terms, and win, because he wouldn't accept anything less.

She saw even more of his determination in the following days as he sweated through physical therapy. The therapist tried to restrain him but Steve insisted on setting his own pace. He swam laps, guiding himself by Jay's voice, and walked endlessly on a treadmill. By the third day of therapy he had discarded the walker permanently and replaced it with Jay. Grinning as he put his arm around her shoulder, he explained that at least she'd cushion him if he fell.

He had gained weight rapidly since the tube had been taken out of his throat, and now he regained his strength just as rapidly. Jay felt as if she could see a difference in him from one day to the next. Except for the bandages over his eyes, he seemed almost normal, but she knew every scar hidden by the comfortable sweats Frank had brought him to wear. His hands were still pink from the burns, and his ruined voice would never be much better. Nor was his memory showing any sign of returning. There were no flashes of memory or glimmers of recognition. It was as if he had been born when he had fought his way out of unconsciousness to respond to her voice, and nothing existed before that.

Sometimes, watching him as he exercised with that frightening relentlessness of his, she caught herself hoping that his memory *wouldn't* return, and then guilt would eat at her. But he depended on her so much now, and if he began to remember, the closeness between them would fade. Even as she tried to protect herself from that closeness, she treasured every moment and wanted more. She was caught on the horns of her own dilemma and couldn't decide how to get free. She could protect herself and walk away, or she could grab for whatever she could get, but she couldn't decide to do either. All she could do was wait, and watch over him with increasing fierceness.

The day the bandages were supposed to come off his eyes, he got up at dawn and prowled restlessly around the hospital room. Jay had gotten there early, feeling as anxious as he did, but she forced herself to sit still. Finally he turned on the television and listened intently to the morning news, a frown knitting his brow.

"Why the hell doesn't that damn doctor hurry up?" he muttered.

Jay looked at her watch. "It's still early. You haven't even had breakfast yet."

He swore under his breath and raked his fingers through his hair. It was still shorter than was fashionable, but long enough to cover the scar that bisected his skull, and it was dark and shiny, undulled by sunlight, and beginning to show a hint of waviness. He prowled some more, then stopped by the window and drummed his fingers on the sill. "It's a sunny day, isn't it?"

Jay looked out the window at the blue sky. "Yes, and not too cold, but the weather forecast says we could have some snow by the weekend."

"What's the date?"

"January 29."

His fingers continued to tap against the sill. "Where are we going?"

Jay felt blank. "Going?"

"When they release me. Where are we going?"

She felt a shock like a slap in the face as she realized he would be released from the hospital within a few hours if everything was all right with his eyes. The apartment Frank had rented for her was tiny, only one bedroom, but that wasn't what alarmed her. What if Frank intended to whisk Steve away from her? Granted, he had once said something about her staying with Steve until his memory returned, but it hadn't been mentioned since. Was that still his plan? If so, where did he intend for Steve to live?

"I don't know where we'll go," she replied faintly. "They may want to send you somewhere...." Her voice trailed off into miserable silence.

"Too damn bad if they do." He turned from the window, and there was something lethal in his movement, a predator's grace and power. She stared at him, silhouetted against the bright window, and her throat contracted. He was so much harder than he had been that it almost frightened her, but at the same time, everything about him excited her. She loved him so much that it hurt, deep inside her chest, and it was getting worse.

A nurse brought in his breakfast tray, then winked at Jay. "I noticed you were here early, so I had an extra tray sent up. I won't tell if you won't." She brought in another breakfast tray, smiling as Jay thanked her. "This is the big day," the nurse said cheerfully. "Call this a sort of precelebration meal."

Steve grinned. "Are you that anxious to get rid of me?"

"You've been an absolute angel. We're going to miss those buns of yours, but hey, easy come, easy go."

A slow flush reddened Steve's cheeks, and the nurse laughed heartily as she left the room. Jay snickered as she unwrapped his silverware and arranged everything on the tray as he was accustomed to finding it.

"Bring your gorgeous buns over here and eat your breakfast," she ordered, still snickering.

"If you like them, get a good view," he invited, turning around and lifting his arms so she did indeed have an excellent view of his tight, muscular buttocks. "I'll even let you touch."

"Thank you, but food wins out over your backside. Aren't you hungry?"

"Starved."

They made short work of the meal, and soon he was again prowling about the small room, his restlessness making it seem even smaller. His impatience was a palpable force, bristling around him. He had spent too many weeks flat on his back, totally helpless and blind, unable even to feed himself. Now he had his mobility back, and in an unknown number of minutes he'd know if his sight had been restored. The doctor was certain of the surgery's success, but until the bandages were off and he could actually *see*, Steve wouldn't let himself believe it. It was the waiting and the lack of certainty that ate at him. He wanted to see. He wanted to know what Jay looked like; he wanted to be able to put a face to the voice. If he never saw anything else, he needed to see her face, if only for a moment. Every cell in his body knew her, could sense her presence; but even though she had described herself to him, he needed to have her face in his mind. The rest of his vanished memory didn't haunt him nearly as much as the knowledge of Jay that he'd lost, and the most piercing of all was that he couldn't remember her face. It was as if he'd lost a part of himself.

His head came up like a wary animal's as he heard the door open, and the eye surgeon laughed. "I half expected you to have taken the bandages off yourself."

"I didn't want to steal your thunder," Steve said. He was standing very still.

Jay was just as still, tension coiling in her as she watched the surgeon, a nurse, Major Lunning and Frank all enter the room. Frank was carrying a bag with the name of a local department store on it, and he placed it on the bed. Without asking, Jay knew it contained street clothes for Steve, and she was vaguely grateful to Frank for thinking of it, because she hadn't.

"Sit down here, with your back to the window," the surgeon said, directing Steve to a chair. When Steve was seated, the doctor took a pair of scissors, cut through the gauze and tape at Steve's temple and carefully removed the outer bandage in order not to disturb the pads over his eyes or let the tape pull at his skin. "Tilt your head back a little," he instructed.

Jay's nails were digging into her palms and her chest hurt. For the first time she was seeing his face without bandages; even the relatively small swathe of gauze that had anchored the pads to his eyes had covered his temples and eyebrows, as well as his cheekbones and the bridge of his nose. He had been a handsome man, but he wasn't handsome any longer. His nose wasn't quite straight, and they had made the bridge a little higher than it had been before the explosion. His cheekbones looked more prominent. All in all, his face had more angles than it had before; the battering he'd taken was evident.

Slowly the doctor removed the gauze pads, then wiped Steve's eyes with some sort of solution. Steve's lids looked a little bruised and his eyes were deeper set than before.

"Pull the curtains," the doctor said quietly, and the nurse pulled them across the window, darkening the room. Then he turned on the dim light over the bed.

"All right, now you can open your eyes. Slowly. Let them get accustomed to the light. Then blink until they focus."

Steve opened his eyes to mere slits and blinked. He tried it again.

"Damn, that light's bright," he said. Then he opened his eyes completely, blinked until they were focused and turned his head toward Jay.

She sat frozen in place and her breath stopped. It was like looking into an eagle's eyes, meeting the fierce gaze of a raptor, a high-soaring predator. They were the eyes of the man she loved so much she ached with it, and terror chilled her blood. She remembered velvety, chocolate-brown eyes, but these eyes were a dark yellowish brown, glittering like amber crystal. An eagle's eyes.

He was the man she loved, but she didn't know who he was, only who he wasn't.

He wasn't Steve Crossfield.

Chapter 7

His heart almost stopped in his chest. Jay. The face to go with the name and the voice, the gentle touch, the sweet and elusive scent. Her description of herself had been accurate, yet it was far from reality. The reality of Jay was a heavy mane of honey-brown hair, eyes of deep-ocean blue and a wide, soft, vulnerable mouth. God, her mouth. It was red and full, as luscious as a ripe plum. It was the most passionate mouth he'd ever seen, and thinking of kissing it, of having those lips touch his body, made a hard ache settle in his loins. She was immobile, her face colorless except for the deep pools of her eyes and that wonderful, exotic mouth. She stared at him as if mesmerized, unable to look away.

"How does everything look?" the surgeon asked. "Do you see halos of light, or are the edges fuzzy?"

He ignored the doctor and stood, his gaze never wavering from Jay. He would never get enough of looking at her. Four steps took him to her, and her eyes widened even more in her utterly white face as she stared up at him. He tried to make his hands gentle as he caught her arms and pulled her to her feet, but anticipation and arousal were riding him hard, and he knew his fingers bit into her soft flesh. She made an incoherent sound; then his mouth covered hers and the erotic feel of her full lips made him want to groan. He wanted to be alone with her. She was shaking in his arms, her hands clutching the front of his shirt as she leaned against him as if afraid she might fall.

"Well, your sense of direction is good," Frank said wryly, and Steve lifted his head from Jay's, though he kept her tight against him, her head pressed into his shoulder. She was still trembling violently.

"I'd say his priorities are in order, too," Major Lunning put in, grinning as he looked at his patient with a deep sense of satisfaction. It hadn't been too many weeks since he'd had serious doubts that Steve would live. To see him now, like this, was almost miraculous. Not that he was fully recovered. He still hadn't regained his full strength, nor had his memory shown any signs of returning. But he was alive, and well on the road to good health.

"I can see everything just fine," Steve said, his voice raspier than usual as he looked around the hospital room that had been home to him for more days than he cared to remember. Even it looked good. He'd disciplined himself to picture everything in his mind, to form a sense of spatial relations so that he always knew where he was in the room, and his mental picture had been remarkably correct. The colors were oddly shocking, though; he hadn't pictured colors, only physical presences.

The surgeon cleared his throat. "Ah . . . if you could sit down for a moment, Mr. Crossfield?"

Steve released Jay, and she shakily sat down, gripping the arms of the chair so tightly that her knuckles were white. They were wrong! He wasn't Steve Crossfield! Shock had kept her mute, but as she watched the surgeon examine Steve—no, *not* Steve!—control returned and she opened her mouth to tell him what a horrible mistake had been made.

Then Frank moved, tilting his head to watch the surgeon, and the movement caught her attention. Ice spread in her veins, freezing her brain again, but one thought still formed: if she told them that she'd made a mistake, that this man wasn't her ex-husband, they would have no use for her. He would be whisked away, and she would never see him again.

She began to shiver convulsively. She loved him. She didn't know who he was but she loved him, and she couldn't give him up. She needed to think this through, but she couldn't right now. She needed to be alone, away from watching eyes, so she could deal with the shock of realizing that Steve...dear God, Steve was dead! And this man in his place was a stranger.

She stood so abruptly that her chair tilted back on two legs before clattering forward again. Five startled faces turned to her as she edged toward the door like a prisoner trying to escape. "I...I just need some coffee," she gasped in a strained voice. She darted out the door, ignoring Steve's hoarse call.

He wasn't Steve. He wasn't Steve. The simple fact was devastating, rocking her to the core.

She ran down the hall to the visitors' lounge and huddled on one of the uncomfortable seats. She felt both cold and numb, and faintly sick, as if she were on the verge of throwing up.

Who was he? Taking deep breaths, she tried to think coherently. He wasn't Steve, so he had to be the American agent Frank had been so concerned about. That meant he had been deeply embroiled in the situation, the one man in the world who knew what had happened, if only he regained his memory. Could he be in danger if anyone—perhaps the person or persons who had set off the explosion that had already almost killed him—knew he was still alive? Until he recovered his memory, he couldn't recognize his enemies; his best protection now was the false identity he wore. She couldn't put him in more danger, nor could she give him up.

It was wrong to pretend he was someone he wasn't. By keeping this secret she was betraying Frank, whom she liked, but most of all she was betraying Steve . . . *damn*, she hated calling him that, but what else could she call him? She had to continue thinking of him as Steve. She was betraying him by putting him in a life that wasn't his, perhaps even hindering his complete recovery. He would never forgive her when he knew, if he ever regained his memory. He would know she had lied to him, that she had forced him to live a lie by putting him in her ex-husband's place. But she couldn't put him at risk. She just couldn't. She loved him too much. No matter what it cost her, she had to lie to protect him.

"Jay."

It was *his* voice, the raw, gravelly voice that haunted her at night in the sweetest of dreams. Numbly she turned her head and looked at him, still so shocked that she couldn't guard her expression. She loved him. Loving Steve, with his need for excitement that she couldn't give him, had been bad enough; what had she done, letting herself love this man whose life consisted of danger? She had walked off an emotional cliff and was now in a free fall, unable to help herself.

He filled the doorway of the lounge. Now that she knew, she saw the differences. He was a little taller than Steve had been, broader of shoulder and deeper of chest, more muscular. His jaw was squarer, his lips fuller. She should have known just by his mouth, the shape of which hadn't been changed by surgery. A funny kind of pain filled her as she realized that she didn't know what he had looked like before. Had his cheekbones been that high and prominent, his eyes that deep set, his nose slightly off center? His face was battered and rough now, but had it been drastically changed?

"What's wrong, baby?" he asked in a low tone, squatting down in front of her and taking her hands in his. His thick, level brows descended in a frown as he felt the iciness of her fingers.

She swallowed, and fine tremors shook her body. Even hunkered down, he was on a level with her. The sense of power, of danger, about him was overwhelming. It had been partially disguised while his eyes had been bandaged, but now, with his fierce will glittering in those yellow-brown eyes, she felt the full force of his personality.

"I'm all right," she managed to say. "It just got to me all of a sudden. I've been so worried...."

He released her hands and slid his palms up her arms. "I wanted to see you so badly I didn't have time to worry," he murmured. The stroking of his big hands warmed her arms, and she felt the heat of his legs as they pressed against hers. "You told me about your blue eyes, but you didn't tell me about your mouth."

He was looking at her mouth. She felt her lips begin to tremble. "What about my mouth?"

"How erotic it is," he said under his breath, and leaned forward. This time his kiss was hard, seeking, forcing her to give way under his onslaught and open her lips for his tongue. Pleasure shuddered through her muscles even though a dim alarm began to sound. While he had been recovering and needed her support so badly, he had been supplicant, asking for her kisses and the intimacy of her touch. Now he wasn't asking, and she realized that he had been holding back all along. He wanted her, and he was coming after her with the full intention of getting what he wanted.

He stood, his strong grip drawing her up, too, without breaking contact with her mouth. He kissed her with the forceful intimacy of a man who intends to take his woman to bed, loosening the reins of control, demanding more. Jay clung to his shoulders, her senses swimming at the hard pressure of his body against hers. He moved his hips, seeking the cradle of hers, and groaned harshly in his throat when his swollen flesh found the warm notch at the apex of her thighs. She would have groaned, too, if she'd had the breath. A wild, hot madness was swirling through her veins, tempting her to forget everything in the demanding urge to satisfy the longings he'd aroused.

A man and woman entered the lounge; the man walked past without more than a sidelong look, but the woman stopped and blushed before looking away and hurrying past. Steve lifted his head, his hands loosening as a crooked smile quirked his mouth. "I think we need to go home," he said.

She panicked all over again. Home? Were they expecting her to take him to the small one-bedroom apartment she'd been using for the past two months? Or would they take him away from her after all, to finish recuperating in some unknown place?

They left the lounge to find Frank leaning patiently against the wall, waiting for them. He straightened and smiled, but his eyes were sympathetic as he looked at Jay. "Feeling better now?"

She took a deep breath. "I don't know. Tell me what's going to happen, then I'll tell you how I feel."

Steve put his arm around her waist. "Don't worry, sweetheart. They're not sending me anywhere without you. Are you, Frank?" He asked the question mildly, but there was steel underlying his tone, and his yellow-brown eyes narrowed.

Frank looked back at him with wry humor. "It never even crossed my mind. Let's step back into your room and we'll talk."

When they were once again behind a closed door, Frank walked over to the window, opened the curtains and looked out, blinking a little at the brightness of the winter sun. "First, you have to let the surgeon finish his examination of your eyes," he said, and glanced back at Steve. "And you'll need a follow-up exam next week, but I'll arrange that."

Steve made an impatient gesture, one that Frank read perfectly. He held up both hands, palms out in a delaying motion. "I'm getting to that. We'd like to keep you safe, but accessible to us. If you agree, we plan to move you to a safe house in Colorado."

Jay's head spun, and she sat down abruptly. Colorado? Her life had been turned upside down in the past two months, so the thought of such a drastic change shouldn't have stunned her, but it did. How could she go off to Colorado? Then she looked at Steve and knew she would go anywhere if it meant she could be with him. It was ironic. When she had been married, the most important thing in her life had been to establish some sort of stability on which to build her relationship with Steve, and the marriage hadn't survived. Now she had to pretend this man was Steve, but she was willing to walk away from everything and everyone she knew just to be with him. Painful sadness filled her, because this pointed out so clearly that she hadn't truly loved the real Steve Crossfield, though she had wanted to. He had held her away, walked his path alone and died alone without anyone ever really being close to him.

"Denver?" Steve guessed.

"No. The closest town is forty miles from the cabin by road, about fifteen air miles. It's a quiet, peaceful place, with no one to put any pressure on you."

"It's really nice of you folks to do all of this, just for the chance to talk to me when I get my memory back," he drawled, watching Frank with a hard gleam in his eyes.

Frank laughed, thinking that some things never changed. Even without his memory, he was so sharp he'd already put part of the puzzle together. "Why don't you go to the apartment and start packing?" Frank suggested to Jay, then lifted his brows in question. "If you want to go, that is."

"She's going," Steve said flatly, crossing his arms as he leaned against the bed. "Or I don't go."

Because she desperately needed the chance to be alone and think, Jay said yes. She slipped from the room without looking at either man, afraid they would see the terror in her eyes.

Steve regarded Frank in silence for a moment before growling, "You told me there wasn't any danger. Why the safe house?"

"So far as we know, you aren't in any danger—"

"Look, you can cut the crap," he interrupted. "I was an agent. I know all of this—" he gestured at the hospital surrounding him "—wasn't done out of the goodness of the government's heart. I know those guards aren't out there for decoration. I also know you wouldn't go to the expense of hiding me away in a safe house unless there was some threat to me, and unless you very badly need some information I may have."

Frank looked interested. "How did you know the guards were there?"

"I heard them," Steve replied shortly.

Now what? Frank looked at the man who had been his friend for over a decade and wondered how much to tell him. Not all of it, for damned certain. Until the Man nailed Piggot, the masquerade had to continue because it was Steve's best protection against any more attacks on his life. He knew too much for them to leave anything about his security to chance, and for the masquerade to be complete, it had to include Jay. The Man didn't take chances with his agents, or his friends, and Steve was both.

"You're right," Frank said. "You're an agent. A very highly trained agent, and we think the information you got on your last assignment is critical."

"Why the safe house?" Steve asked again, not letting up.

"Because the guy who tried to blow you to kingdom come went underground and hasn't surfaced yet. Until we get him, we want to make certain you're safe."

Like a burst of lightning, fury turned his eyes to yellow. "And you dragged Jay into this?"

Frank watched him warily, knowing how fast he could move. "Piggot doesn't know anyone survived the explosion. We just don't want to take any chances with you."

The yellow eyes flickered at the mention of Piggot's name. "Piggot. What's his first name?"

"Geoffrey."

Again there was that flicker in Steve's eyes and Frank watched closely, wondering if the mention of Piggot's name would trigger any real memory. But if it did, Steve kept it to himself. "I want to see the file you have on him," he said.

"I'll see if I can get clearance."

"But don't expect it, right? I'm a security risk now."

"That's the way it's played."

"Yeah. Now tell me why you had to bring Jay into the game. She doesn't know I'm an agent, does she?"

"No. We brought her in to identify you. It's as simple as that. And once she was here . . . you responded to her voice so strongly that the doctors decided it would help you to have her around. So she stayed." That was the truth, as far as it went. Frank just hoped Steve wouldn't ask too many more questions. He'd told him about all he could without clearance from the Man.

Steve rubbed his jaw as he mentally cataloged what Frank had told him. If he'd felt his presence was endangering Jay, he would have walked away from her that minute, but he felt Frank's sincerity. The other man thought they were safe enough. The deciding factor was the thought of living in an isolated house with Jay, just the two of them. He would have another chance. He would learn again what pleased her, and what made her angry. They would have another first time together. After he got all his strength and stamina back, they would lie in bed on cold, snowy mornings and make love until their bodies were damp with sweat even in the chilled air, and she would give him all the fiercely passionate love he could sense inside her. She presented a calm, controlled facade to the world, but perhaps because he hadn't been able to see her and had been forced to rely on his other faculties, he'd sensed the depth of her emotions behind that cool control. Maybe he'd been fool enough to let her slip away from him before, but not again.

"Okay," he said, exhaling slowly. "So we go to this safe house. What kind of security and communications does it have?"

"Bulletproof windows, reinforced steel doors. The cabin is isolated, built on a high meadow. There aren't any roads going up there, so a four-wheel-drive vehicle will be made available to you. The cabin has its own generator, so there aren't any public utility records. You're connected to a satellite-dish antenna for communication and entertainment, with both computer and radio-sending capabilities."

Steve's expression was remote as he concentrated, considering the angles. "Are there any active security systems, or just the passive precautions?"

"Just the passive."

"Why not thermal or motion sensors?"

"To begin with, this cabin is so safe it isn't even on file. And there's a lot of wildlife in the area, which would constantly trigger the alarms. We could set up a perimeter of thermal sensors and program the system to sound the alarm only at a large heat source, but a deer would still set it off."

"How inaccessible is this place?"

"There's just one track leading to it, and I'm being kind by calling it a track. It winds from the cabin across the meadow and down a mountain before it hits a dirt road, then it's twenty more miles before the dirt road runs into a paved secondary road."

"Then a laser across the track would alert us to most visitors, while almost eliminating alarms triggered by wildlife, by covering only a thin strip of the track."

Frank grinned. "You know, don't you, that a bunny is going to hop through that light beam and set off the alarm? All right, I'll have a laser alarm system set up. Do you want an audible or visual alarm?"

"Audible, but a quiet one. And I want a portable beeper to carry with me when we have to leave the house."

"For someone with amnesia, you sure remember a lot," Frank murmured as he took a small pad from his inside coat pocket and began making notes.

"I remember the names of the heads of state of just about every country in the world, too," Steve replied. "I've had a lot of time to play mind games with myself, putting together pieces of the puzzle by cataloging the things I know. I lost everything personal, but I kept a lot of the things related to my job."

"Your job meant a lot to you. It does that, sometimes, takes over so much that the personal side of life kind of fades away."

"Has it done that for you?"

"It did once, a long time ago. Not now."

"How did you get involved in this? You're FBI, and this sure as hell isn't a Bureau operation."

"You're right about that. A lot of strings were pulled, but there are a few people with the power to manage it."

"Very few. So I'm CIA?"

Frank smiled. "No," he said calmly. "Not exactly."

"What the hell does that mean, 'not exactly'? I'm either CIA or I'm not. There's a shortage of alternatives."

"You're affiliated. That's all I can say, other than to assure you that you're perfectly legal. When you recover your memory you'll know why I can't say more."

"All right." Steve shrugged his acceptance. It didn't really matter. Until he regained his memory, the knowledge wouldn't do him any good.

Frank indicated the bag he had brought in with him. "I brought street clothes for you to change into, but first let me get the surgeon in here to finish your exam. After that, I guess you'll be released."

"I'll need more clothes before we go to Colorado. By the way, where did I live?"

"You have an apartment in Maryland. I've arranged for your clothes to be packed and carried to the plane, but they won't fit until you've gained back the weight you've lost. You'll need new clothes until then."

Steve grinned, feeling suddenly light-spirited. "Jay and I will both need new clothes. The snow in Colorado is probably ass-deep to a giraffe."

Frank threw back his head and laughed.

Jay sat on the bed in the cramped apartment she'd been using for the past two months. Her heart was pounding and chills kept racing up and down her spine. The implications, and complications, of the situation terrified her.

Now she knew what it was that had been bothering her off and on for two months; what she had never been able to put her finger on before. When she had been brought here and asked to identify the man in the bed, she hadn't been able to positively say he was Steve Crossfield. Then Frank had said that the man had brown eyes, and she had based her identification on that, because Steve had had dark, velvety eyes, "Chrissy eyes." Probably to a man, or on a vital statistics sheet, brown eyes were simply brown eyes. They didn't allow for chocolate brown, hazel brown or fierce yellow-brown. *But Frank had known that the man had brown eyes!*

She pressed her hands to her temples and closed her eyes. Frank must have known the color of his own agent's eyes, and he had known that Steve's eyes were brown, so it followed that Frank had also realized she couldn't base her identification simply on eye color, yet he had led her to do exactly that. She realized now that he had gently maneuvered her into declaring the man to be Steve Crossfield. He must have known there was at least a fifty-percent chance that the man wasn't Steve, so why had he done it?

The only answer she could come up with, and the one that terrified her, was that Frank had known all along that the man was the American agent and not Steve. He had taken Steve's identity and given it to the man, and given the tale substance by having Steve Crossfield's ex-wife confirm the identity, then maneuvered her into a bedside vigil that would have convinced anyone.

So Steve, the real Steve, was dead, and the agent had been given his identity for... protection?

It all fit. The plastic surgery on his face to alter his appearance; the bandaged hands to prevent fingerprints being taken. Had they done surgery to alter his fingerprints, too? Horrible thought: had they also deliberately damaged his larynx to change his voice? No, surely not. She couldn't believe that. All the doctors had fought so hard for his life, and Frank had been so anxious. No wonder. The man was probably Frank's friend!

But was the amnesia real? Or was the man faking it so he wouldn't have to ''remember'' any of the details of their supposed life together? Amnesia would be a convenient excuse.

She had to believe the amnesia was real, or she would go mad. She had to believe that ''Steve'' was as much in the dark as she was, maybe even more so. And Frank had been sincerely distressed when Major Lunning had told them about the amnesia.

So that left her back at the beginning. If she told Frank she knew Steve wasn't really Steve, the game would be up and they would have no more use for her. She was a screen, useful only to provide incontrovertible proof that the man who had survived the explosion was Steve Crossfield.

So she had to go along with the deception and continue pretending he was Steve, because she loved him. She had fallen in love with him before she even knew what he looked like; she had loved his relentless will, his refusal to give in to pain, to stop fighting. She loved the uncomplaining way he went about recovery and rehabilitation. Except for occasional frustration at his lack of memory, he hadn't let anything get him down. She had fallen in love with the man while he was stripped down to his basic character, without any of the camouflaging layers added by society.

She couldn't give him up now. Yet neither could she take him as hers; she was as caught in the web of circumstance as he was. He trusted her, but she was being forced to lie to him about something as basic as his identity. She knew the man, but she still knew nothing about his life. Dear God, what if he were married?

No, he couldn't be. Whatever game they were playing, they wouldn't tell a woman that she was now a widow, then give her husband another identity. Jay simply couldn't believe that of Frank. But there could still be a woman in Steve's life, someone he cared for, someone who cared for him, even though they weren't married. Was there such a woman waiting for him now, weeping because he'd been gone for so long, and she was terrified that he would never come back?

Jay felt sick; her only choices were twin prongs of the devil's pitchfork, and either would be pure torment. She could either tell him the truth and lose him, very possibly throwing him into danger, or she could lie to him and protect him. For the first time in her life she loved someone with the full force of her nature, with nothing held back, and her emotions propelled her toward the only choice she *could* make. Because she loved him, she could do nothing but protect him, no matter what the cost to herself.

Finally she got up and threw her clothing haphazardly into suitcases, not caring about wrinkles. Two months ago she had stepped into a hall of mirrors, and she had no way of knowing if the reflections she saw were accurate or a carefully constructed illusion. She thought of her chic apartment in New York and how much she had worried about losing it when she'd lost her job, but she couldn't think now why it had seemed so important to her. Her entire life had been thrown off kilter, and now it rotated on a different axis. Steve was the center of her life, not an apartment or a job, or the security she had fought so hard to win. After years of struggle she was throwing it all away just to be with him, and she had no regrets or moments of longing for that life. She loved him. Steve, yet not Steve. His name, but another man. Whoever he was, whatever he was, she loved him.

She found a box and dumped into it the few personal articles such as books and pictures that she'd brought to Washington. It had taken her less than an hour to get ready to leave forever.

As she went back and forth, loading things into the car, she looked around carefully, wondering if any of the people she could see supposedly going about their own business were in reality watching her. Maybe she was getting paranoid, but too much had happened for her to take anything for granted, even the appearance of normalcy. That very morning she had looked into fierce, golden eyes and realized that everything that had happened during the past two months had been a lie. The blinders of trust had been stripped from her eyes, making her wary.

Suddenly she felt a driving need to be with him again; uncertainty made her desperate for him. He was no longer a patient in need of her care and attention, but a man who, in spite of his memory loss, would be more surefooted than she was in this world of shifting reality. The instincts and reactions she had wondered about were now explained, as was the scope of his knowledge of world politics. He had lost his identity, but his training had remained with him.

He and Frank were lounging in the hospital room, patiently waiting for her. Jay barely managed a greeting for them; her eyes were on Steve. He had changed into khaki pants and a white shirt with the sleeves rolled back over his forearms. Even as lean as he was, he still gave the impression of power. His shoulders and chest strained at the cotton shirt. With the bandages gone from his eyes, he had shed the last semblance of being in need of care. He looked her over from head to foot and his eyes narrowed in a look of sexual intent as old as time. Jay felt it like a touch, stroking over her body, and she felt both warm and alarmed.

He got to his feet with lazy grace and came to her side, sliding his arm around her waist in a possessive gesture. "That was fast. You must not have packed much."

"It wasn't actually packing," she explained ruefully. "It was more like wadding and stuffing."

"You didn't have to be in such a hurry. I wasn't going anywhere without you," he drawled.

"Both of you have to go shopping, anyway," Frank added. "I didn't think of it, but Steve pointed out that neither of you has clothes suited to a Colorado winter."

Jay looked at Frank, at his clear, calm eyes and friendly face. He'd been a rock for her to lean on these past two months, smoothing the way for her, doing what he could to make her comfortable, and all the time he'd been lying to her. Even knowing that, she simply couldn't believe he'd done it for any reason other than to protect Steve, and because of that she forgave him completely. She was willing to do the same thing, so how could she hold it against him?

"There's no point in shopping here," Steve said. "Or even in Denver. If we go to a city, we'll have to get what some department-store buyer thinks is stylish for a winter vacation. We'll stop at some small-town general store and buy what the locals buy, but not at the town closest to the cabin. Maybe one about a hundred miles from it.''

Frank nodded at that impeccable logic, as well as the ring of command in Steve's raspy voice. He was taking over the show, but then, they hadn't expected anything else; amnesia didn't change basic character traits, and Steve was an expert at logistics. He knew what to do and how to get it done.

Jay didn't exhibit any surprise at the precautions. Her deep blue eyes were calm. Having made her decision, she was ready for whatever happened. ''Will we need any sort of weapon?'' she asked. ''After all, we'll be pretty isolated.'' She had the urbanite's distaste for guns and violence, but the thought of living on a remote mountain put things in a different light. There were times when guns were practical.

Steve looked down at her, and his arm tightened around her. He'd already discussed weapons with Frank. ''A rifle wouldn't be a bad idea.''

''You'll have to show me how to shoot. I've never handled a gun.''

Frank checked the time. ''I'll make a call and we'll get started. By the time we get to the airport, the plane will be ready.''

''Which airport are we using?''

''National. We'll be flying in to Colorado Springs, then driving the rest of the way.'' Satisfied with the way things had turned out, Frank went to make his call. Actually he had to make two calls: one to the airport to have the plane readied, and another to the Man to bring him up-to-date.

Chapter 8

After a series of small delays, it was midafternoon before the private jet actually took off from Washington National Airport, and the sun was already low in the pale winter sky. There was no way they could make it to the cabin that night, so Frank had already made arrangements for them to stay overnight in Colorado Springs. Jay sat by a window, her muscles tense as she looked down at the monochromatic scenery without really seeing it. She had the sensation of stepping out of one life and into another, with no bridge by which to return. She hadn't even told her family where she was going; though they weren't a close-knit group, they did usually know everyone's location. She hadn't seen any of them at Christmas because she had remained at the hospital with Steve, and now it was as if a tie had been severed.

Steve sat beside her, his long legs stretched out as he lounged in the comfortable seat and pored over several current news magazines. He was totally absorbed, as if he'd been starved for the written word. Abruptly he snorted and tossed his magazine aside. ''I'd forgotten how slanted news coverage can be," he muttered, then gave a short laugh at his own phrasing. "Along with everything else."

His wry tone splintered her distracted mood and she chuckled. Smiling, he turned his head to watch her, rubbing his eyes to focus them. "Unless my vision settles down, I may need glasses to read."

"Are your eyes bothering you?" she asked, concerned. He'd worn sunglasses since leaving the hospital, but had taken them off when they had boarded the plane.

"They're tired, and the light is still too bright. It's a little hard to focus on close objects, but the surgeon told me that might clear up in a few days."

"Might?"

"There's a fifty-percent chance I'll need reading glasses." He reached over and took her hand, rubbing his thumb over her palm. "Will you still love me if I have to wear glasses?"

Her breath caught and she looked away. Silence thickened between them. Then he squeezed her hand and whispered roughly, "All right, I won't push. Not right now. We'll have time to get everything settled."

So he intended to push later, when they were alone in the cabin. She wondered exactly what he wanted from her: an emotional commitment, or just the physical enjoyment of her body? After all, it had been at least two months since he'd had sex. Then she wondered who had been the last woman to lie in bed with him, and jealousy seared her, mingled with pain. Did that woman mean anything to him? Was she waiting for him, crying herself to sleep at night because he didn't call?

They spent the night at a motel in Colorado Springs. Jay was surprised to find there was only a light dusting of snow on the ground, instead of the several feet she had expected, but random flakes were swirling softly out of the black sky with the promise of more snow by morning. The cold pierced her coat, and she shivered as she turned the collar up around her ears. She would be glad to get something more suitable to wear.

Steve was tired from his first day out of the hospital, and she was exhausted, too; it had been a hard day for both of them. She lay down across the bed in her room and dozed while Frank went to get hamburgers for dinner. They ate in Frank's room, and she excused herself immediately afterward. All she wanted was to relax and gather her thoughts. To that end she took a long, hot shower, letting the water beat the tension out of her muscles, but it was still hard to think coherently. The risk she was taking frightened her, yet she knew she couldn't go back. Couldn't—and wouldn't.

She tied the belt of her robe securely and opened the bathroom door, then froze. Steve was stretched out on her bed, his arms behind his head as he stared at the television. The picture was on, but the sound was off. She looked at him, then at the door to her room, her brows puckered in confusion. "I thought I locked the door."

"You did. I picked the lock."

She didn't move any closer. "A little something you remembered?"

He looked at her, then swung his legs off the bed and sat up. "No, I didn't remember it. I just knew how to do it."

Good Lord, what other suspicious talents did he have? He looked lean and dangerous, his battered face hard, his yellow eyes narrow and gleaming; he was probably capable of things that would give her nightmares, but she didn't fear him. She loved him too much; she had loved him from the moment she had first touched his arm and felt his will to live burning in him. But her nerves jangled as he stood and took the few steps he needed to reach her. He was so close now that she had to look up to see his face; she could feel the heat emanating from his body, smell the warm, musky male scent of his skin.

He cupped her cheek in his palm, his thumb rubbing lightly over the shadows fatigue had smudged under her eyes, making their blueness seem even deeper. She was pale and jittery, her body trembling. She had taken care of him for months, spending all day, every day, at his bedside, willing him to live and pulling him out of the darkness. She had filled his whole life to the point that even the shock of having amnesia paled in comparison. She had gotten him through hell. Now the strain was telling on her, and he was the stronger one. He could feel the tension in her, vibrating like a string at the point of breaking. He slid his arm around her waist and pulled her forward until her body rested against his. His other hand moved from her cheek into her heavy brown hair, exerting just enough pressure to bring her head against his shoulder.

"I don't think this is a good idea," she whispered, the sound muffled in his shirt.

"It *feels* like a damned good idea," he muttered. Every muscle in his body was tightening, his loins growing heavy with desire. God, he wanted her. His hands moved over her slender body. "Jay," he whispered roughly, and bent his head to hers.

The hot, needful pressure of his mouth made her dizzy. The stroking of his tongue against hers made her tighten inside with pleasure so piercing it was almost unbearable. Her hands lifted to the back of his neck, clinging as all strength washed out of her legs. She barely noticed as he turned with her still in his arms and forced her backward until the bed nudged against the backs of her knees. She lost her sense of balance, but his arms supported her as she fell back, and then his hard weight came down on top of her.

She had forgotten how the pressure of a man's body felt, and she inhaled sharply as quick response flooded her veins. The wide expanse of his chest flattened her breasts, and the swollen ridge of his manhood pushed against her feminine mound, his thighs controlling the restless movement of her legs. He kissed her again and again, barely letting her catch her breath before his mouth returned to take it away once more. Feverishly they strained together, wanting more. He pulled at the belt of her robe until the knot gave and the fabric parted, exposing the thinner fabric of her nightgown. He made a rough sound of frustration at this additional barrier, but for the moment he was too impatient to deal with it. His hand closed over her breast, kneading the soft flesh, his thumb making circles on her nipple until it tightened into a nub.

She whimpered softly into his mouth. "We can't," she cried, desperation and desire tearing her apart.

"The hell we can't," he rasped, taking her hand and moving it down his body to where his flesh strained at the fabric of his pants. Her fingers jerked at the contact; then a spasm of pain crossed her pale face, and her hand lingered involuntarily, exploring the dimensions of his arousal. He caught his breath. "Jay, baby, don't stop me now!"

She was stunned at how quickly passion had exploded between them; one kiss and they were falling on the bed. Her lips trembled as she stared up at him. She didn't even know his name! Tears burned her eyes and she blinked them away.

He groaned at the liquid sheen welling in her eyes and kissed her again with rough passion. "Don't cry. I know this is fast, but everything's going to be okay. We'll get married as soon as we can, and this time we'll make a go of it."

Shocked, she swallowed convulsively and barely managed to speak. "Married? Are you serious?"

"As serious as a heart attack, baby," he said, and grinned roguishly.

The tears burned again, and again she forced them back. Misery filled her. She wanted nothing more than to marry him, but she couldn't. She would be marrying him under false pretenses, pretending he was someone he wasn't. Such a marriage probably wouldn't even be legal. "We can't," she whispered, and a tear rolled out the corner of her eye before she could catch it.

He rubbed the wetness from her temple with his thumb. "Why can't we?" he asked with rough tenderness. "We did it before. We should be able to do better this time around, with our prior experience."

"What if you've remarried?" She gulped back a sob as she frantically thought up excuses. "Even if you haven't, what if there's someone else? Until you get your memory back, we won't *know*!"

He froze above her; then, with a sigh, he rolled off her to lie on his back, staring at the ceiling. He swore with a precise, Anglo-Saxon explicitness that was all the more jarring for the control in his voice. "All right," he finally said. "We'll get Frank to check it out. Hell, Jay, he's already checked it out! Isn't that why they had to get you to identify me?"

Too late she saw the trap, and saw also that he wasn't going to give up; with his usual steamroller determination, he was flattening the obstacles in his path. "You could still have some...someone who loves you, someone waiting for you."

"I can't promise you I don't," he said, turning his head to watch her with his predatory golden eyes. "But that's not a legal deterrent. I won't let you get away from me because some unknown woman somewhere may be in love with me."

"Until you get your memory back, you can't know that *you* aren't in love with someone else!"

"I *know*," he snapped, propping himself up on his elbow and leaning over her. "You keep coming up with excuses, but the real reason is that you're afraid of me, aren't you? Why? Damn it, I know you love me, so what's the problem?"

He was so arrogantly sure of her devotion that her own temper flared, but only for a moment. It was true. She had revealed it in a thousand different ways. She admitted shakily, "I do love you." There was nothing to be gained from denying it, and actually saying it aloud held its own painful sweetness.

His face softened and he put his free hand on her breasts, gently cupping them. "Then why shouldn't we get married?"

It was hard to concentrate with his palm burning her flesh through the thin cotton of her gown, and her body quickened again. She wanted him just as much as he wanted her, and denying him was the hardest thing she'd ever done, but she had no choice. Until his memory returned, she was in limbo. She couldn't take advantage of him now by marrying him under false pretenses.

"Well?" he demanded impatiently.

"I love you," she said again. Her lips trembled. "Ask me again when your memory has returned, and I'll say yes. Until then, until we're both certain it's what you want, I...I just can't."

His face hardened. "Damn it, Jay, I know what I want."

"We've been thrown together because of the circumstances! We don't know each other under normal conditions. You're not the same man I married—" how true that was! "—and I'm not the same woman. We need time! When your memory returns—"

"That's not guaranteed," he interrupted, his voice harsh with frustration. "What if my memory never returns? What if there's permanent brain damage? Then what? Are you still going to be saying no this time next year? Five years from now?"

"I don't think you have brain damage," she said shakily. "You recovered your speech and motor functions too easily."

"That's beside the damned point!" He was furious. Before she could move, he rolled onto her and pinned her hands to the bed. He was so close that she could see the yellow flecks in his irises, his curling black lashes, and a tiny scar in his left eyebrow she hadn't noticed before. He took a deep breath and slowly relaxed, the anger fading from him as he moved against the softness of her body, letting her feel his hardness. "I won't wait forever," he said in soft warning. "I'm going to have you. If not now, then later."

Then he rolled off her and was gone, moving with a peculiar silent grace that had become far more evident since the bandages had been removed from his eyes. There had been signs of it before, manifested in the superb control he had over his movements, but now it was striking. He didn't just move, he flowed, his muscles rippling with liquid power. Jay lay quietly on the bed, her body burning from frustration and the lingering sensation of contact with his, her eyes on the door he had closed behind him.

Who was he? Terror washed over her again, but it was terror for him. He was an agent, obviously, but not just any agent. He had clearly had extensive training; he was valuable enough that the government was willing to spend a fortune protecting him, as well as setting up this elaborate charade with her as an unsuspecting partner. If it hadn't been for his eyes, she might never have suspected a thing. But if he was that valuable to his own government, then logic told her he was of at least equal value to his enemies. All things were in proportion; whatever lengths had been taken to protect him, his enemies would be willing to go to equal lengths to find and destroy him.

As each new part of him was revealed, the stakes seemed to get higher. Now she knew that he was skilled at clandestine forced entry. She had picked up some of the lingo at Bethesda; what had she heard it called? Light entry? No, soft entry. They called it a soft entry. Going in hard was an attack with weapons. Maybe the lock on the motel door wasn't the sturdiest model available, but she knew that picking it was beyond the average citizen. A good burglar wouldn't have any trouble with it, though...or a good agent.

And the way he moved. He was as controlled and graceful as a dancer, but a dancer's moves were poetic, while Steve's were evocative of silent danger.

His mind. No detail escaped him. He was trained to notice and use everything. Already Frank was deferring to him, another sign of his importance.

And he was in danger. Perhaps not immediate danger, but she knew it was there waiting for him.

The phone rang at two in the morning in Frank's room, and he muttered a sleepy curse as he fumbled for the receiver. It was second nature to him not to turn on a light, which could alert any outside observers that he was awake. Nor did he have to ask who it was, because only one man knew where they were.

"Yes," he said, and yawned.

"Piggot surfaced," the Man said. "East Berlin. We couldn't get to him in time, but we did find out that he's learned there was a survivor of the explosion and has made inquiries."

"Did the cover hold?"

"If Piggot asked at all, there has to be some doubt. Make certain your trail is covered. I don't want anyone other than the two of us to know where they are. How is he doing?"

"Better than I would have, if this had been my first day out of the hospital in two months. He's stronger than I expected. One other thing: I never would have believed it, but I think he's falling in love with her. It isn't just that he's been dependent on her, I think he's really serious."

"Good God," the Man said, startled. He laughed. "Well, it happens to the best of us. I have the final medical report on him here. His brain damage, if any, is minimal. He's a walking miracle, especially the speed of his recovery. He should regain his full memory but it may take a trigger of some sort to release it. We may have to bring his family in, or take him home, but not until we find Piggot. Until then, he stays hidden."

"The day we get Piggot, we tell him—and Jay—what's going on?"

The Man sighed. He sounded tired. "I hope he's recovered his memory by then. Damn it, we need to know what happened over there, and what he found out. But with his memory or without it, he has to stay there until we get Piggot. He has to be Steve Crossfield."

Steve woke early and lay in bed, feeling the fatigue that still weighted his body, as well as the sexual frustration that had been plaguing him for several weeks. He had tried, but even the rigorous exercise he'd been taking hadn't rebuilt his strength to the point he would have liked. Yesterday had exhausted him. He grinned sourly, thinking that it had probably been a good thing Jay had turned him down, because there was a good chance he would have collapsed on her in the middle of making love. Damn it.

He didn't intend to let her refusal stand in his way, but his lack of strength was something else. He had to get back in shape. It wasn't just that he was dissatisfied with his lack of strength and his physical limitations; he had a nagging feeling that he needed to be in top shape just in case... *what*? He didn't know what he expected to happen, but he had an uneasy feeling. If anything came up, he had to be in shape to protect Jay and handle the situation.

After getting out of bed, he first took the pistol that had been on the bedside table and placed it on the floor, within easy reach. Then he dropped down and began doing push-ups, counting silently. Thirty was his limit. Already panting, he rolled over and hooked his feet under the bed, his hands behind his head, and did sit-ups. The new scars on his abdomen throbbed at the strain he was putting on them, and sweat broke out on his brow. He had to stop at seventeen. Swearing in disgust, he looked down at his body. He was in pitiful shape. Before, he'd been able to do a hundred push-ups and sit-ups without even breathing hard—

He went still, waiting for the half memory to become full-blown, waiting for the mental door to open, but nothing happened. Just for a second he'd had a glimpse of what his life had been before; then the door had closed again. The doctor had told him not to try to force it, but that blank door taunted him. There was something he needed to know, and rage built inside him because he couldn't force his way past the block.

Suddenly he heard footsteps outside the room, and he rolled, grabbing the pistol as he did so. Stretched out prone on the carpet, he aimed the pistol at the door and waited. The footsteps halted and a grumpy voice said, "June, come *on*. We need to get an early start and you've wasted enough time."

"Will the town be gone if we get there at four instead of three?" an equally grumpy female voice returned.

Steve let out his breath and climbed to his feet, staring at the pistol in his hand. It fit his palm as if he'd been born holding it. It was a Browning automatic, high caliber, and loaded with hollow-tip bullets that would make a hell of a hole going in and an even bigger one coming out. Frank had given it to him at the hospital while they were waiting for Jay to return and had told him to keep it on him, just as a precaution. When Steve had reached to take it, it was as if part of him had slipped back into focus. He hadn't realized how unusual it had been not to be armed, until the pistol was in his hand.

His reactions just now said a lot about the type of life he'd been living; it had been second nature for him to place the pistol within reach even while exercising, and second nature to regard those approaching footsteps as a possible danger. Maybe Jay had been smart to divorce him the first time. Maybe he wasn't doing her a favor by forcing his way back into her life, considering the dangers of *his*.

The pistol in his hand was a fine piece of hardware, but it couldn't compare to the feel of Jay's body. If he had to choose between Jay and his work, the job had just lost. He'd been a damned fool the first time, but he wasn't going ·to foul up this second chance. Whoever he worked for would just have to reassign him, bring him in, or he'd get out completely. No more clandestine meetings, no more assassins after him. Hell, it was time he settled down and let the Young Turks have their chance. He was thirty-seven, long past the age when most other men had wives and families.

But he wouldn't tell him until his memory returned, he thought cynically as he showered. Until then, he couldn't afford to totally trust anyone, except Jay.

They bought boots, socks and insulated underwear in Colorado Springs, jeans and flannel shirts in another town, hats and shearling coats in another. Jay also bought a thick down jacket with a hood, and a supply of long flannel gowns. The two vehicles Frank had obtained were four-wheel-drive Jeeps with snow tires, so they made good time, even though the snow became deeper the farther west they went.

Frank drove the lead Jeep, with Steve and Jay in the one behind. Jay had never driven a stick shift before, so the driving was left up to Steve. At first Jay worried about his legs, but he didn't seem to have any difficulty with the clutching and braking, so after a time she stopped worrying and began paying attention to the magnificent scenery as they drove west on U.S. 24. The sky, which had been clear, gradually became leaden with clouds, and occasional snowflakes began to drift down. The weather didn't worsen beyond that, and they continued to make good time even after they turned off onto a state highway. Then they left the state highway for a secondary road with much less traffic and a lot more snow, necessitating a slower speed. After that

Frank took a dirt road that wound through the mountains for what seemed like hours, and finally he made another turnoff. Jay could see no discernible road or even a trail; they were simply driving up a mountain by the route of least resistance.

"I wonder if he knows where he's going," she muttered, clinging to the seat as the Jeep jolted to one side.

"He knows. Frank's a good agent," Steve returned absently, downshifting to climb a particularly steep rise. Once they reached the top, they seemed to be in a high, wide meadow that stretched and dipped for miles in front of them. They drove along the edge of the tree line until the meadow abruptly ended, and then they descended sharply down the side of the mountain. Next they climbed up another mountain, where there was a stretch of track barely wide enough to accommodate the Jeeps. On one side was the rock face, and on the other, nothing but an increasing distance to the bottom. Then they crested that mountain, too, and reached another rolling meadow. As the sun dipped behind the western peaks, Steve squinted his eyes at the tree line to their left. "That must be the cabin."

"Where?" Jay asked, sitting up eagerly. Just the thought of being able to get out of the Jeep and stretch her legs was pure heaven.

"In that stand of pines, just to the left."

Then she saw it and sighed in relief. It was just an ordinary cabin, but it was as welcome as a luxury hotel. It was tucked just under the trees, visible only from the front. Because it was built on a slope, the front was higher than the back; there were six wooden steps leading up to a porch that ran all the way across. Built onto the cabin at the back was a lean-to for the Jeeps, and thirty yards to the rear was a shed.

They parked under the lean-to and stiffly got out, arching their backs to stretch aching muscles. The air was so cold and crisp that it almost hurt to inhale, but the setting sun was painting the snowy peaks and ridges in shades of red, gold and purple, and Jay stood motionless, entranced, until Steve nudged her into motion.

It took several trips to carry everything in; then Frank took Steve to the shed to show him how the generator worked. Evidently someone had already been up to turn it on, because the electric lights worked and the refrigerator was humming. Jay checked the small pantry and refrigerator, and found them fully stocked with canned goods and frozen meats.

She gave herself a short tour of the cabin. Next to the kitchen was a small utility-mudroom with a modern washer and dryer. There was no dining room, only a round wooden table and four chairs in one corner of the kitchen. The living room was comfortably furnished in sturdy Early American, with brown corduroy upholstery. A brown-and-blue hooked rug covered the wooden floor, and one wall was almost entirely taken up by an enormous rock fireplace. There were two bedrooms of equal size, connected by the cabin's lone bathroom. Jay stared at the connecting door, her heart beating a little faster at the thought of sharing a bathroom with him. She knew the intimacy of damp towels hanging side by side, toiletries becoming jumbled together, a shared tube of toothpaste. His whiskers would be in the sink, his razor on the side. The small details of living together were at least as seductive as physical intimacies, meshing their lives at every moment of the day.

The back door slammed, and Steve called, "Where are you?" His rough voice was even raspier than usual from breathing the cold air.

"Exploring," she replied, leaving the bathroom and crossing to the bedroom door. "Any objections if I take the front bedroom? It has the best view."

A fire had already been laid in the fireplace. He bent down and struck a match on the hearth, then held it to the paper and kindling under the logs, not answering until he'd straightened. "Let me look at them."

Vaguely surprised, Jay stepped aside and let him enter. He examined the location of the windows and their locks, opened the closet and looked at it, then stepped into the adjoining bath.

"It's a connecting bath," she pointed out.

He grunted and opened the door into the second bedroom. The windows in both rooms were on the side walls, but because the rear of the cabin was closer to the ground than the front was, the windows in the second bedroom were more accessible from the outside. "All right," he said, checking the locks on his windows, too. "But I want it understood that if you hear anything at all during the night, you wake me. Okay?"

"Yes," she said, her throat constricting. All this was second nature to him. He must think there was some danger, too, despite all the precautions Frank had taken. She had wanted to think they were safe here, but perhaps they weren't. The best thing she could do was not argue with him.

He glanced at her, and his rough face softened a bit. "Sorry. I guess I'm overreacting to a strange situation. I didn't mean to scare you." Because the tension didn't fade from her eyes, he walked over to her, cupped her face in his hands, then kissed her. Her wonderfully full, lush, exotic mouth opened for him and his tongue teased at hers. Jay put her hands on his shoulders and luxuriated in the heat of his body against her. The cabin wasn't icy, but it was far from warm.

He held her against him for a moment, then reluctantly let her go. "Let's see what this place has in the way of grub. If I don't eat soon, I'm going to fall down." He wasn't exaggerating, she realized. She could feel a faint tremor in his muscles, a sign of the enormous strain he'd put on his body that day.

Casually she put her arm around his waist as they walked back to the living room. "I've already checked the food. We can have almost anything our hearts desire, as long as our hearts desire plain cuisine. If you want lobster or truffles, you're out of luck."

"I'd settle for a can of soup," he said tiredly, and groaned as he sank down into one of the comfortable chairs. He stretched his legs out, absently rubbing his thighs.

"We can do better than that," Frank said as he brought in an armload of wood, having caught Steve's last comment. He stacked the wood on the hearth and dusted his hands. "I think. I'm not much of a cook." He looked hopefully at Jay, and she laughed.

"I'll see what I can do. I'm a real whiz with microwave dinners, but I didn't see a microwave oven, so I'm a little lost."

She was too tired to do much, but it didn't take a lot of effort to open two large cans of beef stew and heat them, or to brown buttered rolls in the gas oven. They were almost silent as they ate, and after Frank had helped her clean up the few dishes, they all took turns in the shower. By eight o'clock they were asleep, Jay and Steve in their respective bedrooms and Frank rolled in a blanket on the couch.

They rose early the next morning, and after a hearty breakfast Frank and Steve walked around in the snow. The gas stove and hot-water heater operated on butane gas, and the large tank had been filled; it shouldn't need refilling until spring. The fuel tank for the generator would need replenishing, but all Steve had to do was contact Frank by computer, and fuel would be brought in by helicopter. They didn't want a delivery to the cabin by any commercial business or utility, and, at any rate, the cabin was too difficult for an ordinary fuel truck to reach. It was a complicated setup, but it was meant to be an ultrasafe lodging, unlisted in any files. All in all, the place was stocked for a long-term stay, though Frank couldn't help wishing Steve would recover his memory soon and put an end to all this, or that Piggot would be caught.

"The nearest town is Black Bull, population one hundred thirty-three," Frank said. "Go down to the dirt road and turn right, and you'll eventually get there. It has a general store for basic food and supplies. If you want anything fancier, you'll have to find a larger town, but keep a low profile. You should have enough cash to last a couple of months, but let me know if you need more."

Steve looked out over the white meadow. The air was so clear, the early-morning sun so bright on the spotless snow, that it hurt his eyes. The cold burned his lungs. The land was so damned big and empty that it gave him an eerie feeling, but at the same time he was almost content. He was impatient for Frank to leave so he would finally be alone, completely alone, with Jay.

"You're safe here," Frank added. "The Man uses it sometimes." He glanced up at the cabin. "I wouldn't have brought Jay here if it wasn't safe. She's a civilian, so take good care of her, pal."

A tingle, a heightened awareness, had seized Steve when Frank mentioned the Man. It wasn't a sense of danger but a sort of excitement. The memory was there, but blocked from his consciousness by the lingering effects of the explosion. The Man was another piece of the puzzle.

He shook Frank's hand, and their eyes met in the comradeship of men who have been in danger together. "You probably won't see me again until this is over, but I'll be in touch," Frank said. "I'd better get moving. It's supposed to start snowing again this afternoon."

They went inside and Frank got his gear, then told Jay goodbye. She hugged him, her eyes suspiciously bright. Frank had been her rock for two months, and she would miss him. He had also been a buffer between her and Steve; when he left, there would be only the two of them.

She glanced at Steve, to find him watching her intently. His pale brown eyes were glowing, yellower than they had been moments before, like those of a raptor that had sighted its prey.

Chapter 9

Jay had expected Steve to pounce on her, but to her relief he seemed to have other things on his mind. For the next week he spent the daylight hours prowling around the cabin and shed and exploring their high meadow, as tense and wary as a cat in unfamiliar surroundings. The hours passed tromping through the snow tired him, and as often as not he would go to sleep soon after eating dinner. Jay worried, until she realized that it was a natural part of his recovery. The rehabilitation he'd had in the hospital had given him a start, but he was still a long way from full strength, and the many hours of walking served two purposes: to acquaint him with his new territory, and to rebuild his stamina. It was the end of the week before he began to relax, but every day he still walked a perimeter around the cabin, watching, checking for any intrusion.

They seemed so isolated that she couldn't understand his caution, but she supposed it was ingrained in him. Watching him gave her an even greater insight into the man he was.

He was so superbly suited to his occupation! He knew what to do by instinct, without needing to rely on memory.

When he was stronger, he began chopping wood to keep a good supply for the fireplace. They used the hearth for most of their heat, to conserve fuel. The cabin was so snugly built and insulated that it held heat well, and a good fire was sufficient to keep the entire place comfortable. At first his hands were sore and blistered, despite the gloves he wore, but gradually they toughened. After a while he added jogging to his activities, but he didn't jog in the meadow, where it was clear. He ran through the trees, up and down the hills, deliberately picking the roughest path, and every day his legs were a little stronger, his breathing a little easier, so he would push himself further.

Jay loved those first days in the cabin, high in the vast, silent meadow. Sometimes the only sound was that of the wind stirring the trees. Having been accustomed her entire life to the bustle of cities, the space and silence made her feel as if she'd been reborn in a new world. The last remnants of tension from her old life relaxed and faded away. She was alone in the mountains with the man she loved, and they were safe.

He began teaching her how to drive a stick shift. To Jay, it was fun, bouncing in the Jeep over the meadow. To Steve, it was a precaution, against the possibility that something could happen to him and Jay would have to do the driving. It might come down to a matter of saving her life.

There was a heavy snow the third week they were there. Jay woke early to a world where every sound had been muffled. She got up to peek out the window at the deep drifts of new snow, then tumbled back into her warm bed and fell instantly asleep again. When she woke the second time it was almost ten, and she felt wonderfully rested, as well as starving.

She dressed hurriedly and brushed her hair, wondering why the cabin was so silent. Where was Steve? She looked into his room, but it was empty. There was a pot of coffee in the kitchen, and she drank a cup while standing at the window, searching the tree line for some sign of him. Nothing.

Curious, she finished the coffee and returned to her room to stamp her feet into warm boots; then she put on her shearling coat and pulled a thick knit cap over her hair. It was unusual for Steve to go out without telling her where he would be and how long he'd be gone. She wondered what he was doing, and why he hadn't woken her. Could he have hurt himself?

Anxious now, she went down the back steps. "Steve?" she called softly, a little afraid to raise her voice. The meadow was so silent, and for the first time its isolation felt threatening, instead of safe. Was there someone else out there?

His footprints were plainly visible in the new snow. He'd evidently made several trips to the woodpile to replenish the supply in the house, because there was a worn trail between them; then he'd walked up the slope into the forest. Jay dug her gloves out of her coat pocket and put them on, and wished she'd wrapped a scarf around her nose and mouth. It was so cold that the air felt brittle. She turned the collar of the coat up around her neck and began following Steve's trail, carefully stepping in his tracks because that was easier than breaking through the snow herself.

The snow wasn't as deep under the trees, making the walking easier, but Jay kept to the prints Steve had made. The thickly-growing evergreens, their branches weighted down with snow, blanketed noise and muffled it out of existence. She could barely hear herself breathe or the snow crunching under her boots. She wanted to call Steve's name again but somehow didn't dare, as if it would be sacrilege in this silent white, black and green cathedral.

If anything, she tried to be even quieter, picking her way from tree to tree, trying to become part of the forest. Then, suddenly, she lost Steve's tracks. She stood under the drooping limbs of a spruce and looked around, but there were no more tracks to follow. It was as if he'd vanished. It was impossible to walk in the snow without leaving tracks! But there were no tracks under the trees. She looked up, wondering if he'd climbed a tree and was sitting there laughing at her. Nothing.

Common sense told her that he'd played some sort of trick, but his tracks would have to pick up somewhere. She thought a minute, then began walking in a slow, constantly enlarging circle. She would have to cross his path somewhere.

Fifteen minutes later, she was angry. Damn him! He was playing games with her, unfair games, considering his training. She was getting cold, and she was already starving. Let him play Daniel Boone; she was going back to the cabin to cook breakfast—for *one*!

Just to be perverse, she backtracked as cautiously as she'd come; maybe she could leave him in here, sneaking around and hiding from her while she was already back at the cabin, snug and warm and eating a hot breakfast. He'd show up after a while, all innocence, and he could damn well cook his own breakfast! Show-off!

She crept back toward the cabin, sidling as close to the tree trunks as she could, stopping often to listen for any betraying sound before moving to the next tree, and looking in all directions before moving again. Her indignation grew, and she began to think what she could do in the way of revenge, but most of her ideas seemed both petty and paltry. What she really wanted to do was hit him. Hard. Twice.

She had just begun to creep around a tree when the skin on the back of her neck prickled and she froze, her heart leaping in fear at the ancient warning of danger. She couldn't hear or see anything, but she could feel someone, or some*thing*, close by. Were there wolves in the mountains? Or bears? Motionless except for her eyes, she looked around for something to use as a weapon, and finally she saw the outline of a sturdy-looking stick, buried under the snow. A fraction of an inch at a time, she bent to reach for the stick, her senses raw and screaming.

Something hard and heavy hit her in the middle of the back, and another blow numbed her forearm. She was knocked facedown in the snow, her lungs straining for air, her arm useless. She couldn't even scream. She was jerked roughly onto her back, and there was a flash of shiny metal as a knife was laid against her throat.

Stunned, terrified, unable to breathe, she stared up into narrowed, deadly eyes as yellow as an eagle's.

His eyes widened as he recognized her, then narrowed again with rage. He jabbed the wicked-looking knife back into its scabbard and took his knee off her chest. "Damn it, woman, I could've killed you!" he roared, his voice like rusty metal. "What in hell are you doing?"

Jay could only gasp and writhe on the ground, wondering if she might die from lack of air. Her entire chest was burning and her vision was wavering.

Steve jerked her to a sitting position and whacked her on the back several times, hard enough to hurt, but at least the air rushed back into her body. She almost choked as her lungs expanded again, and tears sprang to her eyes. She gagged and coughed, and Steve patted her on the back but his tone was hard: "You'll be all right. It's less than you deserve, and a hell of a lot less than what could have happened."

She didn't plan it. She saw the stick out of the corner of her eye, the one she'd been reaching for when he'd hit her, and the next thing she knew it was in her hand. Red mist fogged her vision as she swung at him with all the strength her fury had given her. He dodged under the first blow, cursing, and leaped back to escape the second one. She moved to the left, trying to back him against a tree so he wouldn't be able to escape so easily, and swung again. He tried to grab the stick, and she caught him on the wrist with a solid *thunk!* then wound up for another blow. Cursing again, he bent low and rushed her. She hit him on the back with the stick just as his shoulder jammed into her stomach with enough force to knock her sprawling again.

"Damn it!" he yelled, kneeling astride her and pinning her wrists to the ground. "Settle down! Damn it, Jay! What in hell's wrong with you?"

She twisted and bucked beneath him, trying to throw him off. He tightened his knees on her sides, forestalling that effort, and his hands bit into her wrists so tightly there was no way she could free them. Finally she stopped struggling and glared impotently at him, her eyes like blue fire. "Get off me!"

"So you can brain me with that damn stick? Fat chance!"

She took a deep, shuddering breath and forced her voice to a relatively calm tone. "I won't hit you with the stick."

"Damn straight you won't," he grunted, releasing her hand to grab the stick and hurl it away from them. Jay used her free hand to wipe the snow out of her face, and slowly Steve eased his weight off her chest. She sat up and pulled the knit cap off her head to shake it free of snow.

Kneeling on one knee beside her, Steve brushed off her back. "Now suppose you explain just what you thought you were doing," he snapped.

Fury burst in her again and she swung at him. He jerked his head back in time to escape her fist, but the wet cap she held in her hand swiped his face with enough force to sting. Like a stroke of lightning she was flat on her back again. From between gritted teeth he said, "One more time and you'll eat standing up for a month!"

She blazed back at him: "You just try it! When I woke up and couldn't find you, I was worried you might be hurt, so I came looking for you. Then you started showing off with your Super Spy tricks, not letting me find you, until I got fed up and started back to the cabin. *Then* you knocked me down and pulled a knife on me, *and* yelled at me! You deserved to get hit with a stick!''

He glared down at her, taking in her tumbled hair and fierce blue eyes, and the stubborn set of those luscious lips. He swore under his breath and thrust his fingers into the honey-brown strands, holding her still while he ground his mouth against hers. His kiss was half angry and half starving. He was suddenly wild to feel her lips, to put his tongue inside her mouth and taste her. She kicked at him, and he moved swiftly, kneeing her legs apart and settling himself between them, his weight crushing her into the snow.

Jay groaned, and his tongue thrust into her mouth. Suddenly she felt on fire, as her fury turned into a different, white-hot passion. Her hands were in his hair, digging into his scalp as she returned his kiss as fiercely as he gave it. His hips rubbed against her in primal rhythm, thrusting as if to deny the sturdy denim between them, and her blood felt like lava.

Roughly he opened her thick coat and shoved the edges aside, his hands covering her breasts, but still she was protected from him by her shirt and bra, and the contact wasn't enough. He jerked at her shirt, popping three of the buttons off to be lost in the snow, and opened it, too. The cold air rushed at her and she cried out, but the sound was caught in his mouth. Her bra had a front hook; he handled it easily and peeled the thin cups away from her white, swollen breasts. Her nipples were hard and tight from the cold, stabbing into his palms when he put his hands over them.

He lifted his head. "Let me inside you," he rasped. "Now." The need was riding him hard, just the way he wanted to ride her. He put his hot mouth over a pouting nipple and sucked strongly at it, rolling it around with his tongue and listening to the incoherent sounds of pleasure she made.

Jay thought she might die from wanting him, even though he had scared her and hurt her; even though he'd made her angrier than she could ever remember feeling at another human being. He'd loosed the passion that had always been in her nature, torn it out of her control. Her hands were shaking, her entire body was shaking, and she wanted more.

He lifted his mouth from her breast, and the shock of the cold air on her wet flesh was so painful she whimpered. Their eyes met, hers wide and dazed with the sudden passion, his narrow and burning, and she knew what he wanted, knew he was silently waiting for her permission. She knew that if she made the slightest sign of acquiescence he would take her there, in the cold and snow, and her entire body throbbed with the need to let him do just that. She started to whisper his name; then terror washed over her like freezing water and she stared up at his hard face as he waited for her answer. *She didn't know his name!* She could call him Steve, but he wasn't Steve. His face wasn't Steve's. She knew him and loved him, but he was a stranger.

He found his answer in the sudden rigidity of her body beneath him. He swore viciously as he got to his feet, one hand rubbing the back of his neck as if that could relieve his physical tension. Jay fumbled with her shirt, trying to draw the edges together, but the buttons were gone and her hands were shaking too badly, so finally she just fastened her coat and got to her feet. She had been burning up only moments before, but now she was freezing. She was covered with snow. She shook it out of her hair and dusted it off her jeans and coat as best she could, then retrieved her knit cap, but it had snow on it both inside and out, and would be worse than wearing nothing at all. Without a word, unable to look at him, she started toward the cabin.

He caught her roughly by the shoulder and swung her around. "Tell me why, damn it," he rasped.

Jay swallowed. She hadn't meant to stop him, and she couldn't explain the dreadful fear she lived with every moment, every day. "I've told you before," she finally managed. "They're good reasons." A single tear tracked down her cheek and formed frozen salt crystals before it reached her chin.

His face changed, some of the angry frustration leaving him, and he wiped at the tear with his gloved hand. "Are they? Your reasons don't make much sense to me. It's natural to want each other. How much longer do you think I can live like a monk? How much longer can you live like a nun? That's not my calling, baby, and damn it all to hell and back in a little red wagon, it's not as if it'll be the first time!"

She thought she would scream. She wanted to cry and she wanted to laugh, but neither would make sense. She wanted to tell him the truth, but the biggest fear she had was of losing him. So finally she did tell him the truth, or at least part of it. "It *will* be the first time," she croaked, strangling on the words. "This time. And it scares me."

She walked away again, and he let her go. She was shaking with cold by the time she got back to the cabin, and she took a long hot shower, then dressed in dry clothing. The smell of fresh coffee came from the kitchen, and she followed her nose to find him frying bacon and whipping eggs in a bowl. He had changed clothes, too, and she faltered under both his physical impact and a sudden realization. He was tall and muscular, as powerful as a puma, his shoulders and chest straining the seams of his shirt. In the weeks they had been there he'd gained weight and muscle, and his hair had grown enough that now it was a trifle long. He looked uncivilized and dangerous, and so utterly male that she quivered instinctively. He was no longer a patient. He had recovered both his health and his strength. She had followed him because she had been worried, but in her mind he had still been a wounded warrior. Now she knew that he wasn't. Her subconscious had recognized it earlier, when she had fought him. She never would have done that before.

He looked up at her, his gaze assessing. "I made fresh coffee. Drink a cup. You still look a little shaky. Does the thought of making it with me scare you that much?"

"*You* scare me." She couldn't stop the words. "Who you are. What you are."

An icy motionlessness seized him as he realized that she had guessed. "You said I was using Super Spy tricks."

"Yes," she whispered, and decided she did need that cup of coffee. She poured it and watched the steam rise for a moment before sipping. Why had she said that? She hadn't meant to. She was in agony, afraid that it would trigger his memory and he would leave, and equally afraid that he might never get his memory back. She was caught, trapped, because she couldn't call him hers until he regained his memory and *chose* her. If he would. He might just walk away, to his real life.

"I didn't think you knew," he said flatly.

Her head jerked up. "Do you mean you did?"

"There had to be more to it than the possibility that I had seen something before the explosion. The government doesn't work that way. I guessed, and Frank confirmed it."

"What did he say?" Her voice was thin.

His smile was equally thin, and a little savage. "That's about it. He can't tell me more because of the circumstances. I'm a security risk right now. How did you guess?"

"The same. There just had to be more to it."

"Is what I am the real reason you turned me down?"

"No," she whispered, an aching, needing expression in her eyes as she watched him. How could loving a man hurt so much? But it did, when the man was this one.

His entire body was taut, his mouth twisted. His voice was harsh. "Stop looking at me like that. It's all I can do to keep myself from pulling your pants off and laying you down on that table, and that isn't the way I want to take you. Not this time. So stop looking at me as if you'd melt if I touched you."

But I would, she thought, though she turned her eyes away. His words made her feel hot and shivery, thinking of the act he'd described, the scene forming in her mind. It would be raw and hot, and purely sexual. If he touched her, they would burn each other up.

He spent most of the day outside, but the tension between them didn't ease; it hung there, as thick and heavy as fog. When darkness finally drove him inside, his eyes burned her every time he looked at her. Instincts she hadn't known she possessed pulled her toward him, despite the reasons her mind presented for not letting their relationship progress. She lay alone in her bed that night, aching with the need to go to him and spend the long, dark hours in his arms. He was right; what did her reasons matter? It was already too late. She already loved him, for good or bad. That was the real danger, and it had been too late for a long time now. Keeping herself from him wouldn't lessen the pain if the worst happened and she lost him.

But she didn't go to him. Things often seemed different in daylight than when lying alone in the darkness, but caution wasn't what kept her in her own bed. Circumstances were hard enough; she had to call him by a name that wasn't his own, had to pretend he was someone else, but she wanted to be able to see his eyes when they made love. More than anything she wanted to know his real name, to be able to call him by it in her heart; failing that, she wanted to see his eyes, for they were his own.

A chinook blew in during the night, chasing away the weather system that had covered them with new snow. Mother Nature must have chuckled to herself as she promptly began melting the high white drifts with her hot winds, teasing them with a hint of a spring that was still over a month away. The melting snow dripped from the trees with a sound like rain, and there were crashes in the night as limbs dropped their white burdens.

The rise in temperature made Jay even more restless, and she was up at dawn. She could barely believe what she saw when she looked out. The hot wind had turned their winter wonderland into a wet, brown meadow dotted with shrinking patches of snow. The melting snow still dripped off the roof, and the heated air made her feel as if her skin would explode. How could it have happened so fast?

"A chinook," Steve said behind her, and she whirled, her heart jumping. She hadn't heard him approach, but he moved like a cat. He looked so ill-tempered that she almost stepped back. His eyes were hard and frosty, and a day's growth of beard darkened his jaw. He glanced from her to the window. "Enjoy it while you can. It'll feel like spring while we have it, and then it'll be gone, and the snow will come back."

They ate breakfast in silence, and he left the cabin immediately afterward. Later on in the morning, Jay heard the solid bite of the ax into wood, and she peeked out at him from the kitchen window. He had taken off his coat and was working in his shirt sleeves, which were rolled up over his forearms. Incredibly, sweat had left dark stains under his arms and down the center of his back. Was it that warm?

She walked out onto the front porch and lifted her face to the warm, sweet wind. It was incredible! Her skin tingled. The temperature was at least forty degrees higher than the day before, and the sun burned down from a cloudless blue sky. Suddenly her jeans and flannel shirt were much too heavy, and her skin began to glisten with moisture.

Like a child made giddy by spring, she hurried to her bedroom and stripped off her heavy, restricting clothes. She couldn't stand them another minute. She wanted to feel the air on her bare arms; she wanted to feel fresh and free, like the chinook. So what if winter could come back at any time? Right now, it was spring!

She pulled her favorite sundress from the closet and slipped it on over her head. It was white cotton, sleeveless, with a scoop neck, and far too flimsy for the temperature, which was probably only in the fifties, but it suited her mood perfectly. Some things were just meant for celebrating; this chinook was one of them.

She hummed as she began the preparations for lunch; it was a while before she noticed that Steve was no longer at the woodpile. If he'd gone off just at lunchtime, she would eat alone and he could do without! She still hadn't quite forgiven him for the day before.

Then she heard a slight noise from out front, and she removed the soup from the stove before walking to the front door. He'd pulled the Jeep around and was washing it. It was such a domestic scene that it lured her onto the porch, and she sat down on the top step to watch him.

He glanced up at her, and his eyes flickered over the dress. "Pushing it a little, aren't you?"

"I'm comfortable," she said, and she was. The crisp air was both chilly and warm, and the sun beating down on her was a delicious sensation. He'd given in to the rising temperature, too, by unbuttoning his shirt and pulling it out of his jeans.

She watched as he alternately scrubbed and rinsed, each time having to stop washing to take up the hose and spray the soap off the Jeep. Finally she went down to pick up the hose from where he'd dropped it. "You wash, I'll rinse."

He grunted. "Do you expect the same deal with the dishes?"

"Sounds fair to me. After all, I'm doing the cooking."

"Yeah, but I'm having to eat all that food so it won't go to waste."

She gave him an awful look. "Poor baby. I'll see what I can do to take that burden off you."

"Just like a woman. Tease her a little bit and she turns nasty. Some people just can't take a joke."

Jay turned the hose on the section of Jeep he'd just washed, but he didn't have time to step back, and the water hit the Jeep full blast, spraying back into his face and onto his clothes. He leaped back, swearing. "Damn it, watch what you're doing!"

"Some people just can't take a joke," Jay said sweetly, and turned the hose on him.

He yelled from the shock of the cold water hitting him and started toward her, holding his hands up to deflect the stream from his face. Jay chortled and darted around the Jeep, then got him again when he looked around at her.

He pushed his wet hair back and his light brown eyes took on that unholy yellow gleam. "You're going to get it now," he said, beginning to grin, and with one bound leaped onto the hood of the Jeep. Jay shrieked and ran to the rear, but the hose caught on the tires as she dragged it after her. She tugged frantically as Steve jumped lightly to the ground. He laughed in a way that made her scream again, and she threw the hose down as she ran for safety.

He grabbed the hose and reversed direction, running back around the front of the Jeep, to free it. He met Jay almost head-on.

"Wait," she said, laughing and begging at the same time as she held up her hand. "It's lunchtime. I came out to tell you. The soup's ready—" A blast of water hit her in the face.

The water was almost unbearably cold. She screamed and tried to run for safety, but he was there every time she turned, and the water soaked her from head to foot. Finally her only means of defense was attack, so she ran straight at him. He was laughing like a maniac, a sound that ceased abruptly when she twisted the nozzle up so the water hit him right in the mouth. They wrestled for control of the nozzle, both of them laughing and yelling as the icy water sprayed all over them.

"Truce, truce!" she yelled, backing away. There was no way she could have gotten any wetter, but then, neither could he. She felt a sense of satisfaction that it had turned out so evenly.

"Are you giving up?" he demanded.

She hooted. "What's to give up? We're both half drowned."

He thought about that and nodded. Then he walked over to the spigot to turn it off and began coiling the hose. "You fight dirty. I like that in a woman."

"That's right, butter me up. You just want to make certain I don't stop cooking."

"The situation being what it is, I'll take anything from you I can get."

Abruptly the humor was gone from the moment. He dropped the hose and straightened, his face hard as he looked at her.

Jay felt her breath catch. He had never been more beautiful to her than he was at that moment, soaking wet, his hair plastered to his skull, badly in need of a shave, and his eyes glittering with masculine intent. Slowly he let his gaze move over her face, then down her body, taking his time as he traced the outline of her form.

Then she realized that he could see more than the outline. The white cotton dress was almost transparent, plastered to her body the way it was. She couldn't stop herself from looking down. Her nipples were hard and erect, plainly visible under the wet cotton, and the fabric was molded to her hips and thighs. With the sun shining through the material, she might as well have been naked for all the protection the dress gave her.

She looked back up at him and froze in place at the look on his face. He was staring at her with such savage male hunger that her heart leaped, making the blood surge through her veins. Her legs trembled as she felt herself begin to grow warm and moist in response, and she inhaled sharply.

His head jerked up. For another moment he was motionless. Her lips were parted slightly, trembling. Her eyes looked heavy. Her nipples were hard little circles plainly visible through the wet dress, her arms limp at her sides as she let him look. He shuddered, and his control snapped.

She couldn't move. He walked toward her without taking his gaze from her, without seeing or hearing anything else, a primal male animal intent on mating. He was breathing hard and deep, his nostrils flaring. Water dripped off him as he moved. She waited, shaking with need and fear, because he was out of control and she knew it. It was an exhilarating terror, freezing her but at the same time filling her with an anticipation so acute she was almost in pain.

Then his hands were on her, and she moaned aloud from the sudden release of tension.

She didn't have time to respond. She had expected to be swept up in his arms and carried to bed, but he had gone far beyond paying attention to niceties. Nothing mattered to him but to have her, right then. He bore her down to the cold, wet earth, which, despite the chinook, still held the long freeze of winter. Jay cried out at the iciness against her back, involuntarily arching upward to escape it. Steve's hard hands pressed her back, and he covered her, his weight pinning her down. He jerked at her dress, pulling the skirt to her waist. "Spread your legs," he said gutturally, though he was already kneeing her thighs apart.

Excitement speared through her. "Yes," she whispered, her hands digging into his shoulders. She wanted him so much that she didn't care where they were or how urgent he was. There would be time for seduction later, as well as worry. Right now there was only this quick, primitive mating.

There was no foreplay, no leisurely petting or stroking. For months there had been too much between them while the final intimacy had been denied, and suddenly the walls were down. He disposed of her panties by the simple means of tearing them apart, then unfastened his pants and shoved them down only as far as was necessary. He pushed her legs wider apart and lowered himself onto her.

She made a little sound of pain as he tried to enter her and couldn't. He swiftly adjusted his position and pushed again, this time sliding deep into her. Shock reverberated through her body as she tried to adjust to his girth, and this time she groaned.

He braced himself on his elbows, and Jay looked up at him dazedly. His yellowish eyes were fierce, his face hard and intent, his neck corded as he drove into her. She arched up to accept him, her heart almost exploding with love. This was what she had wanted, to see his face, to see his eagle-fierce eyes, to imprint his image on her mind and heart even as he imprinted his touch on her body. With the icy earth beneath her and the pure blue sky above, with the bright sun on his face, they were as pure and primitive as their surroundings. No matter what his name or what he did, he was her love, her man.

This was for him. She lifted her hips to meet his thrusts, her flesh quivering under his pounding force. He groaned unintelligibly and slid his arms beneath her to lift her up even more, as if he could grind their bodies so tightly together that they would mesh, then convulsed in release.

She held him tightly, her legs around his hips, her arms about his shoulders as he heaved into her, groaning and shivering. "I love you," she said over and over again, though her lips moved soundlessly and only the warm winds heard her. She closed her eyes, feeling that warm wind on her cheek and his heavy weight both on her and in her, and knew that no matter what happened when he regained his memory, this hard, fast possession had made her his in a way that could never be shattered.

Chapter 10

They lay together, motionless, the only movement that of the wind stirring their hair, the only sound that of the trees rustling together, sighing. Jay felt dazed by what had just happened, her senses buffeted as if she had just weathered a storm. She was totally incapable of action.

Then he braced his hands and lifted his weight off her, staring down at her with an expression so fierce that she almost cringed from it, without knowing why. He swore, his voice low and gravelly, as he disengaged their bodies and shifted to a kneeling position. Uncertainty paralyzed her as her sluggish mind began trying to grasp the reason for his anger.

He pulled his pants up but didn't bother fastening them; instead he tugged her up and into his arms, lifting her from the ground and rising to his feet with a lithe grace that belied the strength necessary to do it. He climbed the steps and strode into the house without saying a word, then carried her into the bathroom. After carefully standing her on the rug, he bent to turn on the water, then straightened and turned back to her. Her dress was unfastened and gently pulled over her head, leaving her naked and shivering from both chill and reaction. She stood docilely, her arms limp at her sides, her eyes wide and dazed and a little frightened as she watched him. What was *wrong*?

He hurriedly stripped, then lifted her into the tub and stepped in beside her, pulling the shower door closed. Jay moved back, a little bemused by how much room he took up, and watched the rippling muscles in his back as he adjusted the water, then turned on the shower. Warm water blasted out of the shower head, immediately filling the small area with steam. Steve pulled her under the water and held her there even when she gasped a protest, because the water was stinging her cold skin.

"No, you need to get warm," he said roughly, rubbing his hands up and down her arms and shoulders. "Turn around and let me wash your hair."

Numbly she did so, realizing that they must have gotten mud all over them. His hands were gentle as he lathered and rinsed her hair, then washed her all over. She began to feel very warm from the combination of water and the stroking of his soapy hands, first over her breasts and abdomen, then her legs and buttocks, and finally between her legs. Her breathing began to hasten as heat built in her.

His touch slowed, and a spasm twitched his tight facial muscles. Her breathing halted altogether as he probed tantalizingly at the entrance to her body, his fingertips barely stroking, one finger barely entering. She caught at his shoulders, her nails digging into his sleek, wet skin. Her breasts were tight and aching as she hung there in an agony of anticipation, waiting for that small invasion, wanting so much more. She felt him hardening against her hip, and a great shudder of pleasure shook her.

He muttered something, but the sound was so rough she couldn't understand it; then she was in his arms, and his mouth was bruising hers. She yielded to his urgency, sliding her hands to the back of his neck. Their water-slick bodies rubbed together, his abrasive chest hair rasping at her nipples, his muscled stomach rippling against the softness of hers, his hardness pushing at her. "Yes," she whimpered.

"I'm sorry, baby," he said, the words rough and frantic and urgent. He slid his mouth down her throat, biting at the sensitive arch, licking the small hollow at the base, where her pulse throbbed visibly. "I didn't mean to be that rough."

So that was why he was angry, not at her, but at himself. But even that wasn't enough to keep him from having her again. She could feel the hunger in his big, powerful body, and again his loss of control thrilled her in a deeply primitive way. She had been married, but Steve had always kept his cool, kept part of himself securely locked away from her, and the passionate part of her had been hurt, because she'd needed more. The man in her arms now was savage in his hunger, driven out of control by his need for her, and his wildness matched the fierce passion of her own nature. All her life she had needed this answering intensity to balance her; without it, she had withdrawn behind a shell of rigid control, and only now was she being freed.

She clung to him like a vine, her wet body undulating against him. "I love you," she groaned, because that was the only thing she could say, the one outstanding truth in the maze of lies and subterfuges.

He lifted his mouth from her throat, his face so close to hers that his burning gaze was all she could see. "I hurt you," he growled.

She couldn't deny it. "Yes," she said, and fitted her mouth to his, her tongue delicately probing. His arms tightened so convulsively that she couldn't breathe, but breathing didn't matter. Kissing him mattered. Loving him mattered.

But finally he did find some remnant of control, enough to allow him to turn off the water and haul her out of the tub. She never released her hold on his neck as he swept her up and carried her, both of them dripping wet, to his bed. She didn't care about the sheets. All she cared about was his hot mouth on her breasts, the rasp of his slightly roughened fingertips on her silky skin, and finally his powerful invasion of her body. It was still such a shock to her senses that she cried out, instinctively trying to close her thighs. But her legs tightened on his muscled thighs and the movement only drew him deeper.

He ground his teeth together, trying to force himself to stillness when every instinct told him to move. The need was so urgent that it smothered everything else in the world except the woman he held in his arms, the woman whose slim body clasped him so tightly and pushed him to the edge of insanity. But for her sake he managed to hold still until she was more comfortable with him. Lying propped on his elbows so his weight wouldn't crush her, he looked down at her and shuddered with pleasure at the intense, absorbed look on her face as she lifted her hips slightly, tentatively, to accept all of him. A deep groan tore from his chest. He knew he'd been too rough and urgent to allow her time to enjoy it before, but this time she was with him.

Her lips parted slightly in a smile so female it took his breath away, and her deep blue eyes beckoned him, dared him. Once again her hips lifted. "What are you waiting for?" she breathed.

"For you," he answered, and even as he lost himself in the mindless ecstasy of making love to her, the truth of that remained. He'd waited for her forever.

He was a light sleeper, so much so that even in the heavy-limbed aftermath he was disturbed by the damp sheets, a discomfort they hadn't noticed before. Jay lay in his arms, exhausted and deeply asleep; he didn't want to disturb her, but neither did he want her to become chilled from the wetness. He eased from the bed and lifted her light weight in his arms, then carried her into the other bedroom to place her on the dry bed. She made a disgruntled noise as he jostled her, then relaxed again, and her breathing evened out as he stroked her back. He joined her on the bed, and she snuggled closer, into his hard, possessive embrace.

The way he felt about her was so intense it edged into pain. Even without his memory, he knew no other woman had ever shattered his control as she did. He'd never desired another woman so intensely, never would have waited as long as he'd waited for her. She overshadowed every other concern. Because of her, he hadn't dwelled on his loss of memory, beyond a peculiar irritation and a certain detached interest in the curiosities of what he had retained. His past life didn't matter, because Jay was here in the present. They were linked in a way that went beyond memory.

A slight frown creased his brow as he held her, his rough hand sliding from the curve of her hip to the warmly resilient mound of her breast. Of all the knowledge he'd kept, why wasn't any of it of Jay? Those were the memories he resented losing. He wanted to remember every minute he'd spent with her, and he wanted to remember why he'd let her slip away from him. He wanted to remember their wedding, the first time he'd made love to her, and the total lack of those memories ate at him. She was the core of his life; why hadn't *something* been familiar? Why hadn't he felt some deep-seated recognition of the silkiness of her skin, the rounded curves of her high breasts or the rose-brown of her small nipples? Why hadn't there been some sense of familiarity in the tight sheath of her body as he entered her?

But everything had been new.

She moved slightly against him, and he stilled his stroking hand, content to simply hold her. They would be married as soon as he could talk her into it, and now he had a very powerful weapon at his disposal.

The scene exploded in his mind. There was a laughing bride and a groom looking excited, proud, wary and impatient all at once. The groom shook his head, beaming, and the bride hugged him tightly. "You made it!" she said exultantly. "I knew you would!"

An older woman and man hugged him just as tightly. "I'm glad you're back, son," the man said, and the woman cried a little even as she smiled at him, the smile full of love. Then there was a rush of other people to shake his hand and hug him and clap him on the back, and the scene dissolved in a confusion of voices.

He lay rigidly, his jaw clenched with the effort required not to jackknife out of bed. Where in hell had *that* memory come from? The man had called him "son," but that could as easily have been a title of affection as one denoting a relationship. He didn't have a family, so they must have been close friends, but Jay had said he'd always been a loner. Who were they? Did they worry about him? Did Jay know anything about them?

Hell, was it even something that had really happened, or a scene from a movie he'd watched?

Movie. Just thinking the word triggered another flashback, but this one was complete with rolling credits. It was a television special on Afghanistan. Then it became another movie, starring a widely acclaimed actor. It was a good movie. Then, in slow motion, the scene shifted. He was standing on a rooftop with the same actor when the man pulled a .45 automatic and pointed it at him. Serious business, a .45. It could have a major impact on a man's future. But the guy was too close, and too rattled. Steve saw himself lash out with his foot, sending the gun flying. The actor staggered back and tripped, fell over the low wall and screamed as he dropped the full seven stories to the ground.

Steve stared at the bedroom ceiling, feeling sweat run down his ribs. Was that another movie? Of all the things he could remember, why a series of films? And why were they so realistic, as if he had stepped into the action? He'd have to ask the doctor about that, but at least it was a sign his memory was returning, just as they'd told him it probably would. He needed to make the trip anyway, to have his eyes checked; it was a real strain to read, and the strain hadn't lessened. He definitely needed glasses. Glasses . . .

An elderly man smiled benignly at him and removed his glasses, placing them on the desk. "Congratulations, Mr. Stone," he said.

He stifled a curse as the scene faded. This was weird; why would that old guy call him "Mr. Stone" unless he'd been using an assumed name? Yeah, that made sense, unless it was just another scene out of another movie. It could just be something he'd watched rather than something that had actually happened.

Jay stirred in his arms and abruptly woke, lifting her head to stare at him in alarm. "What's wrong?"

She had sensed his tension, just as she had from the beginning. He managed a smile and touched her cheek with the backs of his fingers, a different kind of tension taking over his muscles. "Nothing," he assured her. She looked sleepy and sensual, her eyes heavy-lidded, her luscious mouth swollen from contact with his firmer lips.

She looked around. "We're in my room," she said in bewilderment.

"Mmm. The sheets on my bed were wet, so I brought you in here."

Warm color tinted her cheeks as she thought of how the sheets had gotten so wet, but her smile was both secret and content. She lifted her hand and touched his face, much as he had touched hers; her dark blue eyes drifted over his features with aching tenderness, examining each line and plane, feeding the need in her heart. She was unaware of her expression, but he saw it, and his chest constricted. He wanted to say, "Don't love me like that," but he didn't, because it was essential to him that she love him exactly like that.

He cleared his throat. "We have a choice."

"We do? Of course we do. Of what?"

"We can get up and eat the lunch you were cooking—" he broke off to lift his head and look at the clock "—three hours ago, or we can try to wreck this bed, too."

She considered it. "I think we'd better have lunch, or I won't have the energy to help you wreck the bed."

"Good thinking." He hugged her, reluctant to get up despite his own hunger, and found his hands stroking down her sides in sensual enjoyment. Then he paused and moved his hand around to her stomach. "Unless you want to get married this weekend, we'd better do something about birth control."

Jay's heart felt as if it had abruptly swollen so large that it filled her entire chest. For a few glorious hours she'd forgotten how hemmed in she was by this tortuous maze of deception. She wanted nothing more than to simply say "Yes, let's get married," but she didn't dare. Not until he knew who he was—and *she* knew who he was—and he still said he wanted to marry her. So she ignored the first part of his statement and merely answered the second. "We don't have to worry about birth control. I'm on the Pill. My doctor put me on it seven months ago, because my periods had gotten so erratic."

His eyes narrowed a little and his hand lay heavier on her stomach. "Is something wrong?"

"No. It was just stress from my job. I could probably do without them now." Then she smiled and turned her face into his shoulder. "Except for a sudden development."

He grunted. "Sudden, hell. I've been hard for two months. But we could still get married this weekend."

She eased out of his embrace and got up, her face troubled as she put on fresh underwear and got a sweater from the closet, pulling it over her head.

He watched her from the bed. His voice was very soft and raspy when he spoke. "I want an answer."

Harried, she pushed her tangled hair out of her eyes. "Steve—" She stopped, almost cringing at the necessity of calling him by that name. Now more than ever, she wanted, needed, to know her lover's name. "I can't marry you until you've gotten your memory back."

He threw the sheet back and stood, magnificently naked. Jay's pulse rate skittered as she looked at him. All the miles he'd run and the wood he'd chopped had corded his body with muscles. He didn't look as if he'd ever been injured, except for his scars. Her heart settled into a slow, heavy beat. She had cradled his weight, taken his pounding invasion, returned his fire with her own. As tender as she felt now in different parts of her body, she could still feel herself grow warm and liquid as she looked at him.

"What difference does my memory make?" he snapped, and she jerked her gaze upward, realizing that he was angry. "No other woman has a claim on me, and you know it, so don't bring up that crap again. Why should we wait?"

"I want you to be certain," she said, her voice troubled.

"Damn it, I am certain!"

"How can you be, when you don't know what's happened? I just don't want you to regret marrying me when everything comes back to you." She tried a smile, and it only wobbled a little. "We're together, and we have time. That will have to be enough for now."

Steve forced himself to be content with that, and in many ways it was enough. They lived together in the truest sense of the word, as partners, friends and lovers. It was a week before the snows came again, and in that week they explored every inch of their high meadow. He showed her the laser-beam sensor he'd installed across the trail and demonstrated how to operate both the radio and the computer. It was a relief not to have to hide from her how deeply he'd been involved in espionage, though she got a little huffy with him because all the equipment had been hidden from her in the shed and only now had he gotten around to telling her about it.

He liked making her lose her temper. It was exciting, in a primitive way, to watch those blue eyes narrow like a cat's. It was the final sign that he'd tormented her into attack. The day he'd thought she was an intruder and tracked her in the snow, then tackled her, her rage had startled him, caught him off balance, but it had excited him. Most people who knew Jay would never think she was capable of that kind of anger, or that she would physically fight anyone. It told him a lot about her, about the passionate, volatile side of her personality and about what it took to bring it out. Probably very few people could make her angry, but because she loved him, he could. And after he'd provoked her to anger, he liked to wrestle with her and love her out of her temper.

Physically she delighted him. She was still too thin, though she ate well, but he liked to watch her trim hips and rounded buttocks in her tight jeans too much to complain. Her skin was satiny, her breasts high and round, her exotic mouth full and pouty; no matter how she dressed, she turned him on because he knew what lay under those clothes. He also knew that all he had to do was reach for her and she'd turn into his arms, warm and willing. That kind of response enchanted him; there was something so new about it, as if he'd never known it before.

Then one morning they got up to find that it had snowed again during the night, and it continued snowing all during the day, not hard, just a continuous veil of flakes sifting down over the meadow. Except for trips outside to bring in more firewood, Jay and Steve spent the day in the cabin, watching old movies. That was an extra benefit of the satellite dish; they could always find something interesting to watch on television, if they were in the mood. It was perfectly suited to a lazy day when they had nothing better to do than to lie around and watch the fat snowflakes drifting down.

Just before dark, Steve left to check the area, something he always did. While he was gone Jay began cooking dinner, humming as she did so, because she was so contented. This was paradise. She knew it couldn't last; when his memory returned, even if he still wanted to marry her, their lives would change. They would leave here, find another home. She would have to find another job. Other things would take up their time. This was time set aside, out of the real world, but she meant to enjoy every minute of it. Briefly a dark thought intruded: This could be all she had. Perhaps it was. If so, these days were all the more precious.

Steve entered through the back door, slapping snow off his shoulders and shaking it out of his hair before taking off his thick coat. "Nothing but rabbit tracks." He looked thoughtful. "Do you like rabbit?"

Jay turned from the cheese she was grating for the spaghetti. "If you shoot the Easter Bunny..." she began in a threatening tone.

"It was just a question," he said, and grabbed her for a kiss, then rubbed his cold, beard-roughened cheek against hers. "You smell good. Like onion and garlic and tomato sauce." Actually, she smelled like herself, that sweet, warm, womanly scent he associated with her and no one else. He buried his cold nose against her neck and inhaled it, feeling the familiar tension growing in his loins.

"You won't get any points for telling me I smell like onions and garlic," she said, returning to her chore even though he kept his arms looped around her waist.

"Even if I tell you how crazy I am about onions and garlic?"

"Humph. You're like all men. You'll say anything when you're hungry."

Chuckling, he released her to set the table and begin buttering the rolls. "How would you like to take a trip?"

"I'd love to see Hawaii."

"I was thinking more in terms of Colorado Springs. Or maybe Denver."

"I've *been* to Colorado Springs," she said, then looked at him curiously over her shoulder. "Why are we going to Colorado Springs?"

"I'm assuming Frank doesn't want us returning to Washington, even briefly, so he'll fly the doctor out to check my eyes. That means, logically, either Colorado Springs or Denver, and I'm betting Colorado Springs. I'm also betting he doesn't want the doctor to know the location of the cabin, so that means we go to him."

She had known he would have to have his eyes checked again, but just talking about it brought the real world intruding into their private paradise. It would feel strange even seeing other people, much less talking to them. But reading strained his eyes, and enough time had passed for them to realize his sight wasn't going to improve. She thought of how he would look in glasses, and a warm feeling began spreading in her stomach. Sexy. She gave him a smile. "Yeah, I think I'd like to make a trip. I've been eating my own cooking for a long time now."

"I'll get in touch with Frank after dinner." He could have done it then, but filling his stomach was more important. Jay made great spaghetti, and getting in touch with Frank could be time-consuming. First things first.

After the dinner dishes had been cleaned and Steve was in the shed contacting Frank, Jay stretched out on the rug in front of the fire, for the first time thinking about the chic little apartment in New York that Frank had been keeping for her. It contrasted sharply with the rustic comfort of the cabin, but she much preferred the cabin. She would hate to leave it; it would be beautiful here during the summer, but she wondered how much longer they would be here. Surely Steve's memory would return before then, and even if it didn't, how much longer would it be before Frank told him the truth? They couldn't let him live another man's life forever. Or could they? Had that been the plan? Did they somehow know he'd never get his memory back?

The mirrors kept reflecting back different answers, different facets to the puzzle, different solutions. And none of them fit.

"Are you asleep?" he asked softly.

She gasped and rolled over, her heart jumping. "I didn't hear you come in. You didn't make any noise." He always moved silently, like a cat, but she should have heard the back door. She'd been so deep in thought that the sounds hadn't registered.

"The better to sneak up on you, my dear," he growled in his best big-bad-wolf voice. He joined her on the rug, sinking his hands into her hair as he angled her mouth up toward his. He kissed her slowly, deeply, taking his time and using his tongue. Her breathing altered, and her eyes grew heavy lidded. Desire was a heavy warmth inside her, slowly expanding until it completely filled her.

They weren't in any hurry. It felt too good to lie there in the warmth of the crackling fire and savor their kisses. But eventually the heat was too much, and she moaned as he unbuttoned her flannel shirt, parting the edges to press his lips to the swollen curves of her breasts. He lay on top of her, his heavy legs controlling hers even though she twisted restlessly. She wanted more. Moaning again, her voice sharp with need, she turned until her nipple brushed against his mouth. Lazily he extended his tongue and licked it, then clamped his mouth over it and sucked strongly, giving her what she needed.

The firelight burnished her hair with golden lights and her skin with a rosy glow as he unfastened her jeans and pulled them off. Her mouth was red and moist, glistening with the sheen of his kisses. Abruptly he couldn't wait any longer and jerked his own clothes off. The flannel shirt still hung around her shoulders, but even that was too much. He pulled it away from her and knelt between her legs, draping her thighs over his as he bent forward to enter her, fusing their bodies as surely as their lives were fused.

They lay together for a long time afterward, too content to move. He put another log on the fire and pulled on his jeans, then put his own shirt around her to stave off any chill. She sat in the circle of his arms, her head on his shoulder, wishing nothing would ever happen to disturb this happiness.

He watched the waving yellow flames, his rough chin rubbing back and forth against her hair. "Do you want kids?" he asked absently.

The question startled her enough that she lifted her head from his shoulder. "I...think I do," she replied. "I've never really thought about it, because it just didn't seem like an option, but now..." Her voice trailed off.

"Before, we didn't have much of a marriage. I don't want it to be like that again. I want to come home every night, live a normal life." He tightened his arms around her. "I'd like to have a couple of kids, but that's a mutual decision. I didn't know how you felt about it."

"I like kids," she said softly, but guilt assailed her. They hadn't had *any* kind of a marriage before! He was feeling guilty for another man's acts.

"Yeah, I like them, too." He smiled, still watching the fire. "I get a kick out of watching Amy—"

Jay jerked away from him, her eyes wide with something like panic in them. "Who's Amy?"

Steve's face was hard, his mouth grim. "I don't know," he muttered. "I feel as if I just ran into a brick wall. The words just slipped out, then *bam!* I hit the wall and there's nothing."

Jay felt sick. Had she been so wrong in trusting that Frank wouldn't have set this up if Steve had been married? Was he a father as well as a husband?

Steve was watching her and sensed the direction of her thoughts, if not the content. "No, I'm not married and I don't have any kids," he said sharply, pulling her back to him. "It's probably just a friend's little girl. Do you know anyone with a little girl named Amy?"

She shook her head, not looking at him. The terror was back; she felt stiff with it. Was his memory returning? When it did, would he leave? Paradise could end at any time.

Steve lay awake long after they had gone to bed that night. Jay slept in his arms, as she had every night since the chinook blew, her hair streaming over his left shoulder and her warm breath sighing against his neck. Her bare, silky body was pressed all along his left side, and her slender arm was draped across his chest. She had looked so panicked for a second when he'd mentioned Amy's name, whoever Amy was. He held her closer, trying to erase that panic even from her sleep.

This would probably happen a lot, a casual remark triggering flashes of memory. He hoped they wouldn't all scare her so much. Was she truly afraid he wouldn't want her when his memory returned? God, couldn't she feel how much he loved her? It went beyond memory. It was in his bones, buried in the very depths of his existence.

Amy. *Amy.*

The name flashed through his mind like fire and suddenly he saw a little girl with glossy dark hair, giggling as she shoved a chubby, dimpled fist into her mouth. *Amy.*

His heart began pounding. His memory had actually supplied a face to go with the name. He didn't know who she was, but he knew her name, and now her face. The mental picture faded, but he concentrated and found he could recall it, just like a real memory. Just as he'd told Jay, she must be a friend's daughter, someone he'd met since their divorce.

He relaxed, pleased that the memory had solidified. His sexual satisfaction made his body feel heavy and boneless, and his chest began to rise and fall in the deeper rhythm of sleep.

"Unca Luke, Unca Luke!"

The childish voices echoed in his head and the movie began to unwind in his mind. Two kids. Two boys, tearing across a green lawn, jumping and shrieking "Unca Luke" at the tops of their lungs as they ran.

Another scene. Northern Ireland. Belfast. He recognized it even as a tingle of dread ran up his spine. Two little boys played in the street, then suddenly looked up, hesitated and ran.

Flash. One of the first two little boys looked up with a wobbly lower lip and tears in his eyes and said, "Please, Unca Dan."

Flash. Dan Rather stacked papers at his newsdesk while the credits rolled.

Flash. A bumper sticker on a station wagon said, I'd Rather Be at Disney World.

Mickey Mouse dancing ... Flash ... a mouse crawling through the garbage in an alley ... Flash ... a grenade sailing in slow motion through the air and hitting a garbage can with a loud thump; then a louder thump and the can goes sailing ... Flash ... a white sailboat with sassy red-and-white striped sails tacking closer to shore and a tanned young man waves ... Flash flash flash ...

The scenes ripped through his consciousness, and they were truly only flashes, following each other like pages of a book being flipped through in front of his eyes.

He was sweating again. Damn, these free-association memories were hell. What did they mean? Had they truly happened? He wouldn't mind them if he could tell which ones were real and which ones were just something he'd seen on television or in a movie, or maybe even imagined from a scene in a book. Okay, some of them were obvious, like the one of Dan Rather with the credits rolling across his face. But he'd watched network news many times since the bandages had come off his eyes, so that could even be a recent memory.

But... Uncle Luke. Uncle Dan. Something about those kids, and those names, seemed very real, just as Amy was real.

He eased out of bed, being very careful not to wake Jay, and walked into the living room where he stood for a long time in front of the banked fire, watching the embers glow. Full memory was close, and he knew it. It was as if all he had to do was turn a corner and everything would be there; but turning that mental corner wasn't as easy as it sounded. He had become a different man in the months since the explosion; he was trying to connect two separate people and merge them into one.

He had been absently rubbing his fingertips with his thumb. When he noticed what he was doing, he lifted his hand to look at it. The calluses were back, courtesy of chopping wood, but his fingertips were still smooth. How much of him was left, or had his identity been erased as surely as his fingerprints had been? When he looked in the mirror, how much of it was Steve Crossfield and how much of it was courtesy of the reconstructive surgery? His face was changed, his voice was changed, his fingerprints gone.

He was new. He had been born out of the darkness, brought to life by Jay's voice calling him toward the light.

Regardless of what he did or didn't remember, he still had Jay. She was a part of him that surgery couldn't change.

The room had taken on a chill as the fire died, and finally he felt the coldness on his naked body. He returned to the bedroom and slipped under the quilt, feeling Jay's body warmth wrap around him. She murmured something, moving closer to him in her sleep, seeking her usual position.

Instantly desire fired through him, as urgent as if it hadn't been slaked only an hour or so before. "Jay," he said, his voice low and dark, and he pulled her beneath him. She woke and reached for him, her hands sliding around his neck, and in the darkness they loved each other until he had no room for memories other than those they made together.

Chapter 11

They left the cabin early the next morning so they could rendezvous with Frank at Colorado Springs that afternoon. Jay felt a wrench at leaving the cabin; it had been their private world for so long that, away from it, she felt exposed. Only the thought that they would be returning the next day gave her the courage to leave it at all. She knew that eventually she would have to leave it forever, but she wasn't ready to face that day right now. She wanted more time with the man she loved.

She intended to ask Frank the name of the American agent who had been "killed." He might not tell her, but she had to ask. Even if she couldn't say it aloud, she needed to know, she had to put a name to her love. She looked at him as he skillfully handled the Jeep, holding it steady even on the snow, and her heart swelled. He was big and rough-looking, not handsome at all with his rearranged features, but just one glance from those fierce yellowish eyes had the power to make her dizzy with delight. How could they ever have thought they could pass this man off as Steve Cross-field?

Their subterfuge was riddled with holes, but she hadn't seen them until she had been too deeply in love with him to care. They had relied on shock and urgency to keep her from asking the pointed questions to which they would have had no answers, such as why they didn't use blood type or their own agent's dental records to determine the identity of the patient. She had known at the time that Frank was hiding something from her, but she had been too concerned over "Steve" to think it was anything more than protecting the details of a classified mission. The truth was that she had been misled so easily because she had wanted to be; after the first time she had seen him lying in the hospital, so desperately wounded but still fighting with that grim determination of his that burned through unconsciousness, she had wanted nothing more than to be by his side and help him fight.

They were to stay at a different motel than the one they'd been in before, because Frank didn't want to take the chance the desk clerk might recognize them. They even used different names. When they got there, Frank had already arrived, and he'd made reservations for them under the names of Michael Carter and Faye Wheeler. Separate rooms. Steve looked distinctly displeased, but placed Jay's overnighter in her room without comment and went along to his own room. The eye specialist checked Steve's eyes immediately; then he was taken to an optometrist to be fitted for glasses, which would be ready for him the next morning. Jay remained behind, wondering what strings Frank had pulled and whose arms he had twisted to get everything done so fast.

They returned a little after dark, and Steve came immediately to Jay's room. "Hi, baby," he said, stepping inside and closing the door behind him. Before she could answer he was kissing her, his hands tight on her arms, his mouth hard and searching.

She shivered with excitement, crowding closer to his body as she dug her fingers into his cold hair. He smelled like wind and snow, and his skin was cold, but his tongue was warm and probing. Finally he lifted his head, a very male look of satisfaction stamped on his hard face. He rubbed his thumb across her lips, which were reddened from contact with his. "Sweetheart, I may freeze my naked butt off sneaking into your room tonight, but I'm *not* sleeping alone."

"I have a suggestion," she purred.

"Let's hear it."

"Leave your clothes on until you get here."

He laughed and kissed her again. Her mouth was driving him crazy; it had the most erotic effect on him. Kissing her was more arousing than actually making love had been with other women—and just for a moment, before they faded away, some of those other women were in his mind.

"The doctor is already on his way back to Washington. Frank is staying until the morning, so it's the three of us again. Are you hungry? Frank's stomach is still on Washington time."

"Actually, I am a little hungry. We don't keep late hours ourselves, you know."

He looked at the bed. "I know."

Jay hoped to have the chance to ask Frank about the agent's name; she couldn't take the risk of asking him in Steve's presence, because the sound of his own name might trigger his memory, and she couldn't face the possibility of that. She wanted him to remember, but she wanted it to be when they were alone in their high meadow. If the chance to talk to Frank didn't present itself, she could always call him after they'd retired to their individual rooms for the night, provided Steve didn't come straight to hers, but she didn't think he would. He'd probably take a shower first, and put on fresh clothes. She sighed, weary of having to second-guess and predict; she wasn't cut out for this business.

Steve noted the sigh, and the faint desperation in her eyes. She hadn't said anything, but that look had been there since he'd had that first flash of memory the day before. It puzzled him; he couldn't think of any reason why Jay should dread his returning memory. Because it puzzled him and because there was no logical reason, he couldn't let it go. It wasn't in his makeup. When something bothered him, he worried at it until it made sense. He never quit, never let go. His sister had often said he was at least half bulldog—

Sister?

He was quiet as the three of them ate dinner at an Italian restaurant. Part of him enjoyed the spicy food, and part of him was actively involved in the easy conversation around the table, but another part of him examined the sliver of memory from every angle. If he had a sister, why had he told Jay he was an orphan? Why hadn't Frank had a record of any relatives? That was the screwy part. He could accept that he might have told Jay a different version of his life, because he didn't know what the circumstances had been at the time, but it was impossible that Frank hadn't had a list of next of kin. That was assuming he was remembering "real" things.

A sister. His logic told him it was impossible. His guts told him his logic could take a flyer. A sister. Amy. *Unca Luke! Unca Luke!* The childish voices reverberated in his head even as he laughed at something Frank said. *Unca Dan.* Unca Luke. Unca Luke Unca Luke... Luke... Luke...

"Are you all right?" Jay asked, her eyes dark with concern as she put her hand lightly on his wrist. She could feel tension emanating from him and was vaguely startled that Frank hadn't seemed to notice anything unusual.

The pounding left his head as he looked at her and smiled. He'd gladly count his past well lost as long as he could have Jay. The sensory umbilical cord linking them was as acutely sensitive as the strings on a precisely tuned Stradivarius. "It's just a headache," he said. "The drive was a strain on my eyes." Both statements were true, though the second wasn't the cause of the first. Also, there hadn't been that much strain. His problem was the precise, close-up focusing needed for reading; his distance vision was as sharp as ever, which was better than twenty-twenty. He had the vision of a jet pilot.

Jay returned to her conversation with Frank, but she was as aware of Steve's fading tension as she had been of the fact that he'd been as taut as a guide wire. Had something happened that afternoon that he hadn't told her? A feeling of dread almost overwhelmed her, and she wanted badly to be back at the cabin.

When they returned to the motel, she noted with relief that Steve went to his own room rather than stopping to talk with Frank or immediately following her to hers. She darted to the phone and dialed Frank's room. He answered on the first ring.

"It's Jay." She identified herself.

"Is something wrong?" He was immediately alert.

"No, everything's okay. It's just that something's been bothering me, but I didn't want to ask you in front of Steve."

In his room, Frank tensed. Had they failed to cover all bases? "Is it about Steve?"

"Well, no, not really. The agent who died…what was his name? It's been on my mind a lot lately, that he died and I never even heard his name."

"There's no reason you should have. You'd never met him."

"I know," she said softly. "I just wanted to know something about him. It could have been Steve. Now that he's dead, there's no reason to keep his name secret, is there?"

Frank thought. He could give her a fictitious name, but he decided to tell her at least that much of the truth. She'd know his name eventually, and it might help if she could simply think a mistake had been made. It would give her a small fact she could focus on for reference. "His name was Lucas Stone."

"Lucas Stone." Her voice was very soft as she repeated the name. "Was he married? Did he have a family?"

"No, he wasn't married." He deliberately didn't answer her second question.

"Thanks for telling me. It's bothered me that I didn't know." He'd never know how much, she thought as she quietly replaced the receiver. Lucas Stone. She repeated the name over and over in her mind, applying it to a battered face and feeling her heart begin to pound. Lucas Stone. Yes.

Only then did she realize what a mistake she'd made. If it had been difficult before to refer to him as Steve, it would be almost impossible now. Steve had been a stolen name, but one she'd used because there had been no alternative. What if the name Lucas slipped out?

She sat on the bed for a long time while she mentally flailed against the hall of mirrors that trapped her with its false reflections. The things she didn't know bound her as securely as the things she knew, until she was afraid to trust her own instincts. She wasn't made for deception; she was straightforward, which was one reason why she hadn't fitted into the world of investment banking, a world that required a certain measure of "slickery," that balance of slickness and trickery.

Finally, too tired to open any more blank doors, she took a shower and got ready for bed. When she came out of the bathroom, Lucas—*Steve!* she reminded herself frantically—was stretched out on the bed, already partially undressed.

She looked at the locked door. "Haven't we done this before?"

He rolled to his feet and caught her arms, pulling her to him. "With one difference. A big difference."

He smelled of soap and shaving cream, and the underlying muskiness of man. She clung to him, pressing her face into his neck to inhale that special scent. What would she do if he left her? It would be a life without color, forever incomplete. Slowly she ran her hands over his broad chest, rubbing her fingers through the crisp, curly hair and feeling the warmth of his skin, then the iron layer of muscles beneath. He was so hard that her fingers barely made an impression. Bemused, she pressed experimentally on his upper arm, watching as her fingernails turned white from the pressure but had noticeably little effect on him.

"What are you doing?" he asked curiously.

"Seeing how hard you are."

"Honey, that's not the right place."

Her face was bright with laughter as she swiftly looked up at him. "I think I know all your other places."

"Is that so? There are places, and then there are places. Some places need a lot more attention than others." As he spoke he began moving her toward the bed. He was already aroused, his hardness pressing against her. Jay moved her hand down to cover the ridge beneath his jeans.

"Is this one of the places in need of attention?"

"A lot of attention," he assured her as he levered them both onto the bed. He felt her legs move, her hips lifting to cradle him, and all amusement faded out of his eyes, leaving them fierce and narrow. It was a look that made Jay shudder in exquisite anticipation.

She looked up at him, her face soft and shining as his hands began moving tenderly on her body. "I love you," she said, and her heart echoed, *Lucas*.

It was different the next morning, as if the world had altered during the night, but he couldn't quite put his finger on the difference. It was an oddly familiar feeling, as if he were more at home with himself. Jay was in his arms, her sleek, golden-brown hair lying tangled on his shoulder. If they had been in the cabin he would have got up to rebuild the fire, then returned to bed for some early-morning loving. Instead he had to go to his own room to shave and dress. That damn Frank. He'd booked separate rooms knowing they needed only one. But Jay wasn't like all the other women; Jay was special, and maybe this was Frank's tribute to her specialness.

Other women. The thought nagged at him after he left Jay and returned to his own room in the biting cold of dawn. His memory was returning, not in one big, melodramatic rush, like a light switch being turned on, but in unconnected bits and pieces. Faces and names were surfacing. Instead of feeling elated, however, he was aware of a growing sense of caution. He hadn't told Frank his memory was coming back; he'd wait until it had truly returned and he'd had time to consider the situation. Wariness was second nature to him, just as he automatically checked his room to make certain no one had entered it in his absence.

He showered and shaved, but as he shaved he found himself staring at his face in the mirror, trying to find his past in the reflection. How could he recognize himself when his face had been changed? What had he looked like before? He wondered if Jay had a picture of him; it would be an old one, if she'd kept any at all. But women tended to keep mementos and their divorce hadn't been a bitter one, so maybe she hadn't destroyed whatever pictures she'd had. Maybe seeing one would give him a link to the past.

Hell, why should it? He stared at himself in disgust. He hadn't recognized Jay or Frank; why should he recognize his old face? The face he knew was the face he could see now, and it wouldn't win any prizes. He looked as if he'd played too many football games without a helmet.

Still, the sensation lingered that he was on the brink of... something. It was there, just beyond his reach.

It nagged at him in little ways, like the ease with which he slipped his shoulder holster on, and the familiarity of the gun in his hand as he checked it, then slid it into place. The ease and familiarity had been there before, but now they were somehow different, as if the link between past and present were returning. Soon. It would happen soon.

The day was uneventful, but the feeling of anticipation didn't leave him. They all met to eat breakfast; then he and Frank drove to the optical lab and picked up his glasses. On the way back he asked, "Have you found this Piggot guy yet?"

"Not yet. He surfaced a month ago, but he went underground again before we could get to him."

"Is he good?"

Frank hesitated. "Damn good. One of the best. His psychological profile says he's a psychopath, but very controlled, very professional. His jobs are a matter of pride to him. That's why he wants you. You screwed him up the way no one else ever had. You spoiled his job, killed his 'employees' and managed to hit him hard enough that he had to go underground for months to recover."

"I may have hit him hard, but it wasn't hard enough," Steve said remotely. "Do you have a picture of him?"

"Not with me. There's only one. We got him with a telescopic lens, and it's grainy. He's about five-ten, a hundred and forty-five pounds, blond, forty-two years old. His left earlobe is missing, also courtesy of you. His reputation suffered."

"Yeah, well, some days I'm a little cranky."

That was vintage Lucas Stone. Frank felt the shock of it like a slap, but he kept his hands steady on the wheel. "Is your memory coming back?"

"Not yet," Steve lied. He could see Geoffrey Piggot, whiplash thin, malignant, cold. Another face to go with a name.

He was very quiet on the drive back to the cabin. Jay glanced at him, but sunglasses hid his eyes, and she could read nothing in his expression. She still sensed the tension in him, just as she had the night before, during dinner. "Do you have another headache?" she finally asked.

"No." Then he softened the bluntness of his answer by reaching over to rub the backs of his fingers against her jaw. "I feel okay."

"Did Frank say anything that's bothering you?"

Briefly he considered the disadvantages of letting someone get so close to you that they could read your moods, but then he counted that battle well lost in Jay's case, because as far as he was concerned, she couldn't get close enough to suit him. And he hadn't *let* her get close; it had simply happened.

"No. He told me a few things about the guy who tried to make me into beef stew—"

"Oh, gross!" she said, slapping his hand away, and he laughed at her.

"I was just thinking about him, that's all."

After a moment she curled up in the seat and rested her head against the back. "I'll be glad to get home."

He was in total agreement with that. They had been alone together for so long that this trip had almost brought on culture shock. Neon lights and traffic were a definite jolt to a system that was used to fir trees, snow and a deep, deep silence. Right now he would welcome a trip to civilization only if he and Jay were getting blood tests and a marriage license.

Blood tests.

Suddenly he felt alert, just as he'd felt a thousand times before when his life hung in the balance. Adrenaline spurted into his veins, and his heart began racing, but not as fast as his brain. A blood test. Damn it, it didn't fit. Why had they needed Jay to identify him when they had all the means at hand? He was their agent. Granted, his fingerprints were gone, he'd been unconscious and his voice damaged, but they still had his blood type and dental records. It should have been easy enough to establish his identity. It followed, then, that they hadn't needed Jay at all, but had definitely wanted her for some reason.

He went over what Jay had told him. They had wanted her to identity him because they couldn't make a positive ID, and they'd needed to know if their agent had bought the farm, because Steve and this other guy had been caught in the explosion and one of them was dead. That meant there must have been two agents on location, but it wouldn't have changed the fact that Frank had the means at hand to identify both of them. Supposedly he and this other agent had physically resembled each other, about the same height and weight, and with the same coloring. There still wasn't any problem with identification, even if he stretched coincidence and allowed that they both might have had the same blood type. That still left dental records.

Damn, he felt like a fool. Why hadn't he seen this before? They had wanted Jay in this for some reason, but identification hadn't been it. What kind of scheme was Frank running?

Think. He had to think. He felt as if he were trying to put a puzzle together without all the pieces, so no matter how he moved things around they still didn't fit. If he could just remember, damn it!

Why would Frank lie to Jay? Why concoct the story that he and the other agent so closely resembled each other? Why insist that he needed her at all?

Why did they need Jay?

Voices tumbled in on him. *"Congratulations, Mr. Stone"* ... *"I'm glad you're back, son"* ... *"Unca Luke! Unca Luke!"* Stone ... son ... Unca Luke ... son ... Luke ... Stone ...

Luke Stone.

His hands jerked on the steering wheel. He felt as if he'd been hit in the chest. Luke Stone. Lucas Stone. *Damn Frank Payne to hell! His name was Lucas Stone!*

As soon as he'd turned that mental corner, all the memories came rushing at him in a confusing flood, filling his mind with so much clatter that he could barely drive. He didn't dare stop, didn't dare let Jay know what he was feeling. He felt . . . God, he didn't know how he felt. Battered. His head hurt, but at the same time he was aware of an enormous sense of relief. He had his identity back, his sense of self. Finally he knew himself.

He was Lucas Stone. He had a family and friends, a past.

But he wasn't Jay's ex-husband. He wasn't Steve Crossfield. He wasn't the man she thought she was in love with.

So that was why she'd been brought in. There had been only one agent at the explosion, and he was that man. Steve Crossfield must have been there for some reason, and he had died there. Lucas tried to form his memories of the meeting, but they were blurred, fragmented. They would probably never come back. But he did remember seeing a tall, lean man walking up the street, his outline reflected on the wet pavement under the streetlight. That could have been Steve Crossfield. He didn't remember anything after that, though now he was remembering making contact, setting up the meeting with Minyard, going to the meeting site. He'd looked up, seen the man . . . then nothing. Everything after that was a blank, until Jay's voice had pulled him out of the darkness.

His cover had been blown, obviously. Piggot was after him; that was the reason for the charade. Pulling Jay in, duping her into thinking he was her ex-husband, having him positively identified as Steve Crossfield, was the best cover the Man could concoct for him until they could neutralize Piggot. The Man never underestimated his enemies, and Piggot was, as Frank had said, very good. The extent of the Man's deception also told Lucas that the Man suspected there was a mole in his ranks and hadn't trusted regular channels.

So they'd "buried" him, and he'd awakened to another name, another face, another life, even another man's wife.

No, damn it! Savagery filled him, and his knuckles turned white as he automatically negotiated the icy patches on the road. Maybe he wasn't Steve Crossfield, but Jay was his. *His.* Lucas Stone's woman.

Silently and at length, he cursed the Man and Frank for everything he could think of, ranging back over several generations of their ancestors. Not Frank so much, because he could see the Man's fine hand in this. Nobody had a mind as intricate as Kell Sabin's; that was how he'd gotten to be the Man. They had probably—no, almost certainly—saved his life, assuming there was a mole passing information to Piggot, but they weren't the ones who had to tell Jay he wasn't her ex-husband. They didn't have to tell her that the man she loved was dead and she'd been sleeping with a stranger.

What would she say? More important, what would she do?

He couldn't lose her. He could stand anything except that. He expected, and could handle, shock, anger, even fear, but he couldn't stand it if she looked at him with hate in those deep blue eyes. He couldn't let her walk away from him.

Immediately he began examining the situation from all angles, looking for a solution, but even as he looked, he knew there wasn't one. He couldn't marry her using Crossfield's name, because such a marriage wouldn't be legal, and besides, he'd be damned if he'd let her carry another man's name. He would have to tell her.

His family probably thought he was dead, and there was no way he could let them know he wasn't without jeopardizing them. If his cover was blown, his family would be at risk if Piggot ever found out he hadn't died as planned. The way things stood now, he'd have a hard time convincing his family of his identity anyway; he neither looked nor sounded the same. His hands were tied until Piggot was caught; then he supposed Sabin would arrange for his family to be notified that a "mistake" had been made in identification, and due to extenuating and unusual circumstances, et cetera, the error had only now been corrected. The Man probably already had the telegram composed in his mind, letter-perfect.

His family would be taken care of; they would be glad to get him back despite the way he looked, or the fact that his voice was ruined.

Jay was the victim. They'd used her as the ultimate cover. How in hell could she ever forgive that?

Jay dozed, finally awakening as they turned onto the track to the meadow. "We're home," she murmured, pushing her hair back. She turned her head to smile at him. "At last."

He was tense again, surveying every detail of the track. There was new snow on the ground, filling the tire tracks they had made the day before and also obliterating any other trail that could have been made after they'd left. All his training was coming into play, and Lucas Stone didn't take chances. Unnecessary chances, that was. There had been more times than one when he'd laid his life on the line, but only because he'd had no other choice. Taking chances with Jay's life, however, was something else.

As usual, Jay picked up on his tension and fell silent, a worried frown puckering her brow.

The snow surrounding the cabin was pristine, but when Lucas parked the Jeep he put a detaining hand on Jay's arm. "Stay here until I check the cabin," he said tersely, drawing a pistol from beneath his jacket and getting out without looking at her. His eyes were never still, darting from window to window, examining every inch of ground, looking for the betraying flutter of a curtain.

Jay was frozen in place. This man, moving like a cat toward the back door, was the man she loved, and he was a predator, a hunter. He was innately cautious, as graceful as the wind as he flattened his back against the wall and eased his left hand toward the doorknob, while the pistol was held ready in his right. Soundlessly he opened the door and disappeared within. Two minutes later he stood in the back door again, relaxed. "Come on in," he said, and walked back to the Jeep to get their bags.

It irritated her that he'd frightened her for nothing; it reminded her of the morning when he'd tracked her in the snow. "Don't do that to me," she snapped as she threw open the door and slid out. The snow crunched under her boots.

"Do what?"

"Scare me like that."

"Scaring you is a hell of a lot better than walking into an ambush," he replied evenly.

"How could anyone know we're up here, and why should anyone care?"

"Frank thinks someone would care, or they wouldn't have taken the trouble to hide us."

She climbed the steps and knocked the snow off her boots before entering the cabin. It was cold but not icy, because they had left the backup heat system on. She took the bags from him and carried them into the bedroom to begin unpacking while he built a fire.

Lucas watched the yellow flames lick at the logs he'd placed on the grate, slowly catching and engulfing the wood. He couldn't tell her, not yet. This might be the only time he'd ever have with her, an indefinite period of grace while Sabin's men hunted Piggot. He'd use that time to bind her to him so tightly that he could hold her even after she found out his real name, and that Steve Crossfield was dead. She had told him she loved him, but it was Steve Crossfield she'd been saying the words to, and, oddly, it had been Steve Crossfield hearing them. He was Lucas Stone, and he wanted her for himself.

His need was fast and urgent, like a fire low in his belly. He walked into the bedroom and watched her for a moment as she bent over to remove her boots and socks. She was as slim as a reed, her skin silky soft. He caught her around the waist and tumbled her on the bed, immediately following her down to pin her to the mattress with his weight.

She laughed, her blue eyes no longer filled with irritation. "The caveman approach must be fashionable this year," she teased.

He couldn't smile in return. He wanted her too badly, needed to hear her say the words to *him*, not to a ghost. The yellow glitter was in his eyes as he stripped her and surveyed her nakedness. Her nipples were puckered from the chilly air, her breasts standing up round and firm. He circled them with his hands and lifted the tight nipples to his mouth, sucking at each of them in turn. She gasped, and her back arched. Her responsiveness did it to him every time, shattered his control and made him as hot and eager for her as a teenager. He could barely tolerate taking his hands off her long enough to hastily tear at his own clothing and throw it to the side.

"Tell me you love me," he said as he adjusted her slim legs around his hips and began entering her.

Jay squirmed voluptuously, rubbing her breasts against the hairy planes of his chest. "I love you." Her hands dug into his back as she felt the muscles ripple. "I love you." Slowly he pushed and slowly she accepted him, her pleasure already rising to an urgent pitch. Her body was so attuned to him that when he began the rhythmic thrust and withdrawal of lovemaking her sensual tension swiftly reached a crescendo. He held her until her shudders stilled, then found the rhythm anew.

"Again," he whispered.

She wanted to cry out his name, but couldn't. She couldn't call him Steve now, and she didn't dare call him

Lucas. She had to bite her lips to keep his name unsaid, and a moan rose in her throat. He controlled her, his slow, deep thrusts taking her only so high and refusing to let her go any higher. She was on fire, her nerve endings exploding with pleasure.

"Tell me you love me." His voice was gravelly, the strain apparent on his face as he kept his movements agonizingly slow.

"I love you."

"Again."

"I love you."

He wanted to hear his name, but that was denied him. Sometime in the future, when this was all over, he promised himself that he would have her as he was having her now, and she would scream his name. He had to be content with knowing it himself, and with the way her eyes locked with his as she whispered the words over and over again, until his control broke and sweet madness claimed them both.

He couldn't get enough of her, ever, and knowing that he might lose her was intolerable. Physical bonds were the most basic, and instinctively he used them to strengthen the link between them. He would make himself a part of her until his name no longer mattered.

Two nights later, Frank had just gotten into bed when the telephone rang. With a sigh, he reached for it. "Payne."

"Piggot's in Mexico City," the Man said.

Forgetting about the good night's sleep he'd been anticipating, Frank sat up, instantly alert.

"Do you have a man on him?"

"Not at the moment. He's gone to ground again. It's about to unravel, and this move tells me who snipped the thread. I'll take care of that little detail, but you get Luke out of there. The cabin's location has been leaked."

"How much do you want me to tell him?"

"All of it. It doesn't matter now. It'll go down within the next twenty-four hours. Just see that they're safe." Then Kell Sabin hung up, wondering if he'd cut it too fine and endangered a friend, as well as an innocent woman.

Chapter 12

At the first beep from the palm-size pager lying on the bedside table, Lucas was on his feet and reaching for his pants. The tone told him it was the communications beeper, not the alarm caused by the laser beam being broken, but the very fact that Frank was contacting him in the middle of the night was alarm enough. Jay roused and reached for the lamp, but Lucas stopped her.

"No lights."

"What's going on?" She was very still now.

"I'm going out to the shed. That's the communications beeper. Frank's trying to get in touch with us."

"Then why not turn on a light?"

"He wouldn't contact us in the middle of the night unless it was an emergency. It might be too late. Piggot could already be close by, and a light would warn him."

"Piggot?"

"The guy who tried to make me into beef stew, remember?"

"I'll go with you." In a flash she was out of the bed and fumbling with her clothes in the dark. Lucas started to stop her, not wanting her to leave the safety of the cabin, but if Piggot had found them, the cabin wouldn't be safe. A hand-held rocket launcher in the hands of an expert, which Piggot was, could turn the cabin into a shattered inferno in seconds.

He stamped his feet into his boots and grabbed the pistol out of the holster, which he always kept at hand. As he left the room he lifted his jacket from the hook beside the door then shrugged into it as he raced through the dark cabin to the back door. Jay was right behind him; she had on her jeans and his flannel shirt, her bare feet shoved into boots.

They slipped across the snow to the shed, staying in the shadows as much as possible. The ramshackle shed was a revelation; Jay had been stunned the first time Lucas had shown her what lay below its surface. He moved a bale of hay aside and revealed a small trapdoor, just wide enough to allow his shoulders through, then pressed a button on the pager that released the electronic lock. The trapdoor silently swung open. A narrow ladder extended downward, illuminated only by tiny red lights beside each step. Lucas urged her down, then he followed and closed the door, once more sealing the underground communications chamber. Only then did he switch on the lights.

The chamber was small, no more than six by eight, and crammed with equipment. There were a computer and display terminal, a modem hookup and a printer against the end wall, and an elaborate radio system on the right. That left about two and a half feet of room on the left for maneuvering, and part of that was taken up by a chair. Lucas took the chair and flipped switches on the radio. "On air."

"Get packed. Piggot has been spotted in Mexico City, and we have word the location of the cabin is no longer secure." Frank's voice filled the small chamber eerily, with out the tinny sound radios normally produced, testifying to the quality of the set.

"How much time do we have?"

"The Man estimated four hours; less if Piggot has already put accomplices in the area."

"His usual method is to move people in, but keep them at a distance until he arrives. He likes to orchestrate things himself." Lucas's voice was remote, his mind racing.

Silence filled the chamber, then Frank asked quietly, "Luke?"

"Yeah," Lucas said, aware of Jay's sudden movement behind him, followed by absolute stillness. He hadn't wanted to tell her like this, but all hell would be coming down in a hurry. Four hours wasn't a lot of time, and no matter what happened, he wanted her to know his name. For four hours she would know whose woman she was.

"When?"

"A couple of days ago. Any chance of intercepting Piggot before he gets here?" That would be the best-case scenario.

"Slim. Nailing him there would be our best bet. We don't know where he is, but we know where he's going."

"He won't go through customs, so that means he's in a small plane and will land at a private airstrip, one close by. Do you have a record of them?"

"We're pulling them out of the computer now. We'll have men at all of them."

"Where's a safe place for me to stash Jay?"

Frank said urgently, "Luke, you're out of it. Don't set yourself up as bait for the trap. Get in the Jeep and drive, and call me in five hours."

"Piggot's my mess, I'll clean it up," Lucas said, still in that cool, remote tone. "If I'd taken care of him last year, this wouldn't be happening now."

"What about Jay?"

"I'll get her out of it. But I'm coming back for Piggot."

Realizing the futility of arguing with him across two-thirds of the continent, Frank said, "Okay. Contact Veasey, at this frequency, and scramble." He recited the frequency numbers only once.

"Roger," Lucas said, and flipped the switch that cut them off. Then he shoved the chair back and stood, turning to face Jay.

Her entire body felt numb as she stared at him. He knew. His memory had returned. Her time of grace had ended, the mirrors had shattered, the charade was over. The violence that had brought him into her life was about to take him out of it again.

With the return of his memory, he was truly Lucas Stone again. It was there in his eyes, in the yellow gaze of the predator. His face was hard. "I'm not Steve Crossfield," he said bluntly. "My name is Lucas Stone. Your ex-husband is dead."

She was white, frozen. "I know," she whispered.

Of all the things he'd expected her to say, that wasn't one of them. It stunned him, confused him, and irrationally angered him. He'd agonized for days over how to tell her, and she already knew? "How long have you known?" he snapped.

Even her lips felt numb. "Quite a while."

He caught her arm, his long fingers digging into her flesh. "How long is 'quite a while'?"

She tried to think. She had been caught in a web of lies for so long that it was difficult to remember. "You...you were still in the hospital."

Scenarios flashed through his mind. He'd been trained to think deviously, to keep hammering at something until it made sense, and he didn't like any of the situations that came to mind. He'd assumed from the beginning that she was an innocent blind, used by Sabin and Frank Payne to shield him, but it was more likely that she'd been hired to do the job. White-hot fury began to build in him, and he clamped down on his temper with iron control. "Why didn't you tell me?" God, for a while he'd thought he was going crazy, with all those damn memories coming back and none of them connected with the things she had told him. He might have gotten his memory back sooner if he'd had one solid fact to build on instead of the fairy tales she'd woven.

He was hurting her; his grip would leave bruises on her arm. She pulled at it uselessly, gasping as he only tightened his fingers. "I was afraid to!"

"Afraid of what?"

"I thought Frank would send me away if he knew I'd discovered you weren't Steve! Lucas, please, you're hurting me!" At last she could say his name, even though it was in pain, and her heart savored the sound.

His grip eased, but he caught her other arm, too, and held her firmly. "So Frank didn't hire you to say I was Steve Crossfield?"

"N-no," she stuttered. "I believed you were, at first."

"What changed your mind?"

"Your eyes. When I saw your eyes, I knew."

The memory of that was crystal clear. When the doctor had cut the bandages away from his eyes and he'd looked at Jay for the first time, she had gone as white as she was now. That was odd, because he knew Sabin would never have overlooked a detail as basic as the color of his eyes.

"Your husband didn't have brown eyes?"

"Ex-husband," she whispered. "Yes, he had brown eyes, but his were dark brown. Yours are yellowish brown."

So his eyes were a different shade of brown than her husband's had been; it was almost laughable that Sabin's carefully constructed scam could have fallen apart over something as small as that. But she hadn't told them that they had the wrong man, which would have been the reasonable thing to do. She hadn't even told *him*, not then and not during the weeks when they'd been up here alone. Angry frustration made his voice as rough as gravel. "Why didn't you tell *me*? Didn't you think I'd be a little interested in who I really am?''

"I couldn't take the chance. I was afraid—" she began, pleading for understanding.

"Yeah, that's right, you were afraid the gravy train would end. Frank was paying you to stay with me, wasn't he? You were with me every day, so there was no way you could hold down a job."

"No! It isn't like that—"

"Then what is it like? Are you independently wealthy?"

"Lucas, please. No, I'm not wealthy—"

"Then how did you live during the months I was in the hospital?"

"Frank picked up the tab," she said in raw frustration. "Would you please listen to me?"

"I'm listening, honey. You just told me that Frank paid you to stay with me."

"He made it *possible* for me to stay with you! I'd lost my job—" Too late, she heard the words and knew how he would take them.

His eyes were yellow slits, his mouth a grim line of rage. "So you jumped at the chance for a cushy job. All you had to do was sit beside me every day and anything you wanted was given to you, while Frank paid your bills. This explains why you wouldn't marry me, doesn't it? You were happy to accept your 'salary,' but marrying a stranger was a little bit too much, wasn't it? Not to mention the fact that the marriage wouldn't have been legal. You saved yourself some sticky trouble by dragging up all those excuses."

"They weren't excuses. For all I knew you could have had someone who cared for you—"

"I do!" he yelled, his neck cording. "My family! They think I'm dead!"

Jay groped for control, managing to steady her voice. "I couldn't marry you until you'd gotten your memory back and knew for certain you wanted to marry me. I couldn't take advantage of you like that.''

"That's a convenient scruple. It actually makes you look noble, doesn't it? Too bad. If you wanted the gravy train to keep running, you should have married me while you had the chance and just kept pretending I was Crossfield. Then, when I got my memory back, you could have been the poor victim and maybe I would have stayed with you out of guilt.''

She shrank away from him, her eyes going blank. Somehow, during the long months she had spent with him, she had come to believe he loved her, though he had never said the words. He'd been so possessive, so tender and passionate. But now his memory had returned, and he couldn't have made it plainer that his absorption with her had ended. He didn't need her any longer, and he certainly wasn't going to renew his offer of marriage. It was over, and they weren't even going to part friends. The worst had happened; she had lied to him, kept his identity from him, and he would never forgive her for it. He thought she had done it just because the government had been willing to support her for as long as the charade had lasted.

He released her suddenly, as if he couldn't stand to touch her any longer, and she staggered back. Catching her balance, she turned toward the ladder. "Open the door,'' she said dully.

He clenched his fists, not ready to break off the argument. He didn't have all the answers he wanted, not by a long shot. But her movement recalled the need for urgency; he had to get her out of there before Piggot found them. The last thing he wanted was for Jay to be caught in the middle of a firefight.

"I'll go first,'' he said, and shouldered past her. He signaled the door open and climbed the ladder, the pistol ready in his hand. As soon as his head was above ground he looked cautiously in all directions, then climbed out and knelt on one knee by the hole to help Jay out. "All right, come on."

She didn't look at him as she crawled out, nor did she accept the hand he extended. He closed the trapdoor, then replaced the bale of hay over it. She started to just walk out of the shed, but he grabbed her and held her back. "Watch it!" he said in a furious whisper. "We go back the same way we came. Stay in the shadows." He led the way, and Jay followed him without a word.

He still wouldn't allow a light on in the cabin, so Jay stumbled to the bedroom and gathered a few clothes in the dark. He came into the bedroom as she took off his shirt to put on her own clothes, and after a moment of frozen embarrassment, she awkwardly turned her back while she struggled with her bra. Her hands were clumsy, and in the dark she couldn't manage to straighten the straps. Despairing of getting it on, she finally dropped it on the bed and simply pulled her sweater over her head.

Lucas watched her. Her pale breasts had gleamed in the faint light coming through the window, and in spite of his anger, his sense of betrayal and the need for haste, he wanted to go to her and pull her against him. Only a few hours before he had held her breasts in his hands and pushed them up to his avid mouth. He had made love to her until the building anticipation had bordered on agony, and they had writhed together on that bed. She had told him she loved him, over and over, and now she turned her back as if she had to hide her body from him.

It hit him hard, shook him. There was more to it than she'd told him, more than the mercenary motives he'd thrown at her. He needed to know what it was, but he didn't have time. Damn it. If only she didn't look so beaten and remote, as if she had withdrawn inside herself. He had to fight the urge to take her in his arms and kiss that look away. Hell, what did it matter why she had done it? Maybe money had been the reason at first, but he was damned certain i wasn't the reason now, or at least not all of it. Even if it had been, he thought ruthlessly, he wouldn't let her go. He'd get this settled between them as soon as he'd taken care of Piggot, but right now the most important thing was to make certain Jay was safe.

"Hurry," he urged roughly.

She sat down on the edge of the bed and jerked her boots off, quickly put on a pair of thick socks and put the boots on again. Then she got her purse and shearling jacket and said, "I'm ready."

He didn't see the need for her to get anything else, as they would come back to the cabin and pack after he'd taken care of Piggot, and he was pleased that she didn't insist on wasting time. Jay was a good partner, even though she was out of her depth.

He had to find a safe place to leave her. He doubted that Black Bull, the closest town, had a motel, but he didn't have the time to go any farther than that. He drove the Jeep at breakneck speed across the meadow, especially considering that he didn't dare risk turning on the headlights. But he had taken the possibility that he might have to do this into consideration and had walked the meadow over and over, mentally tracing the route he would take, estimating his fastest safe speed, noting all the rocks and ruts in his path. He edged so close to the tree line that branches scraped the side of the Jeep.

"I can't see," Jay said, her voice strained.

"I can." He couldn't see much, but it was enough. He had good night vision.

She held on to the door as they jolted across a hump, rattling her teeth. He'd have to turn on the headlights when they went down the mountainside, she thought; the track was only wide enough for the Jeep, with a steep drop on one side and vertical mountain on the other. Even in daylight she hardly dared to breathe until they had safely negotiated it. But when they made the turn that took them onto the track, he kept both hands on the wheel. The darkness in front of them was absolute.

Jay closed her eyes. Her own heartbeat was thundering in her ears so loudly that she couldn't hear anything else. There was nothing she could do. He had decided not to turn on the lights, to risk the drive in the dark, and nothing she could say would change his mind. His arrogant confidence in his own ability was both maddening and awesome; she would rather have walked down the mountain in ten feet of snow than risked this hair-raising drive, but he had simply decided to do it, and now he was.

She couldn't estimate how long the drive took. It seemed like hours, and finally her nerves couldn't bear the tension, and numbness settled in. She even opened her eyes. It didn't matter. If they went over the side, they would go whether her eyes were open or closed.

But then they were down and bumping across the second meadow. Suddenly he slammed on the brakes, swearing viciously. Jay saw what he saw: a set of headlights playing along the edge of the meadow in front of them. They were still safely out of range of the light, but she knew as well as he did what it meant. Piggot's men were drawing close, closing the net to wait for Piggot's arrival.

Lucas put the Jeep in reverse and backed the way he had come, keeping the Jeep at the tree line. When he reached the rear edge of the meadow he turned, taking the Jeep up the north edge. They were off the track now, and the snow tires dug in deep, spewing snow back behind them.

"Are we going around this way?"

"No. We won't be able to make it. The snow's too deep." He pulled the Jeep under some trees and got out. "Stay here," he ordered, and disappeared back toward the track.

Jay swiveled in her seat, straining her eyes to see what he was doing. She could barely make out his form, black against the snow; an instant later he was out of sight.

He was back in less than two minutes. He vaulted into the Jeep and slammed the door, then rolled the window down. "Listen," he hissed.

"What did you do?"

"I wiped out our tracks. There was only one vehicle. If it goes past us, we'll get back on the track and make it to the highway yet."

They listened. The sound of the other motor came plainly through the night air. The vehicle was moving slowly, the engine toiling in low gear as it cautiously made its way up the slick, snowy, unfamiliar track. The headlights stabbed the darkness, coming almost straight toward them.

"Don't worry," Lucas breathed. "They can't see us from the track. If they just don't notice where we turned and if they keep on going, we'll be okay."

Two ifs. Two big ifs. Jay's nails were digging into her palms. The headlights were close enough that their reflected light illuminated the interior of the Jeep, and for the first time she noticed that Lucas had on his thick shearling jacket, but no shirt. The odd detail struck her, and she wondered if she might be edging toward hysteria.

"Keep going," he said under his breath. "Keep going."

For a moment it seemed as if the other vehicle slowed, and the lights seemed to be coming over the slight rise straight toward them. Then they turned, and the noise of the engine slowly moved away.

She let out her breath. Lucas started the engine, knowing the sound wouldn't be heard over that of the other motor. He put the Jeep in gear and turned it around, praying they were hidden well enough that the red glow of the brake lights wouldn't reveal their position. But at least they were behind the other vehicle now. If he had to, he could make a run for the road. As rough as the track was, the chance that they would be hit by gunfire from a pursuing vehicle was small.

The Jeep lurched through the snow, and then they were on the track again. No other headlights disturbed the darkness, and they could just catch glimpses of light playing through the trees as the other vehicle moved slowly up the treacherous mountainside track.

Jay sat silently, even when they reached the road and Lucas finally turned on the headlights. She was numb again.

They reached Black Bull at two in the morning. The local populace of one hundred and thirty-three souls were all in bed. There wasn't even an all-night convenience store, and the one gas station closed at ten at night, according to the sign in the window. A county sheriff's car was parked at the side of the gas station.

Lucas stopped the Jeep. "Can you drive this well enough to get out of here?" he asked brusquely.

She looked at the gearshift, but not at him. "Yes."

"Then drive until you hit the next town big enough to have a motel. Stop there and call Frank. He'll arrange for you to be picked up. Do you have his number?"

So this was it. It was over. "No."

"Give me a pen. I'll write it down for you."

Jay fumbled in her purse and found a pen, but she didn't have even a scrap of paper for him to write the number on. Finally he grasped her hand and turned it palm up, then wrote the number on her palm.

"Where are you going?" she asked, her voice strained but even.

"I'm taking that county car right there and radioing Veasey. Then we're going to catch Piggot and end this once and for all."

She stared out the windshield, her hand clenched tightly as if to keep the number from fading off her palm. "Be careful," she managed to say, the admonishment trite but heartfelt. She wondered if Frank would even tell her the outcome, if she would ever know what happened to Lucas.

"He ambushed me once. It won't happen again." Lucas got out of the Jeep and strode over to the county car. It was locked, but that wasn't much of a deterrent. He had the door open in less than ten seconds. He looked at the Jeep, staring at Jay through the windshield. Her face was ghostly white. He wanted nothing more than to jerk her into his arms and kiss her so hard that they both forgot about this mess, but if he kissed her now, he might not be able to stop, and he had to take care of Piggot. It was just that he wanted her so badly, wanted to use the bond of the flesh to make certain she knew she was his. A sense of incompletion gnawed at him because they hadn't thrashed out the situation between them, but it would have to wait. Maybe it was better this way. In a few hours he wouldn't have to worry about Piggot any longer, and his temper would have cooled. He would be able to think clearly and not react as if she'd betrayed him. He didn't understand her reasons yet, but underneath everything, he knew she loved him.

Instead of climbing over into the driver's seat, Jay opened the door and got out to walk around. She paused in front of the Jeep, her slim body starkly outlined by the glare of the headlights. "It was the only way I could think of to protect you," she said, then got into the Jeep and put it in gear.

Lucas watched the taillights as she pulled out of the gas station and onto the highway. He felt stunned. Protect him? He was so used to being out in the cold, on his own by choice, that the idea of anyone protecting him was alien. What had she thought she could do?

She could keep the charade intact. She had been right; Frank would have quickly and quietly hustled her away if she'd told him there had been a mistake, that he, Lucas, wasn't her ex-husband. She didn't have his skill with weapons or in fighting, but that hadn't stopped her from literally setting herself up as his bodyguard. The charade had depended on her, so she had kept quiet, and shielded him with her presence.

Because she loved him. He swore aloud, his breath crystallizing in the frigid night air. His damned training had tripped him up, making him look for betrayal where there hadn't been any, making him question her motives and automatically assuming the worst. He had only to look to himself to understand why she hadn't said anything. Hadn't he kept quiet these past two days because he'd been afraid of losing her if she knew the truth? He loved her too much to accept even the possibility of losing her, until Piggot had forced his hand.

Swearing again, he folded his length into the county car and began the process of hot-wiring the starter.

Dawn threw rosy fingers of light across the snow, a sight Lucas had seen many times since coming to the mountains, but the scene wasn't peaceful this particular morning. The meadow was crowded with men and vehicles, the pristine snow trampled and criss-crossed by both feet and tires. Here and there the white was marred by reddish-brown stains. A helicopter sat off to the left, its blades slowly twirling in the breeze.

Ten guns snapped toward him as he stepped out from the trees, then were lifted as the men holding them recognized him. He walked steadily toward them, his own pistol held in his blood-stained hand down at his side. The stench of cordite burned his nostrils in the cold air, and a gray haze lay over the meadow, resisting the efforts of the breeze to disperse it.

There was a tall, black-haired man standing next to the helicopter, surveying the scene with grim, narrowed eyes. Lucas walked straight to him. "You took a chance, setting us up in your own cabin," he snapped.

Kell Sabin looked around the meadow. "It was a calculated risk. I had to do it to find the mole. Once the location of the cabin was leaked, I knew who it was, because access to that information is very controlled." He shrugged. "I can find another vacation spot."

"The mole blew my cover?"

"Yeah. Until then, I had no idea he was there." Sabin's voice was icy, his eyes like cold black fire.

"So why the masquerade? Why drag Jay into it?"

"To keep Piggot from finding out you were alive. Your cover was blown. He knew about your family, and he's been willing in the past to use someone's family to get to them. I was trying to buy time, to keep everyone safe until Piggot surfaced and we could get to him." Sabin looked up at the trees behind the cabin. "I assume he won't be bothering us again."

"Or anyone else."

"That was your last job. You're out of it."

"Damn straight," Lucas agreed. "I've got better things to do, like get married and start a family."

Suddenly Sabin grinned, and the coldness left his eyes. Few people saw Sabin like that, only the ones who could call themselves his friends. "The bigger they are," he jibed, and left the rest of the old saw unsaid. "Have you told her yet?"

"She already knew. She figured it out while I was still in the hospital."

Sabin frowned. "What? She didn't say anything. How did she know?"

"My eyes. They're a different shade of brown than Crossfield's."

"Hell. A little thing like that. And she still went along with it?"

"I think she figured out that the whole thing was to protect me."

"Women," Sabin said softly, thinking of his own wife, who had fought like a tigress to save his life when he'd been a stranger to her. It didn't surprise him that Jay Granger had put herself on the line to protect Lucas.

Lucas rubbed his jaw. "She doesn't even mind this ugly mug."

"The surgeons did what they could. Your face was smashed." Then Sabin grinned again. "You were too pretty anyway."

The two men stood and watched the mopping up process, their faces becoming grim again at the loss of life. Three men were dead, counting Piggot, and four more were in custody. "I'll notify your family that you're alive," Sabin finally said. "I'm sorry they had to go through this, but with Piggot on the loose, it was safer for you, and all of them, as well, if the charade was played out. It's over now. Collect Jay from wherever you've stashed her, and we'll get the two of you out of here."

Lucas looked at him, and slowly the blood drained out of his face. "She hasn't called Frank?" he asked hoarsely.

Sabin went still. "No. Where is she?"

"She was supposed to drive to the next town, check into a motel and call Frank. Damn it to hell!" Lucas turned and ran for the shed, with Sabin right beside him. Suddenly he felt cold all over. There was a possibility Piggot could have gotten to Jay before coming here, as well as the slightly less terrifying possibility that she could have had an accident. God in heaven, where was she?

After leaving Lucas, Jay simply drove, automatically following the highway signs picked out by the headlight beams, and eventually wound up on U.S. 24, the highway that they had taken to Colorado Springs. She turned in the opposite direction. She didn't pay any attention to the time; she just kept driving. U.S. 24 took her through Leadville, and finally she connected with I-70. She took a right, toward Denver.

The sun came up, shining right into her eyes. She was nearly out of gas. She got off at the next exit and had the tank filled.

It would be over by now.

Exhaustion pulled at her, but she couldn't stop. If she ever stopped, she would have to think, and right now she couldn't bear it. She checked her money. She didn't have much—a little over sixty dollars—but she had her credit cards. That would get her back to New York, to the only home she had left, the only refuge.

I-70 went straight to Stapleton International Airport in Denver. Jay parked the Jeep and entered the terminal, carefully noting where she had parked so she could tell Frank where to retrieve his vehicle. She bought her ticket first, and was lucky enough to get on a flight leaving within the hour. Then she found a pay phone and called Frank.

He answered in the middle of the first ring. "Frank, it's Jay." She identified herself in a numb monotone. "Is it over?"

"Where the hell are you?" he screamed.

"Denver."

"Denver! What are you doing there? You were supposed to call me hours ago! Luke is tearing the damned place up, and we have every cop in Colorado prowling the highways looking for you."

Her heart lightened, the terrible dread lifting from it. "He's all right? He isn't hurt?"

"He's fine. He took a little nick on the arm, but nothing a Band-Aid won't cover. Look, exactly where are you? I'll have you picked up—"

"Is it over?" she asked insistently. "Is it really over?"

"Piggot? Yeah, it's over. Luke got him. Tell me where you are and—"

"I'm glad." Her legs wouldn't support her much longer; she sagged against the wall. "Take...take care of him."

"My God, don't hang up!" Frank yelled, the words shrieking in her ear. "Where are you?"

"Don't worry," she managed to say. "I can get home by myself." Totally forgetting the Jeep, she hung up the phone, then went into the ladies' rest room and splashed cold water on her face. As she pulled a brush through her hair she noticed the pallor of her cheeks and the dark circles under her eyes. "You guys sure know how to show a lady a good time," she murmured to her reflection, drawing several startled glances her way.

Yogi Berra had said, "It ain't over till it's over," but this was very definitely over. Jay couldn't sleep on the flight, despite the utter exhaustion weighing down her body. Nor could she eat, though her stomach was empty. She managed to drink a cola, but nothing more.

After the solitude of the meadow, New York's J.F.K. airport was bedlam. She wanted to shrink against a wall and scream at all the scurrying people to go away. Instead she got on a bus, and an hour and a half later she let herself into her apartment.

She hadn't seen it in months; it was no longer home. It had been well taken care of in her absence, as Frank had promised, but it was as empty as she was. She didn't even have any clothes with her. She laughed hollowly; clothes were the least of her worries. Frank would make certain they were shipped to her.

But there were sheets to go on the bed, and towels for the bathroom. She took a warm shower, then even summoned the strength to make up the bed. The afternoon sun was going down as she stretched out naked between the clean sheets. Automatically she turned, searching for Lucas' warmth, but he wasn't there. It was over, and he didn't want her. Acid tears stung her eyes as her heavy eyelids closed, and then she slept.

"Janet Jean. Janet Jean, wake up."

The intruding voice pulled her toward consciousness. She didn't want to wake up. So long as she slept, she didn't have to face life without Lucas. But it sounded like his voice, and she frowned.

"Janet Jean. Jay. Wake up, baby." A hard, warm hand shook her bare shoulder.

Slowly she opened her eyes. It *was* Lucas, sitting on the edge of her bed, scowling at her. Those yellow eyes looked almost murderous, though his tone had been as gentle as his ruined voice would allow. He looked like hell; he badly needed a shave, his hair was uncombed, and a blood-stained bandage was wrapped around his left forearm. But at least he had on a shirt now, and his clothes were clean.

"I know I locked the door." Sleep still muddled her mind, but she knew she'd locked the door. In New York, one wasn't careless about locking the door.

He shrugged. "Big deal. Come on, sweetheart, go to the bathroom and splash some cold water on your face so you can focus your eyes. I'll make coffee."

What was he doing here? She couldn't think of any reason, and though part of her rejoiced at seeing him, no matter why, another part of her cringed at having to say goodbye to him again. She might not be able to stand it this time. At least before, she had been numb.

"What time is it?"

"Almost nine."

"It can't be. It's still daylight."

"Nine in the morning," he explained patiently. "Come on, get up." He lifted her to a sitting position, and the covers fell to her waist, exposing her bare body. Quickly Jay grabbed the sheet and pulled it over her breasts; she couldn't meet his eyes as a flush chased the pallor from her face.

His face was expressionless as he got to his feet and unbuttoned his shirt. "Here, put this on. I packed your clothes and brought them with me, but they're all tumbled together in the suitcases."

She took his shirt, still warm from his body, and pulled it around her. Without another word she got up and went into the bathroom, firmly closing the door behind her. She started to lock it, but decided not to waste her time. Locks weren't much good against him.

Five minutes later she felt much more alert, having followed his advice and splashed cold water on her face. She was very thirsty, after having gone so long without anything to drink, so she drank several cups of water. She would have felt more secure if she'd had on something more than just his shirt, but it almost swallowed her. His scent was on the fabric. She lifted it to her face and inhaled deeply, then let it drop and left the security of the bathroom.

He was lying on the bed. She stopped in her tracks. "I thought you were going to make coffee."

"You don't have any." He got to his feet, put his hands on her shoulders and shook her. "Damn you," he said in a shaking voice. "I went through hell when I found out you hadn't called Frank. Why did you run? Why did you come back here?"

Her hair had fallen over her face. "I didn't have anyplace else to go," she said, and her voice cracked.

He yanked her into his arms, reaching up behind her back to lock his fist in her hair and hold her head back. "Did you really think I'd let you get away from me that easily?" he all but snarled.

"Was what I did so bad?" she pleaded. "I didn't know any other way to protect you! When I saw your eyes, I knew you had to be the agent Frank had told me had been killed, and I knew he'd gone to an awful lot of trouble to hide you, so you had to be in danger. You had amnesia. You didn't even know who was after you! Keeping the lie going was the only way I had of keeping you safe!"

The yellowish eyes glittered. "Why should you care?"

"Because I was in love with you! Or did you think that was a lie, too?"

His touch gentled. "No," he said quietly. "I think I've always known you loved me, right from the start."

Tears leaked from the corners of her eyes. "The first time I touched you," she whispered, "I felt how warm you were, and how hard you were fighting to stay alive. I started loving you then."

"Then why did you run?"

He was relentless, but then, she had always known that. "Because it was over. You didn't want me. I'd been terrified of what you would do when you found out. I was afraid you'd send me away, and you did. So I left."

"I only wanted you away from the danger, damn it! I didn't intend for you to go two thousand miles!" He picked her up and dropped her on the bed, then followed her down. "No excuses this time. We're going to get married as soon as we can legally do it."

She was as stunned as she had been the first time he'd mentioned marriage. "W-what?" she stammered.

"You told me to ask you again when I'd regained my memory. Well, I have. We're getting married."

All she could say was, "That's not asking, that's telling."

"It'll do." He began unbuttoning his shirt, uncovering her breasts.

"Is it because you think you owe me—"

His head jerked up, those eyes fierce and wild. "I love you so much I'm out of my head with it."

She was stunned again. "You never said. I thought—but then you made me leave . . ."

"I didn't think I could have made it any plainer how I felt," he growled.

Very simply she said, "Do you need the words?"

That stopped him. "I need the words very much."

"So do I."

He bent his head and kissed her, his hand stroking her bare body beneath the shirt. His muscled legs moved against hers, and she felt his hardness against her thigh. "I love you, Jay Granger."

The sun was exploding inside her, lighting her eyes. "I love you, Lucas Stone."

At last she could speak his name with love.

Epilogue

"Is Piggot really dead?"

"He's really dead." Lucas watched her face carefully across the breakfast table. He had gone out and bought the necessary groceries, and they had both eaten as if they were starved, which they had been. He hadn't been interested in food before, either. Finding Jay and getting her back where she belonged had been far more important. "I finished the job." The truth wasn't pretty, but she had a right to know that about the man she was going to marry.

She sipped at the hot coffee, then lifted those incredible dark blue eyes to his. "I'm glad he's dead," she said fiercely. "He tried to kill you."

"And came damn close to succeeding."

She shuddered, thinking of the days when his life had hung in the balance, and he reached for her hand. "Hey, sweetheart. It's over. That part is really over. This part—" he squeezed her hand "—is just getting started—if you're sure you can stand looking at this face over the breakfast table."

The smile broke over her face like sunshine. "Well, you're not good-looking, but you sure are sexy."

With a growl he grabbed for her, dragging her around the table and onto his lap. Her arms went around him even as he tilted her face up for his kiss. "By the way, I'm not an agent."

She jerked back, startled. "What?"

"Not any longer. I'm officially retired, as of yesterday. Sabin took me out of it. Once my cover was blown, there was no way I could go back without endangering my family. I've really been out of it since the explosion, but Sabin didn't make it official until Piggot was caught."

"Then I guess we'll both have to hunt for a job." He was retired! She felt like chanting hosannas. She wouldn't have to worry every time he walked out the door that she'd never see him again.

He rubbed his thumb over her bottom lip. "I already have a job, baby. I'm a businessman, in partnership with my brother in an engineering firm. I traveled all over the world. It was a good cover for the work I was doing for Sabin. Speaking of my brother, by now Sabin will have gotten the news to them that a mistake was made in identifying the victims of the explosion and I'm still alive. This is going to be a bad shock to them, especially my parents."

"You mean a good shock."

"It'll be a shock, of whatever nature. Given the changes in my face and voice, they may have trouble adjusting."

"And you're bringing a strange woman into the family," she said, concern darkening her eyes.

"Oh, that. Don't worry about that. Mom has been after me for years to settle down. It wasn't an option I had before, but that's changed." He gave her a raffish grin. "I'd already decided to retire, anyway, so I could spend my time keeping you satisfied."

He certainly did that. Jay put her head on his shoulder, absorbing his warmth and nearness. His arms tightened. "I love you," he said steadily.

"I love you, Lucas Stone." She would never tire of saying it, and he would never tire of hearing it.

He stood up with her in his arms. "Let's go make a phone call. I want to talk to my folks and let them know they're getting a daughter-in-law."

They did make the phone call, but not right away. First he kissed her, and when he lifted his head the expression in his eyes had intensified. He carried her into the bedroom, and then the mirror on the wall reflected the true image of two people entwined as they loved each other.

* * * * *

NORA ROBERTS

Love has a language all its own, and for centuries, flowers have symbolized love's finest expression. Discover the language of flowers—and love—in this romantic collection of 48 favorite books by bestselling author Nora Roberts.

Two titles are available each month at your favorite retail outlet.

In April, look for:

First Impressions, Volume #5
Reflections, Volume #6

In May, look for:

Night Moves, Volume #7
Dance of Dreams, Volume #8

Collect all 48 titles and become fluent in

THE LANGUAGE of LOVE

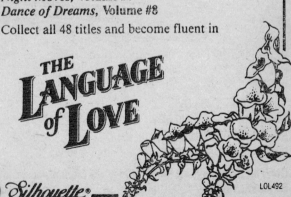

ⓢ *Silhouette*®

LOL492

YOU'VE ASKED FOR IT, YOU'VE GOT IT!

MAN OF THE MONTH: 1992

ONLY FROM

SILHOUETTE® *Desire*™

You just couldn't get enough of them, those sexy men from Silhouette Desire—twelve sinfully sexy, delightfully devilish heroes. Some will make you sweat, some will make you sigh... but every long, lean one of them will have you swooning. So here they are, men we couldn't resist bringing to you for one more year....

A KNIGHT IN TARNISHED ARMOR
by Ann Major in January

THE BLACK SHEEP
by Laura Leone in February

THE CASE OF THE MESMERIZING BOSS
by Diana Palmer in March

DREAM MENDER
by Sherryl Woods in April

WHERE THERE IS LOVE
by Annette Broadrick in May

BEST MAN FOR THE JOB
by Dixie Browning in June

Don't let these men get away! *Man of the Month*, only in Silhouette Desire.

WHEN A TAURUS MAN MEETS AN AQUARIUS WOMAN...

Vivacious Colly Fairchild was out to prove to stubborn-but-sexy Taurus man James Townsend that she could be every bit as persistent as he! He didn't know it yet, but before Colly was through with him, James would be the best dad any lonely little boy could ask for! Find out how Colly works her special magic in May's *WRITTEN IN THE STARS* title—ROOKIE DAD—only from Silhouette Romance. It's *WRITTEN IN THE STARS!*

 Silhouette Romance®